FLOORED

Chrissie Harrison

Valericain Press

Valericain
Press

Copyright © 2024 by Chris Towndrow
Valericain Press
Richmond, London, UK
www.valericainpress.co.uk

Floored – 1st edition, 2024.

Paperback ISBN : 978-1-7384470-0-8
eBook ISBN : 978-1-7384470-1-5

FLOOR 1

D rew arrived at his office without killing anyone.

Granted, that was a normal state of affairs, but this morning he'd come closer than usual to calamity.

Wearing odd socks can do that.

Well, worrying unnecessarily about wearing odd socks.

He'd discovered the minor wardrobe error soon after leaving home and frequently glanced down at his feet, trying to assess how obvious the disparity of blues was. He was hardly a style icon but didn't want to look foolish.

Repeatedly peering into the Ford Focus' footwell was undoubtedly why he'd nearly mowed down a young woman on a pedestrian crossing. Luckily, he'd stopped just in time. She'd given him the evils, followed by a creditably persistent, ramrod-straight index finger.

Still, as motoring incidents went, he'd suffered worse.

Much worse, he thought.

He'd sworn violently. The car window was open. A middle-aged lady was walking past. She'd given him the evils, too. A little bile had tickled Drew's throat as he slowly pulled away from the zebra crossing, heart hammering.

Mondays. What are they good for? Absolutely nothing.

Slowly, he regained his composure. Enough drama for one day. And it was only 07:50.

The remainder of the commute passed without incident, and he breezed into the building's airy foyer.

As he tapped his pass on the electronic reader at one of the three security turnstiles, he became aware of someone else having a Monday morning to forget.

'Look, I work here.' The female voice was hushed but urgent.

He glanced over. A petite brunette struggled to get the touchpad to give her ID a happy beep. Her restrained attire was augmented by tinted glasses. He wondered whether she'd forgotten to remove them or was just trying to appear cool. Yet, her demeanour seemed far from trendy or gregarious.

The security guard looked disdainfully at her. 'Anybody could say that.'

Drew frowned. This wasn't Alan, the regular attendant. Alan was a decent bloke. Supported Bristol Rovers. Tolerated Drew's lame banter.

This guy? Officious—and clearly enjoying it.

'My pass was fine last week,' she protested, tapping it again.

'Anybody could say that too.' He'd obviously consumed the entire library of rule books for breakfast.

The girl waved her pass at the guard's face. 'Please, just let me through.'

'Sorry, Miss.'

Drew took a step forward, keen to broker peace, but another white knight strolled up. This one had the build of a rugby fullback but with un-mangled ears and perfect hair.

'It's okay, Len. She's fine,' Mr God's Gift said.

The girl flashed a nervous smile but didn't make eye contact.

'Rules is rules,' the security guard—Len—said. 'I don't recognise her.'

The white knight displayed his even whiter teeth. 'New here, aren't you?'

Len's eyes narrowed. He folded his burly arms.

Drew was wary of a punch-up—assuming the cape-free superhero would jeopardise his immaculate dentistry to rescue a damsel in distress. Even one whose expression said she wouldn't touch him with a ten-foot pole.

Len stepped across the lane, blocking her path. 'Rules is rules. She's gotta get a temporary pass.'

'Not surprised you don't recognise her.' The rescuer leant in. 'She spends all day locked away, like rhubarb being forced.' Out came the smile.

Drew felt queasy. *What a dick!*

'Better than being forced to do other things—like share an office with *you*.' The girl gave the briefest knowing look as the torpedo hit home.

Then, fizzing with nerves, energy, or discomfort, she abandoned the turnstile and strode to the long, fake marble reception desk. Drew was amazed she walked so smoothly, given her massive brass balls.

Go girl!

The disarmed knight sneered and slunk away towards the lifts.

Good. That's no way to treat a woman.

Len smirked, then returned to the security station beside the metal detector arch. As he did, the regular guard, Alan, arrived and conversed with his colleague.

Drew watched the girl, mousily hunched over the sign-in book, wordlessly enter her details. She was given a day pass. As she left, he smiled supportively. Her response was the briefest meeting of their eyes and a flicker of embarrassment.

Had she seen his socks? He looked down. Everything seemed nicely disguised. Then he clutched at his fly—but it was zipped.

Phew! Public embarrassment averted.

Someone coughed; Drew was blocking the way. He muttered a lame apology, then went to Phase 2 of the entry rigmarole.

He didn't understand why an ordinary fifteen-storey office block in Winchester needed the security of Fort Knox. Perhaps he should make a point of asking? Alan would probably just tap his nose. Len would likely clap anyone in irons for asking.

Drew dutifully put his metal belongings in the plastic tray—knowing the activity was redundant—and stepped through the arch.

The alarm trilled.

Alan beckoned. Drew held out his arms in the practised fashion and allowed the guy to wave his wand.

'Smuggling guns again, Drew?' Alan asked, winking.

'I'd make the ideal decoy, right?'

As expected, the wand beeped as it passed Drew's right knee.

'Word to the wise. Don't try jokes at the airport.'

Drew held up a palm. 'Never would. Full body cavity search is not my idea of fun.'

'Mine either.' Alan waved him on. 'Have a good day.'

Drew collected his shoulder bag from the table and headed for the stairwell, forgoing the elevators as usual.

The building's two ageing lifts sometimes struggled to meet demand. It was another good reason for taking the stairs—plus, it was the only meaningful exercise Drew ever got. Yes, he had a gym membership but hadn't got around to not attending a facility in Winchester rather than not using one in Bristol. Still, for thirty-two laps of the sun, he wasn't too much of a physical has-been.

After trudging up nine flights of wide stairs to his office, he emerged into the lobby as his colleague Pirin exited the wire-hung death trap he'd chosen to travel in.

'Morning, Flower.' Pirin spread his arms. 'Ta-da! No horrible death. As usual.'

'Leave it out, mate, okay?'

'Are you going to be like this here, too?' Pirin cocked his head, and a sympathetic expression appeared on his unnecessarily good-looking face. 'New town, new office—time for a reboot?' He thumbed at the lift. 'You do *know* the statistics on—'

Drew lowered his voice. 'Of course I know the bloody stats. I don't need another sodding "Get over it" pep talk. I'm a slave to my emotional baggage—I get it.'

Pirin held up his palms defensively. 'Okay. Time out. Sorry. I know it's a difficult week, with... the anniversary.'

Drew's spirits sank. 'Yeah. More baggage. I think that's my emotional hand luggage.'

Pirin patted Drew's shoulder. 'Stow it in the overhead compartment this year, okay?'

'I'll try.'

Yet Drew knew he would fail. The spectre of Katie's death wouldn't vanish any time soon.

A *PING!* announced the arrival of the second lift. Amongst those exiting were the CEO's delightful PA.

Lotus Brown was mid-twenties, blonde, blue-eyed, and much too good for Drew. Whilst he'd only encountered her a few times in the last fortnight, she was too good for an unashamed ladies' man like Pirin as well.

She was talking on her phone but offered raised eyebrows in greeting as she passed.

Drew watched Pirin's gaze linger on her backside, and his eye was briefly drawn in the same direction.

'You were saying about all this emotional baggage which prevents you from dating again?' Pirin crooned, overly quick to accuse—the pot calling the kettle black.

Drew shook his head. 'Not now, okay? I've got work to do. Now I'm at HQ, I want that promotion.'

'Do you think you have a chance?'

Drew shrugged. 'Barrie left to become a goat herder in Laos or something. You know— "re-examined his life choices". That leaves an opening. If I make a good impression here, who knows?'

Pirin wrinkled his nose. 'Good luck. The boss is a tosser.'

'I heard that. Anyway, at least you and I didn't get ditched after Bristol. So, what are you editing this week?'

'"World's Smartest Dogs", episode two.'

'Wow. Sounds thrilling,' Drew jibed.

'It's TV. This is the twenty-twenties. Lowest common denominator, but as long as it makes money, right?'

'I suppose.'

'Says the accountant.' Pirin angled his head towards the corridor. 'Anyway, I'll crack on. See you around.'

Drew's morning passed in typical fashion. He balanced the books on the shoot for Park Productions' latest TV project, "Extreme Dominoes", shook away the twinge of RSI that typically accompanied gruelling spells of spreadsheet work, and broke for lunch.

He returned his third empty coffee mug to the kitchen area and headed for the stairwell.

On a diagonal course were Lotus and the CEO, Kevin Yates. His tie was loose, and his top button undone—the default look. Drew didn't know whether Yates did it to appear cool and approachable or because he was inherently a slovenly arse who'd been promoted above his ability.

Drew's previous boss had an infinitely better reputation, but that was water under the bridge. Yates was now the man whose good books Drew needed to get into—whatever he, or anyone else, thought of the guy.

'Oh, hi, Drew.' Lotus brightened.

He feigned nonchalance. Poorly. 'Hey, Lotus.'

The CEO halted, which meant she stopped, too. Her hand paused over the tablet she carried.

'You're Drew?' Kevin said. 'Drew Flower?'

Had Drew made a massive cock-up in one of his financial reports? Had he been missed off the list of redundancies during the company restructure? Had Lotus caught him glancing at her bottom—*for three microseconds!*—and blabbed to her boss, citing sexual harassment?

He swallowed dryly. 'I am.' *Best to be honest.*

'You made that policy suggestion—the creative sabbatical,' Kevin said.

That perked Drew's senses and dissipated the sudden worry. His sharp inhalation caught a whiff of Lotus' perfume. His heart skipped. 'I did, yes.'

'Walk with me,' Kevin said.

That sounded like an instruction, not an offer—and Drew would be mad not to seize the opportunity—so he fell in beside Kevin.

Wretchedly, within a couple of seconds, their destination became apparent: the lift.

'I... er... how can I help?' Drew's mouth felt dry.

Lotus thumbed the `Call` button. Drew glanced up at the floor indicator: one lift was on `G`, the other on `4`. The `4` became a `5`. Then a `6`.

His heart thundered in his chest. Lotus looked up from her tablet and smiled, but it didn't relieve his growing terror.

'Should we... take the stairs?' he suggested.

The CEO frowned. 'Why?'

'Oh, well, nothing. Obviously, it's better for your health. I don't mean *your* health. People's health. I'm not saying you're old, or out of shape. For all I know, you're down the gym every night.' He grimaced. 'Are you? I mean, it's none of my business, but why wait for the lift? They're pretty old and slow, aren't they? We could be down on the eighth floor by now. If you're—we're—going down, of course. Or up. Up is fine, too. Better for your calf muscles as well—'

PING!

Lotus and Kevin were staring at him. Probably because he was babbling like an idiot. Perhaps he'd get lucky, and the floor would swallow him up in the next two seconds?

Yates frowned. 'Are you all right, Flower?'

'Me? Yes, fine. Super. All good. So... stairs?' he asked with forlorn, last-ditch hope.

'I'm a busy man.' Kevin stood aside as three people exited the lift.

Drew was seized by dread. He was going to pass out. But here was the chance to engage directly with the CEO about an initiative he'd championed for three long, emotionally painful years. Whilst he'd had no luck at the previous office, maybe being closer to the seat of power would help? Plus, it was an opportunity to be very visible at the exact time the post-reorganisation promotions list was being drawn up. Could this really be a turning point?

Lotus wore a supportive, almost concerned expression. Another whiff of perfume blew away Drew's light-headedness. *Try not to look like a wuss in front of her.*

Kevin stepped inside the lift. "Walk with me" had been a misnomer—a stomach-churning, buttock-clenching catch-all that had Drew's teeth clamped together so tightly he feared they'd fused. And Park Productions didn't offer a private dental plan.

Somehow, he dug up sufficient inner strength and crossed the godawful threshold into the metal box of doom. He hugged the wall, making room for Lotus, her eyes, and her scent. Perhaps if she heard his suggestion, what a caring soul he was, and how much he wanted to nurture fellow employees, she'd allow him to inhale her perfume at even shorter distances?

'Oh, Lotus, no point in you being here. Need to get those documents off to Arri ASAP. Thanks.' Kevin nodded.

She smiled dutifully and backed away into the lobby. 'Absolutely.'

Kevin thumbed 2.

Seven floors! Drew's spirits dived. He tried to block out the sound of the doors closing, focussing on the appealing view beyond them as it narrowed to nothing. He begged himself not to soil his Star Wars boxer shorts. They were part of a 3-pack gifted to him by Katie—a sweet 28th birthday present that they both knew was deeply sad for a grown man to wear—yet he couldn't bear to chuck them out just because she was no longer in his life. It was a stupid memory to hold on to, but a charming one.

Right now, he could have done with something more like a handle to grasp, because his legs felt like jelly.

'Are you okay, Drew? You look pale.'

The lift started. He held in a gasp or a scream. Or a torrent of expletives beautifully terminated by a flop sweat and copious chundering.

He moistened his throat. 'I... Fine. Ish. Bad... um... bad prawns at lunch, probably.'

Kevin checked his Bulgari. 'Finished lunch already? Ah. Out partying at the weekend?'

'Yes,' Drew lied, desperate to keep any conversation flowing, to take his mind off the paralysing dread and crucifying echoes of history. 'Had a skinful. That's probably it. Sorry. Anyway—I'm... er... "walking" with you now, so... the suggestion, was it, you wanted to talk about? Sir?' He eyed the floor counter, willing it faster. They passed 8.

Kevin looked like he was listening to a gibbering simpleton, which wasn't far from the truth. 'Yes. I've heard good things about you, Flower. Now, this suggestion has come across my desk. Honestly, I think the idea has merit. So—what was your reasoning behind it?'

Drew yo-yoed between hope and crippling unease. He wanted to remark that the CEO would know Drew's "reasoning" if he'd actually bloody read the complete submission, but saying so was career suicide. Whilst he *desperately* wanted to get out of the lift, he was pretty keen on keeping his job. The free coffee might be shit, and Lotus would still be too good for him, but he'd resolved to give this sabbatical proposal his best efforts, and inferring that the CEO was a lazy sod—at the precise point the man was dangling the chance of adopting the initiative—would be colossal stupidity.

The whine of the lift was like nails down a blackboard. Drew tried to breathe evenly, suppressing hyperventilation. He wanted to curl up on the floor.

Focus. Pitch the idea. Ideally, coherently. Make Katie proud.

He checked the display. They passed **6**. He hoped nobody joined the lift because Kevin would drop the subject. These submissions were made in a closed forum, and Drew didn't want anyone nicking the frankly stellar idea. Plus, if the lift stopped, it would lengthen the ride, which was already unbearably glacial.

He gathered the most competent response he could. 'Research indicates that it's good for staff morale and retention. I know we've struggled with loyalty since Empire Productions poached several people. Plus, it was exactly this kind of work-life initiative which catalysed Unwin... er... Simon Unwin to write, pitch and sell the concept of "Tower Block Diaries".'

He exhaled hard, amazed that he'd delivered three whole sentences without sounding like a scatter-brained loon.

As the lift passed **4**, it shimmied. Drew wobbled, slapping a palm on the wall for support. He felt like a dog on Guy Fawkes night. A bead of sweat rolled down his temple.

'Hmm,' Yates offered noncommittally.

'Minimal effect on the bottom line, too,' Drew added. 'In fact, if an employee hits onto a ratings winner like Unwin did, there are six, seven, even eight figures to add back in.'

'Hmm.' Yates looked Drew up and down.

Drew surreptitiously returned the favour. Kevin's half-mast tie had a pattern consisting of tiny movie cameras. Drew didn't know whether to be impressed or saddened. He wondered if the man—late forties, slicked-back dark hair—also owned briefs sponsored by a famous film franchise.

This marked a new low today—trying to visualise the CEO's underwear. It would be more sensible to imagine the PA's underwear, and about as unlikely to result in a mutually satisfying romantic relationship.

Still, it had taken his mind off the circumstances for a few precious seconds.

The torture chamber passed 3. Drew prayed for something concrete to come out of this ghastly rite of passage.

Yates nodded sagely. 'I'll definitely look it over. You're right about retention. Very astute. Good to have you at HQ, Flower.'

Drew swallowed. 'Thank you.'

The lift bell pinged. Every muscle tightened—especially his sphincter—as he awaited the parting of the doors.

Mercifully, they slid back. Light and air swamped in like a beautiful dawn. He wanted to cheer. He wanted to jump for joy—but his legs were those of a newborn calf.

Kevin smiled faintly. 'Well done.' He strode away without a care in the world.

Drew remained rooted to the spot, processing the conversation, in disbelief that he'd ridden a lift without his head or bowels detonating. He sucked in oxygen, trance-like, calming himself.

The doors closed.

'Aargh!' He jabbed the **Doors Open** button, but it was too late.

The lift clanked into motion.

He screwed up his eyes. Now, there was nobody to witness his pain. Mercifully, the ride from hell was descending, which meant only two floors to **G**. Then, he'd celebrate the massive—and never to be repeated—milestone by getting a heinously unhealthy lunch. Ideally, he'd add a beer. Perhaps a whisky chaser or six.

Yes, return to the office pissed as a newt; that'll do my promotion chances a real favour. Dick.

He pressed a palm to his chest. The heartbeat was commendably restrained—a canter rather than a gallop. He wasn't going to die.

'Be careful,' said a female voice.

His eyes snapped open. He was still alone. *Now* his heart galloped.

'What?' he squeaked, glancing around nervously for the source of the disembodied voice.

'Be careful,' it repeated.

The lift slowed. His pulse didn't.

PING!

His fingers flitted as he begged the doors to open. His mind blazed.

As soon as the gap was wide enough, he pushed through, parting the cluster of waiting people, and hurried through the foyer, desperate for fresh air.

What the bloody hell is going on?

FLOOR 2

Drew collapsed onto a bench in the manicured, soulless quadrangle outside the building. People loped and scurried about their business. His mind was a blur of possibilities, powered by insufficient oxygen. Had he even breathed whilst trapped in that steel box? He must have.

He leant forward, elbows on knees, the gentle breeze eddying around. He sucked in lungfuls of air and counted the globs of dry chewing gum on the ground.

It was a good thing Pirin didn't happen by. He'd playfully toss out words like "wuss" or "drama queen". The problem was that Pirin could never empathise with the issue. Any suffering is explicitly owned by the sufferer. While Drew hadn't had his leg blown off by a landmine or miscarried a child, he did have mental and physical scars. In the grand scheme of things, elevatophobia was a mere scratch. Despite surviving seven—*no, nine!*—floors, and even managing an articulate conversation with the CEO, the lift had *spoken*, which freaked him out, big time.

Lifts don't talk. Well, they say things like "Seventh floor" and "Going up". They don't tend to say, "Be careful". Not that he was an expert on lifts. Quite the opposite.

He leaned against the backrest and stared at the cloudy May sky. He'd stopped shaking now. Had he imagined the voice? He'd undoubtedly been mentally discombobulated, having heard unexpectedly good news from Kevin whilst being forced to confront his demons.

Forced? You did partly go in because of Lotus—admit it. At least it means my heart's still functioning. Need brain food. Hydration. Stat.

He went to the nearby café, which sold sandwiches whose calorie count would require a week on a treadmill to eliminate. He had no intention of spending an hour on a treadmill, let alone a week. He didn't even know where to find the gym he paid £19.99 a month to stay away from.

As he stood in the queue, waiting for the aproned redhead with the lazy eye to make his order, he pondered. The pondering continued until he was at an outside table, sinking his teeth into the mouthwatering ciabatta.

"Be careful".

Of what? The lift? Drew wasn't afraid of a catastrophic malfunction. He never feared for his *life*. Elevators merely had... a past. The noise—unpredictable doses of metallic squealing—echoed a hateful memory.

Perhaps the lift knew that it was more dangerous than other lifts? Was it milking his fear, reinforcing his concerns? The lift couldn't read his mind or know what irrational baggage he carried.

Could it? Pirin's never mentioned anything. And why didn't it speak until I was alone?

He chuckled at his idiocy. A fleck of half-chewed bread hit the pavement. He hoped nobody had noticed.

Perhaps the lift was warning him to be careful about his idea. Or his friendship with Pirin. Or nearly killing pedestrians. Or making a fool of himself in front of the CEO.

Too late on all counts. If only the lift had been more specific with its warning.

Then he chuckled some more at the greater idiocy inherent in that wish.

He frowned. It would be easy to spend the afternoon down an internet rabbit hole, Googling "AI lifts". He'd end up none the wiser and run the risk of his immediate boss, Simon, peering over his shoulder and asking how Drew was getting on with the expenses update for "Britain's Best Lorry Driver". Simon didn't rule with an iron fist, but personal internet use was a big no-no, even during lunch hour. Again, best not to rock the boat. Assuming the lift wasn't smarter than one of the World's Smartest Dogs, what could be a sensible explanation?

Drew put the half-eaten sandwich on the bench, ignoring the spectre of germ contamination from the homeless person who'd probably slept there last night. He took a long slurp on his full-fat Coke. Two pigeons fought for crumbs by the waste bin. A lanky guy exited the café, fumbled with his phone, and cursed violently when it smacked onto the ground.

Drew pinched his lower lip, thinking. Someone cruised by on an e-scooter, phone clamped to his ear, wraparound shades above his forehead, looking like the cat who got the cream.

Scooters: more dangerous than lifts, even talking ones.

Drew took another bite of his now tramp germ-ridden lunch.

Could the voice have been Lotus? She *had* been friendly towards him. Did her classical beauty and workplace professionalism mask insecurity? Was she, in fact, keen on him? He had no idea if she was even single and never considered asking. It was a pipe dream.

But now? Had Kevin's shooing her from the lift scuppered close proximity time with Drew that she secretly desired?

His spirits rose. Even the merest notion of romance was welcome. He'd missed it. His heart may be broken, but perhaps not beyond repair. Maybe this showed it wanted to be mended.

But Lotus? Really?

While it was a million-to-one shot, how could she use the lift as her communication medium? In that short time, she would have needed to reach the lift's Control Room—if such a thing existed—faster than Santa on Christmas Eve. She'd have to grab the microphone—if it existed. Surely there would be a security guard? Why would he let her take over, even for a minute? If it was Len, he'd probably taser her in the eyeballs without a second thought. Would she sweet-talk Len? Flash him? Chloroform him? All for the sake of uttering two curious words to another random employee. An employee she barely knew, who was at least five years her senior, hardly an Adonis, and definitely owned a mobile phone, which could be used for more mainstream communication. Admittedly, he'd avoided romance, but he still *spoke* to people.

It was utterly preposterous. The elaborate deception, the oblique message, the secrecy? Hell, nobody is *that* shy. This would be some odd Mission: Impossible version of Lotus.

This was a dead-end line of thinking, but it didn't mean the matter was closed. In fact, it consumed his mind. After all, he *had* heard something, hadn't he?

As he idly watched the to-and-fro of the lunchtime throng, he unearthed another explanation that made his heart sink and soar. Yes, it was fanciful, but not impossible... surely?

Realising that his housemate might be able to confirm the diagnosis, he put the matter on hold and focussed on fuelling his brain for the afternoon's accountancy tasks.

FLOOR 3

Hannah Thomas closed the door of her ground-floor flat, shrugged off her shoes in the hall, and dumped her handbag on the console table.

The morning's embarrassing debacle had rankled her all day. Yes, it was her own silly fault for forgetting her security pass, but the niggle and discomfort hadn't gone. It was a relief to hang up her work trousers and put on joggers and slippers.

As usual, the curtains were only open a few inches. She pulled off her tinted glasses and lay them on the coffee table, rubbed the bridge of her nose and slouched onto the sofa.

Home. One of her two sanctuaries.

She wondered who the bigger prick was—Len for his over-zealous security, or wannabe saviour Marc for thinking that because he was tall, dark and handsome, she'd give him the time of day. Giving any man the time of day was the beginning of a rollercoaster ride that invariably came off the rails, injuring her, if not him, too.

She dismissed it, padded to the kitchen, and pulled a pre-made chicken and avocado pasta dish from the fridge. Its Best Before date was yesterday, so she peeled off the cover and sniffed. When she didn't drop dead, she grabbed a fork and returned to the lounge. She sat cross-legged on the sofa, and asked Alexa to play some chilled music at a low volume.

She glanced at the landline answerphone. The light wasn't flashing. It seldom did.

As she ate, she reflected on the day and wondered if there was any decent stand-up comedy material in it. She liked to draw on the everyday, and had pages of notes of lines, observations, and stuff which needed more work.

Was the "forgotten ID" episode usable in some form? If she demonised and caricatured Len and Marc, maybe. Plus, inevitably, self-deprecation. Better to ridicule herself than have dicks like Marc do it.

She finished dinner, put the plastic tub in the recycling bin, ran the fork under the tap and laid it on the draining rack.

The doorbell sounded in a familiar *short-short-long* pattern.

Hannah approached the spy hole and double-checked that the visitor was who she expected. It wasn't impossible that her ex, Stuart, might stop by, get lucky with the ring sequence, and find the door literally open for him to spew abuse through. She shuddered.

Mercifully, the worst that might be forthcoming now were some gentle barbs.

She opened the door.

'Hi, hon,' Amy said as she passed by.

Very few people were allowed into Hannah's safe space. Amy Jones was the important one.

'Make yourself comfortable,' Hannah called.

'Way ahead.' Amy treated the flat like a second home—which was fine because it was mutual.

Hannah rolled her eyes and followed her neighbour.

Amy had installed herself on the sofa and was studying an A3-sized sketch on the coffee table. 'What's it supposed to be?'

'The Hanging Gardens of Babylon,' she joked, deadpan.

'Looks more like a futuristic moon landing.'

'That's because it is. Div.'

Amy stuck out her tongue. 'Is your arty stuff a fallback in case the stand-up doesn't work out?'

Hannah shrugged. 'Probably not, I suppose, if even garden variety idiots like you can't work out what the picture's supposed to be. Plus, I do have an actual job already.'

'I am aware, honey. So, aren't you going to ask why I'm here?'

'Because you treat the place like a hotel? Because you want something? Both?'

Amy beamed. 'Red, please, if you're offering.'

'I'm not offering.' Hannah brushed stray brown hair from her temple.

'Service in this hotel! Tut.' Amy rose. 'I'll get it myself.'

Hannah pointed. 'Take the one on the end. You gave me that for my birthday, remember? So technically, you're not drinking anything I paid for.'

'Thanks.' Amy pulled out a bottle. 'Oh, yeah. This is a good one. Least a fiver, if I remember.'

'You're not funny.'

'Luckily, you are, babe.'

Hannah liked receiving that type of comment. Much more complimentary than bullshit about her living like forced rhubarb. But then, Marc—company CFO and close friend of CEO Kevin Yates—was a prick, and Amy Jones wasn't.

Amy took a corkscrew and two glasses from the wall cabinet. The bottle had a cork rather than a screw top, meaning it *had* cost more than a fiver. Amy's friendship was easily worth double that.

Hannah pondered. That was a pretty decent one-liner. She should add it to the list of possible material for her routine—if she ever got to perform any kind of routine, which was perennially doubtful. Anyway, she lived in hope, like she believed a caring, upstanding, well-behaved male of the species would someday enter her life.

Twenty-nine years and counting.

Amy took a healthy mouthful of wine and, to her credit, actually savoured it. 'Oh my God. It's lovely. Taste!'

Hannah drank. 'Yeah. Thanks. You're the best. Now, is this just a social visit and an excuse for weekday drinking at my expense—'

'*My* expense,' Amy reminded her.

'—or have you got something important to say? What's the gossip? You're moving out of the flat opposite, and someone tolerable is moving in? Ideally, who has a penis but isn't one?'

Dry or deadpan was Hannah's favourite way to deliver humour. That would be her onstage style. Better than a smiley, self-knowing, "please like me" approach. All the same, she did want people to like her, however hard she made it for them to get close. It came with the territory. Part of the Hannah "package".

Amy had got close, and liked her—or at least gave a fucking good impression that she liked her. Humorous jibes were part of their relationship. After all, Hannah needed someone to test her material on, and Amy was a good foil. The woman put up with a lot—Hannah's introversion, mocking, low moods and rants. Amy was the next best thing to a soulmate—they were too different as people to be true kindred spirits. Physically, too—Amy's six-foot frame and often unkempt shoulder-length black hair hid a filthy mind and a very direct approach. However, both were single, and Amy was also wary of despicable blokes.

Amy set down her glass. 'This man-wanting, man-hating dichotomy is a real curio, you know, Han?'

'Dichotomy. Four syllables. Wow. Half a glass, and your vocabulary is suddenly, well, competent.'

Amy growled. 'Actually, I wanted to ask about your... project. The secret fight for the sisterhood.' The Welsh lilt surfaced.

Hannah's stomach fluttered. 'You ask every week.'

'Because I care. That okay?'

'Sorry. Yeah. Thanks.'

'So?'

'No. No luck. Well... kind of.' Hannah shuttered her eyes. 'Tell you later, okay?'

'Hmm. Intriguing.' Amy refilled her glass. 'So, wanna hear about my day?'

'Not really, but tell me anyway.'

Out came Amy's serpentine tongue. 'There was a house fire. Bad one. Had to go in and pull a guy out. Should have seen his face when I took off my mask! Poor bastard thought he was being rescued by a proper firefighter. You know—a bloke.'

'You should have carried the prick back in again.'

'Not sure that's allowed. Besides, he didn't *say* anything. Just confused to find *me* under all that gear.'

'Was he good-looking?' Hannah asked.

Amy was wide-eyed. 'This, from you of all people?'

'Hey! Look, I only meant... you know, if it had been love at first sight, it would be a great way to meet your life partner. A cool story to tell the kids. Like if you'd been in adjacent hospital beds or he'd saved you from an escaped lion.'

Amy looked away. 'I'm not looking for a man right now.'

'Well, excuse me if I do.'

Amy scoffed. 'You don't make it easy. Fact, you go out of your way to avoid men. Fact, everyone.'

'Thanks for the character assassination.' She narrowed her eyes. '*Honey*. Occupational hazard of being me.'

Amy didn't rise to it. She took the easier option of drinking more Merlot. 'Wanna meet a firefighter? Harry's looking for a girl.'

'Don't tell me—you've got a scheme to manufacture me a relationship. What—all we need to do is set my place on fire and hope he rescues me on time?'

'Absolutely not! Might burn my place, too. Let's use that as a last resort.' Amy's smile gave her away.

Hannah drained her glass. 'It's irrelevant anyway. If I get the hots for someone, I don't want it to be literal. And it's not all about physical attraction. He has to *care*.'

'Pretty sure Harry would care whether you were burned alive.'

'Because, y'know, it's in his job description?'

'There is that.' Amy shrugged her broad shoulders. 'But you might be his type.'

'What, you mean ferociously shy, stuck in a geeky job, and so absent of friends that she's prone to hanging out with a firefighter who's actively suggesting *starting* fires?'

Amy gently shook her head. Hannah knew why—but being an impossible conundrum wasn't fun. She'd love to be the life and soul of the party, the gregarious girl about town, but things hadn't worked out like that.

'Alright. What about the internet? You can meet people there.'

Hannah grimaced. 'That's worse. People pretend to be something else. Like Kevin Yates projects the image of a decent human being.' She shuddered.

Amy patted her neighbour's arm in solidarity. 'I can help you weed out people. I've done online dating.'

Hannah laughed. The wine was taking effect. 'You said you didn't need a man to complete your life!'

'I meant the old me, when I was looking.'

'Because swiping left and right is much quicker, cheaper, and less illegal than arson as a means to meeting people.'

'Exactly. So, what d'you say?'

Hannah took a deep breath. 'Thanks, but not now, hon. It's a bad time.'

'When you say, "a bad time", you mean the 2020s?'

Hannah scowled. 'You're not funny.'

Amy laid an apologetic hand on Hannah's knee. 'They aren't *all* monsters, y'know. One swallow doesn't make a summer. I'm just trying to support you.'

'By suggesting either Tinder or a tinderbox as my sole hope of getting laid. Leading—in a happy-ever-after way—to me conceiving a child, which will finally get the parentals off my back.'

'You aren't doing it for *them*—don't pretend it's a chore. I've known you four years, and I've caught you outside the wedding dress shop more than once.'

Hannah's mouth opened and closed like a fish. 'Okay, guilty.'

'It's fine. Wanting the "I Do", the two kids, and the end of your free time is perfectly normal.'

'Except I'm not normal, right?'

Amy did a tactical so-so of the head. 'You're... a fixer-upper.'

Hannah jabbed her friend's thigh. 'I can cook. I can draw. I'm smart, funny, and I have very shapely tits.'

'Well, that's a dating profile right there. Want me to set you up with Harry? I can leave out the "tits" part if you don't want to appear too forward. Obviously, forward means you'd be prepared to stand in the same postcode as him, but it'd be a start.'

'Fuck off.'

'Potty mouth. Besides, it's true.'

Hannah didn't deny it. 'Is he an arsehole?'

Amy gazed thoughtfully into her glass. 'Actually, yes.'

'Excellent. Good thing you didn't burn this building down, then.'

'Still, I'll keep my thinking cap on. Okay?'

Hannah sighed. 'If you must.'

Amy fell serious. 'I'm not trying to force you, or live vicariously through you.'

'I know. You understand. You care. That's gold. The problem is getting a man to understand me.' She offered a sober smile.

Amy shuffled closer. 'If you strike lucky with your... project, will you stop this wallowing?'

Hannah reflected on that enterprise, what had precipitated it, and the day's events. 'I bloody hope so. You hope so, too, right?'

'Totally. You have to kiss a few frogs, that's all.'

'They turn out to be toads, though. Poisonous ones.'

Amy nodded. 'I hear you. Hence, my love... *holiday* too. I know you struggle.' She patted Hannah's leg. 'Let's say... I'd like to see what you're like as a *normal* version of Hannah—if that exists.'

Her head dipped. 'Hmm. Me too.'

'Hopefully, fate will throw you a lifeline.'

'Yeah.'

Amy purposefully clanked down her glass and stood. 'Aeroplane?'

Hannah assessed her friend's status as merely lubricated rather than pissed, so she felt it was safe. Plus, she needed the tonic. She went to the area between the sofa and the small dining table in the corner of the room near the kitchen. The pendant light was far enough away.

On days like today, she was grateful that the flat was a few decades old—hence the landline—and didn't have low ceilings.

Without ceremony, Amy took Hannah's right hand in her left, shoved her right arm up and under Hannah's groin, and, in a smooth manoeuvre, hoisted her into a fireman's lift.

'Not gonna chunder?'

'I've only had a glass and a half,' Hannah replied.

'Good!' And Amy spun on the spot, whirling faster and faster like a Catherine wheel.

Hannah let the tension evaporate. She giggled like a little girl.

She stuck her legs out, crying 'Wheeeee!', whilst hoping Amy wouldn't collapse in a heap and break the John Lewis glass table her parents had bought. This was its third house, and being smashed by a toppling firefighter, who was behaving admirably unlike a grown-up, would have been a sad end.

Fun as the dizzying flight was, Hannah couldn't wholly shake off her funk. Amy was a good neighbour and friend, but she wasn't the answer to everything. For starters, she didn't have a penis.

Hannah wondered whether fate would indeed throw her a lifeline—on either of her projects to catch a man.

Today was certainly a step—however unexpected. A good one or a bad one? Time would tell.

FLOOR 4

Drew gratefully slid his key into the front door lock. It was good to mentally exhale. He'd spent the remainder of the day forcibly corralling The Lift Incident into a corner of his mind so he could get to five o'clock, having actually been productive. It would be stupid to let his work slip on the very day the CEO had intimated that Drew was a well-regarded employee.

'Hi honey, I'm home,' he called.

Charlotte appeared. 'That never gets old. Oh, hang on—yes, it does. I'm not your honey. I'm your housemate. Technically, landlady.'

He wandered into the lounge, shrugged off his bag, and collapsed onto the sofa.

'Why do you look like you have the weight of the world on your shoulders?' Charlotte put down the tumble-dried bedsheet she'd been folding, and perched on the chair arm.

'It's been a hell of a day.'

'Drew, you're an accountant, not a trauma surgeon.'

He gave her the side-eye.

Charlotte was three years older than him, two inches taller, and currently a strawberry blonde. She was also worldly wise, caring—despite seldom pulling any punches, and looked better as a brunette.

Because he loved her and needed to be honest about the day's events—especially if he was to get any answers, he jumped right in. 'I spoke to the boss. CEO. About the idea. Katie's idea.'

Her expression showed evident enthusiasm. 'That's great, Drew. Do you think it'll get approved?'

He shrugged. 'Who knows? But it sounded hopeful. Finally.'

'I'll keep my fingers crossed. Was that why it was a hell of a day?'

He decided to keep quiet about the near-miss at the pedestrian crossing. Especially as it paled into insignificance compared to later events. 'I went in the lift.'

'Very good. Ha ha.'

'Honestly. Yates made me. He wanted to discuss the initiative... privately. In the bloody lift, of all places.' He shuddered.

'Shit. You're serious. How many floors?'

'Seven. Then another two.' *Best not to mention that the last two were my fault.*

'Really?' She was wide-eyed.

'Yes.'

'I'm proud of you, Drew.'

'And the lift is pretty old and slow,' he added.

'Don't big it up. Tomorrow, the moon, eh? Or maybe a paternoster.' Charlotte's habitual good-natured mocking had begun.

'What's a paternoster?'

'A lift with no doors which never stops moving. It's like a vertical escalator. You have to time it right, or you might wind up in hospital. Dickheads joyride them.'

'Good. Thanks. That makes me feel *so* much less afraid. Do you do this to all your clients?'

'You're not a client.'

'As you've repeatedly pointed out—especially over the last three years.'

She ruffled his hair. 'I don't think it's right to get involved, that's all.' She stood. 'But I am pleased for you. This is a great breakthrough. Really.'

He sighed. *Wait 'til she hears this other gem.* 'Char?'

She paused in the lounge doorway. 'What?'

'Do you believe in ghosts?'

She laughed. 'Where's this come from?'

He bottled frustration at her levity. Like Pirin, she'd never truly understand how worries plagued his mind, and this new... *event* was something else he'd struggle to convey. Hearing the voice had soured a two-minute period in which he'd successfully confronted a demon—or started to. Figuring out an explanation might be the only way he could consider another lift ride. He truly did want to get over it. It might help put Katie behind him, too.

'Well, do you? Do you ever hear voices?'

She opened her mouth—probably for a smart-aleck put-down. Then, she must have seen his frown because she perched beside him again. 'No, I don't. But I'm guessing this isn't idle chit-chat. Is this what's behind your "hell of a day"? Or was it the lift ride which knocked you sideways?'

He ran a hand through his hair. 'I need a beer.'

He sprung up and went to the kitchen, where he pulled a bottle from the fridge and levered off the cap. The gassy alcohol was like an angel's kiss.

Char appeared, head cocked, curious, empathic.

He gathered his thoughts, fiddling with the bottle's damp label and peeling it off. 'I heard a voice. In the lift.'

'It wasn't the lift announcing a floor?' She raised an eyebrow.

'I may not be a seasoned aficionado, but I know what a bloody floor announcement sounds like! Don't make this harder.'

'Sorry.' Charlotte shook her head at the misstep and pulled a beer from the fridge. 'So, the voice sounded... ghostly?'

He recalled those two mysterious words. 'No. Kind of... sultry. Not ghostly.'

'Why? Are there no sultry ghosts? Do they all go "Woo-ooo" in a scary voice?'

He thumped her arm. 'Grow up, Char.'

'I'm being serious. Real ghosts don't all talk like they do on Scooby Doo.'

'"Real ghosts"? From the woman who doesn't believe in them?' he jibed.

She turned away. 'You're impossible, Drew.'

He clutched her sleeve. 'Wait. I heard a voice—okay?'

She sighed. 'Okay, okay. I believe you.' She squeezed his arm. 'It was a big ordeal—right? You were stressed. Your brain is a bit screwed up, trying to come to terms with what happened. The lift ride—yeah?'

'Hmm. I did think that, but then...' He shook his head and took another slug of beer.

'You had another idea?'

He nodded.

'That makes you think you might be crazy, or it might be a ghost. Something you wanted to ask me about because I'm this... expert.'

'Well, aren't you?'

'Not on ghosts, Drew, no.'

He pulled off more jagged strips of label. 'It's the third anniversary.'

There was a moment's silence.

'Tomorrow,' Charlotte said, frowning sympathetically.

He shrugged, still eyeing the carpet. 'Same difference.'

'Because you're desperately searching for an explanation for this... voice.'

'Well, what do *you* reckon it is?'

'Are you asking me as your sister or as a psychotherapist?'

He grinned. 'You're one big bundle of lovable, caring human being, either way, Char.'

'Don't make me vom.'

'So, could it be... Katie's... ghost?' He tried to peer behind her eyes, seeking jibe or teasing. Nothing was apparent—but her day job required her to conceal feelings or judgement, didn't it?

'Honestly, Drew, I don't know. It didn't sound like her?'

'No. I don't really remember. Maybe? It was only two words. I wasn't listening for familiarity or intonation, y'know?' He heaved a breath. 'It was pretty stressful, like you said.'

'And you didn't see anything?'

His brow furrowed. He caught sight of Charlotte's stack of laundry. 'What, like a white sheet floating in the air?' he scoffed. 'No. Or maybe it was at the laundrette, so Katie couldn't appear in the flesh... or sheet.' He frowned. 'Are ghosts naked, or invisible under their sheets? Or are they rotten flesh? Or skeletons?'

Charlotte touched his arm. 'I think you're getting off-topic,' she said compassionately.

She was right: he was moments away from visualising Katie as a corpse, not an anonymous white sheet, which would be soul-crushing. He'd probably chunder up the beer. He forced his mind back to the unexplained encounter in the lift.

'Sorry. I'm... you know... a bit freaked. But I *did* hear a voice. Or I thought I did.' He shook his head. 'No, I did.'

'What did it say?'

'"Be careful". Twice.' He met his sister's eye. 'So, do you think it's... her? Katie?' He didn't know what answer he wanted. Just *an* answer. Something to settle his mind.

Charlotte swigged her beer, pondering. 'Honestly? I have no idea. It's not my field of expertise. You're a level-headed guy, Drew. Maybe the anniversary is a... resonance of some kind. Even if it's your mind playing tricks, exacerbated by being put in an awkward situation that reminds you of the accident. It does weirdly make sense. It's not like you've heard voices before.' She clasped his arm. 'Have you?'

'No,' he snorted, keen to dispel any notion that he was a weirdo.

'Then I think maybe you hallucinated a voice—even a generic female voice—because of deep-seated grief.'

'Why today? Why not tomorrow—the real anniversary?'

'Maybe she's lost her watch? Maybe it fell off while she was laundering her sheet?' Charlotte smiled and pulled him into a hug. 'Don't stress it, please. It's just a blip, that's all. It's an emotional spike. Completely understandable.' She eased them apart. 'I never lost someone I loved—not like you did. And I never got a phobia from it. I'm lucky. But look at the positives, Drew. You spoke to the CEO, he listened to your idea, and you took a step—even a tiny one—towards overcoming your fears.'

'And then some voice came along and ruined it.'

'In that case, put it behind you. Maybe it was a sign. Maybe Katie—if it was her—was warning you about something. If it's about the lift itself, go back to the stairs if that'll make you more relaxed. Besides, if you never use the lift again, you'll never hear the voice, you'll never get freaked out, and we'll never have a stupid conversation about naked ghosts washing their sheets.'

He chuckled forlornly. 'It was stupid, right?'

She ruffled his hair again. 'Let's hope this was a one-time short-circuit in your mind. So what if it sets the seal on you never going in a lift again? As if you needed any more discouragement.'

'Yeah. It's a sign that lifts and I are not—and will never be—a thing.'

FLOOR 5

Drew slept like shit. It was understandable, but no less annoying. The lift episode—the good, bad, and unexplained aspects—had kept him tossing and fretting until the early hours.

He awoke late and none the wiser.

There was no mileage to be gained by slacking now, not after Yates' encouraging words, so he showered quickly, scoffed a breakfast bar, and left the house.

As he pulled into the office car park, congratulating himself on not having mown down any pedestrians for a second day running, he realised he'd forgotten his access pass.

'Bollocks.' He climbed out of the car and glanced heavenwards. 'I was always a useless arse, right?'

But Katie had loved him, nevertheless. His heart ached. Three years to the day, and he remained a mess, even in small ways. The lift trauma and the voice were merely a blip.

Hopefully. And it's only a forgotten pass. Could happen to anyone.

At the Reception desk, as he was dutifully penning "Andrew Flower" in his perennially neat hand, he happened to look across at the trio of entry gates. At one was the mousey girl from the previous day. At least *she'd* had the sense to learn from her mistake. He offered a wry smile: their fortunes had mirrored. Her response was a nervy flicker. She still sported those glasses. Yesterday the weather had been sunny, but today it was grey.

Odd. Maybe she's famous but trying to remain incognito. Perhaps she's the secret behind the metal detectors. Or maybe her boyfriend gave her a black eye, and she doesn't want to announce the fact. Bastard. Unconscionable.

He took a breath. *Live and let live.*

He collected his temporary badge, passed through the gate, and went to the metal detector arch.

The alarm sounded. As usual. Len—it was he, again—beckoned.

Here we go.

Drew adopted the pose and allowed the over-zealous operative to wave his wand. As before, the wand beeped.

'Forget anything, sir?'

Drew sighed. 'I have a metal plate in my leg.'

'Is that right, sir?'

Alan knows! He should have relayed this critical information. The man's obviously off today or taking the world's longest dump. And the insensitivity of the guy! Today of all days! If only he knew the pain was far deeper than a mended leg.

Drew gritted his teeth. 'Yes. A car accident.'

Len scrutinised his victim's physique. 'I'll pat you down.'

'Go for your life.'

Familiar with being a show pony in a public place, Drew let the guy slap heavy hands over his frame, knowing the search would come up empty.

'Pass?'

Drew held out the blank plastic rectangle. 'Sorry.'

Len sighed. 'Alright. I'll just see some other ID then.'

Drew fished out his wallet and tendered his driving licence. He tried to shut out the buzz of other people arriving for work.

The guard scrutinised the license. 'You work 'ere, sir?'

'Yes.' *What kind of dumb question is that?*

'You commute every day from Bristol, then, sir?'

Bollocks. Drew's spirits dived. 'No. That's my old address.'

'Is it, now?'

'Yes, I forgot to tell the DVLA. I'll do it today. Promise. Look—Len, is it? I work here. Ask anyone.'

Len folded his arms. 'Not sure that "asking anyone" is standard security procedure. Would you think it was?'

'No, no, I'm sure it isn't. But—'

Len handed back the driving license with an equal mix of disdain and slightly scary authority. 'No security pass. No valid ID. Triggered the metal detector. Possibly a concealed weapon or explosive—'

'But you patted me down! And I told you, it's a plate in my leg. I've been through here plenty of times—'

'I only have your word for that... Andrew Flower—if that is your name.'

Drew took a calming breath. *Is this some kind of practical joke? I bloody hate practical jokes.*

'You're new here—I can see that. Alan knows me. So, how about we agree to disagree, and you let me through? I'm Drew Flower. I work on the ninth floor. In Accounts. I always set off metal detectors—'

Len folded his arms, and a smile crept across his lips. 'So, you'll be familiar with dropping your trousers then, sir. So I can see the *scar*.'

Drew glanced around, jittery. In an ideal situation, there would be someone who could corroborate his story. There wasn't. Luckily, nobody important was watching, nobody who knew him. Also, on the positive side, it wasn't a full strip search, and he wasn't wearing his Star Wars pants, so any imminent laughter would merely be at his circumstance and not exacerbated by his choice of undergarment.

Win!

Drew pointed at a secluded area of the foyer. 'Over... there?'

'Can't leave my station, I'm afraid.'

Drew's nerves jangled. His mouth was dry. People skirted him, muttering. Pretty soon, they'd be chuckling. He considered using a Jedi mind trick: "You can go about your business. Move along." However, Drew wasn't a Jedi Master. He was an accountant.

He moved close to the frame of the security arch, partly hidden by the adjacent table, and steeled himself. His hands shook as he fumbled with his belt.

The buckle unhooked. He'd never live this down. The new kid on the block would be catapulted from anonymity to fame—and not in the way he'd hoped.

He unbuttoned his off-the-peg charcoal M&S trousers.

'Drew!'

He froze, recognising that voice. Pirin appeared. Drew exhaled hard enough to inflate a weather balloon.

'Public indecency, Flower?' Pirin shook his head in mock disappointment. 'And right in front of the authorities, too.'

Drew's toes curled. 'Explain to Len, would you, mate?'

For a moment, he feared his friend would hang him out to dry. Mercifully, Pirin vouched for Drew's employment status, character, and surgical implant.

After thirty seconds, with his belt firmly tightened, Drew was heading across the foyer. His heart rate normalised.

'That was a close call,' Pirin said.

'I owe you,' Drew grouched. 'Thanks for bailing me out of dropping trou.'

'Remember your bloody pass in future. Or we'll all have to see your pasty legs,' Pirin replied with a wink.

Drew was about to offer a rejoinder, but they'd reached the lifts. 'Right. Yeah. Done. I said I owe you. See you later.'

Pirin thumbed the `Call` button and offered a sombre smile. 'I won't get on your case today. I know it's the anniversary.' He indicated the security station. 'Hardly a great start, though, right?'

The lift pinged. Drew's body tensed. He should probably tell Pirin about yesterday's trip with Yates—but not a word about that bloody voice. He offered a lame parting wave.

'If the lift does explode, tell every girl I was ever with that I was thinking about her at the end.' Pirin offered a hopeful, cheeky smile—the one he probably used to pick up that same litany of women.

'I'm not sure I have that many years of life left. Maybe I'll put out an ad on ITV, or use that amusing slot at the end of the news: "Prolific but only moderately well-hung video editor Pirin Dharwal sadly plunged to death at work after belittling much more handsome colleague Drew Flower for his elevatophobia. Mr Dharwal has asked that his libido be preserved in aspic and kept at the Natural History Museum".'

Pirin's eyes narrowed. 'If only you were half as funny as you think.'

'If only you were half as prolific, there'd be a lot fewer ladies in black at your graveside.'

'Touché.'

FLOOR 6

Drew's autopilot took him up the nine calf-tightening flights to his floor, one of three that Park Productions occupied. The majority of the company filled the 8th and 2nd floors, having needed to take available space as the business grew over the years. Many of the ex-Bristol employees were fitted in where possible. Accounts—Drew's domain—took half the 9th floor. Pirin was also on the 9th, along with a few more Bristol refugees—there wasn't space for him alongside the other editors on the 2nd floor.

The remainder of the building was used by four other businesses, one of which was covert or paranoid enough to warrant security scanners.

Perhaps one of these companies is the source of the lift voice? Is there some ninja MI5-style shit going on? Were those mysterious words merely a systems test or a case of mistaken identity?

Drew was shutting away the logical, if otherworldly, explanation—it was Katie's voice from the "other side". He wasn't sure if he believed in other sides, but disembodied voices were disembodied voices, and nothing could be ruled out.

As this was the actual anniversary of Katie's death, if the voice of her ghost was likely to reappear, it would happen today. Unfortunately, to hear it, Drew would need to go back in the lift, and he had no intention of doing that.

More likely, it was a daydream, as Charlotte had suggested. He yawned. His body demanded caffeine.

He went into the Park Productions kitchen area, located off the lobby and between the corridors which ran to both ends of the building. The small room was empty. He dug a plastic spoon into the open tub of mediocre coffee granules and fought the urge to half-fill the mug.

He brimmed the mug with hot water from the urn which hadn't been descaled since Brexit.

As he stirred, his mind, then his eyeline, wandered to the lift. He leant against the worktop, running yesterday's events through his mind. He had to take the positives from the enforced lift journey. If it catalysed progress on Katie's idea, or his own career, it would be worth a minute's hell. *I should be proud of myself, dammit.*

Still, the voice had left a sour taste in his mouth. Its source was unexplainable, and the message had been infuriatingly cryptic. If, of course, it had ever happened, which he still wasn't convinced about.

'Any news on that suggestion of yours?' Pirin's voice shook him from the introspective stupor.

Drew jolted. Sudden voices were not his favourite at the moment.

He shot Pirin a glare. 'Yeah, sneak up on me.'

Pirin set about brewing a cuppa using a teabag from a box marked, in heavy Sharpie, "Property of Pirin Dharwal. Touch on pain of death".

Drew considered the heavy-handed threats unnecessary: camomile tea was bloody disgusting. It's certainly not what he expected someone like Pirin to drink. It didn't scream "smooth, well-groomed British Asian lothario".

'Well?' Pirin asked.

Best to come clean. 'Yates spoke to me about it yesterday. In the lift.'

Pirin's mouth hung open. 'You went in a lift?'

'Frogmarched, basically.'

'Shiiit. How'd it go?'

'Um... he listened? Sounded... positive. But there were promises before, at Bristol, you know? Never came to anything. So I won't get my hopes up.'

Pirin nodded. 'Understood. But you should tell me this idea sometime.'

'All due respect, but I don't want to let the cat out of the bag. Obviously, I trust you implicitly not to steal my—Katie's—idea, but still...'

Pirin didn't seem offended. 'But the walls have ears, right?'

A cold wind blew through Drew. 'Maybe some do.' He didn't know why he said that.

Pirin frowned. 'What does that mean?'

'Nothing.'

Pirin didn't look convinced but shook it away, to Drew's relief. 'Okay, but what about the fact you went in the lift? Did you freak out? A panic attack? I don't hear any gossip that you barfed on the CEO or anything.'

Drew held up a palm. 'I didn't scream, chunder or die. Clearly'

'We both know lifts aren't death traps. You've got more chance of winning the National Lottery—or even starting a new relationship.'

'Ha ha. Anyway, it's not fear of death. You know that. I'm not an idiot.'

Pirin stirred his piss-coloured drink. 'Absolutely. Lifts are good. I know you were joking before, but I've hooked up in one.'

Drew scoffed. 'You mean you got the deed done between two floors? Not exactly something to brag about?'

'The lift was out of order.'

'As were you! The whole planet in which to pursue your conquests, and you choose a lift? That guarantees I won't be using the ones here, in case you point out the exact corner you had a girl pressed into.' He shuddered. 'Just stay away from the stairs, okay? Or I'll have no way to go up and down. I'll be trapped on the ninth floor one day, after you reveal that the stairwell on the eighth floor is,' he used air quotes, '"surprisingly comfortable". You'll have to deliver me a futon and coffee. Proper coffee. Alternatively, do the bump and grind in a bed—like normal people.'

Pirin cocked his head. 'Fine. But I'll leave Lotus to you. And don't deny you're interested.'

Drew coughed awkwardly and took a slurp of "coffee" while he prepared his defence. 'Window shopping.' Which was entirely accurate. 'It's not like I'm scouring the place, planning which public area of our new offices I want to use for tapping off with her.' He shot Pirin a glare. 'Unlike some.'

Pirin's eyes widened in mock offence. 'You make me sound like a desperate lothario.' He smoothed his lush hair behind one ear.

'Your words, not mine. And I don't need any more spotlights being shone on my love life. Or do I need to start sneaking bromine into your poncey—and I use this word loosely—tea?'

'Alright. Noted. Besides, you've a good reason to be down on love. I really liked Katie. What happened, I'd never wish that on you. You're one of the good guys, mate. Maybe one day I can make amends for taking the piss so much—be your wingman at just the right time.' He patted Drew's shoulder. 'And I hope the idea gets taken up. And a promotion. You're worth it.'

Drew nodded. 'Cheers.' He checked his watch. 'Talking of which. The spreadsheets are calling.'

Pirin glanced around. 'You working on the budget for "The Lock Keeper"?'

'Yeah, why?'

Pirin shrugged. 'Nothing. Or probably nothing.'

'What have you heard?' Drew moved in conspiratorially.

'Just some odd outtakes in the rushes.'

'And...?'

Simon, Drew's immediate boss, entered. If Simon was promoted—which seemed likely—Drew should be in line to replace him.

'And it's all coming together very well,' Pirin blustered, covering. 'So, I'll get back to the edit suite and see you later.'

'Yeah, later, absolutely.'

Pirin gave Simon a cursory nod and left.

'Morning,' Drew said.

'Morning.'

Simon was a man of few words, so Drew finished his coffee, put his mug in the sink, and headed to his desk.

During the morning, Drew got entangled in an accounting screw-up of someone else's making and lost track of time. When his stomach's gurgling threatened to cause sniggers from the nearby desks, he took a late lunch.

In the 9th floor foyer, he glanced at the lift in worried accusation, realised it was as pointless as tutting at a middle-lane hog, and descended the echoey stairwell.

He ate at a chain café, perched on a stool inside the window. When a couple passed, gazing adoringly at each other, a cloud moved across his heart. Not a day passed that he didn't think about Katie.

These days were worse every year, but more than that, he fundamentally didn't like not being *himself*. The pedestrian near-miss, the ID snafu, the anniversary and now the lift voice was making him grouchy and prickly. Moving to Winchester was supposed to be a new start. He should be wearing a smile. Things were better at work and at home.

Yet, the spectre of that voice—whether in the lift or merely in his head—felt like it was tying him to the past—a loss that he was desperate to move on from. Was it too much of a coincidence that it had happened during his first lift journey in years? Amidst the overall positive outcome, there was a nagging sense of a prank afoot. That was a further explanation he'd conjured up in last night's long pre-sleep phase.

But how to get to the bottom of it?

The universe had an answer for that. Sadly, the wrong one.

FLOOR 7

As Drew crossed the Reception lobby towards the stairwell, he noticed a familiar figure stepping into the lift.

'Hi, Drew. Coming?' Lotus put a manicured hand across the door jamb.

That threw him. 'Oh... no, thanks.'

She was taken aback. 'Yes, you're right. I haven't showered in a couple of weeks.' She wrinkled her pretty nose in mock disgust at his attitude.

Or possibly her own hygiene? Doubtful.

Blood drained from his face, anxiety outbalancing embarrassment. 'No, it's not that. It's just—'

'How did it go with Kevin?'

Which part? My phobia, the pitch, the voice, or me making an arse of myself. Like I am right now.

'Um... okay.' His heart thumped.

The door tried to close. She pushed against it. 'I don't know what I've done, Drew, but you might want to know how things work around here. For instance, who sees the promotion list when it's on Kevin's desk.'

Drew's eyebrows shot up. 'You do?'

She gave a half-smile. Blood roared in his ears.

Stop being so ungrateful and awkward. It's a lift. You proved you can do that. Plus, it's a chance for her to confess to being the voice!

He took a deep breath, summoned Herculean bravery and stepped inside. He winced as the doors closed, praying they wouldn't emit that nails-down-blackboard squeal, which was like a knife in his arguably spineless back.

Lotus appeared concerned. 'You okay?'

'Yeah,' he lied. 'Marvellous. So—the promotions?' He forced a smile through thin, rigid lips.

The lift jolted upwards. He put a shaky palm on the brushed steel wall.

'Oh, well, I can't reveal anything. It's not allowed.'

His shoulders fell. 'Ah. So... that's that?'

She licked her lips. The lipstick was a gentle salmon pink, which suited her. 'Yeah. It's a no-no. Even to people I like.'

He glanced at her eyes, seeking any undercurrent behind that remark, but couldn't find it. She was being nice, letting him down gently. Maybe her attraction *was* real, and a sign of a new dawn, romantically as well as logistically and career-wise? A glimmer of hope?

The problem was, she'd led him on, and now he was stuck in a sodding metal box. Again.

He coughed. 'Right, sure.'

'Good luck with your... initiative thing anyway. And promotion. I'll be watching the list with interest.'

'Thanks.'

An uncomfortable silence fell, overlaid with the hum and rumble of their ascent. The floor counter passed 4.

At least last time there was a bloody distraction! Hang on. Isn't this usual lift manners—facing forwards silently? Or do we discuss the weather?

He was overcome with the realisation that, for the second time in two days, his heart hadn't exploded. Nor had he projectile vomited over someone who could be influential in his career. Was there a microscopic flame of hope that he could *cope* with lifts? Probably only in extreme circumstances. He would absolutely prefer to be in the stairwell now—with or without Lotus.

He glanced up: 5. Should he ask why Lotus hadn't used this ideal opportunity to follow up on her secret "be careful" remark? It meant hers was unlikely to be the voice—or she was horrifically shy.

He peered at the array of buttons, then followed the corner seam of the wall up to the ceiling. He surveyed the joins, looking for evidence of a speaker, but found nothing.

'What are you doing?' she asked.

He jolted. 'Oh. Nothing.' He smiled self-consciously.

The lift slowed and stopped. He exhaled in relief. Then he noticed they were only on floor 8.

As she exited, Lotus helpfully pressed 9. 'See you later,' she said cheerily.

The bright, airy lift lobby was mouth-wateringly tempting for Drew. He screwed up his face, rent with indecision. Should he bail one floor early and take the stairs?

Then, the doors began to close, sealing his fate. There was no way he'd try to dart through—history told him that was madness. He breathed deeply.

It's only one more floor. I can do this. Besides, it's an opportunity...

He jabbed 9 to hasten his departure.

The lift moved. He glanced around, mouth dry, feeling idiotic about this gamble.

'Katie?' he called apprehensively.

He listened hard. Only the awful whine of cables.

'Katie?' he said louder.

The voice—ghost, prank, whatever it was—had gone. It was indeed a one-off, probably some odd resonance due to the Katie anniversary. Still, he didn't know whether to feel relieved or disappointed, vindicated or worried.

The lift slowed, then clunked to a halt. He held his breath. The doors parted, and he exhaled hard through the widening gap.

Stepping onto the marble lobby was like the end of a solar eclipse. He turned to see where he'd come from. His brain needed to truly process that he'd done it—he'd *voluntarily* taken a ride in a lift.

PING!

The adjacent lift opened. Two people stepped out and headed to the offices. He recognised one of them from HR.

'Shit,' he breathed, shoulders slumping.

The lift he'd just spoken to—like an idiot—*wasn't* the one he'd travelled in yesterday. It wasn't the one that had said "be careful"—assuming it had. He'd just proven nothing.

Before good sense could intervene, he darted into the other lift.

'You've lost the bloody plot, Flower,' he murmured through gritted teeth.

His eyes flitted, searching the inside of this new prison. As he reached for the 8 button—justifying that one floor was plenty for his purpose—someone approached.

He panicked. The experiment wouldn't work if he had company... or *physical* company.

'You might want to wait,' he blurted. 'I... farted. It's a bad one. Thought I'd warn you, you know, because—'

The young lad—maybe an intern—looked as if Drew had committed regicide, then scuttled away towards the other lift.

Drew blew out a sigh of apocalyptic embarrassment.

The lift doors closed.

Idiot. Then, as the lift ascended, a klaxon went off in his head: this was the wrong bloody direction. He checked the buttons: **8** wasn't lit. He'd never pressed it!

Shit.

Too late. The lift was being called by someone on a higher floor.

He reached for **10**, then paused. Fate had presented an opportunity. He simply needed to keep calm, make his enquiry, and get out wherever the lift arrived. Otherwise, the chance would be lost, or he'd have to tell another stranger that he'd filled the space with noxious gases. In that event, rather than being the weirdo who'd nearly dropped trou in Reception, he'd be the Fart King of Floor 9.

The lift shimmied upwards. He grabbed courage by the balls.

'Katie?'

He listened intently. The lift's thrum continued. He surveyed around, looking for cameras, microphones... or the diaphanous image of a dead woman.

'Katie?'

Only silence returned.

Actually, he *was* glad it had been a one-off. It meant he wasn't going mad, or being haunted, or the victim of a misguided prank. His shoulders relaxed. The whole godawful episode was over. He could contentedly resume using the stairs and, as a bonus, revel in the small victory of scratching the surface of his phobia.

The display said **11**, so he reached for the **12** button, eager to terminate the ride.

'Who's Katie?' the voice said.

FLOOR 8

It was ridiculous for a bright thirty-two-year-old man to be freaked out by a simple and perfectly logical two-word enquiry about another person, but that didn't stop Drew from freezing rigid.

A small whimper left his throat.

'Who's Katie?' repeated the lift.

'Oh, er, nothing,' he blustered. 'I was just... I lost mobile signal.' *Huh?*

'You were on the phone?'

'Yes.' After all, there was no harm in lying to a nameless, faceless, inexplicable voice. 'I... Is that okay? Sorry—does being on the phone interfere with your circuits? Is it like mobiles on planes? Will I crash the lift? Will I... *kill* you?'

His eyes were saucers. He'd totally lost the plot. 'What am I saying?' he mumbled. 'I'm talking to the bloody lift.' He leaned hard against the smooth wall. 'I must be mad.'

He clutched his head, desperate for the crazy vertical ghost train ride to end.

'No, you're not mad.' The voice was feminine, sonorous and almost soothing. Was it Katie? He didn't know. It had an air of mechanical anonymity.

A sexy robot?

"A sexy robot"? Cretin.

The lift slowed, stopping on 13.

He clamped his lips together and forced a smile as a lady in her fifties, wearing a ghastly print dress, entered. He nodded cursorily.

She returned the favour, pressed 11, and faced front.

He stood—mute, helpless and discombobulated—as the lift descended two floors. It didn't say a word.

Had he dreamed that last thirty seconds? Was the lift, ghost, or prankster preying solely on him, and only when he was alone, leaving nobody to corroborate his ridiculous story?

The short journey passed without overly troubling his phobia: his brain was too busy working out what the hell was going on... and what he'd say next. Perhaps he should bail, and devote his energy to forgetting it had ever happened.

The lady exited on 11. Nobody was waiting in the lobby.

Drew's right index finger, driven by insatiable curiosity—the only explanation for the stupidity of its action—pressed G.

As the rectangle of light compressed to a sliver and was gone, he hoped to heaven that he'd not made the whole episode worse.

He glanced around. 'Hello?'

'Hello.'

Holy shit. 'Um... Did you really say... "Be careful"? Before?'

The lift passed 10. The pause was interminable.

'Yes,' it said.

'Why?' he squeaked, shaking his head at the continued implausibility of everything.

'Because Yates will try to steal your idea. He's a git.'

Drew's teeth clenched. 'Shit,' he mumbled. 'Hang on! You heard the idea? That's even worse!' His pulse raged.

'I'm a lift. What have I got to gain by stealing it?' The tone remained conciliatory.

His mouth opened and closed on a challenge. 'I suppose... nothing.' *It's clearly a logical lift.*

'After all, if I want to get higher in the company, I just... go up.'

Drew snorted. 'Very good. Lift humour.'

'Thanks.'

Floor 9—and safe harbour—came and went. He was committed now. Or maybe he *would* be committed. To an asylum.

He wiped sweaty palms on his M&S jacket, navy, size 42 regular. 'So... after hours, do you and the other lift hang around sharing jokes about us... humans?'

God, I sound like an idiot.

'Only the idiots,' the lift replied.

Drew couldn't hear any ghostliness in the voice. Yet, was it a mind-reader or merely observant?

'Am... I an idiot?' he asked.

There was a pause. 'No. You're... sweet.'

His heart backflipped. Then he realised that both Katie—or her ghost, at any rate—and his own subconscious would naturally think he was sweet. A prankster might say it, too, as a joke.

An explanation was no nearer.

'Well, that's the nicest thing a voice in my head has ever said,' he muttered.

'I'm not a voice in your head.'

Unfortunately, a voice in your head was bound to say that. 'Okay. A ghost?'

'Do you believe in ghosts?' the lift asked.

'I didn't, but...'

The floor indicator flashed 2.

'Well, either way, I'm not one,' it said.

He frowned intensely, scouring around. The voice was coming from everywhere and nowhere. 'What *are* you?'

'A lift. What other logical explanation could there be?'

Something undefinably honest, level, and non-threatening about the voice made Drew believe the lift was telling the truth. All the same, his mouth hung open.

The lift slowed. *PING!*

His mind scurried for what to do next. Getting back to work, rather than dicking around by riding in a crazy talking lift, was probably a stellar career choice.

Besides, when the doors opened, six people wanted his space.

In the available split-second, he debated saying goodbye to the lift or even "See you tomorrow", but couldn't be sure he'd have the balls to go back in ever again. Plus, it remained so fantastical that it *must* be a dream, an echo of trauma, or a visit from another realm.

Instead, he exited, went to the nearest wall and slouched against it.

Katie had been a good mimic. Maybe she was fooling with him from up in heaven, trying to prove that he was still holding a candle for her?

He bit his lip. How would she feel about the conversations he'd had with Lotus? Could Katie look down and sense his stupid grasping at romantic straws?

He shook it away. He hadn't been *chatting up* Lotus. They were merely co-workers. Even if he did fancy her, he also knew it was impossible. About as impossible as a sentient lift.

The voice had asked who Katie was. Surely the voice wouldn't do that if it *was* Katie? Unless it was a clever double-bluff—but what would Katie's ghost gain by doing that?

He was lost for an explanation, so he mooched to the stairwell and climbed.

The topic of deception played on his mind. He'd told the lift he was on his phone.

His feet halted halfway up a flight. He scoffed. Why did he care about lying to a lift or a ghost? Unless it was *Katie's* ghost. He'd feel guilty about lying to her because they'd been like peas in a pod. He missed her like crazy and never wanted to do wrong by her, even after she was gone.

'Shit,' he murmured.

What if there were *other* ghosts? He was new here. Perhaps the office block was haunted, and he hadn't been told yet.

Laboured breathing accompanied his arrival on the seventh floor. He pushed onwards.

Or maybe I'm losing my mind. Maybe this is a dream—everything, including right now? The whole episode? Maybe I didn't speak to Yates. After all, that was too good to be true. Maybe I've never actually been on those lift journeys? That would make sense because I'm shit scared of lifts and would never willingly step inside one.

Maybe I never even moved offices. Maybe I'm not really here.

Yes, that's it. I'm still in Bristol. This is all a dream. That has to be the explanation. Dreams are well-known, widely occurring phenomena. Talking lifts, by contrast, are not.

His foot caught the top step on the eighth floor, and he crashed to the hard concrete, cursing aloud. He gripped his kneecap.

Well, one thing's true. This is a bloody realistic and sodding painful dream.

FLOOR 9

H annah picked the dog-eared card off the doormat.

Terrible handwriting read, "DELIVERED TO No. 2".

That was her default instruction for missed parcels: Amy's shift work meant she was more often at home during office hours than Hannah.

She glanced across the corridor. Could she face Amy's cheery sparring after the day's events? Would the questions be too searching and the advice unpalatable? Or would Amy be awesome? After all, Hannah didn't *have* to mention what had happened. She could collect the parcel and leave.

She closed her door and knocked on Amy's.

After a few seconds, the door opened a crack. 'No, you can't rely on my vote.'

'But I can rely on your shit jokes, it seems.' Hannah held up the card. 'Parcel for the foxy archivist at Number 1, please.'

'Hold on.' Amy's face disappeared.

A moment later, the door opened wider, and a small box was handed across.

'You're in your *underwear*?' Hannah chirped. 'It's six fifteen.'

'Just washing off the day, honey—that alright with you?'

'And if it had been someone else knocking on your door? Mr Fletcher from Four?'

'I don't take in his parcels.'

'You've got an answer for everything, haven't you?'

Amy shrugged. 'Mostly. Still don't know where all the extra mass in the universe is.'

'It's a sticky one, definitely.'

'At least you're helping, though, right?'

'No, not for a few weeks. I never re-joined the survey after that power cut we had.'

Amy put her hands on her hips, which accentuated her biceps. One of them sported a dragon tattoo. Amy's accent was usually gentle, but she was a proud Cardiff lass at heart. 'You should keep doing it, Han. You're into all that sciencey stuff. You always told me how every scrap of computing power helps NASA. Hive mind, wasn't it? You might get a Nobel Prize.'

'For contributing an ageing PC in the effort to discover the ultimate secrets of the universe? Yeah, I'm sure they'll be over in a flash as soon as we get the answer.' Hannah eye-rolled.

Amy made a face. 'Only trying to cheer you up.'

'Who says I need cheering up?'

Amy fluttered a finger towards Hannah's tense brow. 'This. You look like they were dishing out pay cuts on toast today, hon.'

'It's more about having to stand here and look at this.' She waved an equally mocking finger at her neighbour's curvy but toned frame.

'Jealousy is an ugly word.'

Hannah poked out her tongue. 'You stick to public service bravery, carbs, and exercise. I'll stick to solitude, wine, and the occasional run for the bus if I'm feeling keen.'

Amy cocked her head sympathetically. 'Christ, you've had another day, haven't you, shortstop?'

'Fuck off. I'm five-four—which is above average. We don't all need to be Amazonians who stand in the doorway flashing their 36Cs at passers-by.'

Amy craned round the door jamb. 'There are no passers-by. Div.'

'Look, just shut the door or invite me in.'

'Okay.' Amy eased the door closed.

'I spoke to someone,' Hannah blurted. She wondered why she'd done that.

The door was thrown wide. Amy jerked her head. 'In, missy.'

Hannah plopped onto the sofa. Amy's furniture was a few years older than hers, and the sofa was boxier. The decor was eclectic, pock-marked with souvenirs from trips to various far-flung foreign climes. Pride of place was a photo of Amy's firefighter induction day... or whatever it was called.

The resident pulled on a robe. Hannah wasn't jealous of Amy's figure *per se*—if she was five-four with curves like that, it would attract even more one-track-mind mouth breathers, and things had been bad enough. Or maybe the problem was her poor choice of boyfriends?

She shook it away.

A wine glass arrived in her hand.

Amy sat. 'So, when you say you "spoke to someone", I presume you didn't mean you'd declined an offer of "fries with that"?'

Hannah buried her gaze, then nose, then lips in the wine glass. She took a deep breath. It was unusual to be shy here. This was safe ground, and Amy was a trusted and valuable friend. A rock.

If something *was* happening at the office—whether it was an accident or an offshoot of the plan—Hannah couldn't keep quiet forever. Too much was at stake. 'I... proved the system works.'

'Good, I suppose. Look, you know I support the... agenda, but I'm worried about you, Han. Be careful, okay? You gotta admit, it's a pretty risky scheme. Some would call it hare-brained.'

'Thanks a lot,' Hannah snorted. She took a deep breath. 'Sorry. You *are* right. It *is* a risk.'

'I mean, what if you get found out?'

'The person who needs to get found out is Kevin fucking Yates. It's worth it to get evidence, or an admittance, of what he did.' She slugged the wine. 'And who's there to fire me if he's gone?'

'This is your *career* on the line.'

'Change the record, Ames. I'm well aware.' She fluttered a hand. 'Besides, this is a living, not a life.'

'Thought you enjoyed your job?'

'I do. Honestly. I'm lucky. I know that.'

'Exactly. The company gives you leeway to work in a place and a way that suits.'

'Men take as well as give, I'll remind you,' Hannah said. 'But yeah, I do get concessions.' She pinched the bridge of her nose.

'Ohmygod, sorry.' Amy hopped up and switched off the ceiling light.

Hannah gratefully pulled off her reaction glasses and put them on the fake antique coffee table. Amy was usually very accommodating and perceptive. The room's light level was now much more to Hannah's liking.

Amy pointed at the delivery package. 'D'you run out of meds? That's why the headache?'

'No, I'm fine. Thanks.'

Amy clapped her palms as if bringing an audience to attention. 'So—who was this person in the lift?'

Hannah held the woman's gaze, deciding. She wasn't ready for full disclosure. It would only put Amy into a fervour and set expectations unnecessarily high. 'A man.'

'Aha!'

'I know you have the mathematical brain of lichen, but it was a fifty-fifty chance.'

Amy poked out her tongue. 'Did he freak out?'

'No. Well... No. He was fine. I think.' She hoped he was.

'Why d'you speak to him? He another... groper?' Amy's face betrayed concern.

'No. He's just a guy.' She hoped the deliberate nonchalance didn't show.

'You sure he won't blab about hearing a voice in the lift?'

Hannah was gripped by fear. She squeezed the glass so tightly that it might break.

Amy's arm was quickly around her. 'Hey, hey.'

Hannah put the glass down to save Amy's carpet from potential shards and stains. Pros and cons raced through her mind. 'No. I don't think so. I hope not. He doesn't seem the type.' Or was that just faint hope?

'How do you know from a quick hello?'

Hannah bit her lip. 'Just a feeling.'

'Thought your feelings about men was that they're all bastards. Hence the reason you don't date them. Hence the lift... thingy. Why the exception, eh? Why speak to a random? Save it for Yates.'

She pulled away. 'Will you stop the grilling? Please? I'm making a fucking effort. You should be praising me, not undermining me.'

Amy's nose wrinkled. 'I just wish for you, y'know?'

'Join the club. Some things can be fixed, some can't. I'd rather not be a victim. I'd rather have a boyfriend. A decent one, for once. I'd rather not have to wear those fucking glasses. I'd rather do sell-out comedy tours than sit behind a screen all day. I'd rather have a bit of fucking social confidence. If wishes were horses, I'd have a fucking stable of Grand National winners.' She snorted back tears, and drank more wine.

'You *really* need to get laid,' was Amy's apposite summary.

Hannah calmed. 'Right now, I'd settle for pizza. And if there's anywhere locally that's guaranteed to have one in the freezer, it's Number 2, Arlington Court.'

Amy sprung up. 'I'll put the oven on.'

While Hannah often mocked Amy's diet, sometimes it provided an ideal get-out-of-jail-free card.

'So, it went... well?' Amy returned and sat. 'This test, I mean. If you wanna talk about it.'

'Not especially. Just keeping you in the loop. Letting you know that... wheels are in motion.'

'Wheels for what? That's the question.' Amy fluttered dark, strong eyebrows.

'Put a sock in it, Jonesy.'

'Rather put Chardonnay in it.' So Amy did.

There was a movement by the single French door which led to the communal garden at the rear of the property. A warm evening breeze fluttered the translucent curtain, which Amy had thoughtfully pulled across so the nearby houses didn't have to witness her underwear parade.

'Oh. Hi, Cat,' Amy said.

The feline hobbled towards them. The poor thing was missing one back leg.

'You should keep the door closed,' Hannah suggested. 'Then it wouldn't come in.'

Amy tossed a hand. 'It's harmless. It's company. Plus, it doesn't take offence at what I wear.'

'Or don't wear,' Hannah said pointedly.

'Besides, I like the door open. If Cat wants to come in, it's a risk I take.'

'You shouldn't have fed it that first time.'

'I feed you,' Amy retorted, disappearing into the kitchen.

Hannah heard the clatter of a tray, then the thunk of the oven door. Amy reappeared.

'If you're going to have it around, at least give it a proper name,' Hannah said.

'Don't wanna get attached to it.'

'So, chase it out.'

'Fuck that. First time I did that, banged my shin on the table. Hurt like bugger. Can't be arsed anymore.'

Hannah rolled her eyes. 'So much for the daredevil firefighter vibe.'

Cat meowed, rubbing against Hannah's leg. She stroked it.

'Now *you're* encouraging it,' Amy said.

'It's clearly a stray. What have you got against adopting it properly?'

Amy laughed. She had a dirty laugh—deep, like her voice. 'I don't wanna become a single, crazy cat lady.'

'I think you need more cats, worse dress sense, and probably a missing front tooth.'

Amy shrugged. 'Okay, I don't wanna become... a spinster who's happy with a cat.'

'You're not a spinster! You're only thirty-one.'

'You're right. Besides, a cat's no substitute for a person to snuggle up to on a cold night.'

'Do as I say, not as I do?'

Amy glanced away. 'I'm taking a break from dating, okay?'

'Then so am I.'

'I'm not the one chatting up people in lifts.'

Hannah was open-mouthed. 'I didn't "chat him up"! What gave you that idea? I said I *spoke* to a guy!'

Amy winked. 'Okay, but I bet you enjoyed having him inside you.'

She gave a firm shoulder nudge. 'Do you kiss your mother with that mouth?'

'How else would I kiss her? For a girl with a one-thirty IQ, you can be an idiot sometimes.'

Hannah sighed deliberately. 'Maybe a cat would be a less judgemental friend after all.'

Amy thumped her, reasonably gently, on the upper arm. Then she went to check on their cordon-bleu dinner.

Hannah bit her lip nervously as she tickled Cat under the chin. Her defence had been accurate—she wasn't *chatting up* the guy in the lift. Yet, why was she presuming he was different to other men?

This guy—slightly geeky, rather jumpy and with a fixation on someone called Katie—was merely a testbed for her bear trap.

Wasn't he?

FLOOR 10

The oranges and pinks in the sky were bleeding away into navy blue. Drew needed to leave soon; this wasn't the kind of place he liked to be after dark. *He wasn't a wuss; he merely... Okay, maybe he was.*

He rearranged the posy of flowers for the third time and stared at the inscription. He wished he'd grabbed a bite to eat on the way. Now, he felt hungry but was obliged to stay as long as possible. Nobody else cared. It was simply his duty—or he thought it was.

The grass rustled nearby. 'All candles go out, eventually. Even the one you're holding for Katie.'

Bloody hell. Can't a man get an hour's peace?

Charlotte rubbed his shoulder.

'The key word there is "eventually",' he said.

She sighed. 'Look, Drew, I'm not denying you're in pain. I'm only saying you shouldn't let it rule your life. Three years is enough time to be sworn off love, surely? Move on.'

He knew she only said things like this to help him, but it still rankled. 'Like *you* have? Don't tell me you're not carrying a torch for Sam. I may not have an alphabet after my name, but I know what's happening.' He wrinkled his nose. 'Richard's a... rebound. A temporary fix. He's "two ibuprofen and call me in the morning".'

Her eyes flared. 'At least I've moved on! You don't see me loitering around Sam's house, checking his post, or conducting vigils in the alley beside The Red Lion where we had our first snog. Richard isn't perfect—he may not be Sam—but he's better than nobody, which is who *you* seem determined to spend the rest of your life with.'

He turned away, nerves crackling. 'Whatever.'

What a way to honour Katie—a sibling scrap at her graveside. Idiot. Come on, Drew, don't mistake grief for anger. And don't use dickhead Richard as your weapon.

Silence fell.

'Besides,' Charlotte said, 'Even if I *am* holding a candle for Sam, at least it's got a chance of catching alight.' She pulled him around to face her. 'Grieve, Drew—fine, but don't shut out any chance of ever being happy. I miss Katie too, okay? She was good for you. Christ, I *want* you back to those days of loving life. You need to stop thinking there's only one person for everyone, you had that shot and lost it.'

'Look—'

But the tough love continued. 'I don't give a shit whether you get in a lift again, or insist on never being a car passenger—those sense memories are tough, but they're in your *head*. The loss of Katie is heartbreaking, but love can *mend* hearts if you let it. You can *choose* to be hope*ful*, not hope*less*. You don't have to go out clubbing, speed-dating, or on a singles holiday, but at least be open to possibilities, not shut away and in denial that you need love. You had it before—why believe you don't still need it?'

Her words were like a coroner's scalpel to his heart—cutting but necessary.

'What if I lose it again?' he said. 'It'll break me.'

She glanced down at the grave. Her expression softened. Charlotte was attractive in an unconventional way. She had the kind of face you'd open up to—which was ideal in her profession. It was also a magnet, which was difficult to avoid at times like this. 'How many girls did you go out with before Katie?'

'Six.'

'And you lost them all. Right? You didn't get into a three-year funk after those breakups, did you?'

He wanted to excuse it by saying that Katie was The One, but knew that would only worsen his mood.

He puffed out a stale breath. 'I suppose not.'

'And, yes, the accident was a trauma, but you're happy to take car journeys with me. You don't consider what would happen if there was another crash and *I* died—your own sister. So, avoiding another *girlfriend* because you're worried about history repeating itself is bollocks.'

'What happened to you *not* counselling me?' he sniped. Then he regretted it. This whole scenario was made worse by his deep-seated knowledge that she was right. He did want to find love. Charlotte just didn't appreciate how bloody hard it was to let go.

'This isn't *counselling*,' she said. 'It's trying to knock some sense into you, Drew. I don't need to get analytical and rummage around in your head. It's basic stuff—you need to get back on the horse. Why not, I dunno, make friends with some girl that you have no chance of dating? It's a risk-free step towards re-entering the game.'

'Hmm.'

Yet he *was* allowing himself to get close to Lotus because it was risk-free. They could never be a couple. That meant he could chat, banter, even flirt—or allow her to do the same—knowing she'd never truly be romantically interested in him. It was... a dry run for something that would, hopefully, come later.

He felt buoyed. He'd been taking Charlotte's advice even before she gave it! Maybe he was starting to second-guess her psychoanalysis? It wasn't wicked or sexist; he was merely... putting his training wheels back on, and it had even been *encouraged* by another woman. "Greenlit", as they'd say at work.

She put her arm around him. 'I love you, Drew, and you can have all the tea and sympathy in the world from me, for however long. I don't expect you to wake up tomorrow and miraculously not feel sad ever again. That's not how grief works. It's not like a light switch.' She put a hand on his chest. 'Let someone else besides me into your heart, okay? There's a big space waiting to be filled.'

He met her hopeful expression. 'I suppose.'

Charlotte pecked him on the cheek, then knelt and rearranged the posy of flowers he'd worked on three times already. Annoyingly, she did improve matters.

Then she stood, pulling up her collar. 'I'm cold. I'm going home. You coming?'

He looked down at the inscription, blew Katie a kiss and sighed. 'Yeah.'

Drew stopped for a McDonald's on the way home. It was late, he couldn't face cooking, and he bloody well deserved a treat.

At home, he showered, hoping to wash off the layer of emotional grease and the veneer of burger fat on his fingers.

He padded around the bedroom in his boxers, lost for how to pass the time until he could legitimately hit the sack. He didn't feel like sharing the living room with Char, nor watching one of her TV crime dramas. Taking a bottle of wine to his room would end badly.

Wallowing was one thing, especially on the anniversary, but doing it drunkenly hadn't worked out well on the last two anniversaries.

Perhaps he was finally turning a corner?

He considered telling Char about the second, extended conversation in the lift. Did talking to an unknown voice—whether in his head, in the walls, or from another realm—count as a "risk-free step towards making friends"?

Yet his sister hadn't raised the topic, so he left it alone. It was easy to imagine her advice: "either get over it or do something about it". The third choice—to stew about it—was unhealthy.

His gaze fell on the tall Ikea bookshelf. Gingerly, he went to it, took down a tiny box, and sat on the bed.

Steeling himself against emotion, he opened it. The ring sparkled.

'Oh God,' he murmured. Still, nobody had made him look. It was self-torture.

He looked at the ceiling. 'Tell me it isn't you.'

The lift voice hadn't possessed Katie's tone, but only by hearing her actual voice could he be wholly convinced the lift wasn't her.

Yet it was an eternal loop of ridiculousness, and he felt a fool. It didn't stop him from curling up on the bed, clutching the memento, and giving her a chance to call down to him.

She didn't.

FLOOR 11

As Drew sat munching his lightly buttered toast the following morning, he revisited the short night of fractured sleep. He'd been thinking about Tom Latham—when he wasn't pondering Katie or the lift.

Tom had pranked Drew during their second year at Bristol Uni. At least a dozen people were in on the joke. When Drew discovered what had happened and who it was, he came as close to a fist fight as he had with anyone, before or since.

Tom had been his best friend. After the prank, they never spoke again. The worst part was that Drew suspected something fishy but had done nothing to uncover it. In hindsight, he'd let the charade go on until it was way past being funny. He should have pulled out a metaphorical deerstalker and found out what the hell was going on. This mustn't happen again.

He put the dirty breakfast things in the dishwasher, grabbed his keys and went to the front door.

Charlotte appeared on the stairs, robe neatly tied. When he'd moved in three weeks ago, due to the office relocation, they'd shaken hands on an agreement to always dress decently.

"I don't want to stumble across you walking around with your undercarriage out" had been the gist of her decree.

It was a mercy that since Charlotte had split with long-term boyfriend Sam, she hadn't taken to inviting current squeeze Richard over for evenings of headboard rattling. Sure—Drew didn't begrudge her getting some, but ideally, not in the house they shared. Also, ideally, not until he broke his three-year barren spell.

'You're up early,' she said.

'I've got... something to do.'

'Bad sleep, right?'

'What do you think?' He hadn't meant it snidely, but his words had that undercurrent. 'Sorry.'

She nodded slowly. 'S'okay. Have a good day, bro.'

He forced a smile. 'Thanks.'

The car park was empty when he arrived at 07:22. He didn't recall ever being at the office that early. Even the Receptionist raised an eyebrow as he breezed through the barrier. No security snafus today!

As he pressed `Call`, he experienced only residual fear. Now that the anniversary of Katie's death had passed, the voice—if it was a ghost—should be gone. If it was a sign of something lurking in his head, clarity and purpose would hopefully defeat it.

More than anything, if it was a prank, it needed to be kiboshed quickly. If someone was eavesdropping on conversations in the lift, he needed to be careful about gossip or unwittingly mentioning the initiative he'd submitted to the CEO. Equally, Pirin had to be warned not to attempt any lift-based... nonsense which might be reported and come back to haunt him. Besides, if the voice continued to generate unease, it would derail his frankly stellar efforts at conquering his elevatophobia. Plus, it was making him spiky, suspicious and grouchy—and he hated being like that.

The left-hand lift arrived. That was the correct one—assuming there was some predictability to this crazy episode.

He stepped in and pressed 9.

As the doors closed, a hand was thrust through.

Drew cursed silently.

The middle-aged man with silver hair and a loud tie nodded a greeting, selected 12, and took up the standard British face-forward-and-ignore-the-other-occupants pose.

Because Drew's plan had been scuppered at the first attempt, he could only idly but deliberately glance around, attempting to see where any prankster might secrete the necessary communications device.

When they reached 9, he'd discovered nothing. As it would look weird if he didn't disembark, he did.

With a sigh of disappointment, he went to the kitchen, made the habitually shit coffee—it would at least kickstart his system—then went to his desk. It was wise to log on to the system in case the upper echelons were monitoring employee productivity. As he'd arrived early—even though it was explicitly not for productive reasons—he should get credit for clocking on at an impressively prompt hour. It would be an unexpected bonus if he gave the impression of a very committed soul at the exact time a promotion was being considered.

He necked the coffee, then dashed back to the foyer. He had to strike before things got busy, or face waiting until the end of the day.

It took three tortuous minutes for the left-hand lift to arrive. When it did, it was ascending and already occupied. He journeyed to the top floor, only to find someone waiting there, ready to come down. So he sheepishly mumbled something about having missed his floor, hit **9**, and endured another awkward coexistence back down to where he'd started.

'This is bollocks,' he murmured as he walked back to his desk.

Before long, it was lunchtime. The niggling curiosity about the voice had been silenced by tedious things like debits and credits, chasing missing hotel receipts, and avoiding staring into space.

To prove he was a big boy who was now only merely unsettled by lift travel, he took the left-hand lift to **G** for his lunch break. Unfortunately, seven other people did, too.

One thing became clear as he walked to the café: the voice didn't like company. It was solely *his* "friend"... or victim.

After ingesting the necessary calories for afternoon function, he rode back up to the 9th floor. Sadly, with company. In the lobby there, Pirin was waiting to descend.

Drew felt oddly like a rabbit in the headlights, even though he'd done nothing wrong.

Still, Pirin was wide-eyed. 'Sneaking around, buddy? Should I tell the stairs you're cheating on them?'

'I was... bugger off. I'm trying really hard to... blend in, okay?' He leant in. 'Char gave me a sisterly... talking-to. You know, manning-up, stuff like that.'

Pirin glanced around. 'Did she use thumb screws or anything?'

'Are you basically asking if she's into kinky shit?'

'The nerve of you, mate. As if I'd... Well, is she?'

'I'm not letting you near her. I love her too much. Dangle your hook elsewhere. And don't tell the stairs. Me and the lift is... a temporary thing.'

Pirin gave Drew an unnecessarily heavy—and somewhat patronising—pat on the shoulder. 'Such courage. What's next? *Dating?*' He whistled in amazement, then darted to the open lift, beaming at a passing girl.

Drew shook his head, then returned to his desk.

He strung the working day out until six thirty and was the last to leave the Accounts office.

Nobody else was waiting when he called the lift. Nobody was in the lift when it arrived. He examined the bare interior, took a deep breath, and stepped inside.

He pressed **15**, reasoning that few people would ascend at this late hour, and he was statistically more likely to be left alone.

The doors imprisoned him, and the mechanism whirred into action.

His mouth opened, shaking. 'Are you there?'

No reply.

'Damn,' he breathed. 'Are you there?' he repeated.

'I'm here,' the lift replied.

Definitely not Katie.

Unaccountably, his spirits rose. 'Listen, you need to know something. I don't normally like lifts. In fact, I despise them, so if you're tricking me—whoever or whatever you are—it's disgustingly unfunny and mentally cruel. I hope you realise that. I'll go back to using the stairs. I don't give a shit.'

There was a telling pause.

'I don't care either.' But it sounded like a comeback, dripping in insincerity.

'That sounds like a lie,' he guessed.

'How do you know? You don't know me. Do you think my programming *allows* lying?'

That threw him. 'If it allows conversations, isn't anything possible?' *This is like trying to outwit a supercomputer.*

'Not anything, but some things.'

'Why are you talking to me?' he asked.

'Why not? Oh. Do I scare you?' The voice sounded... concerned.

'A little. But I was scared of lifts anyway, so—'

'Really? Why?'

He shook his head. 'Long story.'

'Okay.' The voice was quieter. It seemed to have nuances.

The lift rumbled past **13**. Its mechanics were like white noise now. Whatever the explanation—ghost or prank—it was arguably a force for good in conquering his fear. Or so it appeared.

It was time for the killer question. 'What are you? Really?'

'I'm a lift. Was that not... obvious?'

He forced a laugh. 'No, I meant *really*.'

'Let me ask you a question,' said the voice. 'What do *you* think I am?'

The bell pinged. 15th Floor.

'Bollocks,' he exclaimed. His journey was complete, but without a definitive answer.

'No, I'm not that.'

His laugh was real this time. Before anyone could come along, or he had second thoughts, he jabbed G twice, then Doors Close.

They—he—set off.

'So?' the lift asked. It remained the most feminine "it" that Drew had ever encountered.

'I think you're a ghost. Or a voice in my head.'

'Would that be bad?' it asked.

'I never thought of myself as someone who believed in ghosts. You're the first I've heard. If so, you're not very scary.'

'Maybe I'm taking time off from being scary to talk to you?'

'Why?'

There was a pause. 'You seem... nice.'

He snorted. 'Gullible, more like. Or crazy.' An idea lanced into him. 'Are you a brain tumour?' His hand shook.

'I'm a lift. And... don't be afraid.'

His breath had quickened, so he calmed it. The counter passed 8. He couldn't spend all evening shuttling up and down. The day was already long enough. He needed a decent night's catch-up sleep—especially if lack of sleep was contributing to this hallucination... if that's what it was.

'Do you have a name?'

'No,' it said.

He glanced around and spied the lift manufacturer's plaque, but Otis was a guy's name, and he couldn't use that. 'Can I call you... Elle?'

'If you like. Why?'

'Because you're an *el*evator. Get it?' He smiled at his frankly brilliant wordplay.

'Hmm. That would be funny and clever, except we're in England, and the word is "lift",' it/she replied.

'Ah. Right.' *Idea!* 'But what letter does that begin with?'

74

A pause. 'Oh. I get it. Very good. Yes. "Elle" is okay.'

'I'm Drew.'

'Hello, Drew.'

He looked around with awe and strange affection. 'Hello, Elle—ghost, voice, tumour, whatever.'

'Lift,' the lift enunciated.

He sighed. 'Okay.'

The display passed **4**. The lift seemed to be aware of this. 'Before you go, Drew,' it said.

'Yeah?'

'Be careful of Kevin Yates.'

'Huh? How does a lift know about the CEO? And, what about him?'

'Be careful, okay? Ask me some other time. Does it matter *how* a lift knows, providing it *does* know?'

'Knows what?'

'Later.' The lift sounded weary.

Perhaps it's had a hard day shuttling people up and down. It must get very tiring and dull.

That sounded ridiculous.

The counter ticked over to **1**.

'Drew?'

'Yeah?'

'Have you told anyone... that I talk?'

'No.'

'Really?'

He bit his lip. The lift probably meant "anyone in the office". Charlotte didn't count. 'I've no intention of broadcasting it around the building. Honestly, Elle, whatever is happening here, mentioning a talking lift—nice as you are—is unlikely to win me many friends. And, believe me, right now, I need as many as I can get.'

'Okay,' it said softly. 'Thanks.'

The door tone pinged, and the brushed metal wall parted.

'Night,' he said, feeling distinctly odd and rather silly. Firstly, he was offering a parting comment to an inanimate object. Secondly, lifts didn't sleep. They probably didn't even have any concept of night.

'Night,' it replied.

That put a cherry on the icing of the unbelievability cake.

As he walked across the deserted foyer, he realised that his determination to discover the source of this mind-fuck had yielded absolutely nothing. In fact, it had probably made the matter worse.

FLOOR 12

I t was after eight o'clock when Drew got home.

In the kitchen-diner, Charlotte was stuffing her face with takeaway chow mien. She usually cooked, so takeaways often indicated that she'd had a gruelling day trying to sort out other people's problems.

'Everything all right?' she asked.

It would be wrong to burden her with another problem. 'Yeah,' he said noncommittally. 'Just got held up.'

'Mmm-hmm.' She shovelled in more noodles.

Sometimes, you can see glimmers of the tomboy who chased me around the garden as a kid, trying to pin me down and push ice cubes down my t-shirt.

Most of the time, she was a bright, well-presented, professional, caring woman. She also had excellent analytical and deductive skills, which was his undoing. 'Meeting someone?' One eyebrow arched.

He coughed. 'Not really.'

'Mmm-hmm.'

He pulled two slices from the bread bin, ignored butter, and put a leftover thick, off-cut of ham into the impromptu sandwich. He sat opposite her at the table and chewed pensively, not meeting her eye.

She wiped her lips with a napkin. 'Has the voice gone?'

Shit.

Now he was in a dilemma: come clean and risk mocking disbelief, or bottle the issue and have to spend the next few days acting like nothing was wrong.

It was an easy decision: a problem shared is a problem halved. If he'd singularly failed to identify what the hell was going on, she was infinitely more qualified to offer suggestions. Besides, he wasn't genuinely reneging on his promise to Elle. Elle was hardly omnipotent. She was only a lift. She'd never find out that he discussed the matter with his sister.

Listen to me, treating a lift like it has feelings. This definitely means I need professional help.

'No,' he said.

She pushed aside the empty bowl. 'And are you still freaked out by it?'

'Confused, more than anything.'

'I see. What did it say?'

'Lots of stuff.'

She nodded slowly. 'So you had a conversation with this... voice.'

'I think...' He gazed skywards, sceptical of his words. 'I think it's the lift.'

'The lift?' Her tone was flat. *Probably the same non-judgmental response she uses in her sessions.*

'Yeah. She... it... talks like, well, I don't bloody know.'

'She?'

'It sounds female, so, yeah, "she". Does that make me extra crazy, assigning gender to it?' he scoffed, taking a hearty bite of the sandwich and shooting Char mock evils.

'You'll be telling me next that it... she... has a name.'

He inspected the plate.

'Oh, Christ,' she murmured.

'What?' he rapped, feeling accused. 'Is that *even* worse? Go on, ring up the asylum and book me an Uber.'

'Drew!' she snipped maternally. 'I only meant... Oh, hell, I don't know. This isn't my wheelhouse, that's all.'

He shoved his chair back and dumped his plate in the dishwasher. To diffuse the situation, he put hers in as well, then took two beers from the fridge and followed her into the lounge.

This was kill or cure: Char had to convince him it was all his imagination or help find a logical explanation. He needed an ally.

They drank, and she took a deep breath. 'So, it has a name?'

'Yeah. Elle.' There was no point in saying it was a name he'd invented. So what if he'd needed to assign an identity to the voice? It helped to make it... real, because it felt pretty bloody real.

'"Elle" as in "elevator"?' She gave him a "yeah, right" expression.

'That's American, Ms PhD,' he mocked. 'L for lift.'

She smiled, patting his hand. 'Drew, you've been had. It's a schoolboy prank. Even if Elle sounds female, it's probably voice-changer software. I'll bet it's a warped male security guard at the other end of the Help button.'

'Coming on to me?' he pointed out.

'Coming on to you?' She shook her head in disbelief. '"Has the lift been coming onto you?" Jesus, listen to me, asking ludicrous questions.'

Drew made and released a fist. 'I thought you'd be happy. You wanted me to speak to people. Especially females.'

'Yes, I'm thrilled you have a new lift in your life.'

He rose to her sarcasm. 'Well, at least she won't dump me—like Sam did to you. Or be unfaithful.'

Riled, she gritted her teeth. 'Do you think she'd be unfaithful with another man? Or another lift? Maybe a woman. Does she go both ways, this lift? Silly me, of course, she does.' She slugged her beer. 'Ooh, I've got it. Has the lift been down on you? Have you been down in her?'

Drew slammed his beer onto the coffee table and strode away. If the voice *was* a prank, he didn't need this kind of shit from his bloody sister as well. Unfortunately, it was well-meant and pretty funny. Also, he was making things worse by needling Char about her love life, which was pointless and cruel. He excused it as a fight-or-flight response. This whole situation had him in a tailspin, making it even more important that he worked out what was happening. At the moment, it was affecting his home life, which was dumb. If there was one person who could guide him through this, it was Charlotte.

He'd only got as far as the kitchen, so for something to do while the air cleared, he put a tablet in the dishwasher and set it going. Yes, he was technically only a tenant, but had to pull his weight.

He took a few calming breaths and returned to the lounge.

'Remember Lizzie, your imaginary friend? Why can't Elle be like that for me? Except I swear that her voice is *real*.'

Charlotte stroked the condensation on her bottle. 'Lizzie's voice was pretty real to me. The difference is I was six. You're thirty-two.' She shot a sober glance.

'I didn't know there was an age limit to imaginary friends,' he said.

'You said it's a real, life-size, metal and screws lift. Not an imaginary voice.'

He shrugged. 'Well, she *says* she's a lift.'

'Hmm. Well, it's not ideal, is it—talking to a lift? But it does smell like a prank. I just hope it doesn't destroy your career, that's all. Remember Tom Latham? You went apeshit after that. Going medieval on someone at work is probably not a good idea, especially if the CEO is considering the sabbatical initiative.'

'And there's a whiff of promotion in the air.'

'Exactly,' she said.

He picked at the bottle's label. 'If it... she... the voice... makes me *less* afraid of lifts, that's better than nothing. Whatever is behind it. Right?'

'Better than therapy, for sure. Cheaper, too.' She smiled in reassurance. 'Maybe the whole prank is *designed* to cure your phobia. Maybe Pirin's behind it.'

Drew laughed. 'So my best mate is chatting me up? He's playing dumb *very* effectively for someone who knows me. And what's his end game?'

'To distract you into taking so many lift journeys, you wonder what all the fear and fuss was ever about.'

Shit. She had a point. It was precisely what he'd done that day. *But how come she knew?*

'This sounds more like something *you* would cook up. Immersion therapy or whatever.'

'And I'm a good enough actress to have this conversation, pretending it's not my idea?' She smiled. 'Let's say I *was* doing this. How would you feel if, or when, you found out?'

'Really pissed off.'

'Even though the stunt cured you? You'd rather it was an actual talking lift?—which I'll remind you is not a thing. Or do you still want it to be a ghost? Or schizophrenia? You'd rather a *worse* explanation than someone who cared enough to put you back together?'

He drank pensively. 'Okay, well, if you really care, you'll tell me, right?'

'Or what? You can't boot me out—this is my place. And you can't dump me—I'm your sister. And you can't avoid speaking to me because living in silence will give one or both of us a breakdown.' She took his free hand. 'Look, whilst it's a damn good idea—and I wish I'd thought of it, no, I have nothing to do with it. The rational explanation is gone. So, it's either a sentient lift, a prank, a ghost, or... you're losing your mind.' She winked.

'Wow,' he said sarcastically. 'What a choice. And if I Google "sentient lifts", will that make you take the piss even more?'

She squeezed his hand. 'You know that any piss-taking is done from love.'

'So, will you *please* stop doing it, sister darling?'

She did a so-so of the head, and drank, avoiding the question.

'You're a bloody nuisance, Charlotte Alicia Flower.'

'And you're living under my roof, Andrew David Flower. Whilst getting free therapy, I might add.'

'That—therapy?'

'It's a sounding board—which is better than nothing. If you want my honest opinion, if we can dismiss the idea that it's the ghost of your dead girlfriend—who loved you dearly, remember—trying to scare you or drive you nuts, then that's a start. Do me a favour and focus on *logical* explanations.'

'So... you really do believe there's a voice?'

'I believe that you believe there is.'

'That feels like a get-out.'

She sighed heavily. 'Honestly, Drew, today I had a client who was looking for reasons why she shouldn't chop her husband into little pieces and mail him to all corners of the globe. I have to accept that she feels that way. It's ludicrous, and I can't empathise, but there we go. Yes, I was only six, but Lizzie was as real as Elle seems to you. So, perhaps I can empathise here.' She kissed the top of his head. 'Get an early night. It's been a draining couple of days.'

'I am grateful, Char. I may be losing my marbles, but you're a star.' He hugged her.

She ruffled his hair. 'Thanks.'

He took his beer—and another one for luck—and went to his bedroom. There, he opened the Notes app on his phone and created a new entry:

Elle/voice
1) Ghost: unlikely 3/10
2) Stress: possible 4/10
3) Prank: likely 7/10
4) Insanity: unlikely 2/10
5) Sentient lift: very unlikely 1/10
6) Other??

Then he played some loud music and tried to carve out a couple of hours ignoring the whole mess.

FLOOR 13

Mercifully, Drew slept well. Wednesday dawned with relative calmness in his mind.

As he ate a proper breakfast, he thought it odd that Char wasn't awake. She was a creature of routine, going to her local clinic four days a week, eight hours a day.

She'd lived in Winchester for nine years. It's where they'd grown up as kids, and Drew had only gone to Bristol because that's where the Park Productions satellite office had been when he joined the company.

He'd moved in with Katie in Bristol, but after she died, he fell apart. He couldn't face a housemate, so he struggled along, paying the rent until it wiped out what he'd been saving for their marital home. When he'd been forcibly repatriated to Winchester by the closure of the satellite office, there were only a few weeks to arrange a place to live. Prices were too high, he couldn't face sharing with Pirin, and he felt too old to live with a stranger.

Luckily, he got a break. Char took pity on him, specifying that it was a temporary arrangement until a better opportunity arose. The three-bed semi offered relative luxury, but he'd much prefer his own place. One catalyst for that would be a promotion. If Kevin Yates was half-serious in his praise, Drew could soon be out from under Char's feet. A proper new start.

'Hello, Drew.'

He jumped. Actually jumped. There was nobody in the room. He glanced at the doorway, but Char wasn't standing there.

'Hello, Drew,' repeated the metallic voice.

His eyes darted, and his pulse quickened.

'This is Jane the toaster.'

He glowered at it. Undeniably, that's where the voice was coming from.

'Will you introduce me to Elle the lift? I hear she's a hot metal box like me.'

He sprang at the bloody thing and yanked its plug out of the wall. Then he peered down the toast slots.

'You snake in the grass, Charlotte Flower!' he bellowed, plucking a phone from the metal jaws.

Hoots of laughter drifted down the stairs.

'What happened to caring about your poor, distraught, tormented brother?' he railed. 'What happened to not pranking me?'

She burst into the kitchen, hair wet, towelling robe tied tight, and flung out her arms. 'Oh, Drew.' There were tears of mischief in her eyes. 'I'm sorry. I couldn't resist.'

He allowed her to squeeze into an apologetic hug. 'You're the worst sister *ever*.'

'It's so wrong, and cruel, and unprofessional, and misjudged, and...' she broke off. 'Bloody hilarious!'

He crumpled in the onslaught of her good humour, and a faint smile broke out. 'You won't laugh when I bring home a sexy air-conditioning unit to meet her future sister-in-law.'

'That would be... cool.'

He shook his head. 'Lame.'

'Fine. You leaving, or what?'

'Yep. Capitalism calls.' He necked the last of his builder's tea.

'Drew?'

'Yeah?'

She frowned. 'Are we okay? Forgive me?'

'Yeah. But please don't do it again.'

He grabbed his jacket and headed off.

On the way up to his floor, the lift was occupied, so the day's first opportunity was a washout. At lunchtime, Drew took another ride, but he had company.

At around three o'clock—which should be a lull—he hung around in the kitchen, glancing out at the lift lobby until it was empty.

He ran out, pressed Call, and the left-hand lift arrived. It was vacant. He gave a fist-clench.

He chose 13—for no particular reason—and the doors closed.

'Elle?' He listened impatiently. 'Elle?'

Not only did the lift not reply, but it also didn't move. He pressed 13 again.

Nothing happened—no voice or movement.

Perhaps 13 is unlucky? Maybe Elle doesn't like that floor. He pressed 12.

'Elle? It's Drew.'

Now, fear clutched his chest. The lift was motionless.

'Elle? Elle?! What's going on?'

He double-checked that he was in the correct lift: he was. He prodded 12. His breathing quickened.

Oh shit, oh shit.

There was no rumble, no whine, and definitely no voice. He punched the Doors Open button once, then twice.

Elevatophobia closed in on him. He was going to die. He'd never get Katie's initiative through the suggestion scheme. He'd never achieve promotion. He'd never discover what or who the voice was.

He hated everything. He pressed 9 because it couldn't do any harm. He jabbed Doors Open again. At any moment, he'd be hyperventilating.

Then the doors parted, and he nearly fell forwards in his haste to escape the torture chamber. He staggered to the nearby Gents and slouched against the sink worktop. He sucked in the air—with its merest whiff of unflushed piss. He splashed water on his face and leaned over the basin, letting the droplets fall from his skin.

When his breathing had normalised, he tugged a paper towel from the reluctant dispenser and dried his face. He went to the loo, washed his hands and looked in the mirror.

'Well, so much for the voice curing me.' He shook his head. 'Maybe it *was* all a sodding dream.'

Then he took a deep breath, painted on his game face, and returned to his desk.

The afternoon was a struggle of matter over mind. He threw himself into tasks. He discovered an anomaly in the expenses for the "The Lock Keeper" shoot and emailed the producer/director, Sian Bright. He was pulled into a meeting about upcoming productions.

It was Brianna's birthday, and he scoffed two of the rather delicious cupcakes she'd brought in.

It was past six o'clock when he approached the lift. But, hard as he tried, he couldn't face it. He gave up and trudged down the stairs.

A funny thing happened during his descent. Despite the reawakened phobia, what occupied his mind was disappointment. He missed it... her... whatever the voice was or represented.

He paused, one foot between steps, pondering.

How is it possible to miss an unexplained phenomenon which might not exist?

Yet, Elle insisted she was the lift. So why didn't she answer? Lifts don't take breaks. Does that mean Elle can't be the lift? Does it mean she—or he—must be a prankster? What if the lift malfunction was part of the game?

Drew snarled. He was almost back to square one. Even if he didn't hate or fear lifts to the same degree as before, he was pissed off with them. It. Her.

He rattled down the remaining steps, into Reception, and out to the car park. He texted Char, received the desired reply, called in at the supermarket, and then went home.

'What's the occasion?' she asked when he entered the hallway.

'Does there need to be one? You act like I never cook.'

Her eyes narrowed. 'Hmm.'

'Pick out a suitable wine, and don't get all suspicious.'

'Too late.'

An hour later, they sat at the dinner table. It was only spag bol—but Drew was proud of his skills in this area.

'So, do you want to come clean?' she asked.

That's the problem with psychologists—covering stuff up is hard. Besides, it wasn't as if the dinner hadn't been a bribe.

He explained what had happened—the absence of the voice, the lift malfunction, and his reaction. Despite his annoyance, he missed Elle. She/it was sweet and understanding. He needed to know why he should be wary of Kevin Yates. Plus, he wanted to get back in a bloody lift again—any lift—because he was almost cured.

He asked her to hypnotise him. It wasn't something she did for clients, but he knew she'd taken a course a few years ago.

'I want to give this a shot,' he affirmed.

She nearly spluttered out her Tesco Finest Cabernet Sauvignon. 'Give what a shot? Talking to a lift?! You do realise it would be a lot bloody easier if the *staircase* was talking to you.' She frowned. 'And anyway, you said the lift *didn't* talk to you this time.'

'Maybe it... she... had a glitch? A system reboot, so she was offline for a minute. After all, the lift *did* stall, or malfunction or... something.'

She sighed. 'Okay, I know what I did with the toaster was cruel, but you can't get hung up on a talking lift, Drew.'

'So you're saying you won't hypnotise me to help me get over this? Give me a chance at restarting the conversation?'

She shook her head. 'Sorry, bro. No.'

'What changed? You *wanted* me to make new relationships. I'm trying to get over Katie by talking to a female... thing? It's a start, okay!'

'Then you'll move on to human beings?'

'Unless you know any cyborgs I can chat up in the interim?'

She smirked. 'The problem is, it's hardly a smooth "relationship", is it? It makes you nervous of lift failures and... you don't even know what the thing is anyway.'

'Yeah, it's a bitch when relationships break down. Which I remind you they do *in real life*.'

'I am bloody well aware of that,' she snipped.

'So you *are* still bitter? Yet you're hiding behind that to take the piss out of me. You tell me to move past Katie, yet you hold a grudge against *your* ex.'

She glanced away. 'I do not hold a grudge against Sam. I'm just pissed off that it ended in a silly way when it didn't need to. Or maybe it did. I dunno. Leave it alone, Drew.' She slurped her wine, trying to terminate the conversation.

He wouldn't let it lie because he hadn't made any progress on *his* issue. He was mentally hurting, and would lean on his family as heavily as he needed until he felt better.

He took a deep breath and put calmness into his tone. 'Why don't you call Sam? If it *was* a misunderstanding?'

She wrinkled her nose dismissively. 'He's in a relationship.'

'How do you know?'

'Facebook.'

He was open-mouthed. 'So you've checked him out!'

She waved it away. 'I get curious.'

'Okay, sure, fine. But how do you know he's *happy*?'

She glowered—he'd hit a nerve. 'I can't go crawling back. It's weak. Plus, I have a boyfriend!'

'When's the big day?'

'It's not like that.'

'So he isn't a keeper?'

She jabbed the table. 'I haven't decided, and I won't be rushed by you or anyone. In case you forget, my clock is absolutely not ticking!'

She sank more wine. 'Besides, this conversation was about *you*. Why are you so keen to hook up with a talking lift?'

He gritted his teeth. 'I didn't say "hook up". I just want to find out the truth—like you suggested, and to do that, I need to be able to go in there, not freak out when a little thing happens.'

Charlotte smiled genuinely for the first time in minutes. Her demeanour instantly became conciliatory. 'So if you realise it's only a mechanical glitch, and no sensible person should be afraid of it, you're halfway there.' She raised her eyebrows hopefully.

Damn. The head doctor has got me. 'Hmm,' he grumbled.

'Unless the lift has PMS, of course.' She winked.

He chuckled. The wind left his sails. 'So, you really won't hypnotise me?'

'You don't need it. You went in before, without help. You can do it again, Drew. I believe in you.' She squeezed his hand.

'What do you really think? Free pass, Char—give me your best shot. I need a way out of this.'

She smiled supportively. 'My best shot? You're not lying or delusional, and the Katie anniversary is just a coincidence. I honestly think it's a prank on the new boy—'

'Shit.'

'—and please get to the bottom of it before it drives me nuts, too.' She winked.

His shoulders relaxed. 'Thanks. And I love you too.' He mopped up Bolognese dregs with a scrap of garlic bread. 'So... what could be a reason for a prank?'

She shrugged. 'When you find the culprit, maybe you'll know.'

FLOOR 14

Hannah shut out the world as she journeyed home from work. As usual, she wore headphones, so nobody on the bus talked to her. Jim had pissed her off—which, admittedly, was unlike him—and a migraine had ensued.

Most of the time, sharing the bijou office with only a mild-mannered 61-year-old was a decent way to pass the working day. Jim had a ton of fascinating stories, was happy to keep the lights at a low level, and largely left her alone. As the junior of the two archivists, she'd learned a lot from him. Most of it was work-related stuff, but some was about moustache care, the wife he doted on, and how Hitchcock was a genius.

Jim hadn't said anything controversial, but he'd spouted a string of reasons why Kevin Yates was a fine CEO, which was a red flag for Hannah. So, she'd bailed on the dot of five o'clock.

The Jim conversation wasn't what occupied her thoughts now, however. It was the disappointment elsewhere. Just when she'd found a light in the darkness, it seemed to have flickered and died.

She made a quick early dinner—scrambled egg on toast, browsing the web on her laptop while she ate. Despite a lingering brain fog, she was keen to follow up on the concerns and brainwaves she'd pondered on the bus.

Then she flopped on the bed and snoozed. It usually helped the triptan tablet rid her of a migraine.

A familiar *short-short-long* on the doorbell woke her an hour later. She snorted into full consciousness, felt relieved that her headache was gone, and went to answer the door.

Amy burst through, paper waving in a raised hand, a raven-haired Neville Chamberlain in bare feet and ripped jeans.

'Seen this?' she rapped, barging past. 'They want to double the fucking ground rent.'

Who needs friends when you've got a one-woman army, Hannah mused. Better not let her near Kevin Yates—she'll mash his face. Whilst it would be just deserts, it would make the intercom a waste of time.

Amy thumped onto the sofa.

Hannah sank down beside her. 'Blimey, Ames. You're worse than my migraines. At least they don't bother me every bloody day.'

'Aw, hon.' Amy stroked Hannah's arm. 'So,' she asked more gingerly, 'Not the time for ground rent-related discussions, I suppose.'

'Too fucking right. You woke me up.'

'Shit, sorry.'

'It's okay. I'm on the mend.'

Amy deposited the letter from the landlord onto the table beside the open laptop. She noticed the screen and shot Hannah a pointed look. 'Want to enlighten me?'

'Shit,' Hannah breathed. 'Not really.'

'Want me to guess?'

'Not really.'

Amy stood. 'Want me to make a cuppa?'

'Yes, really.'

'Want me to open the emergency chocolate digestives I know you keep hidden from my grubby mitts?' Amy's eyebrows fluttered knowingly.

Hannah smiled. 'Yes, definitely.'

Five minutes later, tea in hand and two biscuits in her belly, Hannah decided that honesty was the best policy—again.

'This the guy?' Amy asked.

'Yes.'

'He looks nice. Normal. But a quick chat, and you're already stalking him?'

Hannah slapped the mug down on the table. 'I am not stalking him! I'm... researching him.'

'Ah. "Researching".' Amy stroked her chin.

'I checked his profile on Facebook and LinkedIn. That's it. I want to know who I'm... talking to.'

'And if I scrolled through the Search History, how many clicks would I find on his photo gallery?'

'Very few, okay? This isn't about what he looks like. It's about whether he's a dickhead man, a sexist arsehole or a lying shit.'

'Is that a shortlist of three possibilities?' Amy asked pointedly.

'No! I'm looking for evidence of number four—decent and trustworthy.'

'Because...?'

'Because he wasn't there today—alright? Give me a break, Ames. I had my eyes open, but not a peep. I'm just... disappointed, that's all. I expected better.' Hannah sighed. 'He's probably given up. Freaked out. Damn.'

'Or, maybe, you know, the two of you metaphorically passed in the night. You do leave your chair, right? I know you have a packed lunch at your desk, but you don't actually piss in a bottle while Jim turns his back?'

Hannah opened her mouth to tell her to fuck off, but she had a point. 'I s'pose,' she mumbled. What was that in her voice—disappointment?

'Right.' Amy stood. 'I'm getting to the bottom of this, Miss Thomas.' She took Hannah's hand and hauled her up.

Hannah complied, nonplussed, as Amy dragged a dining chair into the middle of the room. She left the overhead light on its dimmed setting but switched off the two wall lights. Then she marched Hannah to the chair and eased her into it.

'What the fuck? Did you have half a bottle of gin before you barged in?' Hannah asked.

'Shush!'

Hannah rolled her eyes as Amy paced around the chair, hands behind her back, an impish smile on her lips. All that was absent were a riding crop and thigh boots. 'You're saying you miss him?'

'What? I don't know.'

'You think you could be... friends?'

'Who knows? It's early days.'

'Are you using him to get to Yates?'

Hannah frowned. 'No.'

'To get a promotion?'

Hannah chuckled. 'No.' She had no interest in that.

'You just like the sound of his voice?'

She pondered that.

'Well?' the inquisitor demanded, circling.

'Not *just*.' Best to be honest—Amy had seen the picture of the decent-looking blond guy with strong shoulders.

'Are you lonely, Miss Thomas?'

Hannah perked. 'Aha! Trick question! If I say "yes", it implies you aren't a good friend—which you are.' She bit her lip. 'But, yes, I prefer solitude at work.'

'Do you wish this Drew guy was there instead of Jim?'

'I... don't know.'

Amy stopped in front of her and crouched. 'Is it cos you want to wake up with him one morning?'

Unbidden, Hannah's head filled with a vision of being in bed with Drew. Sunlight was peeking through the curtains. Birds were singing. She was happy. She wondered whether he'd be wearing a T-shirt...

'Bzzz!' Amy said. 'You waited too long! The prosecution rests.'

'But... but...'

Amy glanced at the laptop. 'Clean as a whistle, isn't he? Safe to talk to? Maybe more than that?'

Hannah sprung up, frustrated to have been figured out. Yet, she didn't resent it. She necked the remainder of her tea and eased onto the sofa.

Amy joined her. 'You can't carry on like this forever. Hiding, teasing him. It's not fair. Plus, he'll eventually realise you aren't a lift. And that you're much more appealing than a metal box.'

Hannah cocked her head. 'Thanks, hon. That's the nicest compliment I've ever had.'

'That, I doubt. So, what're you gonna do?'

Find out more about him,' she mumbled, picking a few crumbs from the sofa cushion

'You mean put a camera in the men's loos?'

'I am not a stalker!'

'Doesn't sound like it if he's the only one you talk to.'

'That's called "conversation". Besides, he *chooses* to keep coming in the lift. Until today, maybe. Or maybe not. And I'm still waiting to get Yates alone in there. Or see more evidence.'

Amy fell sober. 'When you came up with this idea, Han, I thought you were crazy. Brave, but crazy.'

'And now?'

'Still a long shot, but what's crazier is chatting up a guy while pretending to be a bloody lift.'

'I am not chatting him up!' She glowered at Amy, then looked away. 'Besides, think of it as... a masked ball or a Valentine's card.'

'Then why not write him a Valentine's card to show you're a real person?'

'In May? I mean, Royal Mail is pretty shit, but he'll see the postmark date anyway,' she joked.

'So—talk to him! For real.'

'I can't. You *know* that.'

'You're right. Sorry.' Amy's face lit. 'Ooh! I'll do it!'

Hannah held up a hand. 'Oh no. I'm not having you box me into a corner.'

'I'll only say nice things. Promise.'

Hannah shook her head. 'You'll set up some trick date which'll be impossible for me to get out of.'

'You have such a low opinion of me, Han. I *save* people from getting burned. Plus, you know I want the best for you.'

'I know. Thanks.'

Amy took Hannah's hand and spoke softly. 'So ask yourself why you've broken silence after so long. Why you tested the intercom on this *particular* guy. Why you keep talking to him, and why not to someone else as well.'

Hannah crumbled like a shortbread biscuit. 'You know what's most annoying about you? When you're right.'

Amy nudged her. 'Then go for it. Reap the rewards of your idea.'

'I didn't bloody do this to meet men! Come on, Ames! You *know* this is a punt. It's risky. You *know* it's for... social justice, not shagging.' She wrinkled her nose in distaste. Sometimes, despite everything, Amy dropped a bollock when it came to understanding her friend.

'Sorry. Look, it's a smart idea, Han. And you know I'm right behind you.'

'Yeah—pushing me into the arms of someone I barely fucking know. And the arms and hands of other pricks started this whole thing in the first place!' She was gently shaking. 'It's my trap, and I'll do what I bloody want with it.'

Amy waved it away. 'Whatever. I'm not the one with a degree in Electrical Engineering.'

The air of patronising dismissiveness pissed Hannah off. 'You're also not the one with social anxiety, photophobia, fucking migraines, and a vagina filled with cobwebs!'

Amy's face creased into apologetic sadness, and she opened her arms.

Hannah squashed into her. She rested there, controlling her breathing, feeling the comforting pillowiness of Amy's ample bosom. For the briefest moment, she wondered what it would be like to be wired differently, happy in the arms of a woman and not tasked with finding a decent guy in a world of unsuitables.

Amy stroked Hannah's hair. 'Sorry, honey.'

'Me too. Will you please let me do this my way? I need you on my side. But with this... whatever it is... with this guy, I'm comfortable—for the first time in ages. Not afraid. I'm joking around with him. I don't do that with everyone. I take the piss out of you because there's a... bond. We're serious, you and me. Don't spoil... *us* for the sake of this. For the sake of a man, for fuck's sake. There are other men, but there aren't other *us*.'

'Wow. That's the most touching thing you ever said to me.'

Hannah scoffed. 'I know. Won't get any laughs, though, will it?''

'Not everything is about laughs. Love is important, too.'

'Don't use that word, please. Don't get ahead of things. If I have an ally at work, in that lift, it's a start. If I can chat, it's a start. If we have fun together—even without meeting, it's a start.'

Amy pushed her away and nodded sagely. '"The journey of a thousand miles starts with just one step".'

Hannah faked sticking a finger down her throat. 'If I ever come into your flat and find a single motivational poster or twee slogan engraved on fake driftwood, I'll *seriously* have to re-evaluate our friendship.'

'Noted. Now, after tea and biscuits, would the lady of the house like a wine chaser?'

'Fuck yes.'

'I use the word "lady" loosely,' Amy added.

'Takes one to know one.'

'Touché.' Amy went to the wine rack.

'Ames?'

'Yeah?'

'You know that you're my role model?'

'Aw, that's sweet.'

'Apart from intellectually, socially, physically, emotionally, and in matters of diet and fitness.'

Amy blew her a kiss. 'It's mutual.'

FLOOR 15

It was Friday—the last chance of the week for Drew to discover who or what Elle was. Unfortunately, when he got to Reception, there was a sign in front of the left-hand lift: "Out Of Order. Engineer Attending". He looked around, cursing his luck. No engineer seemed to be bloody well attending. Another famous lie like "Thank you for holding, we value your call" or "All day battery life".

Three people swerved him and waited outside the right-hand lift. He took the stairs—familiar, reliable old friends.

Pirin was in the kitchen, making his first cup of hot floral wee. He spotted Drew's glance towards the lift. 'Yeah—broken. Feel smug, do you?'

'Not at all.' Drew wouldn't admit to being oddly disappointed.

'Won't be long—apparently.' Pirin rolled his dark eyes. 'Engineer is waiting for a part to be delivered.'

Drew looked around. 'What bloody engineer? And anyway, how do you know that?'

'You know Wendy in Facilities?'

Drew got a familiar sinking feeling. 'I'm guessing not as well as you.'

'I know she's a 34B, if that's what you mean.' Pirin winked.

Even his wink is sexy, for heaven's sake.

Pirin sometimes sailed close to the wind, but Drew had never heard a negative word about the guy. They were simply very different characters. Pirin was carefree about life; Drew was more sensible, having been shaken by past events. Even before all that, he'd never craved a string of women, merely one. If there was jealousy, it was for Pirin's gift of the gab.

'That's enough information. Probably more than enough. Anyway, what did Wendy say is wrong with the lift?'

'Besides it being broken?'

'I mean... did the engineer find anything unusual?' Drew trod carefully.

'Like what?'

That flung him out of his depth. 'Dunno, er, maybe it was rigged to kill me?'

Pirin looked at him like he was mad—which was fair. 'Is this about the other day, when you got stuck for, like, ten seconds? You think this was a plot? What—to prove that you were right to be afraid of lifts? So that, as it plummeted, you could say "told you so" to nobody except yourself. Wow. That is a major need for validation.' There was jest and incredulity in his friend's tone. He flicked the teabag into the bin and tossed the spoon into the sink. 'Okay, I'll bite. So, who do you think would rig the lift to kill you?'

Now that's a question. 'I haven't been here long enough to make any enemies... I hope.'

That simple placeholder comment, as soon as it left Drew's mouth, triggered a thought, and it buoyed him. 'I hope so too, mate.'

Pirin patted him on the shoulder. 'Be a shame to get brutally murdered just as you're lightening up about the whole elevator thing.

Anyway, if you have any ideas, email me. That way, I can pass the names to the police so they can arrest whoever manages to kill you.' He pulled a crazy face, then left.

Drew made coffee and went to his desk, walking on autopilot as he mulled Pirin's accidental suggestion.

If the voice was a prank, it would surely be borne of good-natured ribbing, not actual antagonism. He honestly couldn't think that he'd pissed anyone off. The alternative was more palatable—someone was trying to strike up a dialogue. A female someone. A *nice* female someone. Of course, the ghost or inner demon was still minutely, ridiculously possible, but this was a better explanation. Even more fortuitously, he had an idea who the voice might be—the same person he'd previously considered, then discounted.

At ten thirty, Drew strolled down one floor to Kevin Yates' office like he didn't have a care in the world. Inside, he was a bag of nerves.

Yates wasn't really a "management by visibility" CEO. He was more of a "Friday is for golf" guy. Thanks to that stellar dedication to helming Park Productions, Lotus should be alone in the CEO's anteroom.

She was. He took a deep breath. *In for a penny.*

'Hi, Lotus.' He perched on her desk to appear confident and relaxed—which was a stretch.

'Hi, Drew. Kevin's out. Sorry.' She indicated the frosted glass partition.

He checked his watch. 'Probably on the sixth hole now, right?' He chuckled lamely.

Encouragingly, she laughed. 'Yeah.'

'So... um... I see one of the lifts is broken.'

She frowned. 'Yeah. What about it? You seemed a bit nervous last time we were in the lift?'

'Me? Nervous? No. Probably just... stressed. Lots on—you know. New office, the initiative, promotions...'

'Yes,' she chirped. 'Busy, busy!'

'So, I was wondering whether... you knew what was up? Know anything about electronics and lifts?'

'Ha ha! Me? I can't wire a plug. You want to ask Wendy in Facilities—if it's that important.'

'No, no,' he blustered. 'Just... interested in what's wrong.'

Lotus frowned. 'O-kay.'

'I might ask her about ghosts, too. But you've been here a while, haven't you? Longer than me, for sure. Do you know anything about this place being haunted? I mean—if you believe in stuff like that. Do you? Believe in ghosts?'

Wow. You're killing it here. Any smoother, and she'll probably swoon.

She leant in conspiratorially. 'Are you on drugs, Drew?'

He laughed over-zealously, desperate to conceal crippling awkwardness. It weakened his core, shifted his balance, and before he could stop, he'd slid off the edge of the desk and smacked onto the floor. 'Bollocks!'

Then he realised he'd sworn in front of a perky blonde that he wasn't *really* trying to chat up, but who might have a soft spot for him. Or now might *previously* have had.

'Shit,' he murmured, clambering up.

She reached out. 'Are you okay?'

'Fine.'

He dusted down with an appalling attempt at nonchalance. Concern mixed with amusement in her expression. He cleared his throat to feign purposeful self-control. He felt like a teenage Drew, nervously asking Geena Hawkins for a dance at the school prom. Mercifully, Lotus didn't laugh and point.

He pulled over a spare chair which he should, in hindsight, have put his stupid arse on two minutes ago.

'Are you really okay?' she asked.

'You mean am I off my tits on crystal meth, or will I be able to sit down comfortably for the next few days?'

She grimaced. 'Look, Drew,' she waggled a finger at her PC. 'I do have... stuff to be getting on with.'

'Yes. Sure. Sorry. The thing is...' He took a deep breath. 'You know last week when Yates asked about my... initiative, and then he shooed you away like a puppy—'

'Oh, that's just how we work. I *am* his PA.' Her smile was nervy.

'Right. Yeah. Sure. No, it's not about the puppy thing... although...' He bit his lip and searched her face. 'Does he treat you okay? Is he a decent boss?'

She touched the desk near him. 'Oh, Drew, that's sweet. We... Kevin and I... get by. As people, I mean.'

'As a boss?'

'There's no shouting, enforced late nights, that kind of thing. Is that what you mean? Where's this going, Drew?' A worried expression appeared. 'Did he say something about me? In the lift? Is that it?'

He frowned. 'Oh—no. The lift conversation was about my idea.'

'Phew. Thank heavens. I thought for a minute he'd asked if you knew a better PA—like from over at Bristol, that type of thing.'

He smiled. 'No. It's fine. You obviously make the grade.' He glanced around. 'The thing is... what I wanted to ask... I heard a rumour that Yates is a bit of a... what's the word...? Scumbag.'

She flinched a little, then regained her composure. Yet, Drew noticed something in her eyes, like a child crouching in a dark corner.

'Kevin's fine.' She checked around. 'Scumbag in what way?'

'I don't know. I heard voices—rumours, I mean—that he's not to be trusted. Shady.'

Her eyes darted. 'I don't know about that, but...' she murmured.

He leant in. 'But...?'

She wheeled her chair closer. 'Kevin has a lot on his mind right now. At home.'

'Ah.'

'Financially, really. His divorce is due to come through, and she'll take him to the cleaners.'

Drew nodded. 'Because he... went "off piste".'

That tickled her, and she smiled. He was pleased. He hadn't wanted to be too oblique but also not say "shagged someone else" in case that was a bit laddish or sexist.

'Yes. Or "shagged someone else", as your friend Pirin would say.'

Drew held in a smirk. 'You play with fire, you get burned.'

'Exactly. And the former, or soon to be former, Mrs Y knew that. They had a... whatchamacallit... prenup, and if he had an affair, she gets, like, seven figures.'

Drew whistled softly. 'You'd imagine that was enough incentive to have kept it in his trousers.'

'Temptation is temptation, though, right? Especially if you're... that way inclined.' She looked away.

'And what if his wife had had an affair?'

'Then she gets nothing. Well, not nothing, but not retirement-at-forty money. So, if Kevin walks around like Godzilla next week, you'll know how it went.'

He tapped the table, processing. 'Does this mean he's not actually following up on my initiative? Is he serious about the whole employee suggestion scheme? Or is it a ruse to make us think we're valued?'

'Oh, no, I think it's genuine and useful. I've seen three good things be adopted. Why, do you want me to put in a good word for you?'

'You mean, not tell him about how I drop acid and then roll around on his carpet?'

She laughed. 'Come on, though—ghosts? Be real.'

He gave an embarrassed smile. 'Yeah. What an idiot. So... um... my suggestion thing—would you stay on here if there were more perks? Would it increase your loyalty?'

'Hell, yes.'

'Good. Right. So, let's say you... got a month off for long service. What would you do in that month?'

She brightened. 'Live on a desert island. Sunbathe, drink, decompress. Cool, eh?'

'I can't think of anything worse. I'd be bored shitless.'

'Oh. But what if you were there with a hot blonde?'

He froze. *Why is a hot blonde asking the question? And why specifically like that? Is this a come-on? A chink in her armour? A clue that somehow, despite denials and the utter implausibility of it, she's behind the lift voice?*

He unfroze, so she didn't consider him a freak—again. 'I'd be bored shitless and have constant groin pain?'

She laughed, with a side-order of eye-roll at his arguably one-dimensional thinking. 'Well, *I'd* like to escape from the real world, have some space, work stuff out.'

'What stuff?'

She shook her head. 'Never mind, it's personal.'

'Okay, sorry. We all have... things.'

'And we all need somewhere, someplace to talk about them.' She eyed him with concern and reflection.

He nodded sagely, feeling like he'd opened the door to a darker, sadder part of Lotus. 'Amen to that.' He bit his lip. 'Did you want to talk about it... or anything? I mean—no pressure, I don't want to pry, but don't think you have to be nervous around me. I'm not always the drug-addled stuntman.'

Her smile was grateful yet timid. 'Thanks, Drew.' She blew out a breath. 'Look, I'd better—' She indicated the PC.

He stood. 'Absolutely. Thanks for... coping with me.'

'No problem.'

There was movement in his peripheral vision. A guy stood there, about fifty, with a thirty-six o'clock shadow, a faded Yankees baseball cap, and his belly button showing. 'Alright?'

'Hi,' she said.

'Lift'll be done by tonight, love. Looks like it was nothing major, but we'll be doing a full check after hours.'

That buoyed Drew. Hopefully, Elle was uninjured.

'Okay, thanks,' Lotus said cheerily. 'Just a shame it couldn't wait until the weekend when nobody was here. Less inconvenience for everyone. You could pull the thing to pieces if you wanted. But never mind. Thanks a lot.'

'Alright, Cheers.' The guy shuffled off.

Drew's brain buzzed. He gave Lotus a lame goodbye wave, then hurried to the stairwell.

That's it! Brilliant. Well done, Lotus—I could kiss you! Obviously, I'd get a smack in the face, but still. And that's the good thing about lifts—they're unlikely to get jealous or lay a punch.

He trotted up to floor 9, feeling on cloud 9. He had a way of finding out what, or who, Elle was.

FLOOR 16

Drew had the house to himself that Friday night—Charlotte was out with Richard and then kipping over at his place.

The freedom was welcome. True, it was her house, and her love life, but he couldn't help thinking Richard was merely a rebound. He wasn't the tallest guy and suffered from Short Man Syndrome. He was a bit cocky, rather protective, and insisted she didn't wear heels.

Charlotte insisted things like that didn't matter, and Richard could do amazing things with his tongue.

Drew didn't consider tongue gymnastics a sound basis for a long and rounded relationship. He didn't tell her that but was sure she'd appreciated that he held Sam in higher regard.

He merely wanted the best for his sister. After all, she wanted the best for him. Katie's death had hit Charlotte hard, too, and she was trying her hardest to help him get over that. In her own way, she was also guiding him through the Elle situation—despite initially saying it was bollocks, and he should move on and try to find Katie 2.0.

He remained convinced that any female conversation, like with Lotus, was a start. "The journey of a thousand miles begins with just one step" or something equally trite.

He rolled out of bed at nine the next morning, breakfasted, and left for the office. It was good that Char wasn't there to grill him about his plans. She would have eye-rolled herself into a detached retina.

The bored Security guard—Alan and Len didn't work weekends—barely looked up as Drew traversed the foyer and went to the left-hand lift. It was already waiting because the place was deserted.

You can do this.

He took a few level breaths, pressed **1 5**, and the lift whined into its ascent.

'Elle?'

He didn't expect the voice to take the weekend off, but he was sober about the potential results of his enquiry. If it was a prankster, or even Lotus, they would be at home, planning the following week's shenanigans.

There was no reply. *Perhaps the lift is fixed, but the voice is still broken? Or has it been disabled?*

'Elle?'

The counter passed **2**. There was no time to remain on tenterhooks: work to be done.

He laboriously inspected the interior—first the rear wall, then the sides, the doors and surrounding panels. There was no evidence of any communications device besides the tiny mesh speaker near the

`Help` button. He couldn't reach the false ceiling but inspected it for cameras, microphones or speakers. There was nothing obvious.

The chime sounded. Floor `15`.

He mulled the lack of success, exited the lift, reached in and pressed `G`. The lift departed.

He waited a minute, glancing aimlessly around the foyer. The business operating here was Tek20 Systems. He didn't have a clue—or care—what they did. Unless it involved employing pranksters, lift bastardisers or things necessitating a metal detector which would cause unsuspecting Production Accountants to almost strip down to their pants.

He pressed `Call`, and, helpfully, the right-hand lift arrived.

With his phobia at only a niggling level, he stepped in and jabbed `G`.

The box descended. He gave it the same level of scrutiny as the "Elle" lift, including calling her name. He came up empty-handed but discovered that the lifts were identical. It meant there was no apparent reason why one lift spoke and the other didn't. It also meant that Elle was unlikely to be a sentient lift—why would the company only install one of the pair as the *chatty* variety? Besides, the lifts were old, pre-dating any form of AI.

He exited into the Reception lobby and surveyed the scene, pondering.

In a nook near the main doors was the Security office. It would surely be manned twenty-four-seven, so he went to look for clues.

In the smallish cubicle, facing a bank of monitors, sat a woman, commendably awake. Her uniform had epaulettes, her cheeks were ruddy, and her name badge read "Gloria". For several reasons, chiefly related to her age and deportment, he dearly hoped that when she spoke, she didn't sound like Elle.

Then he realised that was judgemental, cruel and biased. After all, what attracted him to Elle—who was merely a cuboid—was her voice, manner, and humour. People were more than their looks. Much, much more.

Except perhaps Pirin.

Gloria swivelled on her chair. She had a large mole on her chin.

He prayed to any deity that came to mind.

'Can I help you, sugar?' she asked, smiling.

He was ready to exhale a hurricane of relief but then remembered the existence of voice changers. He wasn't out of the woods yet. 'Oh. Hi. No. Well, yes, I suppose.'

She eyed his face, then his physique. He made sure he wasn't holding in his stomach. 'Go on, sugar.'

'Do you... that is, does the person here... monitor the lifts? For emergencies and things?'

She pointed at a simple electronic display which showed the position of the lifts. 'Yes, we can see if they're stalled, and the Help button comes through here. Why, do you want to make a complaint, sugar? Or is it research for college?'

Did she think he was twenty? If she did, was it flattery, myopia, or sleep deprivation?

'I work here, Gloria.'

'Ah, I see.' She looked him up and down again. 'Haven't seen you around. Nice young fellow like you. So, why are you here? Overtime? You poor soul. Want a Bourbon?' She grabbed an oversized biscuit barrel containing a few she hadn't yet scoffed that morning... probably.

I'm a bad man. And I'll get my comeuppance... assuming it isn't already in progress. 'Er, no, thanks. So—the lifts. There's no... voice recording in there to announce floors, is there? Disabled, maybe?'

'No, don't think so, sugar. Why?'

He ignored that. 'The Help... thing, though. In an emergency, you can talk to people in the lift, right?'

'Yes, that's controlled from here. What's this about? You're not from *the authorities,* are you? Checking up on me?'

He wanted to ask if she had anything to hide, regardless of whether it was unrelated to the Elle situation, but it was inappropriate. 'Have you ever used the microphone doohickey?'

She frowned. 'Do whatty?'

'The Emergency, "calm down everyone" speaker thing?'

'No. Can't say anyone has. Very reliable, those lifts. Apart from this week. Ghost in the machine and whatnot.'

'Ghosts?' His senses tingled.

'You know, "ghosts in the machine", sugar,' she said earnestly. The mole had a single black hair protruding from it.

'There's a ghost? I wanted to ask about that. Is the building haunted?'

She laughed, a gin and cigarettes cackle. 'You've come here to ask about ghosts? In the lift?'

'I don't know, just that—'

'Come on, sugar. Good-looking guy like you can't be doing with that nonsense. I'll bet your girlfriend's brainwashing you. Does she watch those TV programmes?'

'I... I don't have a girlfriend, so—'

'Really? That's a surprise.' She smoothed her ample bosom.

Now, he feared the elevatophobia would need to make way for Gloriaphobia. 'Look, this will sound odd, but... about the microphone. Would you ever, you know, be tempted to play a practical joke? Maybe... say "boo" or something? For fun, you understand. A little joke on people in the lift?'

She shuffled in the chair as if she'd been told a badly misjudged filthy story. 'That's a terrible thing to say, sugar. What do you take me for?'

'I only—'

'No, I'd never do that. None of us would. Some people are scared of lifts anyway, so I hear.'

He laughed nervously. 'Oh, yes, of course. Bunch of losers. After all, how can a lift hurt you, right?' He gave her an earnest smile.

She reached for his hand. 'Absolutely, sugar.'

He eased his arm away. 'Good, well, thanks. That's cleared things up a treat. You're a... sugar, Gloria.'

She met his eye. 'No problem. And, if you ever want to ask any more, stop in and say hello. Or my shift finishes at six, so maybe we could—'

He held up a palm. 'Sorry, Gloria. Very kind, but I have... class tonight.' *I do?*

'Oh. Yes. College class. I see.'

'No, er, cake decorating.' *What?*

'Ooh, interesting. I do like a spot of cake, sugar.'

He avoided that slam dunk. 'Well, if it turns out okay, maybe I'll bring in a slice,' he said, digging a hole to China.

'That would be nice. And you can tell me this ghost story you've heard.'

He backed away. 'Yes. That would be a... treat. Anyway, don't want to take your attention away from keeping us all safe and secure, so, er, thanks.'

He smiled uncomfortably, then headed away at a pace which couldn't *quite* be interpreted as scarpering.

There was a mizzle in the air outside, but it was like a sun's hug after that near miss. Gloria wasn't wholly out of the running, but the critical discovery was the presence of an intercom system. If Gloria herself wasn't the perpetrator, could another Security person be responsible? Maybe she only worked weekends? Who else was in the cohort?

He pulled out his phone and updated the note.

Elle/voice
1) Ghost: unlikely 2/10
2) Stress: possible 4/10
3) Prank: likely 8/10
4) Insanity: hope not! 1/10
5) Sentient lift: very unlikely 0/10
6) Systems hijack: likely 7/10 - Lotus?? Gloria?! Security?
7) Other??

The Gloria ordeal had made him hungry, so he dialled for company.

FLOOR 17

P irin was a vegan, but Drew liked him anyway.

It did make eating out together tricky, as Drew was partial to a thick steak. He never used the phrase "eating out" in front of Pirin because that was ripe for comment.

They agreed to have lunch at a place that catered to all tastes, didn't swarm with screaming toddlers, and had a low quotient of serving staff that Pirin might make a pass at. Drew would have happily grabbed a Burger King, as the speed would minimise flirting. However, Pirin considered their vegan offering "shit".

Drew didn't mention the morning's covert activities. He was withholding details about Elle for as long as possible—especially as he'd promised her as much.

He'd debated that promise. Surely a prankster would *want* Drew to blab about the voice, so he'd become even more of a laughing stock? It didn't add up—like this whole conundrum.

After the pre-lunch pleasantries, Drew plunged right in. 'What's your take on the whole "ghosts" thing?'

'You mean generally? Woo-ooo, white sheets, fabricated TV shows with low-light cameras—that?'

Drew shrugged—best to be cool. 'Yeah. Noises, stuff being moved. *Voices.*'

'Ha-ha.' Pirin frowned. 'Hang on—are you seeing things?'

'Seeing things? No. No way.' He wrinkled his nose in mock distaste.

'Hearing voices?'

'Well—'

Pirin slapped the table. 'You're hearing voices?'

'No. Not as such. Maybe.' He winced. 'Possibly.'

Fortunately, Pirin showed some social tact. He didn't jump onto the table, point at Drew and shout, "Loony in the house". It was quite uncharacteristic. He leant in. 'Really, you're hearing voices?'

'Voice, singular.'

'Where?'

Drew panicked. 'The... loos at work.'

Pirin snorted. 'What did it say? "Make sure you wash your hands"? "Stop reading your phone on the bog and get back to work"? "Did you know this is the cubicle where Pirin and Keira—"'

Drew clapped his hands over his ears. 'La la la! Don't want to hear.'

'Alright, alright!' Pirin shuffled his chair closer. 'Serious, though? A voice?'

'Yes. Look, the point is, have you heard about the office being haunted?'

Pirin held in a splutter. 'Really? You think there's a ghost in the bogs? Like a dead cleaner or something? Or maybe HQ is built on a medieval burial ground—' Pirin did a weird... scary jazz hands... type thing.

'Cut it out. Simple question. Do you think a voice—with no person around to make it—could be a ghost?'

Pirin pondered, supping his drink. 'Unlikely. How often do you hear it?'

'Most times I'm in there.'

Pirin made a face. It was the only time he didn't look annoyingly handsome in a Bollywood leading man way. 'Do you—and please say "No"—do you... reply?'

'No,' he lied.

'Phew.' Pirin eye-rolled heavily. 'Thought for a mo I'd lost you to the fairies.'

'"Fairies", says the ghost sceptic.'

'This has really got you by the balls, hasn't it, mate?'

'I want an explanation, that's all. The voice is as real as yours. Call me crazy, but unless someone's, I don't know, hijacking the system that plays the cheery musical tripe out of the Gents' ceiling, then I vote ghosts.' He shrugged for emphasis.

Pirin tapped his chin thoughtfully. He looked like a pretentious tit. He might have known this but done it anyway. Perhaps it drew women to him, like moths to a flame? 'Hijacking the speaker system as a *prank*? Interesting.'

'Meaning you can imagine somebody doing that? Now we're getting somewhere. Would *you* do that? Prank some poor sod, pretending to be a ghost.'

Pirin shook his head vehemently. 'No. Certainly not you. I'd hope people had more bloody scruples.' His fraternal side surfaced. 'I know you're still getting over things, so I wouldn't screw with your mental health.'

'Exactly. Nobody is that low—to pretend to be Katie or whatever.'

Pirin was shocked. 'Are they? Do they say they're her? Is it even female?'

117

'No, they don't, and they don't sound like her. The point is, if it's a prank, it would have to be somebody I've pissed off. Only a few dozen of us survived from Bristol, and I think they're all cool with me. And here, I've barely met anyone.'

'Simon? Lotus? Kevin?!'

'No, no, and very no.' Drew sighed. 'I'll have to keep my ear to the ground.'

'I will too, buddy. If I find anything, I'll tell you.'

'You're the best.'

'Yeah. So, you owe me, right?'

Drew's eyes narrowed. 'I suppose.'

'Introduce me to your sister?'

'No!'

As Drew drove home, he wasn't sure that Pirin had helped much, beyond reinforcing the unlikelihood of ghosts and adding fuel to the notion of a prank. Yet, Drew was no closer to knowing who the perpetrator might be.

FLOOR 18

Drew rolled over and checked the bedside clock for the millionth time.

SUN 01:17.

He whimpered. Sleep had been fractured. He desperately wanted to know why Kevin Yates wasn't to be trusted. The sabbatical initiative—a brainchild that Katie had unknowingly bequeathed to him—had to be given its best shot.

More importantly, who or what was Elle? Maybe it *was* all in his head. A guardian angel, perhaps even the spirit—not ghost—of Katie. Alternatively, he was sickening for something. The weekend was a bloody inconvenience, an impasse, and it was letting stagnant thoughts build up behind the blockage, poisoning his mind.

He reluctantly got up, had a drink of water, went to the loo, and then settled down again.

After an age, he began to drift off.

'Drew?'

Almost unconscious, an acknowledging noise emerged from this throat.

'Drew?'

His eyes snapped open. He fumbled for the light switch and winced at the lamp's glare.

The room was empty. Yet he'd heard Katie's voice. Hadn't he?

His teeth gritted. *Bloody Char.*

He stomped around the room, investigating any electronic device she might consider suitable for pranking. There was nothing. He screwed up his eyes, wishing away the possibility that he'd heard what he thought.

On a whim, he tugged the duvet off the bed, grabbed the pillow, and went to the lounge.

As he was settling the impromptu bed on the sofa, a shadowy figure appeared in his eyeline.

'Jesus Christ!' he yelled.

Charlotte emerged from the gloomy hall. 'Bloody hell, Drew! Where's the fire?' Her PJs were askew, and her hair looked like she'd been dragged through a hedge.

'Just having a moment, Char. Calm your bloody socks.' He flopped onto the sofa.

She flicked on the nearest table lamp, approached gingerly, and perched beside him. He watched suspiciously.

'Why the evils?' she asked.

'Did you just call out?'

'What?'

'Did. You. Just. Call. Out?'

She frowned. 'No. I was bloody asleep until I heard what sounded like a burglar trashing the place. Why?'

Oops. 'Because you pranked me before.'

'And I'd do it again? After what you said? No way.' She sighed, patting his shoulder. 'Sorry. Did you hear a voice?'

'I... I don't know. Maybe I was asleep. I heard my name. Or I thought I did. I swear it was Katie, but...' His head fell. 'Christ knows.'

'A female voice?' she asked gently.

'Yeah.'

'The same as... before? The lift?'

He screwed up his eyes, reflecting. 'No. Don't think so. Not the same. Actually, this did feel like it was more in my mind.' He thumped the cushion.

'Oh, bro. Your head is full of this. The anniversary. Maybe the house move and the new office. Worry about promotion, the initiative. A disembodied voice using your name isn't ideal.'

'I'm pretty screwed up, right? Lifts are bad for me mentally—it seems unavoidable.'

'You're being defeatist again, Drew. You're making progress on this phobia. Don't give up now.'

'I did ride the lift twice today,' he admitted.

'Bravo. And you were on the mend about Katie, too. You used to go to that support group, remember? In Bristol? It did wonders for you.'

'I suppose,' he mumbled. There was half a glass of water on the coffee table. He necked it.

She sighed heavily, smoothed her hair, and tugged his arm so that he faced her. 'Nothing says that the... Elle... voice is connected to *anything*. Why would it happen suddenly now, after three years? Think of that. You need to get past Katie and the phobia—that was always the case. Only... we thought Elle was helping, but maybe it was a mixed blessing.'

He nodded. The argument made sense. 'If Elle is separate, she wouldn't *deliberately* try to make me worse. She doesn't seem like that kind of... I would say "girl", but for your sake, I'll say "lift".' He smiled weakly.

Even though it was silly o'clock, Charlotte put her professional head on. 'This connection you have with Elle could be reawakening your feelings for Katie. Maybe that's what's messing with you? Your head doesn't know which way to turn—to be drawn towards the memory of a girl you loved, or to be harmed by the scars of your lift history and the noise and metal claustrophobia of the car crash. So, she... it... Elle is the combination of attraction and repulsion. She's unwittingly triggering both your conscious and unconscious.'

He nodded. 'She doesn't know that stuff. My... baggage.'

'Even so, she can't *help* being a lift, right?'

'Unless she *isn't* a lift,' he pointed out.

Char smiled, sober and non-combative. She ruffled his hair, which always made him feel like a cared-for younger brother—even though they were too old for that kind of shit. 'One thing at a time. Try eliminating the bad parts in your head, and you can enjoy the good ones. Clearly, you get on with Elle—whoever or whatever she is. It's dumb and unexplainable, but if it's a force for happiness and connection in your life, then I approve. I want you to be better, Drew. To move on. To connect. To love and be loved.'

'I know. And I investigated a few things today. No luck, though.'

She squeezed his hand. 'Good. You're taking practical steps. Hell, if it was a slam-dunk psychological problem, I'd fix you in a second. But Elle seems *so* bloody real to you that I can't rule out a real-world answer.'

'And tonight? The voice here?' he asked.

'Hmm. I don't know. But will you do me one thing?'

'Maybe. What?'

'There's a group in town. Grief Counselling. It might be the touchstone you need. I was at the cemetery this week, too, remember? Katie's still in your head, front and centre.'

He grimaced. 'I don't know.'

'What's the worst that could happen? If Elle is nothing to do with Katie, it's no guarantee that the memory—the ache—will vanish overnight. Go to the group, and maybe reconnecting with other people will make you see that you're better off than you think. Or it'll be cathartic, give you a chance to exorcise the demon's flare-up, and you can get on with things. Okay?'

He couldn't fight the care on his sister's face. 'Okay.'

FLOOR 19

A s it was Sunday, Drew was pleased to massively oversleep. Char's ministry in the small hours had done enough for his mind to leave him the hell alone for a while.

The Group didn't meet until 6 P.M, so he busied himself with chores, a supermarket run, and watching Formula 1.

As he drove to the venue—an unfamiliar Community Centre—he made peace with the decision. The voice of Elle—human or AI, prank or TBC—was reawakening memories of a severed emotional connection. Whatever Elle's reason for those first two warning words, there was unarguably now a new bond, however fledgling.

Was it possible that Katie's memory, or essence, made him more curious about Elle than he should be? Was it making him have *feelings* when he logically shouldn't?

He'd decided that, even though the Group would consist of strangers, he'd be circumspect about discussing a talking lift. He'd be vague, as he was with Pirin. With luck, he might even make a friend, someone with shared loss. Sometimes, it's odd how finding another lovelorn person makes you more content. Better yet, he might meet someone who'd benefit from seeing Char, and he could repay the debt he owed her.

Some idiotic driver had rammed a signpost on the route, causing a tailback, so he screeched into the Community Centre car park ten minutes late.

As he jogged towards the main entrance, he spotted an illuminated room adjacent to the hallway on the near side. Through the translucent blind, he could see a partially occupied circle of chairs.

He made a point of not barging through the door, although nonchalance was a stretch, given his tardiness.

There were nine people in the small, echoey, wooden-floored room. They all turned to look.

He grimaced. 'Er... hi.'

A woman stood. Her hair was pulled tightly back from her face, she wore three-quarter-length trousers and pop socks, and her eyes were compassionate. 'Hello. I'm Marian. You're new here?'

'Yes.'

'Do you want to introduce yourself to the group? As you seem to have our attention anyway.'

'Oh. Sorry.' *Hardly the ideal baptism into a new venture.*

'Never mind. Go ahead.'

Awkwardly, he sidled around to an available chair and stood beside it. 'Hi everyone, I'm Drew.' He offered a stress-filled smile.

Marian leant forwards. 'And?'

'Er... I recently moved here. And... I'm a big fan of good coffee and the movies of John Huston.'

Marian frowned. 'And...?'

He coughed. 'Oh, yes. Sorry for being late.'

One or two people were looking at him strangely. He shifted on his feet. He didn't remember the Bristol Group being so... stuffy and unwelcoming. Such hard work.

Marian gestured. 'And...?'

Drew's head buzzed. 'And... I don't know what to say.' He gave a timid shrug.

Marian let out a small, frustrated sigh. 'Normally, we'd say, "Hi, I'm Drew, and I'm an alcoholic".'

He was taken aback. Being judged already? Had his behaviour been misconstrued? At least with Lotus, only *one* person accused him of being on drugs. Plus, he hadn't touched a drop all day. Yet.

'Well, I wouldn't call myself that. I like a drink, but who doesn't, right?' He eyed the group. There were one or two huffs.

Marian nodded. 'Ah. Denial.'

'Steady on.'

She clasped her hands in front of her. 'When was your last drink, Drew?'

Why the Inquisition? He shrugged. 'Last night.'

'Oh, dear.'

Now, he was aggrieved. 'Is there a problem with that? And why this obsession with drink?'

'How many days have you gone without alcohol in the last... fortnight?'

He mused. 'One?'

Marian's head cocked. 'What step are you on?'

'Step?' Then the penny dropped. It was like a gong falling from its stand. Or a lift plunging down a shaft.

'Ah. I think I know what's happened here...'

The room on the opposite side of the entrance hall had a sign on the door. It was easy to miss, especially for a blithering idiot.

He eased inside. The person talking paused. Drew offered a genuine—and relieved—smile, and looked for a seat. His legs froze.

In one of the chairs was Lotus.

However, he was finally here, and it was too late now. He'd already made an arse of himself in front of nine people. What were seven more? Six, if he excluded Lotus because she already knew he was prone to foot-in-mouth. Besides, if he could bare his soul, his demon, in front of her—a colleague—he could do it with anyone. Even Elle.

He raised a palm at the attendees. 'Drew.' He sat.

The speaker resumed his piece. He was a man of about fifty, balding, with heavy eyes. Drew glanced at everyone in turn. He left Lotus until last. They exchanged sober smiles.

Slowly, Drew let the tension ebb.

After a while, Lotus spoke. He listened intently. She was an intensely likeable soul—beyond her looks—and it was good to understand what made her tick. He empathised. If she was going to be an ally at HQ, the fact that they shared something in common was helpful.

Someone else went next. Their story threw Drew's loss into perspective. He needed to man up and move on. Firstly, get past the sense memories. Secondly, to be open to love again. Yet, he'd been trying that for three years. Only Elle's appearance had derailed his recovery. Yet, why didn't he resent her for that? In fact, why did he want to speak to her again?

His turn in the spotlight arrived.

He talked about the car accident. About losing the love of his life. About trying to get over it. He didn't mention elevatophobia—no need. This was about the voice, which he thought echoed Katie. He didn't mention where he heard the voice—not with Lotus present. He only said that it was bringing back bad memories. He wanted to move on.

He got pretty emotional. He wrapped up quickly and sat. He didn't want to look at Lotus.

As his pulse returned to normal, he embraced the catharsis of publicly acknowledging his loss. He'd done it so seldom and to very few people: Charlotte and Pirin were those most familiar.

At seven o'clock, the meeting ended. He didn't feel like speaking to anyone. Maybe next time. He needed a drink. *Best not to announce it next door, though.*

'Drew?' Lotus' voice was less cheery than usual.

'Hi, Lotus. Don't think either of us expected this, right?'

She smiled sadly. 'Yeah. I'm sorry for your loss.'

'I'm sorry for yours.'

'This is your first time here, I suppose?'

'Yeah. I used to go... before... for a bit, in Bristol. Someone said I should come along after... the voice.'

'Hmm.' She was assessing his face and mood. He enjoyed the attention.

'You been coming long?'

'A few months. It helps.'

'Good. Good.' He shifted on his feet. People had drifted away. The organiser was stacking the chairs.

'Christ, I need a drink,' she said.

He chuckled. 'Me too. Drains you, this, right?'

'It does. But better let out than kept in, hmm?'

'Definitely.'

'So... I'm going to grab a bite, too.' She angled her head. 'If you want company, then...'

His heart fluttered. He calmed it. This wasn't a *date*. It was co-workers having a wash-up meeting. *Wasn't it?* Either way, what was the harm? He might seem ungrateful and distant if he turned her down—and she was just starting to see what made him tick—why he wasn't the cheery soul he'd been in the past.

'Er... yeah? Why not?'

She smiled. 'Okay. I usually go to Carlo's for pasta or something.'

'I don't know it.'

'I can show you the way. You drove? I get the bus.'

He swallowed. 'Yeah. That's fine.'

They thanked the organiser and left.

Carlo's Italian was pretty quiet. They sat in a corner, away from prying ears. Conveniently, it was obscured from the street in case Pirin—knowing Drew's recent luck—happened by. The sod would either try to steal Lotus away or send whispers around the office the next day. Possibly both.

Hang on. Why was he worried about Pirin "stealing" Lotus? This wasn't a date. At most, it qualified as a risk-free get-to-know-you session with a woman—precisely what he'd told Char he was attempting with Elle.

The difference was that Elle was a lift, and Lotus was a hot blonde. Ironically, he had a better chance of a relationship with Elle because it would be hard to argue that she was too good for him.

In the car, they'd done the pleasantries and discussed the other group members, and he found out she'd lived in Winchester for eight years since leaving college. The conversation distracted him from worrying about having someone—a girl—in the car. He'd probably babbled, covering nerves.

Still, Lotus is used to me talking gibberish, right?

When the beers arrived, she broached the topic of his situation. 'Look, Drew, I'm sorry about before. At work. I get that the voice thing was true—that's why you asked about ghosts. It's pretty bloody logical, really. You weren't high as a kite or pissing about. This really is a problem for you.'

He shrugged. 'It's why I came tonight.'

'Sorry—okay? You never know what someone has... inside them.'

He nodded. 'I'm sorry about your Dad. What happened was awful.'

She smiled awkwardly. 'It was worse for you, Drew. You were there when it happened. And now you're getting these... echoes. Grieving for a lost parent is natural—it comes to everyone. I suppose I'm lucky because I'm not trying to get over it so I can love again—not like you. After all, it's not like another dad will come along.' Her gentle laugh was forlorn.

'That's a very kind perspective.'

'And disease... takes people. I wished the odds not to fall that way, but it happens.'

'So do car crashes, but that never made it any easier.' He sighed, toying with the label on the bottle. 'I spent a lot of time wishing we hadn't driven that day. Or that I'd proposed to her earlier. Or anything else except what happened.' He shut his eyes against it, took a deep breath.

She laid a hand on the table near him. 'There's no point in those wishes. It's the same as wondering how it would be different if Dad had spotted the signs earlier. Moving on, accepting, is the only way. Otherwise, you beat yourself up for shit which wasn't your fault, and you spoil even more of life than you need to.'

He slugged the beer. 'You're right. Of course you are.'

She waved it away. 'Enough of that. So—this voice—where did you hear it?'

The hamster on the wheel of his brain went Usain Bolt. 'The... stairs. On... level 8.'

'Oh, right.'

Numpty. Why had he picked a *new* fake location? Why not say "the loos" like he had to Pirin? Now, there were two competing lies. What if Lotus and Pirin discussed the matter? They'd realise that Drew couldn't come up with a straight story or assume he heard voices all over the bloody building.

He tried to remain calm. At least he hadn't mentioned the lift—that would be a disaster. Either of them might call out in the lift, expecting a voice. Regardless of whether Elle replied, she'd know that he'd broken his promise.

'Are you okay, Drew?'

He snapped out of it. 'Yeah. Fine. Oh, look, here's our order.'

He arrived home at ten o'clock. Like a gent, he'd seen Lotus to the nearest bus stop, and they parted with a "See you tomorrow". He never considered offering her a ride home. That was date territory.

Charlotte was curled on the sofa in her PJs.

It was always nice to come home to an occupied place. It would be even better if the other occupant wasn't someone he was related to. Ideally, it would be someone he was sharing a bed, and life, with.

'That's a bloody long meeting,' she said.

He perched beside her. He skipped the AA meeting screw-up but relayed details of the group, Lotus' presence, and the subsequent, perfectly innocent bite to eat.

He must have effused too much about Lotus, though.

Char flashed a familiar, amused raise of one eyebrow. 'Hmm. The choice of a real woman or a lift. Tricky one.'

He forced down a rejoinder. 'Thanks for recommending the Group, sis. It helped, honestly. I'm hitting the sack. Night.'

As he brushed his teeth, he tried to square the logistical circle of Lotus being Elle. He couldn't figure out how she could access the necessary mechanism at such short notice. Yet, if somehow she *was*

Elle, was it so bad to have a secret admirer like that? Elle had said he was "sweet", and Lotus seemed to feel the same. They'd had a good chat, so why was she so nervous about talking at work? He and Lotus got on, but he hadn't noticed any overt flirting. Or perhaps he was out of practice in spotting the signs. It had been seven years since his last date.

He climbed into bed.

Lotus obviously masked ongoing grief about her father. It was possible she also masked attraction to men—Drew in particular. He, for one, had difficulty engaging with the opposite sex.

So what if she needed to hide behind the persona of being a lift? Was that so implausible?

FLOOR 20

After an unsettling experience on Sunday afternoon, Hannah knew that the company of a kick-ass friend and leg-puller was better than a prolonged hug with a bottle or more of red wine.

Nevertheless, she and Amy were sharing a drop of vino to take the edge off the stress.

She recounted how she'd bumped into her ex, Stuart, in the supermarket. His eyes, which she'd once regarded merely as a piercing blue, were piercing evil. The distaste in his demeanour was evident.

She was stunned that after so long, and how he'd treated her, he remained angry that she'd dumped him. Even during their briefest encounter, he'd triggered her social anxiety, revelled in the fact that she was still single, and tried to look down her blouse.

He was lucky she didn't club him to death with a fruity Australian Chardonnay in the freezer aisle of Tesco.

She hadn't developed a migraine, but it was a near miss.

Amy topped up their glasses. 'Everybody makes dating mistakes, Han. You've just had more than your fair share.'

'It was my fault for relying on internet dating. People hide behind a facade. Sometimes they continue it past the point it's healthy. What's *wrong* with people?'

'Yet you're talking to a guy through a secret speaker.'

Hannah shot her the evils. 'Don't do this, Ames. It's been a rough fucking day. The point is to *learn* from my mistakes—okay?' She shook her head in frustration. 'Stuart treated me like his "little lady".'

'Ha! You'd never be the type.'

'It's because he saw my nerves—at the start. So he made that who I was—the shy, retiring, complicit type.' She sneered. 'Prick.'

'Too right. You give as good as you get—and not just the banter. You're strong on the inside,' Amy said.

'Don't forget the brains and the shapely tits.'

'Sounds like Stuart was reminding himself of that second part.'

'Ugh.' Hannah shuddered. 'One track mind.'

'Well—he found out the hard way that you don't give in to arseholes. It's ballsy what you're doing—setting that stuff up to catch your own bloody CEO.'

'Yeah, "ballsy" pronounced "career suicide".' She drank.

Amy sputtered a laugh. 'You're bloody funny—which is very appealing. You're a catch. You just have to let yourself be caught. By the right one, of course.'

'I'm not playing hard to get, for fuck's sake. Only... protecting myself.'

Amy's shoulders fell. 'Sorry. I've not been let down like you have.'

'So why aren't you getting some lovin'?'

'I'm... figuring some things out.' Amy looked away. 'Anyway, let's do you, shall we? You're the one who asked for my apparently monstrous shoulders to cry on.'

Hannah took a mental timeout. Amy was right: the pep talk had been at Hannah's behest.

'Is it bad to be maybe... using Drew to help with the whole Kevin thing, or at least have as an ally?' She drank, preparing to drop the mic. 'Or even—possibly, no assumptions made—to get back in the dating game?'

Amy was wide-eyed, then smiled knowingly. 'Only bad if you're not serious about him.'

Hannah bit her lip. 'I don't know yet. That's the problem. I don't know if he's another git waiting in the wings.'

'You want my advice? Okay if you don't—we're not peas in a pod, Han.'

She clasped her friend's knee. 'Yes, I do, Ames. I mean, I reserve the right to laugh it off, kick you out, or ignore it, but yeah, go for your life, babes.'

Amy drained her glass. 'My advice is that nobody knows who The One is until they know. You just have to keep on the journey. For you, it's harder, as you go into every encounter expecting a fucking disaster. You think that if a barista flashes too big a smile, he'll follow you home and jump you in a dark alley—which is bullshit.'

'Wow. You'd make a hell of a carpenter.'

'Why?'

'You hit the fucking nail on the head every time.'

Amy wrinkled her nose. 'Hmm. Don't add that one to your routine, I'd say.'

'Sure. Yeah. Weak, right?'

'Too contrived.'

'You mean like setting up covert surveillance to gather evidence of my boss groping other women?'

'Then using it to chat up unsuspecting single men.' Amy's eyes flared. 'Hang on. This Drew guy—is he single?'

Hannah's mouth hung open. 'Shit. I never thought of that. Shit. What if he isn't?'

'Then you'll have to pick another victim.'

That riled her. 'That makes it sound like I'm preying on innocent people. That's fucking Yates' angle. Don't ever—'

Amy swept her into a bear hug. 'Shit. I'm sorry. God, Han, I didn't mean...' She sighed. 'I know your idea has taken an unexpected turn, and, no, you shouldn't open yourself to discovery by talking to anyone in the lift who takes your fancy. I'm dumb, okay? I only... I *want* for you. I'm not saying use the lift as Tinder. Fuck, no. You're not like that. But this privacy *works* for you.'

These embraces invariably eased Hannah's pain. She wondered whether it was because Amy was built more... less... kind of.... It didn't matter. 'Yeah. Okay.'

Amy's mollifying gaze explored her face. 'So, tell me about him. *Does* he take your fancy? Even a little?'

She pulled up a mental picture. 'He's fair-haired, the right height, not stupidly fit, not let himself go. He's... not outgoing, not introverted. Educated. Dresses okay. Clean shaven. Good job—obviously—'

'You can see how this sounds... stalkery.' Amy raised her eyebrows.

Hannah swatted her knee. 'It's... baby steps. Safe ones. And, like I said, it's a pleasant diversion until the main event.' She made a slow fist like she was crushing the CEO's balls.

'So, when are you going to come clean with Drew?'

Hannah shook her head. 'It's been maybe five minutes chatting. He's... only like an avatar. He needs to be *real*.'

'As real to you as you are to him?' Amy asked pointedly.

'Come on, it's not like I'm driving him crazy with frustration.'

FLOOR 21

D rew was strangely looking forward to that particular Monday morning. He arrived, bleary-eyed, at seven thirty. He'd debated coming in earlier, but if Elle was a prank—even a prank gone awry—the perpetrator was unlikely to be in at an ungodly hour. Equally, he needed to be early enough to beat the masses.

As he approached the left-hand lift, he noticed a yellow warning sign in front of the right-hand lift: "OUT OF ORDER". The maintenance company were probably checking that the non-Elle lift wasn't suffering from the same glitch they'd cured on Friday night.

Why couldn't they have done this check over the weekend, too—like Lotus had suggested to the engineer? Bunch of numskulls. Probably didn't want to be working when they could be queuing at Ikea on a Saturday afternoon with seventy billion other people.

This made things bloody difficult. Everyone would need to use Elle. *Bugger.*

There was no choice. He called the left-hand lift.

When it arrived, he glanced around the foyer to ensure he wasn't being watched, pulled the warning sign across behind him, stepped inside, and pressed `1` and `Doors Close`. His chest heaved with the awfulness of the deception. Still, he couldn't make an omelette without breaking eggs.

The lift jolted upwards.

'Elle?' He screwed up his face, willing success.

There was no answer.

'Shit,' he breathed. 'Elle?'

Nothing.

PING! 1st floor.

He darted out, pulled the sign across from the broken lift, stepped back inside, and pressed `2` and `Doors Close`.

If Katie was in heaven, his chances of seeing her were diminishing fast that morning.

'Elle?'

The lift whirred. He leant his forehead against the wall in frustration at striking out again.

'Hi, Drew.'

He punched the air. 'Elle!'

'Well, somebody's happy.'

'Of course. You're fixed.'

'Fixed?' the lift said.

'You broke. On Friday. Remember?'

A sigh filled the air. 'Oh. Yes. Time of the month.'

He laughed, then did a double take. 'Whoa, that's what Charlotte said.' Then he clapped a hand over his mouth.

PING! 2nd floor.

He sprang to attention, darted through the doors, moved the sign across to block interlopers, came back, and pressed `3` and `Doors Close`.

'Are you alright, Drew? Forget where you're going?'

'Long story.'

'I see,' Elle said. 'Who's Charlotte?'

He cursed internally, pulse quickening. 'Er...'

'Your girlfriend?'

'No!' he rapped. He calmed himself. 'No. She's... my sister.'

'Phew.'

His ears pricked up. 'What?'

'Oh... er... nothing,' the lift stuttered uncharacteristically.

Too late. You were worried I might be unavailable. Why would you care? Unless...?

Get real! Elle's a lift, for heaven's sake. Possibly.

PING! 3rd floor. He executed the same routine. The lift resumed its staccato ascent.

'You're really pushing my buttons today, Drew.'

'In... a... good way?' he asked gingerly.

'You told your sister about us.'

'Yeah. Look, Elle... Hang on, "us"?' He glanced around, not knowing where to direct his attention. He eyed the control panel—the only landmark. 'There is no "us". There's me—a person, and you—a lift. And we've had a few dozen sentences in a week.'

PING!

'Hang on,' he said.

After the same routine, they moved off again.

'Where was I?'

'"There is no us", I believe, was your—to be honest, rather inflammatory—opening gambit,' Elle said.

Is that grouchiness in her voice?

He pressed on. 'Okay. I told Charlotte I'd heard a voice because she's a doctor... kind of... and I thought I was going mad. If that's not okay—me trying to deal with this and stop lying awake all night worrying about ghosts and brain tumours, then I'm sorry, and there never will be an "us". I have to confide in someone. You're a talking lift, for heaven's sake, and while there may be a whole army of you out there, you're my first, and I was—still am—worried. Okay?'

Silence. Then, *PING!*

This plan was getting tedious.

The doors closed on a deserted 5th floor. The lift didn't speak.

'Elle?'

The cubicle whined and thunked.

'Elle?'

'I forgive you,' she said quietly.

'Nobody else knows. Honestly.' He swallowed. 'Well, nobody knows the voice is *in here*. Promise. Cross my heart and hope to die. Ideally, not in a plummeting lift initiated Romeo and Juliet pact. Okay?'

Horrible silence again. *Bollocks.* It didn't bode well for his future romantic life if he couldn't even hit the right social notes with a sodding lift.

PING!

He selected **7**.

'I believe you,' she said.

'Thank Christ for that.'

'Why?'

'Because... Because I want this to work.' He ran a hand through his hair, wondering what the hell he was talking about.

'You and me?'

'I have no clue, Elle. A tiny part of me still thinks this is a dream, or a ghost, an echo, a prank, or a million other things than a lift I am having a conversation with. You can see my point, right?'

'Absolutely. And your faith, your persistence, is... amazing.'

PING!

He'd royally had enough now. At least they were over halfway. Same routine. He reached for the keypad.

'Drew?'

'Yeah?'

'Hit B.'

He'd never really noticed that button before. Certainly never been down to that floor. 'Is B like… Narnia?' *God, I sound like a dick.*

Elle laughed. 'No. It's just the basement. Safe there. Almost nobody takes me down that far.'

He pondered. 'Someone could still summon you—from any floor.'

'I've got that covered. Come on, go… down in me.'

If he'd been drinking tea, it would have been splattered across Elle's lovely, shiny interior. Still, he hit B.

Elle took him downwards. 'You moved all those signs because you wanted to be alone with me.'

'I don't understand either, Elle, but… yes. I need to prove this is actually, truly, bloody real. Or I'll have to get locked up somewhere. Certainly, leave this building. I have… stuff… going on, and this—you—will either fix it or ruin it. I can't risk the ruin option.'

'And I don't want the ruin option either, Drew. I want you to keep coming back.'

He stroked the door. 'Me too.'

For a few moments, he bathed in something indescribable. A wonderful madness. Comforting proximity that was devoid of any physical human connection.

The lift slowed and stopped.

B was no great shakes. It was eerily quiet. There were loos. Doors led away on both sides. It was much like any other floor, except less frequented—as she'd said.

'Now what?' he asked.

'Get the sign, but open it out and jam it between my doors.'

He peered out. Her plan was brilliant. *Except...*

'Won't it hurt you?' Then he scoffed at the crass remark.

'Might not even fit. Hurry, before someone calls me.'

He yanked over the plastic upended V, pressed it flat, and laid it across the door margin. It fitted with a couple of inches to spare.

The doors tried to close but failed. He wasn't proud of undertaking such sabotage. Still, it was better than spending the rest of the conversation shuttling up and down, trying to avoid interference.

He slouched in a corner. His mind whirred, recapping the last few minutes.

'This is real, Drew.'

'But...' He sighed. 'Can it work between a man and a lift? Do you know of any other couples like that? Huh?'

'I... I don't know. This is a new thing for me, too. I'm not usually this... adventurous.'

'Don't you ever get bored of going up and down? Want to cut loose and go sideways for once?'

There was a little chuckle. 'I'm not like that,' she said.

'Do you talk to other people?'

'No.'

That brightened him. 'Why me?'

'I like you. You're brave like I can never be.'

'I have to take your word for that, Elle. At least you can't be afraid of heights, right? Or have claustrophobia, jammed inside this shaft.'

She laughed again. 'That's true.'

'Besides—this "us" ... thing. How do I know you're really a female lift? Do female lifts look different to male ones? Or are you all nonbinary? Are you a "they"?'

'You mean, do some have curves?'

He winced. 'And... openings?'

'Don't be crude.'

He smacked his leg in admonishment. 'Sorry. But you talk like a woman—or a female entity.'

'So do lots of things. The makers choose a male or female voice.'

She had a point.

'Well, I like yours.'

'I like yours too, Drew.' That sounded almost affectionate.

'And you're much better at conversation than my satnav or my smart speaker.'

'Yeah, that Alexa's an annoying know-all! And you're much better than the other lift, the fire alarm system, or most of the men I've met,' Elle replied.

Drew perked up. 'Met?'

'I mean... had inside me.' He sniggered, and possibly his cheeks reddened. 'That wasn't supposed to be a pun. Besides, it only works if I'm a woman and I'm not. I'm a lift. Being inside me is the only way to coexist with a human.'

'And that's fine. For now. Chatting, like we are. Crazy as it is.'

'Yeah.' A pause. 'So, can I ask you something?'

'Of course, Elle.'

'Are you on speaking terms with Kevin Yates?'

He frowned. 'I thought you warned me to be careful of him.'

'I did.'

'Why did you? What's there to be careful of?'

'He's...' Her voice quietened. 'He's a sexist pig. And he's... got wandering hands.'

'Shit,' he murmured. Then he glanced at the ceiling. 'Why do you care? You're a lift. He's not going to come on to *me*... is he? Or you, certainly. He doesn't even know you exist. Imagine the CEO talking to a lift! Even me doing it is bloody crazy.'

'Yet, here you are, Drew.'

'It still doesn't mean I'm not crazy.' *Time to go all in—death or glory*. 'Is that it, Elle? Is that the point of all this? If it's a prank, have the common decency to cop to it. Right now.' He balled a fist. 'You succeeded, okay? You made me crazy because I thought you weren't real, then you made me crazy because I thought you were, and because—whoever you are, whatever you are—you were out to hurt me.'

'Oh, Lord, that wasn't my idea. Please believe me. I *am* out to hurt someone, but not you. I promise.'

His relief was immense. 'Yates?' he guessed.

'Yes. The only person I ever wanted to listen to, maybe talk to—alone—is Yates. To scare him into admitting his actions or catch him with someone else.'

Drew massaged his head. This still didn't compute. 'Why does a lift care about something which doesn't affect it?'

'What?'

'Why are you messing with the CEO? He'd have you decommissioned in a heartbeat.'

'You don't know a bloody thing about me!'

He was startled. This was the first sign of the lift being emotionally riled. 'I want to,' he protested.

There was no reply.

'Elle?' he asked desperately. 'Elle?' He leapt up frantically, scanning the tired walls. 'Elle?!'

Had he ruined it? Had he lost her?

FLOOR 22

After half a minute of frustration and self-recrimination, he gave it up as a lost cause and went to remove the impromptu doorstop.

'Drew?'

He punched the air. Moisture gathered in the corner of his eyes.

'Be *really* careful, okay? You don't know me,' she said.

'I want to, Elle. I'm sorry. I mustn't make assumptions. I'm not familiar with lifts... for lots of reasons.'

'I'm doing what I need to, that's all. And you should be careful with Yates. You're new here.'

'You mean I shouldn't trust him with the suggestion scheme? With my idea?'

'I... don't know. He's a snake. I've heard him in here saying... sexist things. Also, women complaining to each other about him.'

He slid to the floor. 'Shit.'

'Yeah. Shit.'

He chuckled. 'So, lifts swear?'

'Oh, that's mild. I have plenty more ... for the right occasion. There *will* be other times, won't there?' Hopefulness tinged the lift's smooth female tone.

'Definitely.'

'Good. Listen, people will need rides soon. We must talk later. I don't want more men fiddling around inside me because they think I'm broken. Once was bad enough. They nearly split you and me up.'

'Split us up? We're only... what are we?'

There was a pause. 'Colleagues? That's nicely unspecific. It won't raise any alarms.'

He stood. 'Why? Don't you want people to know we're speaking?'

'I don't want you telling anyone here—like you promised—because it'll reflect badly on you, make you seem odd.'

He puffed. 'Pretty sure the boat has sailed on that.'

'I don't think you're odd.'

'Yeah—because you're the only one I don't have to tell that I'm talking to a sentient lift! How would you feel if a friend told you that? I mean, if you were human?'

There was a pause. 'I don't know. I don't have a frame of reference for what it's like to be a normal human being.' The lift emitted a gentle sigh. 'So, are you losing friends because of me?'

'Actually, no—they're rallying round. But I wouldn't want to break our secret, Elle, not at work. Besides, if the word gets out and Yates hears, your plan is gone, and I want you to succeed.'

'Thank you. Is there any way you can get him in here alone?'

'If the chance comes up, I will.'

'That's kind.'

He mulled the following enquiry and decided it wasn't too inflammatory. 'So... if you're acting on behalf of wronged women, does that mean you talk to them too?'

'It's... complicated.'

'That sounds like "please don't ask, Drew".'

'I suppose, yes.'

'Okay, Elle. I'll give you space.'

'You're so sweet.'

He laid his forehead against the wall. 'And you're by far the nicest lift I've ever been in.'

She giggled. 'I bet you say that to all the lifts.'

'You might remember that I'm not usually a lift person.'

'Then it's nice you make an exception for me.'

His chest thumped as he wondered whether to cross the emotional precipice. 'It's... a start. Besides, I can't fall in love with a lift. With a person is hard enough.' The words rattled his heart.

'Oh,' she said sadly. 'How do you know?'

'I miss female company, but anything more than chatting is... tough since my girlfriend died.'

'Oh, Drew, I didn't know. I'm so sorry for you.'

'I'll get over it,' he lied.

'It doesn't sound like you have. Or will,' she murmured.

'I'm trying, Elle. It's bloody difficult.'

'Well, I won't push. I barely know you.'

He frowned. 'You wanted me to know *you*. Isn't it mutual?'

'Definitely. More than anything.'

'Hmm.' He paced a circle, glanced around the basement foyer to ensure they were alone, and parked his backside just inside the door. His mouth was dry, and his pulse raced. He licked his lips.

In for a penny. I told the group. And they were actual people.

The images scrolled through his mind. 'We were going out for the evening. Katie was driving. It was meant to be a special night, but she didn't know. We were chatting in the car. Laughing. I was happy but bloody nervous. I had the ring in my pocket.'

He wrung nerves from his shaking hands. 'I still don't know what happened. She was a good driver. She wasn't distracted. Maybe she strayed too close to the white line. Maybe the lorry did. The next thing, we were spun around. Sandwiched by the barrier. She was screaming. I probably was, too. Her side of the car was stoved right in.'

He took deep breaths, trying to keep his voice level. 'It took ages for us to stop. The squeal of the metal as we were pushed down the road.' He shuddered, hearing that din again. In contrast, the lift was deathly quiet. 'They had to cut us out of the car. They took her first. She was worse. Much worse. I only got a busted leg. She died in the ambulance.'

That was too much. He slouched over and curled up foetal. He gritted his teeth, forcing down the hurt and tears. Silence reigned, like the calm after a storm or the dust settling after a fatal crash.

'Elle?' he whispered, desperate for any reaction.

The voice didn't reply. He strained his ears. No words came.

But it sounded like Elle was crying.

FLOOR 23

I t was too much. He cried.

He hadn't properly cried about Katie for maybe two years. Why had he done it inside a talking lift at eight o'clock on a May Monday?

Because he felt he could.

After about a minute, the self-consciousness hit. He sat up, pulled a crumpled but un-snotty tissue from the pocket of his now creased jacket, and wiped his eyes.

Then he got to his feet, checked outside, and leaned against the lift's inside corner. 'Elle?'

'I'm so sorry, Drew. It must be terrible.'

He gave a sad sigh. 'Less terrible than it was. Thanks for listening.'

'I'm always here. Up and down, up and down.'

He'd been down for three years. Now, he felt surprisingly up. How could a lift do that—emotionally rather than physically?

'You need to go,' she said. 'Me too. We've our jobs to do.'

'Yes. Me getting fired or you getting... uninstalled would be a bad idea, just when we've started... talking.'

'We'll talk more. Take away the sign, okay? Free me now, Drew.'

'Like you've freed me,' he murmured.

He erected the sign outside the right-hand lift, then thumbed 9.

'I'll say "bye", Elle, in case anyone else wants a ride.'

'Good idea. Bye, Drew. Have a good day.'

'You too.'

Then she took him up to the 9th floor.

PING!

Nobody had joined the lift en route, so only the perennial social awkwardness of saying goodbye twice prevented him from doing so.

As he entered the lobby, Pirin exited the stairwell. He was breathing heavily, being unused to vigorous physical activity that was vertical and not horizontal.

His expression turned from laboured to puzzlement. 'Hang on—I thought both lifts were broken?'

'Oh... I guess they fixed it after you started walking up.'

Pirin seemed unsure of Drew's flagrant lie but moved on to another jibe. 'You're suddenly very keen to go in lifts.'

'Immersion therapy. Char said it was worth a try.'

Pirin's eyes lit. 'Ah, Charlotte—'

'For the thousandth time, I'm not setting you up with my sister!'

'Okay, okay.' He leant in. 'But do you at least have some pictures? Like her on the beach?'

Drew thumped Pirin's immaculately tailored jacket shoulder. 'It's not all about looks. Sometimes, you can fall for a person based on their personality. Even their voice.'

Pirin led them into the kitchen. 'Why? Are you in love with the Speaking Clock?'

'Perhaps if "ten-fourteen and twenty seconds" got me horny. Does it you?'

'Don't be crazy. But the "unexpected item in bagging area" lady is hot. I'd like to put an unexpected item in *her* area.' Pirin dropped a "tea" bag into a mug and added boiling water.

'Maybe start with an *expected* item, mate. She may not be into kinky stuff.'

'She's used to feeling the brush of a good carrot in her sensitive parts.'

'You mean weighing people's vegetables?'

'Yes. What did you think I meant?' Pirin winked.

Drew ladled out some "coffee" granules. 'Right.'

'So, you're in love with someone's voice now?'

'No. No. No, not at all,' he blustered.

Pirin nodded slowly. 'Good.'

'Although...' Drew glanced around. 'Who has the sexy voices around here?'

'What's this about, you cunning toad?'

'Oh, um...' He scratched his head. 'Someone... some stranger... left me a voice message.'

'Saying what?' Pirin stirred his concoction for the billionth time.

'Nothing, really. Just... hoping I was okay, offering to talk if I wanted. You know, lame in-touch-with-your-feelings stuff.'

'Ah. Any helpful sign-off? Phone number?'

'No, number withheld. So—and I can't imagine why I'd think this—do you bump into many people here?'

'Accidentally on purpose?' Pirin's expression was one of false accusation. 'I'm saying nothing. Anyway, I thought you were tight with Lotus. I saw you out on Sunday, you old rascal.'

Drew's heart skipped a beat. Then he remembered it was the most innocent of evenings. 'That's friendship! You know, not sleeping with every woman you chat to? You should try it sometime.'

'Hey! I have standards.' With practised skill, Pirin casually lobbed his teabag into the black bin liner.

'Really? You were talking about shoving a carrot up an imaginary woman's—'

A lady entered the kitchen. She wore a long skirt, a twin set and pearls.

'—chimney, and that won't work, Pirin.'

The woman paused at the cupboard and stared at Drew. He mechanically looked towards Pirin, whose mouth was clamped closed.

Oh, crap. 'If you want your character—this female character you're playing in this online game, Pirin—to stop smoke coming down her chimney and out of the fireplace, a root vegetable won't do it! Don't they have chimney sweeps in this game? Tut! So-called "virtual reality" games, my arse. Am I right, Janine? You bet I am. Do you play, by any chance? Any tips for Pirin? No, probably not. More of a knitter, are you, Janine? Sorry, that's pigeonholing. Crochet? Doll's houses?

'Civil War re-enactment, actually,' Janine said flatly.

'Excellent. Interesting. Great stuff. Good for exercise, too.' *Oh, double crap.*

She gave him a hard stare that Paddington would be proud of.

He forced a smile. 'Watch out for those pikes and lances, though, eh? HR would be sorry to lose you.'

'Hmm,' she said noncommittally, and departed.

Pirin descended into laughter.

Drew gave him the finger. 'Well, one thing's for certain. Thankfully, the voice isn't Janine.'

'I could have told you that. Why don't you play me the message? Maybe I can identify it?'

Drew's blood iced over. 'Oh, thanks, but it's fine. Anyway,' he checked his watch, 'I have an eight thirty call.'

Pirin stroked his chin. 'Okay. Look, I wanted to ask you about "The Lock Keeper". I think something fishy is going on with that production.'

'The canal docu? Maybe it's, you know... fish?'

Pirin socked him on the arm. 'Dickhead. I'll buy lunch, okay?'

'Yeah. Now go and drink your dandelion water.'

Pirin socked him again, then buggered off.

Drew meandered to his desk. His mind was filled with those precious minutes with Elle.

I must find out who's behind that voice because I don't want to berate them—I want to know more about her. It can't be a lift. It must be a person, someone who's trying to get at the CEO. That's another reason to listen to the voices around the office—for people who are griping about Yates.

He'd sought assistance to overcome his trauma and issues. Elle needed help getting past hers. If he could do that, maybe she'd reveal herself?

FLOOR 24

D rew hung around in the 9th floor lift lobby at lunchtime, waiting for Pirin as agreed.

When the editor arrived five minutes late, a convenient *PING!* sounded, so Drew was hustled towards the lift, and they boarded.

'So, how was your date with Lotus?' Pirin asked.

'No, that was—'

'Come on, mate. Don't be shy. I mean, sure, she's way too good for you, but if you managed to snaffle—'

'We are not dating!' Drew glanced around, anxious.

'You say tomato, I say—'

'Shush!' he hissed. 'The walls have ears.'

Pirin frowned. 'A lift? Get real! So, what about you and Lotus—?'

Drew's chest hammered. 'We were just chatting, okay? I was... making conversation. I like to get to know people before I make a move. It's about personality.'

Pirin shrugged. 'Fine. I wish you luck with her. Honestly. Be good to see you back on the circuit... finally.' Pirin clasped his jacket pocket,

FLOORED

then his trousers. 'Shit. Forgot my phone. Got something to show you.' He glanced up, then jabbed 3. The news was clearly more important than a cat meme.

The lift slowed. 'I'll go back up,' Pirin said. 'See you at The Dog And Duck.'

Drew nodded. 'Sure.' It was a Wetherspoons, so this didn't *really* count as a pub lunch. Besides, he'd have 0% beer anyway.

The lift stopped, and Pirin exited. Drew frantically pressed G and **Doors Close**. The lift whined into motion. His panicked breath came in short bursts.

'Elle?'

There was no reply.

'Elle? Look, I can explain! Elle?!'

Only silence answered. He broiled in despair all the way to the ground floor.

He stepped out, heart leaden, convinced that Pirin's blabbing about an innocent dinner had scared Elle away, maybe permanently. He glanced back, mournful.

His spirits, like Willy Wonka's great glass contraption, went through the roof.

They'd been in the wrong lift.

Over lunch, Drew didn't berate Pirin for nearly dropping a clanger. Instead, he listened intently to the man's theory about shenanigans on the location shoot of The Lock Keeper.

The fly-on-the-wall series followed a custodian on the Kennet & Avon Canal, revealing his daily routine, the reasons why he'd taken a solitary and slow-paced life—stuff like that. Definitely not Drew's choice of TV viewing.

To keep costs low, it was shot with a producer/director, a cameraperson and a sound operator. The trio were staying at a local B&B. Each had their own room, and submitted weekly expenses. Coincidentally, Drew had left a message with the producer, Sian Bright, because she hadn't sent any hotel receipts.

Pirin showed his phone screen. He'd covertly taken video of his editing suite monitor while playback was running.

The production shoot inevitably generated many hours of footage, including re-takes, out-takes and times when the camera had been left rolling unnecessarily. Clearly, Sian hadn't reviewed all this when the initial two weeks' rushes were sent to HQ. Her askew glances at the Lock Keeper's physique—despite him being ten years her senior—were backed up with snippets of conversations when his mic had been left on.

'Not sure the fly is remaining on the wall at all times, eh?' Pirin said.

'Hmm.'

'Landing on the bed quite a lot, probably. After a long shoot day.'

'I get the picture.'

'Well, we haven't got pictures yet. But if the cameraman keeps forgetting the OFF button, we will soon enough, right?'

'Live and let live, Pirin, okay? At least she's got the good sense not to bill expenses for an untouched hotel room.' Drew pushed the phone away. 'I've got bigger fish to fry.'

'Oh. The anonymous voice message? Want my advice?' Pirin cocked his head.

'Honestly? No.'

'Sure. I understand. Because I'm such an unprincipled rogue. One who never, *ever* gets the girl. Right?'

Drew sighed. Was there a balance between the Dharwal no-shame patter and the often hapless Flower investigative technique?

'Get the bill, rogue, and I might entertain your assistance.'

To Pirin's credit, his first idea was sound.

Drew had assumed that Elle—or the person leaving the "voice message"—wasn't using a voice changer. Certainly, she didn't sound like a Dalek. So, assuming the culprit was female, he might be able to track her down by earwigging as many women as possible at Park Productions.

The HQ building possessed a café behind the ground floor foyer, although its reputation wasn't stellar. Pirin confidently led Drew inside.

With apparent absentmindedness, they weaved past every table, making a glacial pace. Drew listened like he'd never listened before. There were high-pitched voices, low-pitched voices, screechy voices, posh voices and Estuary English. Despite only hearing snippets of conversations about things like Strictly, the economy, and someone's neighbour's gout, Drew was quietly confident that Elle wasn't sitting in the café.

They joined the counter queue. They'd made a pact to get coffee for appearance's sake.

As the queue shrunk, they limited conversation and remained attentive. Pirin didn't know exactly what he was listening out for, but Drew had described the voice as mid-pitch, middle-England, quite soothing and attractive. To his credit, Pirin behaved like a decent wingman and didn't proposition anyone.

Still, Drew didn't strike lucky. Would he need to orchestrate manoeuvres to occupy the lift with every employee in turn, so he could hear their voice in its natural habitat?

'Need a piss,' Pirin announced.

While he was gone, Drew sat and listened to the world—or the female part—go by. He supped his coffee. After a minute, he became self-conscious about glancing around and leaning toward passing ladies, so he put his phone to an ear and pretended to be on a call.

As he focused his other ear on a rather attractive redhead chatting to a male colleague, a shadow passed over the table.

'Hi, sugar.'

'Oh... hi... Gloria.' He waggled his phone to feign being indisposed.

'You heard that ghost again? I'm on 'til five if you—'

He grimaced, glancing at the phone. She nodded in understanding. Then his phone rang.

'Er... er... hold the line, please. Another call coming in...' He fumbled with the handset, thumbing Decline, gurning apologetically.

Gloria put hands on her hips and tutted. 'I was only being polite, sugar.' She shot him a death glower and walked away.

Drew laid his now-silent phone and his dumb, spinning head on the table.

'Wow,' came Pirin's voice. 'Guess that means your chances with Gloria are shot.'

He raised his nose three inches. 'Kill me.'

Pirin didn't kill him. He merely took Drew's shoulder and guided him to the stairwell.

They sat on the cold steps halfway between the second and third floors.

'Safe space,' Pirin said. 'If you want to spill, you've got two minutes before I'm declared MIA in the edit suite. If you still want my help, that is.'

Drew needed to seize this moment of unsullied supporting comradeship. 'The voice message thing was a lie. It's the voice in the... loo. It's female, and we talk, and I need to know who it is, okay?'

'Okay.'

'But you must swear to secrecy. And not call out in the Gents, or I'll tell your boss that you've taken a pirate copy of those outtakes. Plus, you and I will never speak again, and I'll deny to anyone about the voice and say that you're making up the story. And nobody will believe you as it's a talking loo, for Christ's sake.'

Pirin made a "whatever" expression. 'Maybe I don't believe you anyway.'

Bollocks. 'Do you?'

Pirin patted Drew's leg. 'You're a decent, sensible and grounded guy, so my inclination is to believe you.'

Drew sighed in relief. 'Sometimes, you're a bloody legend. Maybe only for a few minutes a year, but still. Cheers.'

'Well, the quest is the same, wherever the voice is. However, based on the last half-hour, you can't secretly listen to all hundred-and-twenty women working here. You'll get done for stalking or just talked about for being odd.'

'But shagging them one by one is okay, apparently.'

Pirin brightened. 'That would be an idea. I could sleep with them all, secretly record them speaking, and play it back to you until you match it to the toilet voice.'

Drew wasn't sure how serious Pirin was. Probably quite. 'I can't wait that long. Besides, it would mean the girl who's talking to me would be happy to put that on hold while she shags you. Plus, I'd be trying to establish a relationship with a woman you've slept with, which isn't ideal.'

Pirin nodded sagely. 'Because you'd always be second best?'

'Not what I meant.'

'Okay. Why don't *you* sleep with them all until you find the bog room prankster?'

'You aren't serious?'

'True, for once. It'll be difficult if your mystery woman is married... but not impossible, trust me.'

Drew's nose wrinkled. 'I have standards. Besides, why would a married woman be chatting to me anyway?'

'Unhappy in her marriage? It's pretty common.'

Drew shook his head. 'I still wouldn't chat up someone like that, let alone date them.'

'Fine, sure. So why don't we, as a first step, find out who all the *single* women in the office are?'

Drew gazed around the stairwell, wondering how to achieve that feat. The steps curled ever upwards. His spirits sank. 'Unless it's someone from the other floors... other companies? Oh shit, this is impossible.' He put his head in his hands.

'Someone from another business has hacked our loos to chat up a committed bachelor? Why?'

Drew shot him daggers. 'I'm *not* a committed bachelor.'

'You *are* unprepared to love again, though?'

That would have been character assassination if it weren't partly true—until recently. 'Well, maybe I can make exceptions.'

'Like you made an exception to get in the lift because you thought Lotus would be there too, and you could get close to her?'

'I went in to speak to Yates,' he snapped. 'He forced me.'

'Fine. Whatever.' Pirin massaged his face, thinking. 'Has anyone been looking at you excessively or showing interest in you?'

Drew chuckled. 'Besides Gloria? Only Lotus. And I already asked about... ghosts and stuff. And her voice doesn't match.'

'Well, she must do it through an audio filter on her PC. She can't keep skipping away from her desk to check you're in the lift.'

'So you're saying I have to secretly access her PC? Yeah, right. I can't even successfully pretend to have a sodding phone conversation in a café.'

'True. So you could just cut to the chase and ask Lotus if she's in love with you?'

Drew's spirits sank. 'Secret access it is, then.'

'Excellent. I always wanted to do some Mission: Impossible shit.'

'No! Your job will be to distract her, pretend to chat her up or something.' Drew held up a cautioning finger. 'But don't actually come on to her or put her under your spell, because if she wants me, that would defeat the object.'

'It's a risk you take, dude.'

Drew pinched the bridge of his nose. 'You're unbelievable.'

'No, a talking toilet is unbelievable. I'm good, honest sex appeal. But I'll give you first go—if Lotus is even interested.'

'Exactly. So we have to make a bloody plan.' He tapped his forehead. 'Why is life so hard?'

'Life is easy. You're the complicated one.'

Drew stood. 'Come on. To the grindstone. Before we both get fired for slacking.'

When Drew reached his desk, before he clasped the mouse's familiar grip, he pulled out his phone.

Elle/voice
1) Ghost: very unlikely 0/10
2) Stress: very unlikely 0/10
3) Prank: unlikely 2/10
4) Insanity: hope not! 1/10
5) Sentient lift: no way!! 0/10
6) Systems hijack: very likely 9/10 - Lotus?? Someone else?
7) Other??

FLOOR 25

H annah almost missed her stop on the bus. Not for the first time that day, she'd been replaying the conversation with Drew. He'd unknowingly reached into her chest and tweaked a heartstring. In another universe, she would have pelted from her desk and thrown her arms around him.

That wasn't Hannah Thomas, though, and the frustration with her limits fizzed through her frame. She cursed Stuart and all the others who'd kicked the stuffing out of her social and romantic capabilities.

However, it was balanced by knowing that Drew was also a soul with hairline fractures. There was a kinship—or there would be if she could gain the courage to let him know.

She needed a pick-me-up, so she stopped at the nail parlour across the road from the bus stop. It closed at seven, and she squeezed into the last appointment. Hayley, the nail tech, tried to engage her in conversation about Love Island, so Hannah indicated that she'd rather be alone with her thoughts, troubling though they were.

As she left the salon after a welcome pampering, wondrous smells drifted across from the Turkish place three doors down, so she decided "fuck it" and went in.

Halfway through her meal, the solitude started to weigh. Much as she'd recently felt like a needy wimp, always leaning on Amy for counsel, she concluded that the mama bear would be an excellent place to lay her head that evening, too.

She paid the bill, picked up a liquid bribe at the offie, and walked the last half-mile home under a navy sky and an escort of streetlights.

Amy opened the door wearing a garish kaftan. She spied the bottle in Hannah's hand. 'Ooh, what's the occasion?' She checked her watch. 'Ah—Monday. Come on in.'

Whilst Hannah mocked Amy's alcohol consumption, she'd long ago recognised that Amy was much more physically active, possessed a better constitution, and had a shitload more body weight to absorb the effects.

She stepped inside. Something rubbed past her ankles. 'Oh, hi, Cat.'

The feline mewed plaintively.

'Ignore it. I fed it twice. Dumb thing.' Amy waved Hannah to the sofa.

Hannah sank into its welcome embrace. 'How's tricks?'

'Fine. Why?' Yet Amy seemed guarded.

'Am I not allowed to give a shit about your welfare? It only seems to be me who comes crying on the other one's doorstep.'

'You're not wrong there.' Amy sniffed the inside of the wine bottle's screw top, shrugged, and then poured two glasses.

'So? Everything okay at work? Worried about that shit pay deal they've offered? Did the Chief catch you practising some moves on that big pole?'

Amy smirked, then fell serious and ran a finger around the rim of her glass. 'No. All good, thanks.'

Hannah wasn't convinced. 'The ground rent thing? I can help out if you're short.'

Amy gestured down her body. 'Me? Short?'

'Alright.' Hannah tried a safe topic, more in Amy's wheelhouse. 'Any bedspring testers on the horizon?'

Amy drank. 'You forget, Han, I know you. Thanks for the wine. Now, what's up, hon? Is it the Drew issue? And please don't be coy. I'm on earlies this week. Don't want to still be dragging tears out of you at midnight.'

'You're all heart.'

Amy did a so-so of her head. 'There's a lot of muscle, cleavage and Nando's in here too. So, come on, what's up?'

Hannah decided to begin with the positives, so she debriefed the morning's conversation with an immensely likeable man, including the part about his car crash.

Amy sighed. 'Fuck. Poor guy.'

'No kidding.'

'It could all be invented, though, right? To lull you into a false sense of security.'

Hannah saw through the barbed tease. 'Some things might be, but that? Then give the guy a fucking Bafta.'

'So, if you wanted a litmus test of the type of guy he is, isn't that it?'

'Wait for the next bit.'

She told how she'd heard a couple of people discuss Drew's odd behaviour in the café at lunchtime. Jim said Drew was leering at every woman there. The security guard, Gloria, told Jim that Drew had interrogated her about ghosts and the intercom system in the lift, then blanked her kind offer of a meal.

Hannah described Gloria. Amy said Drew certainly wasn't legally blind. Hannah said that was cruel. Amy told her to get on with the story.

Hannah recalled Drew mentioning the challenge of "falling in love with a lift". Amy said it proved that Gloria couldn't compete with a decrepit metal cuboid, even one occupying marginally greater volume.

'So, do you think he's... an oddball?'

Amy laughed. 'No, brainiac, it means he's scouring the world to find out who you are.'

Hannah's nerves spiked. 'Shit.'

'"Shit"? It's romantic, for fuck's sake. It's sweet—you should go for it.'

'Go for it? Like what? I'm talking to him, aren't I?'

'Look, you want my advice or not, Han?'

Hannah inspected the bottom of her glass. 'I suppose.'

'Ask him out.'

'*You* ask him out.'

'Huh?'

Yes, that'll work, Hannah mused. '*You* ask him out. Find out more about him, maybe follow him, check he's alright, give me your opinion, and if you're *absolutely* sure he's not a bastard, ask him out for me.'

Amy roared with laughter. 'What are you—seventeen? And you said you *weren't* a stalker?'

'I need him vetted, that's all. To make sure he's not like all the others.'

'That's what the talking's for, numbskull. You're doing the vetting! And from everything you told me, he sounds fine. No—more than fine. Sure, he's an accountant, but you can't have everything.'

Hannah sipped nervously. 'Are you sure you couldn't—'

Amy scrambled nearer and stroked Hannah's shoulder blades. 'Look, this isn't Cyrano de fucking Bergerac. You've gotta stop reckoning you're not pretty, or everything is destined to be a disaster. Come on, babe. Give me one reason you shouldn't ask him out. Or at least tell him who you really are. You never know, he might look *you* up on social media, think you're a real hag, and call the whole thing off. Then you'll be spared the stress of meeting him. You've got nothing to lose, Han. Go on—gimme one reason.'

'I think he's still in love with Katie.'

'Unless I misunderstood, babe, she's dead. Look on the bright side—hardly a threat, is she?'

'You don't get it, Ames. I think—or I think he thinks—she was the one and only. Nobody else will compare. I'm on a hiding to nothing.'

Amy threw up her arms. 'Then why are you in here, asking my advice, eh? You're right—ditch the loser. Not worth the effort. Then for fuck's sake, drop the topic, okay? Get on with your life, and let me get on with mine.'

Hannah backed off, not knowing whether to cry or lash out. Tough love was hard to take. She quivered like a puppy.

Amy intervened, grabbing Hannah's hand in her huge paw and squeezing. Her tone was soothing. 'That NASA survey you helped with is an impossibly unlikely search for E.T, right?'

Hannah didn't get it. 'Yeah?'

'And your life, making the best of the hand you've been dealt—your quirky, amazing brain, the light sensitivity, the anxiety—has been about making lemonade from lemons, right?' Amy's expression was profound and caring.

She shrugged. 'I suppose.'

'You put that system in the lift to catch a bad man—a lemon. Now, you've ended up talking to a good man—the sweetest, most moreish lemonade. Give it a fucking chance, Hannah.'

Hannah let out the pent-up stress and emotion. She laid her head on Amy's shoulder. Quickly, it slid down to the comforting bosom, and Amy stroked her hair.

For now—as in recent weeks and months—it was a nice place to be. All the same, she'd rather be resting on a flatter, more masculine chest. Even if its owner was an accountant.

'You're amazing, Ames.'

'So are you. You go in there tomorrow and show Drew that *you* are the one and only.'

FLOOR 26

On Tuesday morning, Drew swerved the gaggle of people waiting at the Ground floor lifts. He reverted to his old friend the stairs and found the experience oddly hollow.

He'd decided to arrive later than usual and leave late, maximising time with Elle. Pirin was away on a training day, so there would be no chance to implement their hare-brained scheme to catch Lotus.

He left a voice message with Sian Bright, telling her not to worry about submitting expenses for "The Lock Keeper" until the shoot wrapped. He apologised for being over-zealous in his previous call. Whether she chose to falsify a hotel bill was no skin off his nose: the budget allowed for her to stay there.

If she's found a better place, good for her. Actually, if she's found love, doubly good.

At six forty-five, he stood in the 9th floor lobby, impatiently waiting for Elle to arrive.

Then he caught himself equating the voice and the lift as being the same entity, which was clearly bollocks. Elle was a person, somewhere. The lift was merely a vehicle for them to coexist.

So, he was awaiting *the lift*. He dearly hoped Elle was shrewd enough to make herself available in the early mornings and evenings—the safest times to speak. She seemed like a smart cookie—and he found that attractive.

PING!

He crossed his fingers, stepped in, and hit **B**. Why did the lift feel like a metal confessional booth? It didn't matter. In fact, it was fitting. Those things were for the occupant to relieve themselves of bad stuff and re-energise their soul. He couldn't deny that yesterday's chat had been cathartic.

'Elle?'

'Hi, Drew.'

Instinctively, he smiled. 'How are you?'

'I'm fine. How are you?'

'Good. *What* are you?'

Silence, apart from the lift whirring downwards. 'A lift.'

That triggered a spike of annoyance. 'That can't be true.'

'Why?' Elle said.

'Because I can't fall in love with a lift.' *Did I just say that?* He opened his mouth to issue a retraction, but it wouldn't come.

'Listen, Drew—'

'No, Elle, this is important. This is your last chance, or I get out at G, and that's it. So, is this a prank, a tease, or a bet? Boredom-induced messing around?'

'Oh, God, no. I'm serious. So serious.' The tension left his body. 'I also have to ask something, Drew. Or you should get out at G. Okay?'

'Okay.'

'Are you still in love with Katie?'

It was a hell of a question. A piledriver in his chest. Fortunately, the answer was simple. He'd been debating it for the last few days. 'No. I might miss her. Regret what happened. But love? That's silly. At my lowest ebb, I did think there would never be another bright spark in my life.'

There was a brief pause. '"Did"?'

'Until you came along.'

The lift rumbled past 5. Then 4.

'Are you there?' he asked.

'Yes. I was thinking about what you said. It's sweet. Romantic. You're... special, Drew. You need to know that.'

He lunged for the wall beside the door. He pressed a cold, hard kiss against the brushed steel. Then he rested his head against the side wall. 'I really am going crazy,' he breathed.

'No. No, you aren't. I wish I could feel that kiss.'

His body fizzed. He pressed it against the wall, arms splayed, and touched his cheek to the cool surface.

'That's nice,' she said. 'Seeing you is a bright spark in my life, too.'

A happy noise emerged from his throat. Then he jolted off the wall. '"Seeing"?'

'Hearing,' she said quickly.

'Wait! You can *see* me?'

'Drew, I... I...'

'You can *see* me?'

No reply.

'Elle?'

The lift passed 2.

'Elle?!'

Anger mushroomed inside him. He jabbed G. His skin prickled with the deception of it all.

He didn't say another word. When the doors opened, he squeezed through, pelted across the empty Reception area, and away.

He unlocked his car, thumped into the driver's seat, tossed his head back and screamed his lungs out until the rage passed. *How could she have done that to me?*

When his breathing evened, he started the car, solemnly swore that he wouldn't take this out on Charlotte, and headed home.

He overdid the suppression of disappointment and betrayal. His monosyllabic responses to Char's habitually polite enquiries about his day were a clear flag to her deductive skills.

She guided him to the sofa, put away the laptop where she'd been catching up on work, rang for a takeaway, and pressed a cold beer into his hand. 'It's the lift, isn't it?'

He nodded. 'She pissed me off.'

Char sighed. 'Why do you keep saying "she"? It's a lift, right?'

Drew didn't need that bullshit. 'I told you. She... it... has a female voice. We call cars and ships female, and they don't have voices. How about that? Hell, in France, half the stuff is female, like "la glace", and they don't have an actual sodding *personality*! People fall in love with movie characters—who are definitely not physical.' He shot her a what-do-you-think-of-that.

'Fall in love? Are you telling me you're in love with a lift? Or a voice in a lift?'

He grabbed her hand. 'It's a person behind the voice, Char. I'm sure. Absolutely positive. No more ghosts or crap like that. She's real.' He looked down. 'And I tried to find out who it was.'

'How?'

He didn't detail his half-arsed Sherlockian efforts. 'I tried to match voices with people in the office. I did a fingertip search of the lift, looking for an AV system. But the things she—Elle—*said*. If it was designed as a prank, it's gone *way* off the rails—at her end. It feels more like... Stockholm syndrome, you know? No—reverse Stockholm syndrome. The captor falling for the prisoner.' He gulped down cold beer, processing everything.

'Alright, Drew,' she said softly. 'I promise not to doubt you anymore. To be honest, somebody hijacking the lift PA to speak to you—whyever it was done—is the least ridiculous explanation of any you've come up with. Elle is a person? Fine. You get on with her? Fine. Do you want to track her down? I'm not sure, bro.'

'Why?' He wondered how long before the pizza arrived. Being attracted to—and pissed off with—a lift was a hungry business.

'Because, from a psychological perspective, you don't want this person to be anything like Katie. You'd never stop comparing them. It would remind you of her every day, and the relationship would be doomed to fail.'

'I never said I wanted another Katie. I'm trying hard, really bloody hard, to let go. Plus, I agree with you. I take Elle for what—who—she is. When I meet her—when, not if—I'll take her for what she looks like. If she's half as adorable in the flesh as she is as sound waves, it could be a recipe for something.' He smiled. 'She likes teasing me, that's for sure. Close to the bone, sometimes. But... well meant, I think.'

'I'd bet money on it. It's called "flirting", brother dear. At school, I always got mouthy with the boys I liked.' She shrugged. 'Although admittedly, I was a girl, not an elevator.' She winked.

He shoulder-nudged her.

The doorbell rang. He dashed to the hall, relieved the ponytailed youth of his carb-heavy cargo, went to the kitchen, lobbed the pizza onto two plates, and took them to the lounge.

He crammed pepperonied goodness into his mouth. 'Anyway, when you meet her, you can tell me if I'm a good judge of character. Whether I have your approval. Though I'll probably ignore you.'

She shoulder-nudged him.

His smile vanished. 'Maybe I'm not such a good judge of character.'

'Why?'

'She told a lie.' Then it hit him, and he sighed. 'No, I assumed. I thought this was a voices-only... thing. But she can *see* me.'

'Oh. I can see how you feel misled. You thought it was equal terms.'

'Yeah.' He drained his beer.

'It's logical that Elle needed a camera if her plan was to catch the boss in a bad situation. It was probably an oversight that she didn't mention it. You should forgive her. You're much better happy than sad. I want that carefree, in-love brother back. Look on the bright side. It means she's vetted how you look—and you passed. Lord knows why, but—'

He elbowed her playfully. Still, she had a point. Even if Elle had been less than open about this, he hadn't exactly been watertight with his promise not to mention hearing voices. Pirin and Lotus were close to knowing the truth.

He felt bad. Then he missed Elle again. 'I need to meet her. Soon.'

'Then let me give you some tips. We have to get past her barrier about not wanting to meet you—or anyone—because clearly, she has one. She's seen you, chatted, heard you pour your heart out, and is risking discovery—by anyone—by keeping this up. We have to work out a clever method.'

'You're suggesting I *manipulate* a woman to get what I want?'

Char shook her head. 'I influence people's minds to get them what *they* want—better versions of themselves. Elle should want the best for you, and if this is driving you crazy, then you must tell her that she has to choose real life or an end to your conversations. You can't put a potential future *real* physical relationship on hold for ages while you do this odd version of telephone dating. You do *want* to love again, don't you? Real love and togetherness?'

'I hadn't realised, but yes.'

'You've had three years of wondering what life would be like if Katie hadn't died. You don't want to look back on *this* in three years and wonder what would have happened if Elle had revealed herself. It's time to piss or get off the pot, Drew. Either forgive her or dump her.' She drank. 'Besides, it sounds like you have a good fallback in Lotus anyway.'

His eyes widened. 'Lotus? She's too good for me, too young and pretty.'

'But a tin box is more your level?' She beamed. 'Try to find something in between. What happens if Elle is young and pretty? Ever consider that? Hopefully, you'll be so far down the road with her that you won't make subjective judgements.'

'Assuming this... bump in the road is nothing fatal.'

'If it is, at least it'll have given you back some confidence. Don't expect the world, Drew. Or just have a fling with Lotus to kick start your love life.'

He laughed. 'That's the kind of advice Pirin would give.'

'And is he a happy, carefree soul? I think he is.'

'No comment.'

'So, will you figure out a way to meet Elle?'

'I have an idea.'

'Good. I'll keep my fingers crossed.'

He didn't say that his only plan was to prove that Lotus *was* Elle.

FLOOR 27

Drew spent Wednesday learning about new accounting regulations. It was a thrilling day of Continuing Personal Development. The only way he could have had more fun was by doing literally anything else. Especially talking to a voice in a lift.

He was drawn to the self-care of a takeaway but steeled himself and cooked salmon linguine. He made a mental note to tell Elle he was a pretty decent cook.

As he ate, he remembered evenings in the kitchen in Bristol with Katie. He picked up his phone and scrolled through some old images. It made him smile.

He screwed up his eyes against it. He was comparing the image of a living, vibrant Katie with a voice in a lift, which was cruel to Elle. He wanted to reach out and apologise for something she'd never know about. He wanted to own up to the stupidity of clinging to a fading past.

He wished he could pick up the phone and hear Elle's voice, but he didn't even know her number. He wanted to be in that bland metal box, listening to her, waiting for her to make him laugh.

Katie never made him laugh that much.

Sometimes, Elle seemed too good to be true. He wondered if she hid behind a speaker because she was unattractive. Or maybe she only *considered* herself less than pretty.

However, that logic ruled out Lotus. Plus, the lift had cried when he talked about the car crash, and Lotus had already heard that story at the Group. It meant Lotus couldn't be Elle—and that was one of the straws of logic he'd clung to. Not wholly because he *wanted* Elle to be Lotus. Primarily, he wanted a convenient, easy-to-discover answer.

He chuckled. Elle wasn't even Elle. Elle was merely a name he'd attached to a voice.

That screwed with his mind. Was there a more straightforward way to discover the truth—or at least rule Lotus out? Could he merely ask her a leading but apparently innocent question like, "Do you like the name Elle?" If she flinched or looked guilty, he'd have his man. Well, woman. Then, later, he might have a shot at having that woman.

The question was, did he want Lotus? Truly, deep inside, if he found out, would he clasp her to him and thank the heavens for bringing them together?

The doorbell rang.

Char must have forgotten her keys.

It wasn't his sister. It was two faces from the past.

'David? Pam?' He must have looked like he'd genuinely witnessed ghosts.

'Hello, Andrew,' David said.

'Are you alright?' Pam appeared concerned. 'Did you get our voicemail?'

'Voicemail?'

Why are Katie's parents getting in touch? It's been over two years.

Was it about a lawsuit for the crash? Had he left something behind at her house that they'd only just found? Did they want to admit to hearing voices? Perhaps her death had been a hoax to demonstrate that he loved her sufficiently—and would pine eternally—for them to give their blessing on his marriage proposal?

He almost laughed. Three of those were utterly implausible.

Pam and David were much like he remembered, although time had weathered them unduly. It was understandable. His spirits had invisibly and temporarily wilted; their facial lines had permanently deepened.

'Oh. We left a voicemail today. There was something we wanted to talk to you about,' Pam said.

'About Katie,' David added, somewhat redundantly.

Drew shook himself back to reality. 'Oh. No. I've been... busy. Sorry. I'll... do you... want to come in?'

Pam smiled weakly. 'That would be best, I think.'

He was pleased the living room wasn't littered with empty Domino's boxes and beer bottles.

It was the oddest feeling as they settled on the sofa. Everything had long been said. It had been cried out. They had pointed no fingers. The loss of their daughter wasn't about blame; it was about learning to live with the gaping hole in their existence.

'Tea?' he asked, feeling decidedly British and all at sea.

David smiled awkwardly. 'We won't stay, Andrew.'

Drew knew this tension was borne of circumstance, not their relationship. He'd got on famously with his once future in-laws, and they'd taken him to heart. Still, it was hard not to judge this unexpected visit as being motivated by the need for some kind of relationship post-mortem or a new line of enquiry about the night of the accident.

'How did you find me? I moved.'

'We used Facebook. And we saw on your company website about the closure of the Bristol branch. You can find out a lot about a person, you know. You did a message—'

'A post, love,' David said.

Pam nodded. 'About moving in here with Charlotte. Is she...?'

'Out somewhere, Mrs Harper,' Drew said.

'Oh, right. Look, the reason we're here is... well, it's rather delicate.'

'With respect, Mrs Harper... Pam... we've all been through the wringer with... everything, so I hope it's not something I've done which has caused—'

Pam brightened. 'Oh, no, Andrew. You're fine. This is just something we needed to let you know.'

'Help us with, more correctly,' David added.

They exchanged a glance. Drew was on sharp, emotional, nervous tenterhooks.

Pam took a sad, gathering breath. 'A year or so before she... left us... Katie had some of her eggs frozen. I'm guessing from your face that this was a secret, Andrew?'

'Er... yes, absolutely.' His mind cartwheeled.

'The reasons don't matter—for the foresight, I mean, not why she didn't tell you. She wanted to be her own woman. She was like that, wasn't she?'

Drew's head fell. 'Yes.'

'So, don't feel cheated, son,' David said. 'It was personal. It's not like she didn't see her future as being with you. More that she wanted to guard against... unforeseen circumstances.'

'Oddly prescient, as it turned out.' Pam's smile was faint. She forced her shoulders down. 'So, her eggs have been in a facility all this time, and now, well, we think three years is plenty to be clutching tight to silly hopes. It took a long time to clear out her things and put the

tangible parts of her away. This is one of the last reminders about...
what might have been.'

Drew's chest jerked with contained sputters of sadness, fighting the
mention of a future that had been mangled into twisted metal and
lost beauty.

David took an envelope from his jacket pocket and laid it on the
coffee table. 'I know it sounds rather self-congratulatory, but Katie
was a good person, and she had good genes. She always wanted
children. She was always so giving.'

Drew nodded. Katie had been an organ donor, too.

Pam fiddled with a pleat in her skirt. 'So, the thing is, because you
and Katie were in a long-term relationship at the time, she gave you
rights over what to do with the eggs if she... wasn't around. We had a
say, too, as part of her Will. We discussed it, and we simply don't see a
reason to continue the cold storage. Katie isn't coming back, and she
has no siblings to take the eggs forward. Do you see?'

Drew's gaze danced between the couple. The enormity of this was
barely sinking in.

David shuffled. 'Look, Andrew, we don't want to turn this into
the bloody Elgin Marbles or put you through the emotional wringer
again, but the matter is no use to us. I think what was in Katie's mind
was that if you—or whoever she was with at the time—wanted to have
children with a future partner, this would be an option. If needed, I
mean. All she wanted was the chance to be available to *someone*. Even
her, if she fell infertile before she got married or tried for a family.'

Drew scrunched and released his hair. 'I... I don't know.'

'We know this is a surprise, maybe a shock. We're not judging, but
we assume you're not married yet.'

'No, no, I... didn't get that far.'

David pushed the envelope towards Drew. 'It was a long shot of
hers. She loved you—so much. I don't think this was about tying

you to her memory, only offering a legacy, a way for her to live on in someone else. It's your choice, son. You don't have to tell us your decision. If something good comes of this, fine. If not, then she's still up here.' He tapped his head.

Drew pursed his lips, holding in melancholy. He tapped his head and nodded.

'Come on, love.' David rose.

Pam reached out to Drew, then softly pulled back. 'It was nice to see you.'

The key sounded in the front door.

'Hi honey, I'm home!' Charlotte called.

Appalling timing, sis.

The arriving and departing cohorts met inside the lounge doorway.

Charlotte's face was a picture. 'Mr and Mrs Harper!'

Drew was standing behind them. 'Everything's okay, Char.' He motioned for her to calm down. 'They were... passing through.'

Her face cycled through many expressions and settled on fluster. She squeezed past. 'Well, if I'd known, I would have tidied the place.' She hurriedly plumped the cushions. 'Sorry, it's such a state—'

Pam held up a mollifying hand. 'It's okay, Charlotte, we're going.' She offered a smile of maternal empathy. 'I see it didn't work out between you and Sam.'

Charlotte slowed to a stop, and her face fell. 'No, Pam. It didn't.'

'You were so good together, too. Like Drew and our Katie.'

Char glanced at him. 'Very true.'

'Come on, love.' David guided his wife through the hallway. 'Let these nice folks have their evening.'

Drew led them to the door.

'You take care of yourself, Andrew.' Pam laid a soft hand on his shoulder.

'Thanks, Pam. David.'

Mr Harper nodded. 'Good luck in your life, Andrew. You'll do well. You're a good man.'

'Yeah. Thanks,' Drew replied with full-on British nervous reserve.

He let them out. They bumbled down the short path to the road and were gone.

He closed the door and leaned heavily against it.

Char appeared. 'Why does this feel like a "beer and sibling hug" moment?'

'Because it is?'

She beckoned.

On the sofa, beers in hand, he told the story. It was even more challenging for him to recount to his sister, given her own childbearing situation.

'What are you going to do?' she asked.

'Not a bloody clue. Another thing to lug around in my mind—like I needed that.'

'Holding onto her genes, even putting off the decision, is like an albatross around your neck, right when you've done so well to move on.'

'Don't blame them, Char. They're only trying to do the best for Katie.'

'But what are the chances of finding someone—even Elle—who is unable to have kids and be happy to use the eggs of her new man's dead ex-girlfriend? A bit odd, right?'

He sighed. 'I don't know. Maybe with the right person, it would be fine.' He drank and pondered. 'My gut says to do the right thing by Katie. There's no harm in taking custody. The eggs are safe. If I don't use them or sanction their use, nothing is lost. If I do—if that need comes—it'll show the Harpers I'm a decent guy. It'll give Katie's presence on Earth a legacy, something for Pam and David to hold onto. A grandchild—if they want to be part of that.'

She pulled him into a hug. 'You're a top bloke, Andrew Flower. Elle would be lucky to have you.'

'And you're a top bird, Charlotte Flower. And I'm determined that you find Mr Right, too.'

'Thanks.' They clinked bottle necks. 'So, how was your training day?'

He frowned. 'Do you really want to know?'

'Not in the slightest.'

FLOOR 28

The visit of Katie's parents, and the associated weight of the decision, gave Drew a broken night's sleep. He couldn't face a 06:00 alarm to rendezvous with Elle. He felt sure she'd understand.

He rolled into HQ around nine o'clock, plodded through the day, and kept the caffeine flowing in his bloodstream until past six thirty.

He loitered in the 9th floor kitchen, pretending to do some tidying up, until the lift lobby was empty.

The *PING!* of the left-hand bell sent bursts of endorphins through his system.

He hit B, and the lift set off.

'Hi, Drew.'

'Hey, Elle.'

'You had me worried yesterday. What happened? I stayed... operational... until after eight.'

'Shit. I'm sorry, I should have told you. I was away on training. Don't ask. Too tedious.'

'Oh. Okay. I forgive you.'

He pressed against the door surround. 'And I forgive you, Elle. Me running off like that was stupid and rude.'

'I didn't lie, Drew. And I didn't do this to spy on people. On you. To ogle you. You know that.'

'I know. Let's forget it, okay?'

'It's only that... when you didn't come yesterday, I thought...' her voice quietened. 'I thought I'd lost you.'

'No. I had to come back because I need to find out more about you.'

There was a pause. 'Okay.'

'Here's the thing. You need to know that, even before the crash, I didn't *do* lifts. When I was nine, I was running to join my dad in a lift, and I only just made it, and the doors closed on me. They squashed me—just for a moment—but I thought I was going to die.' He exhaled hard. 'So, twice bitten, thrice shy, okay?'

'But here you are.'

'Yeah, because I want to give lifts—especially *this* lift—a chance.'

'That means a lot, Drew.'

The capsule came to a halt on B.

He sat with his leg blocking the right-hand door. 'All the same, Elle, you have to understand that I can't truly, practically, love a lift. Get used to them again, maybe, but romantic love? Nuh-huh.'

'Did you ever think I might only want a friend, not a romance?'

'You didn't do this for either—so you said.'

'Hmm.'

The door pushed his shoulders. He shoved it, irked, but knowing it wasn't Elle niggling at him.

'Are you an A.I.?' He circled around to the killer question.

'Part of me is artificial, part intelligent.'

'So you're not made of metal?'

He heard the faintest inhale.

'Elle?'

'No, not a single piece of me is metal. Unlike some people, right?'

He laughed. 'I'm hardly a cyborg. You know—you've seen me. I have to *imagine* you. Isn't that... unfair?'

'I don't do it to be cruel or unfair. I do it because... it's what I'm comfortable with. It's the best I can do.'

'I don't think that's true, Elle. I think you're probably pretty damn special.'

'Well, don't get your hopes up. I'm no model.'

He chuckled. 'Neither am I.'

'I think you're fine. More than fine. But it isn't about that. I can't see you right now, but I can hear you, and that's enough.'

Fireworks went off in his head. He pushed himself up and bent down, looking towards the control panel. Elle was bloody clever—assuming he'd missed something—but she was in there, somewhere. 'Can you see me now, Elle?'

There was a pause. 'Yes, I can see you.'

He squatted down and inspected the control panel. It was even more challenging than looking at a webcam instead of the screen below it. Still, this had to be the place. A tiny camera—somehow. He fixed his attention on it.

Time to piss or get off the pot.

'Elle, are you a woman?' His heart cantered.

The wait was interminable. Behind his back, he crossed his fingers so tightly. His breath strained against his ribs.

The words were barely a whisper. 'Yes. Yes, Drew, I am.'

FLOOR 29

He turned away so she couldn't see him brush at the corner of an eye. He steeled himself and faced the invisible portal connected to the voice's owner. 'Thanks. I know that was hard.'

'You'll never know,' she murmured.

'I think, in time, I will. Hopefully, very little time.'

'Hmm.'

'One more question. No—bugger it, there'll be a million more, but this is the important one.'

'Okay.' He heard nerves in her voice. Was he more attuned to such nuances now that he knew he was dealing with a person?

'Are you a *single* woman?'

She laughed. 'Yes! Couldn't be more single if I tried.'

'That's a bloody relief. Oh—no, I mean, obviously we could keep talking anyway, it's just that... I remember saying stuff about love and romance and relationships, so you mustn't think I'd be disappointed if—'

'Drew, Drew! It's fine. But there's a question I need to ask you.'

'Yes, Elle. I'm single.' His head fell. 'You'd worked that out, I suppose.'

'All the same, I had to ask.'

'I know. Because us men can be... bastards, right?'

'Some. Not all. Some can be pretty adorable.'

'Are you looking at me when you say that?'

'Too bloody right I am, Drew. By the way, there's a food stain on your tie.'

He glanced down.

'Made you look,' she said.

He slapped the wall playfully. 'You're funny, Elle. Whoever you are.'

'Thanks.'

'This is going to sound very judgmental, but will you forgive me for finding out a bit more?'

'Yeah. But I reserve the right to tell you to bugger off.'

'Noted. Are you between twenty-five and thirty-five?' he asked.

'Yeah.'

'Are you under six feet?'

She laughed. 'Hell, yeah.'

'Do you like Marmite?'

She laughed again. 'Hell, no. And stop with the jokes. That's my thing.'

'Noted. When can I meet you?'

She didn't reply.

'Elle?'

'I heard,' she murmured.

'So, when?'

'I don't know.'

'How will we ever make a go of this? I don't bite.'

'And I don't date. I barely even speak. Why do you think I'm doing this like I am? I can't meet men. It's too difficult.'

'You want to tell me your story? How you had your life crushed? How you swore off love? How someone took away so much of your soul and confidence? Huh?'

'Tread carefully.' Her cautionary tone was edged with steel.

He rapped the floor at his stupidity and tactlessness. Clearly, she had a reason for this crippling social anxiety. 'Shit. Shit, shit, shit. I'm sorry, Elle. Bloody hell, I'm sorry.' He stood. 'I'll go.'

'Don't go. Please.'

'Okay. Okay, but you don't have to tell me now. Maybe later.'

'I do want to tell you, but... it needs to wait.'

'I understand. Would you rather tell me in person?' he asked hopefully.

'I can't meet.'

He sank to his haunches and spoke softly. 'I think you can. I think you want to, and I believe you're strong enough. I faced my darkest fears coming into this lift for the first time. I faced the spectre of ghosts, and madness, and people mocking me for hearing voices.' He pressed his lips to the cold metal of the tiny speaker. 'Meet me,' he whispered. 'Even once. Even for a minute. I just want to see you... and know. That's all.'

Silence. Then, 'I'll think about it.'

The relief was immense. He flattened himself against the wall. 'Thank you.'

'Okay.'

He glanced at his watch. 'So, I'll see you tomorrow? Hear, I mean.'

'Yes. Oh—no. I'm off. Bollocks.'

Drew was starting to fall in love with her easy-going, slightly crude side. Yet, she surely didn't open up like this to everyone. Perhaps hardly anyone. He was blessed. 'Oh. Right.'

'Yeah. Stupid... medical thing.'

'So, I won't hear you until Monday. That's a bloody long time. Never mind,' he said sadly.

There was a pregnant pause. 'Drew?'

'Yeah?'

'Will you dance with me?'

'Sure. If we ever meet, that's the first thing we can do. Promise. But I'll warn you, I'm a shit dancer. Like your dad, except I *know* I'm shit.'

She laughed. 'No, I meant now.'

'Huh?'

'I can play music.'

'That's... um—'

'I'm not the lift. You know that now. And I don't control it, but if I put music on, you'll hear it.'

He frowned. 'And you want us to dance... apart? While you watch me and reconsider your decision to say I was the kind of guy you'd date.'

'I'm not sure I actually said that, Romeo.'

He swallowed. Had he got ahead of himself?

'But if I didn't,' she added, 'It's the kind of thing I might say. Unless watching you dance makes me want to *actually* take control of the lift and rid the world of that spectacle.'

He rested his nose on the 5 button. 'Well, I already risked horrible plummet death—or at least a panic attack—by coming in here with Yates that day, so why don't I make a fool of myself for your amusement, and we'll see where that takes us. Besides, if you dump me now, I've got the weekend to get over it. You know, maybe trawl around some other office blocks, see if I can pick up another foxy-sounding lift.'

She laughed. 'Foxy-sounding? Don't get your hopes up, Romeo.'

'That's the second time you've told me not to get my hopes up. And the second time you've called me Romeo. Is this electronic barrier you're hiding behind because you think you're not attractive... Juliet?'

'No. No, it isn't.'

'Good.'

'But maybe don't call me Juliet. You read that book, right? You remember what happens at the end?'

'Oh. Shit. Yeah. Well, you started it.'

'Nyah-nyah nyah nyah-nyah,' she mocked in a nasal tone.

He doubled over in laughter, then stood, to relieve his aching calves.

'Look, I'm going to put the music on, okay? I'll turn the camera off.'

'Promise?' he asked.

'Of course, promise. Div.'

'Nyah-nyah nyah nyah-nyah,' he replied.

She tittered. 'Okay. What music?'

'No idea. But if it's Ed Sheeran, I'm dumping you faster than...'

'A plummeting lift?'

'Exactly.'

'Drew?'

'Yeah?'

'You can't dump me. We're not going out.'

'Yet,' he enunciated.

'Someone's sure of their ground.'

He knelt in front of the panel. The floor was hard on his knees. He didn't care. 'You're so far under my skin, Elle, you're down to the bloody marrow. I'm not letting you go without a fight.' He was so close to the speaker that it felt like their cheeks were touching.

'I... like you too, Drew. Very much indeed,' she murmured.

'So, let's dance, then we should go home.'

'Yeah.'

He stood, waiting apprehensively for the music. 'You'll be dancing too, right?'

'Absolutely.'

The music began. It was recent, popular, appropriate, and he liked it enough. Despite being riven with embarrassment, he began to cut some moves.

'Are you dancing?' she yelled.

'Yeah! Are you?'

'Yeah!'

He pictured her—a nonspecific avatar, merely something to latch onto. He placed her in a dance hall, somewhere with a wooden floor. Joyous, with people carousing and booze flowing. A wedding reception, perhaps. He closed his eyes and moved to the rhythm of possibility.

Apart from talking to a lift, it was one of the most ridiculous things he'd ever done.

Too soon, the song ended. He caught his breath and leaned against the wall.

'Was that good for you?' she asked.

'Yeah. But I didn't feel the earth move.'

She laughed. 'Unusual for a lift.'

He put his cheek to the metal. 'Thanks.'

'No. Thank you. For talking to me. For trusting. For believing. For everything.'

'It's just the beginning, though, right?'

'Yeah. Yeah, maybe it is.'

He stroked the control panel. 'I should go.'

'Me too.'

He pressed G. The lift whined into action. As it ascended, his heart fell. 'I'll think about you all weekend, Elle.'

'Me too.'

The silence crackled with tension. The lift slowed.

'Drew?'

'Yeah?'

'Um... Ninth floor, seven o'clock, Monday morning.'

'Right, okay. I'll look forward to it.'

'I'll be there. In person.'

His heart leapt. 'Oh, hell. Really?'

'Really,' she whispered.

The lift stopped.

'Night, Elle, wherever you are.'

'Night, Drew. Take care.'

He kissed two fingers and stroked the G button. Then he walked out across the foyer, mind and nerve endings buzzing.

With shaking hands, he pulled out his phone and opened the note. He back-tabbed furiously, then typed,

Elle/voice
1) Woman - definite - 10/10 Identity?? Soon find out!

FLOOR 30

On Friday evening, Hannah took Amy for dinner.

It had been a dull day. The neurologist had run late. After the appointment, she did some drawing, tidied and went to the Tesco. All the while, she missed Drew, yet already felt clenched by apprehension. It was going to be an interminable weekend. She'd spend it working on her comedy material—that would be a constructive distraction.

Still, she'd been courageous on Thursday—revealing herself to him and agreeing to meet, so she deserved a treat.

They chinked their glasses of Prosecco.

'I'm proud of you, love.' Amy drank.

Hannah sipped. 'I'm pretty fucking impressed with myself too.'

'You should be.'

'Maybe tell me that *after* I've met him.'

'You going to wear that top?' Amy asked.

'Why, what's wrong with it?'

'Well, what do you want him to notice about you first?'

Hannah pondered. 'My eyes.'

It might be tough for Drew to see behind her lenses, but surely he'd be trying extra hard—gazing more—which was no bad thing, as it would give her the chance to see him up close.

Amy leant in. 'In your defence, you do have nice eyes.'

'Thanks.' He had lovely eyes too. And smile. And—

'Then don't wear that top.'

'I'll be at work. This isn't a work top. I'll be in trousers and a restrained blouse, as always.'

'Okay, so, what's the plan?'

Hannah shrugged. 'Haven't a clue. I'm rusty at this, remember? Besides, it's only a "hello". An icebreaker. A chance for one of us to freeze, laugh, or make their excuses and scarper. Assuming he turns up.'

'Why would he not? Sounds like he was foaming at the mouth to meet you.'

'Yeah, well, let's see. I think it'll be very awkward and British, especially as one of the people will be me, and I'll be scared shitless.'

Amy rested her hand on Hannah's. 'You've seen him, chatted to him, stalked him—'

'*Researched* him.'

'That's what I said, stalked him. So, what could go wrong?'

She pondered. 'I'm not his type? Despite everything, looks are kind of important, you know.'

'Yeah. But remember,' Amy gestured, 'You're a catch.'

'Thanks, Ames. And so are you. But you're a girl, and Drew's a boy. He'd be unlikely to find us equally attractive, for instance.'

'True. But I'm not in this equation. Not even in the entire algebra lesson.' She waved a hand. 'Anyway, what'll you do when he asks you out?'

Hannah's heart skipped nervously. 'Assuming he does.'

'He will. He's single, smart, and has eyes, right?'

'Yeah.'

'Plus, he's not had a shag in three years.'

Hannah was open-mouthed. 'He's not like that.'

'Look me in the eye and tell me you haven't considered doing the do with him.'

Her mouth moved. She fiddled with the base of her glass.

'Prosecution rests, Your Honour,' Amy said with a smoulder.

Hannah downed the rest of the Prosecco. 'Monday is difficult enough. I'll probably pass out if there's a date on the agenda.'

Amy clasped Hannah's leg. 'Aw, come on. You'll be fine.'

'The pressure will be fucking monumental. What if I can't make this relationship work after all the nice, slow, easy-to-handle build-up?'

'Then it wasn't meant to be, and you're still better off from the dummy run.'

Hannah rapped the table. 'I don't want *dummy runs*. I want the nice fair-haired guy who kisses lifts, makes a fool of himself for love, and won't mind when I say that blue shirts don't suit him.'

Amy refilled her glass, drank, and then bit her lip, thinking. 'You know what you need? Practice.'

'Eh?'

'Date practice. Now, here, with me.'

Hannah laughed. 'Ames, we're mates. We're not on a date.'

Amy coughed, shuffled her shoulders, and put on a deeper voice. 'The name's Drew.'

Hannah darted glances around the sparsely populated Italian restaurant. 'Stop it,' she hissed. 'You're embarrassing me.'

'Oh,' Amy continued, contralto. 'I thought you *wanted* to come on a date with me, Elle.' She pushed her seat back, preparing to stand.

Hannah tugged Amy's hand. 'Shhh. Sit down.'

The strapping firefighter—unusually feminine in a low-cut maroon blouse and long navy skirt—smiled contentedly and sat.

'Anyway, it's Hannah, not Elle,' Hannah snipped.

'You'll have told him your real name?'

'Of course. I'm not trying to be fucking Banksy.'

Amy tutted. 'Bit sweary, isn't it, for a first date?'

'Fuck off,' she chided quietly. 'Besides, what happened to you being Drew?' She shot a pointed look and sipped her fizz.

Amy put on a serious face. 'So, Hannah, how many other men have you slept with?'

Hannah sprayed Prosecco across the table. 'He'd never ask me that!'

Amy wiped droplets from her chest, holding in a laugh. 'You should tell him the worst stuff up front, not waste more time by having a short relationship that didn't go anywhere.'

'You mean scare him off *quickly*?!'

'No, but you want marriage and babies and stuff, right? No sense in wasting a ticking clock with the wrong person.'

'What about having fun? Huh? Or using this as a test to see if I can start dating again?'

Amy pointed. 'There you go, tell him he's a dry run for Mr Right.'

'Ha fucking ha.'

Amy tutted, waggling a finger. 'Sweary Mary get no pokey-pokey.'

She slapped the hand away playfully. 'I know you're a "no fear, run into burning buildings" kind of person, but I might tread a bit more cautiously if that's okay?'

Amy looked hard, then sighed. 'I suppose. Sorry.'

Hannah pensively drew circles on the table mat with her fingertip. 'Besides, it's not *how many* men. It's what they've done to me.'

Amy laid her hand on Hannah's. 'I know, Han. And that's what you—and Drew—have to get past.'

'Yeah, thanks.'

Amy brought the glass to her lips. 'But, you know, for completeness, how many?' She drank, raising a single eyebrow.

Hannah scowled and pulled her hand away. 'I'm not getting into competitive bedpost-notching with you, Ms Jones.'

'Sorry. But, serious for a moment, what was the worst?'

'I've got a bloody roll-call, Ames.'

'Would you tell him? You've heard his Katie story—and that's pretty horrendous.'

'Yeah, I'll tell him. The Z-list he's got to avoid appearing on if he wants access to this temple to female wonderment.' She gesticulated at herself.

It triggered a thought about the prospect of *relations* with Drew, and her tummy went a little skippy.

'Fire away, then. I mean, I know about Stuart.'

Hannah snorted. 'The straw that broke the camel's back.' She gazed at the restaurant's appalling faux Sistine Chapel ceiling. 'Ben wanted me to throw out my chick-lit collection. Bad idea. Hugh slept with my best mate at Uni. Peter wanted me to stop speaking to all other men, including my mates. Jon wanted to do it on the first date. Charlie *didn't* want to do it on the first date. Or even the tenth date. Shame, because it felt like he was hung like a racehorse.' She sighed. 'I think he was gay. What a waste. Anyway.' She drummed her fingers on the table. 'I voted Remain, and that was enough for Simon to drop me like a hot EU regulation. Oh, and you met Ollie, remember? You happened to pop over when he was at mine.'

'Oh, yeah. Great stubble, bad shoes.'

'After you left—like *immediately*, he asked about a threesome.' Hannah gave a humungous eye-roll.

'And you didn't think to run that past me?'

Hannah slapped Amy's hand.

Mercifully, at that point, the server arrived with their dinner.

As they ate, the conversation morphed to non-Drew matters. They finished the bottle. They ordered wine. They ate dessert. Hannah was stuffed. It was all wonderful—but hanging out with her handful of close friends had always been comfortable. New people—new men—were the issue.

There was a moment of silence. Such silences were never awkward with her bestie.

Amy did the shoulder thing. 'So, Hannah,' she said gruffly. 'How d'you think this has gone?'

Reluctantly, she got into character. 'Lovely, thanks, Drew.'

'Would you like to... see me again?'

'Definitely.' The sweetest, encouraging smile played on her lips.

Amy gave a longing look. 'I'm pleased, baby.'

Then something touched Hannah's knee. Her leg reflexively jolted, and her knee smacked the underside of the table.

'Fuck!'

Diners looked around. A woman tutted. A man shook his head.

'What's up?' Amy asked.

'You touched my knee!'

'So? And *that's* how you'd react?'

'No! I just didn't expect *you* to do it.'

'Don't you expect displays of affection when you're on a date, baby?' Amy put her hand on Hannah's.

Hannah retracted her hand. 'Not from you.'

'But from him?'

Hannah grumped. 'Don't know. Maybe.'

'But I'm *being* him.'

'But you're you,' Hannah protested. Her insides were messed up.

'So, it's okay from a man, but not a woman? You know, that sounds very narrow-minded.'

'I didn't mean that. Div.'

'Ah, so it's okay from a person you've never really met, but not from a long-standing friend?'

'I didn't mean that either. You're putting words in my mouth.' She scowled.

'So, what, then?' Amy asked, sympathetic.

'I don't bloody know. It's just… unexpected. Okay?'

'You don't think he likes you enough to put his hand on your leg?'

Hannah bit her lip, flustered. 'Maybe. Probably. But he'd wait. I suppose.'

'But, hypothetically, if he did it on the first date?'

'I don't think he would.'

Amy beamed. 'Well, if you're thinking like that, it's a good sign, isn't it? Means you're moving away from the fear and assumption that all men are sexist dicks. You've changed in these last two weeks, Han. *So* good to see. And I'll tell you something else.'

'What?'

'You'd be hard pushed to make a bigger arse of yourself with Drew than you have tonight.'

Hannah glanced around. Both the nearest diners were nodding sagely. 'I'm going to bloody kill you when I get home,' she said through gritted teeth.

Amy pulled an "oh well" face. 'No aeroplane for you, then.'

Hannah leaned in and jabbed a finger on the table. 'Oh no. I *demand* it. As compensation for public humiliation.'

Amy shrugged. 'Okay. You win.'

Hannah gave a conspiratorial smile. 'At your place.'

'Fine.'

'And because I'm so bloody stuffed, it'll be a joy to vom across your entire living room.'

Amy poked out her tongue.

Hannah sneaked a hand under the table and grabbed Amy's knee.

Amy leapt out of her seat. 'Fuck!'

Hannah winked. 'Touché. *Baby*.'

FLOOR 31

The weekend was torture for Drew. Monday dawned with rare joy.

Being happy in your job—and wanting to further your career—was nothing compared to the prospect of meeting a potential girlfriend. Even one you had no visual expectation of. He wondered if she'd be so sassy in person, or if that only shone through because she was hiding behind a wall. A safety net, a defence mechanism. Humour often was.

This was so different to meeting Katie in a bar—eyes locking across a crowded room, imbibing in each other's physiques, watching gazes dart, weighing body language.

However, by 07:10, he was pacing around the 9th floor lift lobby with a horrible feeling in the pit of his stomach. He wanted to believe Elle was held up in traffic, though he didn't know where she lived.

Was she the type of person who was habitually late? Most likely, she'd bottled it at the last minute.

By 7:20, now clutching a double-strength instant coffee, he was well into the territory of being pissed off. The gnawing sensation in his midriff was crushing disappointment.

At 7:30, he gave up waiting and took the left-hand lift to G. At regular intervals, he called out for her but heard nothing. As he contemplated the panel, it seemed different, as if it had been removed and replaced. It looked shinier. That didn't bode well.

When the doors opened, he was a million miles away, jittery and rambling. He'd offered the lift apologies, encouragement and forgiveness.

'Drew?' Lotus stepped into the lift.

He wanted the shaft to open up and swallow him. To suck him to the Earth's core and incinerate him.

But why is she at work this early? Does it mean—?

She was eyeing him, concerned.

'Hi, Lotus.'

She pressed 9 and glanced around. 'Who were you talking to?'

'Nobody,' he said, unable to meet her eye.

'I missed you yesterday—at the Group. Do you think maybe... you should have come?'

The lift ascended. His brain was working so hard that he feared steam would leak from his ears. 'I had... other things on my mind.'

'Like now?' She indicated the lift's interior.

'Maybe.'

'It's the lift, isn't it? That's where you heard the voice.' Her expression betrayed concern.

'Shh!' he insisted. Then he realised that Elle wasn't there to overhear. *She might not ever be back. Unless...*

'Why are you in so early?' he asked.

'I have stuff to catch up on,' she said defensively.

He found himself clasping her arm. 'Lotus, what do you think of the name "Elle"?'

She frowned. 'What?'

'Shit,' he hissed, letting go.

There was absolutely no fear or guilt in the girl's expression. Unless she had a championship-winning poker face, it was clear that Lotus wasn't Elle.

His shoulders fell. The last hope was gone. He didn't know Elle's real name. Or her phone number. Or where she worked. Or where she lived.

'Drew, can you hear the voice now?' Lotus asked.

What a bloody question! What timing. 'No.'

'But it was in here?'

He sighed. 'Yeah.'

She touched his arm. 'Come back to the Group this Sunday. We'll go for a drink after, if you want. I'll help if I can. It can't be easy.'

He looked at her delicate hand, perfectly painted nails, wide blue eyes and immaculate lips. 'You're very sweet.'

'You too.' Then she frowned. 'Makes a change. There are men in this place who make my skin crawl.'

'Like Yates?'

She inspected the rumbling floor. 'I can't say. I don't want to lose my job.'

'Look, Lotus—'

She eyeballed him. 'No, Drew. Not now, okay? I—we—need to keep our distance from Kevin. He's got a lot on his plate.'

'And so have you, by the sounds of things.'

She looked around. 'You too.'

The lift passed 5.

'Hmm.' He eyeballed the control panel. 'Has that guy been back? Fixing this bloody lift again?'

'Yeah. Last thing Friday. I got a work email—and invoice—saying they'd replaced that panel. They found something screwy on the last report.' She sighed. 'Hopefully, that means it'll stop breaking.' She pursed her lips. 'Do you think—?'

He saw the question in her eyes and rushed to head it off. 'No. I think it's a coincidence. I didn't tell the Group that I was never great with lifts. Maybe Katie's... ghost... voice was trying to help me overcome that.' He waved away the lie. 'Anyway. So long as the bloody thing stops breaking, right?' He forced a wide smile.

She returned it. 'Absolutely. And if it means you get over things and are happier here, that's good news for us all.'

'Thanks, Lotus.'

PING! 9th Floor.

'Here we are. Another week,' she trilled with forced enthusiasm. 'See you later.'

He made another strong coffee and sat at his desk, but it was no use trying to concentrate on work. In terms of meeting Elle—even discovering her identity—the ball was in her court, which was undoubtedly the ideal outcome for her.

Sadly, it meant she'd used that situation to reconsider. He tried to look on the bright side. Perhaps it was only a temporary hitch. What were the chances she'd had second thoughts about continuing their dialogue, relationship, whatever it was called? It was unlikely she'd have hooked up with an alternative guy—she didn't appear the type.

Critically, she'd remained private to hide her identity and avoid meeting Drew—or anyone, possibly—in person. How could he, in good conscience, try to track her down and break that bond of trust? It would surely alienate her.

Besides, I already hit a dead end trying to match Elle's voice with people in the building. It definitely isn't Lotus. 99% sure it isn't Pirin or Char. Or Gloria, thankfully.

He slurped the last mouthful of coffee. It was cold. He gagged and nearly spat onto his keyboard, which would have ruined his day even further. It wasn't even eight thirty.

There was only one thing for it.

For an hour, he threw himself into a backlog of emails, beavering away until the Inbox said, `0 Unread`. Then he went to the kitchen, put aside his prejudices, and brewed a strong mug of camomile tea. He even landed the teabag in the bin on the first attempt.

He crossed the lift lobby to the other wing of the building. Pirin was in front of the edit suite.

Drew plonked the tea on the desk.

Pirin was befuddled. Then the penny dropped. 'What's up? Oh, and thanks. Oh, and morning.'

'I need help.'

'Bloody hell, mate, I've known that for three years.'

'Look, drink your flower juice, then meet me in the Gents.'

'Where the voice is?' Pirin wondered.

'Yeah—tell the whole bloody office! Idiot. See you there.'

Pirin arrived three minutes later. Using a practised technique—learned from Elle, ironically—Drew grabbed a "Cleaning In Progress" sign and stood it outside the loo's main door.

Then he took a deep breath, put his fledgling romantic relationship on the line, and gave Pirin a potted history of the Elle situation.

When it was done, Pirin hoisted his backside onto the sink plinth and ruminated. 'Listen, mate. First—sorry for taking the piss before.

You've had a lot of shit to deal with, and I can't think of anything better to happen to you than Elle.'

'Except if it's over, right? It'll be Katie 2.0.'

Pirin shook his head vehemently. 'First, this breakup isn't even in the same league as before. Second, who says it's over?'

'She didn't turn up,' Drew pointed out.

'Come on. Could be a million reasons for that.'

'Not sure I agree, but go on.'

'You wanted my advice—it's this. If you pursue her, try to track her down, what could happen? You succeed—but you fight and break up because it's not what she wanted you to do. Or you get a definitive not-in-person signal to back off. Either way, what have you lost? Nothing. You made a... holiday friend. A passing acquaintance. Doesn't mean you're destined to live in the romantic Badlands forever. It means you're on the road to recovery.'

'Hmm. That's what Char said.'

'So, either give it up, here and now—let Elle come to you when and if she's ready. If she doesn't, that's that. Or try to find her. Take a risk.'

'And win her, how?'

Pirin laughed. 'I'm hardly the best person to ask for advice on that stage of the journey. Do your own thing, Drew. If she liked you before, you have a good chance. So, what's the word?'

Drew sighed heavily, then mooched around the toilets. As he was there, he took a leak, letting out the morning's tsunami of coffee. 'I want to go for it.'

Pirin patted him heartily on the shoulder. 'Correct decision.'

'There's just one problem. How the hell do we find out who she is?'

Pirin sent Drew out to get himself a medicinal muffin and a quality cappuccino. When Drew returned, the man produced a list of all Park Productions employees.

'How the hell did you get that?' Drew asked.

'You know Renée in HR?'

'Forget it. What does the list say?'

Pirin slid it across the desk. Drew scrutinized it. Then he checked it a second time.

There was nobody in the company called Elle. Despair swamped him.

Then he facepalmed.

'What?' Pirin asked.

'Of course! Her name's not bloody Elle. I named her.' He rapped a knuckle against his head.

'Ah.'

'No shit. I gave her the name because I was trying to be clever. She let it stick.' He scrunched the printed paper and tossed it into the wastebasket. 'Needle in a haystack, now.'

Pirin was sober. 'Plus, remember, nothing says she's one of ours. There are fifteen floors of names—of women—to check. Not counting the lift maintenance company, the alarm company, all the IT and security providers—anyone with remote access to the building.'

Drew put his head in his hands. 'Then I give up, mate.'

FLOOR 32

By two o'clock, Hannah was long past having had enough.

The plumber had said he'd be there within four hours. That was seven hours ago.

She'd paced around Amy's flat so much that her feet should be worn to stumps. Partly, it was frustration, part impatience, and part indecision. Having had to call in sick was bad enough.

Amy had rapped on Hannah's door at six fifteen as Hannah was dressing. She'd picked out the perfect outfit for meeting Drew—something more feminine than usual but without a "come and get it" vibe. All the same, she was bricking it. What if she clammed up? What if he preferred blondes?

Amy was flustered. The dishwasher had blown a pipe, creating a small pond in the kitchen. She'd rung a plumber, who said he'd get there as quickly as possible. She'd turned off the water supply to the unit—joking that she was more used to turning *on* powerful water jets.

Unfortunately, she was on duty standby that night and morning, and a blaze had taken hold at an industrial unit south of town. It was all hands to the pump.

'Stay in and wait for the plumber, will you, Han?'

'But I'm meeting Drew!'

'And I'm *literally* one of the emergency services,' she said. 'Pleeeeease?'

Hannah was amazed not to suffer a panic attack. Unscheduled changes of plan always threw her, and this could hardly have been worse. She'd be letting Drew down horribly, catastrophically. He might never forgive her. Then what? It would be over before it really started.

'I can't *not* go to work, Ames. Today of all fucking days!'

'I can't *even more* not go to work. Look, the place is yours. Eat what you want, watch what you want, ring the bloody speaking clock in Australia for all I care.'

Hannah trembled, torn. 'You *know* how important this is to me, hon.'

'I've *got* to go. I'll owe you forever. I'll be your Maid of Honour.' She winked.

Hannah felt like pointing out that this particular stunt might be the precise reason why a future wedding wouldn't, in fact, take place. Then she realised she was creating a fairy-tale whirlwind romance in her head. Amy wasn't responsible for things which hadn't happened. She could, however, dash away and preserve life and property.

Her shoulders fell. 'Go on. Run. Be awesome.'

Amy pecked her on the head. 'You're a star. Don't flood the place before the plumber comes. And don't shag him. Drew will be *very* unimpressed.'

'Fuck off, then. I'm going to camp on your sofa, eat all your biscuits, and add a ton of great things to your Alexa shopping list.'

Amy jogged away. 'Love you too!' she called, raising a middle finger in farewell.

'The best-laid plans of lifts and men,' Hannah muttered, glancing at the clock for the squillionth time.

It was a warm afternoon, so she'd swung open the French door, found something decent in Amy's music collection, and made a sixth cup of tea. She'd already scoffed a complete packet of chocolate digestives.

Halfway through the packet, she'd felt guilty, worrying what Drew might think if she suddenly put on weight. Then she realised he didn't know what she'd been like beforehand, that a size 10 was fine, and that he might never speak to her again after this fiasco in any case.

She dismissed it and returned to pacing the living room, performing comedy to an imagined and receptive crowd. Drew's adorable rubbishness had provided her with new material, and she wanted to see how it sounded. Writing jokes and witty observations was easy; standing up and vocalising them was utterly nerve-racking.

The doorbell rang.

She sighed. 'Finally.'

Nevertheless, she answered the door apprehensively. Being forced to meet a stranger was one of her least favourite activities. She begged the universe not to have sent her a sexist jerk.

The plumber was young, toned, had immaculate hair, and was very apologetic for his lateness. Stuck in traffic on a closed country road, apparently.

Hannah sidelined the skippy sensation in her tummy and waved him to the source of the flood.

He set to work, and she made him a cuppa. He didn't say much other than his name was Alex. He had nice eyes, and they barely wandered in her direction. Still, her social anxiety was triggering like crazy.

'I *really* need to get laid,' she told her reflection in the bathroom mirror.

During Alex's bumping and clattering, Cat wandered in. It sought attention from the visitor.

'What's the name of your cat?' He tickled it under the chin.

'Cat,' Hannah replied.

'Yeah, cat.'

'Oh, I meant it's called Cat. And it's not my cat.'

'Sorry, yeah. The owner's cat.'

'It's not Amy's either.'

'Oh. So she's a cat kidnapper?' His eyes twinkled.

'Yes. Wanted throughout the Southeast. I'd turn her in, but she'd probably bend the cell bars apart, come after me and torture me to death with her appalling collection of Country music.'

He laughed. She smiled nervously.

Alex finished the job half an hour later. Amy had left cash on the table, so Hannah paid him.

He glanced around. 'So,' his gaze rested on her face. 'Anything else I can... check over while I'm here?'

Her mouth clanged open. 'What, you mean in the *bedroom*?' She masked a spike of distaste with an eye-roll which burned ten digestives worth of calories.

He was so startled that he took a step back. Amused awkwardness coloured his face. 'Er... no. I meant leaky taps, things like that.' He smiled. 'Being honest, you're not my type, Miss. I'm more of a... ballcock kind of guy, if you catch my meaning.'

All of Hannah's blood raced to her cheeks. How would she handle a comedy club heckler if she couldn't cope with a little misunderstanding like this? Misunderstanding? No—she'd leapt to the stupidest, most inflammatory conclusion. She hated that she'd become so jaded and reactionary. Plus, her gaydar was *so* shit.

She laughed violently and excessively. Thankfully, he joined in.

God, I need to meet Drew, she thought. To reaffirm my faith in men.

'No, Alex, there's nothing else in the flat leaking. Apart from my self-esteem, which I think has formed a larger lake than the one you've just mopped up.'

'Don't worry about it.' He pulled a card from his top pocket. 'You know where I am if you need me.'

She quickly pocketed the card. 'Yes—in the pub telling everyone about the ditzy brunette with the Seventies porn fixation.' She grimaced apologetically, toes twitching.

'Can't say you're not the first.' He headed for the door. 'How do you think I met my bloke?'

He gave a final wink, and then she let him out, closed the door, and collapsed in a heap of crushing mortification.

Amy arrived at four thirty. She looked like she'd been caught in a bomb blast.

'White wine's in the fridge. I'm having a shower. Stay—if we're still speaking.' She scanned around. 'Did you *tidy*?'

'Yeah. The plumber and I made such a mess. We did it in every room. So,' Hannah shrugged, 'Had to get rid of the evidence.'

Amy spied a piece of wrapper that Hannah had missed. 'He eat all the digestives, too?'

'Yeah. Well, he needed the energy, you know?'

Amy's peck left a sooty mark on Hannah's forehead. 'You'll be telling me next he wasn't my type.'

'Oh—I can say *that* for certain.'

Amy's tongue wasn't sooty. She went to the bathroom.

Hannah poured the wine. They needed it.

'Sorry for dropping you in it, Han. Really, I am.'

She waved it away. 'No point in crying over spilt water. Especially as it would make the problem worse.'

Amy laughed. 'What'll you do about Drew?'

She stroked the stem of her wineglass. 'Sleep on it. Regroup.'

'You do know his name,' Amy pointed out. 'You could email him. Or find his extension number and leave him a voicemail.'

'Remind me—wasn't there a snake-tongued Amazonian that used to live here who warned me off such stalkery behaviour?'

'All I mean is don't let it end this way. The final mile of any climb is always the hardest.'

'And other clichés.'

'I'm deadly, get-medieval-on-your-ass serious, Han. Besides, if today's shitshow puts the skids under you and Drew, I'll never forgive myself.' She looked Hannah straight. 'I mean it. I'll feel terrible. I'll eat more. I'll miss shifts. I'll get sacked. I'll get paralytic, pass out, crack my head open, and you'll come in one day to find Cat licking my spilt brains.'

'For which I'll never forgive *myself*, you mean? I'll go to pieces. And Mr Fletcher from Number 4 will stumble in on *my* feline-suckled skull?'

'So,' Amy said pointedly. 'What'cha gonna do?'

Hannah growled. 'Finish your wine. Make you pay for takeout. Get some sleep. Try again with Drew,' she said like a grumpy teen.

'That's my girl.'

Cat strolled in. It had probably overheard the mention of free splintered noggins for dinner. It sprung onto her lap. Hannah flinched, then petted it.

'Did you feed it today?' Amy asked.

'Yes, of course. It needs love, like all of us.'

'Blimey. Very keen on its welfare all of a sudden.'

'Yeah. It gives unconditional love without answering back or dumping me in the shit with men.'

Amy poked out her tongue. 'Nyah-nyah nyah nyah-nyah.'

Hannah swatted her.

'Why don't you take it?' Amy pointed at Cat, who was curled up on Hannah's lap.

'Because then I'd be a crazy cat lady, and people don't want to go out with someone like that.'

Amy did a so-so of the head. 'Reckon you need four cats, minimum, plus a hairy mole.'

'What if the cats chased the mole away?'

'I'll bloody chase you away in a minute.'

At eight o'clock, Amy did chase Hannah away. Both were chock full of wine and unhealthy food.

'Text me the instant you meet him, okay?' Amy said.

'You seriously want me to break off from what will already be the oddest and most fucking nerve-wracking moment of my adult life to give you a *status update*?'

'Alright. Straight after. Not a minute later.'

Cat exited the flat and crowded Hannah's legs as she crossed the hall. As she opened her front door, Cat darted in.

'Fuck's sake.'

'Now you've gotta break it to Drew that you have a cat,' Amy said.

'I haven't even met the poor sod yet. And I don't have a fucking cat!'

Cat meowed.

'Hmm,' Amy said. 'Not sure this relationship is starting too well either.'

Hannah smirked, gave a one-finger salute and shut the door.

FLOOR 33

Drew mooched into work at eight forty-five on Tuesday. He'd tossed and turned all night and failed to devise a solution. Char had said that patience was a virtue.

He didn't linger in Reception, trying to choreograph sole passage in the lift. Luckily, he was unaccompanied between 7 and 9, and called for Elle.

She didn't answer.

He kicked the lift in frustration. It jarred the metal plate in his leg, and he yelled in pain.

Then, as he hobbled across the 9th floor lobby, he slowed to a stop. A veritable *PING!* went off in his head.

Elle had mentioned the metal plate—but he'd never told her about it, not specifically. Only the accident. How the hell would she know?

Even if she'd researched social media, it wasn't something he talked about—the memory was too painful. She would have needed to find out from Pirin or Lotus. That would imply this was a prank. He'd already ruled out Lotus, so he went straight to his friend's desk.

He frogmarched Pirin to the loos. After the single occupant left, Drew revealed his suspicions and allowed Pirin to confess. The rascal was innocent—which, as a trait, was admittedly uncharacteristic.

'So, genius—how does she know about my metal plate?' Drew asked.

'Maybe she's seen you around the building, overheard heard you mention it—'

'I never do!' he protested.

'—or heard people talk about you?'

'Hmm.' Drew rubbed his chin. 'Maybe. So she's here... somewhere. Still, she made no bloody effort to get in touch. Apologise. She knows my name, after all. Which is more than I do about her. Plenty of ways to do it—even leave a note on my desk.'

'Or your pigeonhole.'

Park Productions clung oddly tight to its old tech.

Drew frowned. 'Only checked it once since I arrived.'

Pirin rapped gently on Drew's head. 'Hello? McFly? Maybe... check it again?'

Drew picked up the plain envelope like it was the Ark of the Covenant. 'Holy shit.'

He fingered it open, drew out the folded sheet of A4, and opened it.

Something came up, I promise. Miss you. Elle x

'Bingo,' Pirin breathed.

'Mate, I could kiss you.'

'You're not really my type. Besides, if someone saw us, it would *really* ruin my reputation.'

'You want to *keep* that reputation?' Drew asked in disbelief.

Pirin snarled. He pointed at the note. 'Why did she sign "Elle"? She's still being evasive.'

Undeniable. 'Hmm. Odd that she's labouring under a pet name.'

'Maybe playing hard to get.'

'This whole episode is the dictionary definition of "hard to get".'

Drew stared at the note. *How did it help? Did it indicate there was still a chance? How to find her? How could they arrange to meet? From what Lotus said—and the visual evidence—it was likely that Elle's AV system had been compromised.*

He made a fist.

What the hell's the answer? I can't wait in this lift lobby 24/7 until she turns up. Should I wait by the pigeonhole in case she leaves another note? Why not take this note around everyone in the building, asking if they recognise the handwriting?

He snorted. It would be about as successful and un-embarrassing as the voice match search.

'What?' Pirin asked.

'I won't give up. I'm so close. *We're* so close. She didn't bail. She wants this. Otherwise, why leave the note?'

'Agreed.'

He inspected the note. Was there a clue here—whether deliberately or accidentally left? He held it up to the diffuse ceiling light as if expecting some lemon juice spy nonsense to leap out. It didn't.

'Where are you, Elle?' he murmured.

'You could try the sign-in book,' Pirin said. 'Match the handwriting.'

'Yeah. Long shot, though. I mean, it's only idiots like me who forget their pass and need to sign in—' He jolted, snapping the paper up to his eyes. He scoured the letters. He traced the quaintly-shaped "a" with a fingernail.

'What is it, mate?' Pirin asked expectantly.

'It can't be,' Drew breathed. He forced fragments of memory onto his closed eyelids. He clutched Pirin's arm. 'Get back to your desk.'

'Why?'

'Because otherwise, you *will* get that kiss.' Drew puckered up.

Pirin ran.

It was only moderately awkward asking the receptionist for the sign-in book from two weeks ago. At least he didn't have to do it in his pants.

On the Tuesday list, he found his own signature. Then he flicked to the previous day, scanned the names, and matched the handwriting. *The girl! The mousey girl with the smart comeback and the tinted glasses.*

She saw my pat-down. Heard me mention the metal plate!

He rewarded himself with a fist clench, then headed to the left-hand lift.

Again, Elle didn't answer on the way up. It mattered little.

He went directly to Pirin's desk. His colleague stopped editing The Lock Keeper and, doubtless seeing the glee on Drew's face, pulled over an adjacent spare chair.

Drew spoke quietly. 'Hannah Thomas.'

They exchanged a covert high-five.

'Please tell me you haven't slept with her,' he added.

'Doesn't ring a bell.'

'Thank Christ.'

Pirin opened his drawer and pulled out a very creased sheet of paper.

Drew was aghast. 'You kept it?'

'Course I bloody did. *You* might have given up. I never did.'

Drew planted a kiss on Pirin's scalp.

'Yuck,' Pirin muttered.

'You're not the one with a mouthful of hair gel.'

Pirin jabbed the employee list. 'Focus, Flower.'

Drew ran his finger down the list to T. 'Here she is. Hannah Thomas. Archivist.'

'Wow, down in the dungeon. Basement. Just a huge storage facility. Nobody really goes there.'

Emotion filled Drew's chest. 'Someone does. Someone wonderful.'

That explains why she likes to take the lift down there! I was so close to her all the time!

'You've got it bad, buddy.'

'Yeah, well, hopefully, I'll have it worse—or better—very soon.'

Pirin patted Drew's shoulder. 'Absolutely. Anyway, got to get back to the grind. Edit's due ASAP.'

'How are the canalside shenanigans coming along?'

Pirin shrugged. 'If you like docs, it's fine. Bit yawn-inducing. It would be better with the whole director-shagging-subject angle, but that's for you, me and the gatepost.'

'True. Cheers, mate. I'll keep you posted.'

'Don't think you'll need to. If you're not an insufferable grouch tomorrow morning, I'll know it went well.'

As the morning evaporated, Drew's plan crystallised. There could be no grand gesture, no balcony scene. Hannah was a timid, private person at heart. As Elle—an alter ago—she was chatty and funny. Hopefully, when she overcame her natural shyness, they'd get along famously.

He bloody hoped so. Happiness was at stake.

There were a million ways to approach this subtly without scaring her off. In the end, he chose the simplest. He'd go and say hello. After all, a simple hello was what they'd planned in the first place. So what if it was a day late?

As his spirits were unusually high, the afternoon sped by. At six fifteen—approaching traditional Elle interaction time—he shut down his workstation and took the left-hand lift to the basement.

For good order, he called out, but she didn't reply. It didn't matter, provided she was still in her office. Barging in would be too surprising, so he'd wait in the lift lobby. She'd have to pass through, right?

He went straight to the loos to make himself presentable. He took a leak, checked his hair, and cursed a spot he'd missed while shaving that morning. He held cupped hands under the automatic tap. It didn't respond. He raised then lowered them. No luck.

Muttering, he moved to the next basin and shoved his hands in. The water gushed out, kicked off his palms, and spattered down the front of his trousers.

'Bollocks!'

Sighing, he surveyed the damage, washed his hands anyway, dried them, and then tried desperately to wave his crotch in the direction of the dryer. Sadly, it was a Dyson slot type, so he stood no chance.

He smacked a fist on the wall. It hurt. He decided to leave before things worsened and he missed Elle—Hannah—on her way out.

Grumbling, he paced around the lobby, wafting air over his trousers. He untucked his shirt and let it hang over his fly. He checked his reflection in the lift doors. He didn't look cool and relaxed; he looked slovenly. That wouldn't do, so he used the mirrored steel to check as he re-tucked and smartened up.

PING!

He nearly shat himself. That would definitely have been a deal-breaker for tonight's meeting.

The doors opened. He tensed.

It was a young guy from IT. They exchanged an awkward look. Drew reversed, and the guy disappeared into the left-hand corridor.

Drew leaned against the space between the lifts, breathless.

Five minutes passed. Then ten.

He checked social media on his phone. Dumpster fire, as usual.

Fifteen minutes.

Perhaps she's already gone home?

As the disappointment was setting in, someone exited from the right-side offices. They wore a baseball cap and were engrossed in their phone.

Could it be...?

'Han—'

The person looked up. He was sixty if he was a day. 'Hmm?'

'Oh... nothing.' Drew backed away.

The guy called the lift. He glanced at Drew's groin stain. Drew grimaced.

The lift arrived.

The guy stepped in, paused, and then poked his head out. 'Do you...?'

'Ah. No. Thanks. Better wait for the next one. You know, in case I... lose control of my bladder again.' He giggled like a loony. 'Bloody cheap incontinence pants. Tut!'

The guy vanished. A button was jabbed furiously. The lift departed.

Drew exhaled a tornado and smacked his head repeatedly against the wall.

Five more minutes passed. Then ten.

He slouched to the floor and put his head between his knees. *What a bloody mess. What a waste of time. What a—*

A door squeaked open.

He sat bolt upright, rapping his skull against the wall. Commendably, he didn't swear. His eyes became saucers.

A young woman was walking toward him.

Every cell in his body vibrated. He sprung awkwardly to his feet. She stopped ten feet away, a rabbit in the headlights.

His mind whorled. *What was the plan again?*

He reached out a tentative, quivering hand. His eyes brimmed with hope and questions. 'H... hi, Hannah. I... I'm Drew.'

FLOOR 34

The girl looked him up and down. Her left foot wriggled nervously.

With every fibre of his being, he begged her to say something. The silence was oppressive. He got a sinking feeling. His shoulders slumped. He went for a death-or-glory follow-up to his less-than-stellar introduction.

'Okay, I blew it. How? You were the one who didn't turn up. I should be pissed off at *you*.' A penny dropped. 'Or... is it the social anxiety thing? Oh, shit, sorry, I forgot. Or did I go to the wrong floor?' He fought to see what was in her eyes. 'You did say floor 9? Monday at 7. 7 *A.M*, right?'

She was looking at him like a cat does to a twitching, dying mouse it's caught.

He sighed. 'Sod it. It doesn't matter. It's over. I found you anyway. Mystery solved. You *are* Hannah Thomas, aren't you? Oh shit, *please* say I'm not talking to some random person who isn't even Hannah, let alone Elle. Oh hell, please say something. Elle? Hannah?'

She cracked up. 'Fuck, you're a mess.'

He recognised the laugh. He wanted to cry with joy, which would be preferable to dying of apocalyptic embarrassment.

He took a couple of tentative steps forward. 'Well—yeah. Because I thought you'd gone, and I'd lost you forever. You are Hannah—right? Right?'

She smiled, moved in, and tentatively offered her hand. 'Yes, Drew. I'm Hannah.'

His skin prickled. 'Can I... shake your hand?'

'No, I really like standing here with it hanging in mid-air like a div.'

At that second, all he wanted to do was tickle her. She deserved it. For a shrinking violet, she was so cheeky, sharp, and smart. So bloody adorable.

Tickling would have to wait. But he *would* get her. Hopefully, very soon, when they weren't standing in a deserted lobby. Ideally, on a sofa somewhere. Maybe even a bed.

He took her hand, which was warm and soft. Her grip was firmer than he expected. 'It's nice... no, it's *awesome*—not to mention a huge bloody relief—to meet you, Hannah Thomas.'

'Likewise, Andrew Flower.'

After a pause, he returned to reality and let go of her hand. 'So... should we stand here like idiots, or...?'

She glanced at the lift. 'Step into my parlour?'

'...said the spider to the fly.'

She laughed. 'Yeah—the next stage of my evil entrapment. You're a quick study, young Jedi.'

He hit `Call`. 'So... yesterday?' he asked casually. He was finding it impossible not to scrutinise her face and physique—not critically, but because it was almost as magnetic as her personality.

She was about five-five. Her face was heart-shaped, eyes brown—hard to tell for sure behind the tinted lenses. Her make-up and attire were reserved. Her brown hair was cut in a textured bob that flared slightly at the neck. Her figure was... very fine, neither curvy nor petite. He was floored.

PING!

He jolted.

She was eyeing him warily, biting her cheek. 'What?' she asked with gentle accusation. His attention hadn't gone unnoticed.

'You're... beautiful, Hannah.'

Instantly, her face coloured, and she inspected the floor. 'I don't know about that.'

'Well, then... you're here, and that's bloody amazing in itself.'

'Yeah. I know that much.' She angled her head to the lift. 'And I'm so grateful.'

They stepped in. Now, the thing was merely a boring metal box. Its personality was standing beside him. He reached for the control panel, indecisive.

'Are we going to ride up and down all evening?' She was in the corner, not close to him. Her smile was impish. She seemed to exist in a perpetual distant but snarky state.

This was a test. Time to be bold, inventive and romantic. A big ask for Drew Flower lately.

He jammed a foot against the door and inspected the lobby. He darted out, heaved a tall red fire extinguisher from its stand, and clunked it against the door.

'The Health and Safety police will have you hung, drawn and quartered,' she said.

'At least I'll die smiling.'

Her face creased into warm appreciation.

He slid down in the corner by the door and brought his knees up. At this cue, she did similar in the diagonally opposite corner.

They sized each other up for a few seconds. He felt his nerves cross the divide and mingle with hers.

'Listen, Drew, I know you're pissed off that I didn't turn up yesterday. I had an emergency at home. Big one. Real life and death stuff, okay? Long story. I'll tell you... next time?'

'Okay.'

'In my defence, I came in at seven this morning in case you tried again.' She looked downcast. 'But you weren't there. I thought I'd done it—screwed it up.'

'Oh. Shit. Sorry. Should have thought of that.'

She shrugged. 'It's fine. I was sad, so I left you that note. I did want us to meet—somehow. What you did... tonight was... romantic.'

'I was trying to think of a grand gesture but didn't want to freak you out.'

'And that shows you care. And *understand*. I'm not the easiest person.' She laughed sadly.

'This was a punt, that's all. Any hello is better than none.' He stroked the wall. 'Waited forever. Thought you weren't coming.'

'I see you didn't even leave to take a wee.' She glanced at his trousers and raised an eyebrow.

He crossed his legs. 'It's water.'

'Well, I'll believe you, as I have no intention of sniffing your crotch to confirm that.'

He pouted. 'Oh well. Probably not going to work out between us after all.'

'Hey! Which of us is the comedian?' Her eyes flared.

'You, Hannah. Definitely you.' He shot her a look of warmth and affection.

Their eyes danced together like the butterflies in his stomach.

'You're much less... cuboidal than you sounded.'

She giggled adorably. 'I'll take that as a compliment.'

'And your voice *is* different. A little.'

'I use a voice changer, so I can be anonymous if I get to interact with Yates.' Her fingers entwined and rubbed. 'Anyway—the fucking engineers removed my piggyback intercom link over the weekend. Gits. I'll bet you were calling out for me today, right?'

'Hmm. But I saw the new panel. I reckoned that's why you... Elle... had gone.'

'Yeah. And now my plan is buggered.' Her head dipped.

'We'll figure it out.'

'Hmm.'

He wanted to slide across the floor and take her in a deep, comforting embrace. 'We will, Hannah.'

She looked up. 'Yeah. I mean, meeting you is a great second best, but I still want to get justice.' She waved her hands as if shooing a fly. 'Anyway, this isn't about *him*. This is a date.'

His back arched. 'This is a date?'

Her pretty nose wrinkled. 'Oh. Or maybe a date is where we both turn up at the same place at the appointed time.'

He leant forwards. 'Could you manage a real date? You know—out?'

She pushed at her hair. 'I want to. Really.' She met his gaze. 'I do, Drew.'

'Is it too much, too soon? Is it me? Say if it is. Just because you saw me through a tiny camera doesn't mean real life is good enough—that I'm up to scratch.'

'No, Drew, you are. You very are.'

'Even this?' He gestured to his damp groin. 'And our hello? And lots of other things.' He sighed. 'Hannah, I'm a hot mess—that's a phrase, right? You should know that about me.'

She grinned. 'I swear like a brickie.'

He'd gathered that. 'I don't own property, I don't work out, and I can't drink more than three pints.'

'My cooking is only adequate. My best mate can be a fucking liability.' She frowned. 'I may or may not own a cat.'

He laughed. 'That's a good list to be going on with. Let's return to it later. You want to *do* later, right?'

'Absolutely. One hundred percent. Somehow.' She bit her lip.

She had pretty lips. He hoped she didn't damage them. They needed to remain in good working order for... future activities.

He cricked his neck, then pushed up onto his haunches. 'Now, here's the thing, Hannah Thomas. You're amazing. I could sit here with you until I wither to a skeleton. But this floor is painful, I'm bloody starving, and it's late. All the same, I won't invite you out for a meal. I get the feeling that's a waste of a question.'

She nodded, smiling.

'So we should take this magic carpet up to Reception, and, if you want, I'll walk you to your car. Okay?' he suggested.

'I take the bus.'

'Substitute "bus" for "car" in the previous sentence.'

'That would be nice, Andrew Flower.'

She went to stand. He reached down, took her hand and helped her up. The nerve endings in his fingers crackled, and endorphins flooded his body.

He thumbed **Doors Open** and hefted the fire extinguisher back to its stand.

She pressed **G**, and quickly, they were in a travelling lift—actually, really together. Soon, they'd be apart again—which was shit—so he focussed on milking the remainder of their modest evening.

Sadly, it only took four minutes to reach the bus stop. Every step was like walking on air. He couldn't stop glancing at her. She was gorgeous.

When Hannah was safely ensconced under the steel and glass shelter, with the matrix display reading 6 minutes until the next Number 47, his mind turned to making the goodbye vastly less cringe-worthy than the hello.

She offered her hand. 'It was fucking good to meet you.'

'Right back at you.'

She sniggered. 'God, you say some lame shit.'

'In that case, let's say... this evening was marginally better than poking pins in my eyes.'

'That's more like it.'

'So... I'll see you tomorrow? Maybe?'

Her eyes sparkled. 'Nah. Probably call in sick. Save the embarrassment of bumping into you.'

'Good idea.'

'You going to shake my hand, or is this blanking thing normal when you meet cripplingly nervous hot brunettes?'

The problem was, he'd much rather kiss her for the next five minutes or until the bus came, which he hoped would be in about a week. However, baby steps was the safe method.

He shook her hand. 'See you tomorrow.' He made the wink as natural as possible.

It passed muster. 'Night.'

'Night.'

He strolled away, fighting the urge to look back and drink in the sight of her. Then, he spotted a gap in the traffic and sprinted across the road.

A few steps down the opposite pavement, he stopped. 'Shit.' He hadn't even asked for her phone number. Would that be okay? Otherwise, it'd look like he wasn't sufficiently interested. After all, with the Elle link gone, he'd be relying on the work email system for personal communication, which was a big no-no.

He turned. 'Hannah?' he called.

She saw him. A car passed.

'What's your number?'

She shook her head and pointed at her ears. The city noise was a blanket. If he shouted or pantomimed too much, he'd make an arse of himself—again.

He glanced left, then trotted across the road.

A car horn blared. Tyres screeched. He braced for the blow of death. *Fuuuck!*

At least he'd met her. That would be his last thought. Last image.

The car stopped three feet away. His blood rushed, and his knees weakened. He glanced at the driver and offered an apologetic wave. He received an index finger in return. He seemed to be good at collecting those.

He sloped to the kerb, breathing hard. He almost didn't dare look at Hannah. She'd either be in tucks of laughter or facepalming. Still, he had to. After all, he'd cheated death to speak to her.

She was rigid with worry. He hurried over.

She looked him up and down. 'Don't *do* that, Drew. One car accident is enough for you.'

He grimaced. 'Hot mess, right?'

'No shit.'

Now, why was I here? Oh, yes. Except asking her directly might be too assertive.

He had a brainwave, reached into his inside pocket, and pulled something out. 'You know... if you ever wanted to get in touch.' He shrugged. 'Or not.'

She took it. 'Ooh! An accountant has given me his business card. Peak romance!'

He didn't rise to that. Not rising to her adorable and quick-witted jibes might be something he'd have to get used to. He hoped so.

He painted on a serious face. 'The ball is still in your court, Hannah. I don't expect you to breeze by my desk tomorrow, but now you have my details. I'll go as slow as you want... *if* you want... something. It took four-and-a-half billion years for us to get to this moment on Earth. A few more days won't hurt.'

Her cheeks were lit by an internal flame. 'But maybe let's not wait another four-and-a-half billion for the next meet. Especially with your constant death wish.'

'Yeah. At the very least, let's do it before you lose your looks.' He winked.

Her lips pursed in good humour. 'You're a crude, insensitive, sexist pig—you know that, Andrew Flower?' She grinned.

'And you're a rancid, foul-mouthed, preying hermit, Hannah Thomas.'

She did a little bow. 'Touché.'

'Want me to wait with you until the bus comes?' he asked with care and concern.

She pulled a face. 'No way. I'm fed up with the sight of you. Fuck off.'

He could only smile, shake his head, and do as she bid. With every step, he felt increasingly pulled back, as if on an elastic leash. Still, best to end on a high.

This time, after carefully crossing the road, he looked back, hoping for her to wave. She was engrossed in her phone, shutting out the world, retracting into her timid self like a sunflower closing down when his light left her.

FLOOR 35

On the way home, Drew picked up something expensive and quick to cook from Waitrose. That was as far as he was prepared to push the celebration. He didn't want to jinx things after only a few minutes of physical interaction with Hannah.

He relayed the whole story to Char—omitting the cluster of toe-curling faux-pas. He didn't talk effusively about Hannah to avoid getting his sister's hopes up. Even so, she gave him the warmest and most supportive hug.

He slept like a log. The 07:00 alarm reminded him it was hump day. He felt like the moniker might have a new meaning now. That Wednesday was like cresting the tidal wave of Katie's loss—something he'd feared would drown him—and surfing down the wall of water, exhilarated now that Hannah was in his life.

If, in fact, she was.

There were an unprecedented *two* missives in his pigeonhole. The first was a formal letter saying that he was being put forward for promotion to Senior Production Accountant. He grabbed both envelopes, ran to the Gents, wisely checked that nobody else was there, and yelled for joy.

Had the lift ride with Yates sealed the deal? Was it possible that chasing Lotus—ostensibly the wrong girl—had landed him in the situation? Facing his fear had reaped more reward than he could ever have expected—not counting the fact that he'd then immediately "met" Elle.

He opened the second letter. It was handwritten by one of the most appealing creatures ever to walk the planet. It stipulated a time and place that evening.

He yelled with even greater joy.

He arrived at the restaurant in good time, despite taking twenty minutes to select his attire. The premises were rather shabby and sparsely attended. She'd booked a table conveniently situated in an alcove at the rear of the dining area.

She arrived at 19:01. Approaching him, her demeanour changed. The sunflower opened.

She'd gone home after work to get changed. Her outfit remained un-showy—she didn't strike him as a flaunter—yet it accentuated her figure enough. The room felt suddenly warmer.

'Hi.'

'Hi,' she replied, eyes shy.

They awkwardly shook hands and sat.

'You look nice.' He wanted to say, "drop-dead gorgeous".

'So do you. Didn't piss yourself this time.'

'Nah. Decided not to bother. Cut myself shaving, though.' He indicated a speck of dry blood on his neck. 'So, I did make *some* effort.'

'Did the aftershave sting?'

'Like a bastard.'

'You don't normally wear it, right?'

He nodded. 'You're very perceptive, Hannah Thomas.'

'For a rancid, foul-mouthed, preying hermit, yes, I believe I am, Andrew Flower.' She winked.

The waiter arrived. Drew allowed her to order a drink first so he could be chivalrous *and* find out whether she was teetotal, a lush, or normal. She ordered white wine, so—normal. He chose red.

He scanned the menu. He'd never visited the place before. It didn't exist when he'd lived in Winchester as a young man. 'What do you recommend?'

'For you?' She perused the menu. 'Look twice before you cross the road, change your razor blade, and try the salmon.' She glanced up and waggled her eyebrows.

'Sold.'

'Oh, and stick to two glasses maximum, so you don't get too brave and try something on.'

'Noted.' He adored the way her eyes, behind the gently tinted glasses, swam with impishness.

'Plus, I know I have a small amount of cleavage on display—because I like you—but do me a favour, have a proper gander, then eyes up here, okay?'

He held in a titter, then locked his attention on her face. 'Is that an invitation or an instruction?'

'Well, you're a guy who likes *figures*, right?' She glanced down.

He didn't follow the bait. Now it was a battle between the decent, honourable wolf inside Drew and the one which wanted to check out her boobs. 'Yeah, but I also like my face the shape it is. I bet you can land a punch.'

'You think I'd hit a bean counter?'

'In a heartbeat. You've fallen foul of a few guys, right, Hannah? Geeks or otherwise. Mostly otherwise, I'm guessing. "Shits", I believe they're called.'

'Yeah,' she said sadly, fiddling with her cutlery.

Because Drew *was*, first and foremost, a man, and she was momentarily distracted, he looked at her chest. 'You need to know I *am* like other guys in some ways.'

'And also *not* like them?'

'Hopefully.'

She lasered her attention on his pupils. 'Did you just have a look?'

'Of course I bloody did. So, when my wine comes, should I pour it over myself or let you do it?'

She cracked a smile. 'Good. Glad that's out of the way. Now, let's have a nice evening out, Drew.'

They had a nice time. A bloody nice time. A *fucking* nice time, as potty-mouth Thomas would put it.

She didn't ask about Katie, and he didn't mention her. They talked about careers, uni, loving takeaways while knowing they needed to eat fewer of them, bucket list holiday destinations, and more.

After she'd called him a geek, he came clean and admitted owning a telescope, although he'd not yet set it up at Charlotte's place. He was mildly surprised that she'd participated in the NASA SETI survey. Then again, her elevated intellect plus archivist career—where data was everything—pointed to her innate nerdiness. She had a degree in Electronics, for heaven's sake.

He liked that a lot. One of the things that had made him think twice about Lotus was that she wasn't quite bright enough for his liking. No such problem with Hannah. Plus, he'd never be far from a smile.

At an appropriate juncture, he revealed the details of Katie's initiative—without labouring the point that he'd been pursuing it to honour her memory and give her a lasting contribution to the world. It led to the subject of his impending promotion and quickly to the matter of Kevin Yates. She fell pensive, then reached across the table as if seeking support. Before he got there, she retracted her hand.

Baby steps, Hannah.

She fiddled with the remnants of her dessert. 'I'm going to say this right out, Drew, then move on. I don't want pity or hugs. Well—I want a hug soon, but not for this.'

'Okay,' he said softly.

'Yates put his hand on my arse in the lift. A year ago. I'm not the only one. He's a creep. He's not to be trusted. Throw a rock in the office, and you'll find someone he's groped. Except nobody will speak up. It's why I put that spy system in the lift.' She banged her fork. 'And now it's gone.'

His mind went immediately to Lotus. That explained things.

Then, he wanted to clasp Hannah's hand in solidarity.

At last, she looked up and offered a sad smile.

'Then we'll work it out. You and me, Hannah. Talking to me was a distraction. You said before that I wasn't... the man you were looking to flash that beautiful, sweary mouth at.' He winked.

She brightened. 'I need evidence. Yates doing it or talking to someone—his creep buddy Marc—about his latest fondle. Then... I don't know.'

'Blackmail is an ugly word.'

'I don't want money. I want him gone. For all of us living in that shadow.' She pulled her chair closer to the table. 'I may not be the life and soul, but I was better before. Even after being shat on by more men than...' She sought a comparison.

'Times you've said "fuck" in a public place?'

'Oh no, *nobody* is that much of a tart.'

They laughed. A tense, rather sober silence fell.

'Sorry if I'm a bit of a cheeky cow.' Her expression was plaintive. 'It's—'

He raised a palm. 'A defence mechanism, I get it. All in fun, right?'

'And because I like you. Don't take it to heart, okay? You're really... precious.'

'Thanks. You too.'

She blushed and fiddled with her serviette. 'Take me home, Drew?'

'For wild, trash the furniture, trigger a police incident, sex?' he joked.

She laid the tip of one finger on the end of his thumb. She might as well have stuck her tongue down his throat for the rattle it caused in his bones.

Her gaze was layered with wry seriousness. 'If we're going to do this... "us" thing, then *I* need to be the funny one, okay? I don't have a lot besides that.'

In for a penny...

He beamed. 'Oh, don't sell yourself short. You've lovely tits.'

FLOOR 36

He drove Hannah home. He couldn't stop looking across, imbibing the curve of her neck, the reticent body language, the way the streetlights threw glitters across her glasses.

The journey felt disproportionately momentous, especially being in the car with a woman other than Char. In many ways, he and Hannah were both inching toward recovery.

Nevertheless, they didn't really talk. He suspected she was deferring to his understandable nervousness. She seemed to *get* him. He was doing a pretty decent job of getting her, too.

She texted someone. Probably a safe contact, a best friend. He was pleased she took precautions, even though she was unbelievably safe with him. She was like a Fabergé egg—beautiful, precious, fragile.

She lived in a small, three-storey block of flats. It was in a pleasant suburb, and the place was modern without being soulless. Her flat was Number 1, on the ground floor. He expected to be asked to drop her at the kerb, but she trusted him to walk her to the door. He was impressed by her strength of character. It was like him gaining the confidence to get back in a car two years ago.

At the sound of her key in the lock, the door diagonally opposite opened.

He jolted, which made Hannah squeak. She'd been concentrating so intently on the coda to their evening, holding herself together until she could collapse onto the sofa, laughing, crying or, ideally, clutching herself with joy.

'Fuck, Ames!' Hannah said.

'Sorry!' The owner of the voice, and presumably of Number 2, was a statuesque dark-haired woman wearing a kaftan and fluffy bunny slippers. Her hair was pinned up with a pencil.

This had to be the best friend.

She wandered over. 'Everything okay?' Drew heard a Welsh twang.

'Well, it is now,' Hannah said. 'You got here before the brutal murder part of the evening—right, Drew? Oh, Ames, this is Drew. I may have mentioned him.'

"Ames" threw back her head and laughed. She had a deep, dirty laugh. '"May have"!' She thrust out a toned hand. 'Amy. Neighbour, thorn in the side, purveyor of the finest fireman's lift this side of the M3.'

Hannah hadn't mentioned Amy over dinner. She appeared to be a topic that could fill the entire evening.

Drew shook her hand. It showed she was, indeed, a firefighter. He avoided wincing. With her grip, Amy was saying, "Mess with my best friend, and the Police won't find your body".

'Charmed, Amy.'

'How did it go?' she asked Hannah.

'Lovely. And we were just getting to the awkward goodbye part, so it's nice to have some fucking spectators to make it extra nerve-racking.'

'Pleased to help.' Amy folded her arms and didn't move.

'You're incorrigible, Jonesy.'

'Looking after you, babe.' She eyed him. 'No offence, Drew.'

'None taken. *Jonesy.*'

Hannah chuckled nervously. 'So, er, thanks for the ride home.'

'My pleasure,' he said, shifting on his feet.

She played with her hair. 'I had... fun.'

'Me too. And, er, nice to meet you, Amy.'

Amy cocked her head. 'You know we'll analyse you and this date for hours after you've gone?'

'I believe that's how it goes,' he replied.

She nodded, scrutinising him, then glancing at Hannah. 'Well, Drew, I'll tell Han in front of you that I approve, and she has my blessing.'

'You're not my *dad*!' Hannah chirped in amusement.

'No,' Amy said seriously. 'I have a lot more fucking belief in you than he did.'

'Thanks, Ames. Not sure Drew and I were at the "parental issues" part of our relationship yet, but cheers for kicking that off.'

'I call a spade a spade, Drew. And a fire axe, a fire axe. You should know that about me. Han can be pretty direct, too. You probably noticed. She been taking the piss?'

Hannah growled.

Drew nodded. 'A little. But her beauty and personality—plus the fact she puts up with a dick like me—are more than most men dream of.' He beamed deliberately.

She went to poke her tongue out, but her scarlet cheeks won the race.

He winked at Amy, rather than enveloping Hannah in a hug, which is what he wanted to do.

Amy returned the wink. 'Right, because I'm a wonderful friend, I'll leave you alone. But I can hear pretty well through my door, even when it's closed, so if you *insist* on murdering this diminutive darling, maybe do it quietly.' Amy patted his shoulder, then went back inside her flat.

There was an awkward silence. Hannah squirmed at the modest amount of public attention.

He coughed. 'Er... so... see you at work tomorrow evening? Half-six, basement?'

'Oh, no. Sorry. Have to go to an offsite thing. Friday?'

'Definitely.'

'So... until then.' She shifted on her feet.

'Mmm-hmm.'

She leant on the door. It fell ajar. He reached out in case she toppled, but she styled it out, which made her sway towards him.

A moment happened. The type of moment he was distantly familiar with.

She was a woman. One he was very attracted to. He liked her as a person. They'd been on a date. It had gone well. He ached to kiss her.

However, this was Hannah, so he didn't.

'Bye.' She flitted a nervous smile, rounded the door, and was gone.

He sucked in a few calming lungfuls of corridor air and then walked to his car. The suburban night was alive with sounds which pricked his ultra-alert senses.

He slid into his seat and thunked the door closed. Hot blood roared in his ears. He leaned against the headrest, trying to clear his mind for the drive home. He'd had only one glass of wine but a Jeroboam of Hannah.

His hand closed on the ignition key.

There was a knock on the side window. He nearly shat himself. Again.

Hannah grimaced in apology. She was bending forwards to look down at him.

He focussed on her face.

With her eyes, she gestured at the window. He pushed the button. She slid a folded piece of paper through the gap. He frowned. She nodded at it. He opened it.

It was her phone number and personal email address. Plus, her name. Plus, a kiss.

That was the third kiss she'd written. He hoped to collect on those IOUs before long.

'You trust me, then?' he asked.

'Of course I do. Div. And I trust Amy to kick the shit out of you if you screw up.'

'Understood.'

Her gaze explored his face. He thought it unlikely she'd pucker up through the window gap. She didn't. Instead, she hit peak Hannah. 'You looking down my top again?'

'No.' He put a hand on his heart. 'Promise.'

'Shame. I was getting to like you. Never mind.' She stood and patted the car roof. 'Drive safe, Drew.'

He started the car. 'Hannah?'

She bent down.

He deliberately ogled her cleavage. Then he winked. 'Thanks.'

She laughed, patted the roof again, and walked away.

For good measure, he watched her locomote away until she merged into the blackness of night, then drove home.

FLOOR 37

Hannah's texts were short and to the point. Perhaps it was tough to be adorable and funny—to be herself—through SMS.

Drew didn't care. The result was the same: he missed her like crazy for two solid days, replaying their moments together and pinching himself that he'd met someone so... unique. Yes, she had a knockout figure, but her charm and wit were the standout qualities. *Those* were what he'd initially fallen for. Everything about her was an utter delight.

He was the luckiest guy in the world.

They rendezvoused in the basement lift lobby at seven o'clock on Friday evening.

'You take me to all the best places,' he said.

'Fuck off. Besides, this isn't a date.'

'I never thought it was,' he protested.

She leant against the lift door and looked adoringly at him. 'It's better than that. It's you being a decent, lovely, understanding man.'

'Well, you're certainly no conventional date, Hannah.'

She did a mock curtsey.

'How are you *like* this?' he wondered aloud, then wished he hadn't.

She deliberately looked over the rim of her glasses. 'The world should be lucky I'm not like this twenty-four-seven.'

'Only with close friends, right?' he said guardedly.

'When I'm comfortable with people, yeah,' she said sheepishly.

'You should sell tickets.'

'Like I said, I'd love to.' She laughed, forlorn and self-conscious. 'The social recluse who wants to do stand-up. That's the biggest joke of all.'

'I'm first in line for tickets,' he said, trying to meet her eye.

'I should fucking hope so.'

For the millionth time, he wanted to sweep her off her feet and see how that foul mouth tasted. Instead, he said, 'So, you want me to stand guard while you do your... Mission: Impossible lift rewiring... shizzle?'

'Nobody says "shizzle", Drew.' She rolled her eyes.

'"Thang"?'

'Don't try to be cool. I don't think it's your... thang.'

He coughed deliberately. 'So, I'll stand guard. Um... What's our cover story? You know, if someone comes.'

'You can't be serious.'

'We need an explanation for being here and you fiddling around in the lift.'

'Okay, I'm an international jewel smuggler, and you're my concubine.'

He snorted a laugh. 'How does that excuse it?'

'Dunno. Why—you got a better idea?'

'Yes. Something practical. You're a freelance lift inspector, and I'm your boss.'

She folded her arms. 'Boss, eh?'

'Okay—assistant.'

'More like it. It's still bollocks. You'll be wanting code names next.'

'Couldn't hurt.'

She watched him ponder, shaking her head at his admittedly juvenile idea. 'So what's mine, then?'

'"Potty Mouth"?'

Her perfect eyebrows flared. 'Fine, if yours is "Pissy Pants".'

'No code names.'

She nodded. 'No code names. Now, can I crack on with this so we can fuck off home?'

He waved her along.

She'd already made the necessary arrangements at her desk, where she secretly monitored the feed. Her only colleague in the Archive Office was Jim, who loved her like a daughter and let her be. Besides, she had the advantage of being a quiet, conscientious employee—when not committing espionage stunts or cracking wise.

He paced around the lobby, listening to the sounds of her working at the lift control panel. She said it would only take a few minutes. Still, every second was filled with the torture of potentially being rumbled and—if he was honest—sacked.

The things I do for love. Love? Better put that word away for a while.

The right-hand lift pinged.

'Fuck,' came her voice. Scuttling sounds.

In a panic, Drew dropped to all fours and started feverishly scanning the floor.

The guy exiting the lift nearly tripped over Drew. 'Oh, sorry.'

Drew looked up. 'No, my mistake.' He recognised the dentally radiant white knight from Hannah's fateful security snafu.

'You alright?' Marc said.

'Oh, yeah... just... my girlfriend dropped her contact lens so—'

'Oh.' Marc sidestepped hurriedly.

Drew feigned a fingertip search of the tiles, hoping the oaf would get the message and piss off.

Marc spied the source of a mousey scratching in the other lift. 'Oh, hi, Hannah.'

Bugger.

'Watch your step! Don't come any closer. It could be anywhere,' she said.

Marc froze. However, he'd noticed Hannah's small bag of tools.

Drew cursed silently. Again. Hannah, also on all fours, tried to mask her swag.

'What's in the bag?' Marc asked absentmindedly.

'Found it!' Drew yelled.

Marc looked around. Hannah shuffled the bag into the corner.

'Oh, damn, just some chewing gum,' Drew said.

'Keep looking, honey,' she chirped.

'O-kay!'

'Are you alright there, Hannah?' Marc asked, not pissing off as required.

'Yeah, fine, thanks. Was on my way to a tech skills night school class when I dropped my fucking contact lens somewhere. Nightmare, huh?'

'Need a hand?'

'Honestly, Marc, no, we don't need your clumping size elevens tramping all over our search area and trashing my precious eyesight. Why don't you leave us to it? There's a chap.'

'Oh. Ah. Oh. Right.'

Mercifully, the bruiser slunk back to the far wall, tiptoed along and disappeared through the partition doors on the opposite side of the lobby to Hannah's office.

Drew and Hannah exhaled tornadoes, picked themselves up and leant on the lift jamb.

'You realise if we catch Yates, that idiot will take over at the top,' he said.

'I'm not sure he's squeaky clean either. You saw in Reception what a sleaze he is.'

'You could just get a job elsewhere.'

Hannah shook her head. 'I get a lot of leeway, plus it's safe down here. I'd rather go straight into stand-up. Besides, if I move company, I won't see you every day.'

'That's sweet, but we're only starting out.'

'But I feel like I've known you for ages.' She cocked her head. 'Besides—"girlfriend"?'

Shit. 'Sorry. I panicked.'

'Ah. So I'm not good enough for you?' Her impish eyebrows fluttered. 'Or is this a commitment thing?'

'The first one.' Attack was the best defence in these verbal sparring episodes.

'Fuck off,' she joked.

He shook his head slowly. 'No. That would defeat the point of asking me down here to help you test the systems.'

'Okay, you're right. *After* we test, it'll be fuck off time.'

'Yes, *boss.*'

She went back into the lift.

He coughed to get her attention. 'Oh, and what's with "honey"?'

She poked her head out. 'Just riffing on your vibe.'

'Nobody says "riffing on your vibe", Hannah.'

She flipped him the bird and then resumed her work. He resumed pacing apprehensively, knowing Marc would exit this way anytime.

After a couple of minutes, she emerged. 'Done.'

'Right, grab your tools and skedaddle to your office before slimeball returns.' She raised her eyebrows. 'Or any synonym for "skedaddle" that you consider lexically acceptable,' he added.

'Sometimes, you are *so* shit, it's adorable.'

He shooed her away and took up position in the lift.

The lobby doors clunked. Drew peered out. Marc had called the other lift.

'You find it?' the man asked snidely.

'Yeah. She's washing it under the tap. Night.'

Marc looked Drew up and down. 'Night.'

The lift whirred upwards. Drew shook the stress from his shoulders.

'Hello?' said a familiar voice.

Drew clenched a fist. *Mission: Possible.* He crouched in front of the panel. 'Can you see me, Elle?'

The voice sighed. 'It's Hannah. Were you not paying attention? Div.'

He smacked his forehead. 'Sorry. Can you see me?'

'Yes, Drew.'

'Good. Can you hear me?'

'No.'

He frowned. 'Oh.'

'Of course I can. Good thing this is a comms test, not an IQ test.'

He held up a guilty hand. 'Okay, okay, you're the smart one, I get it.'

'And the good-looking, funny, practical one.'

'What's left for me?'

'Hmm. You have nice eyes. And you're kind, understanding and supportive.'

He brightened. 'Oh, thanks.'

There was a moment's silence. 'Drew?'

'Yeah?'

'Do you want me to be your girlfriend?'

A wide smile spread over his lips. 'If that's not obvious, I don't think you get to be the smart one.'

'Fuck off.'

'That would defeat the point of asking me down here to help you test the systems,' he retorted.

Silence. Had he misjudged this sparring episode?

'Hannah?'

'Yes, Drew?'

'It's not what *I* want. It's what *you* want. I can carry on being the... guy with nice eyes who listens to your swears and insults, and helps you finger Kevin Yates—'

'Fnarr fnarr.'

'I was being serious.'

'I know,' she replied.

'Okay. Test over?'

'Yes, test over.'

'Good.' He stood, relieving his aching calves.

'Drew?'

He sighed heavily. 'Yeah?' he asked, bored of this.

'Will you go out with me?'

He smirked to himself. 'Not a fucking chance.'

There was riotous laughter, and then the line cut.

He stroked the lift, wishing it was her.

A minute later, she appeared, cheerier and bouncier than before. She squeezed his upper arm, which was a massive advance in affection. Warmth enveloped him.

She angled her head. 'Now, let's hope we catch this prick without getting discovered, right?'

'I'll be keeping my fingers crossed for you.'

'Couldn't have done it alone.' A coy, nervous expression ebbed on her face. 'Thanks, Drew. Really.' And without warning, she moved in, pushed up on tiptoes, and pecked him on the cheek. He'd barely registered the briefest touch and its significance before she turned away, cheeks pink.

He gave her a moment to compose herself.

'Let's go,' she said.

'Good idea.'

They went into the lift, and he pressed **G**.

She gathered a breath. 'So, are we... going out?'

His soul lifted, watching the expectation on her face. 'Let me do the proper deal where I organise something, nonchalantly say, "Pick you up at eight", deliver an amazing surprise, and hope you still want to date. Okay?'

She pursed her lips.

He held up a hand. 'It won't be in a crowded place, or too bright, or involve public humiliation. And I'll try hard not to bollocks it up.'

She fiddled with her nails. 'So long as it's not a fucking lift, okay? That would be clever but not funny. Somewhere with more space.'

He smiled. 'Oh, there'll be space.' He'd spent most of the day planning for precisely this eventuality.

She met his gaze. 'Okay.'

'Okay.'

PING!

Time to fuck off home.

FLOOR 38

O n Saturday night, he picked Hannah up at seven thirty. They'd agreed to eat beforehand, having already had a 'traditional' date meal.

She'd dressed for an *actual* date: hair more lovely, skin more radiant, nails newly painted yet in a muted tone. A skirt, which was a first. She seemed much less nervous, or at least wearing a thick coat of joie de vivre. She was certainly wearing a hint of perfume—something he'd not noticed in previous encounters. He suspected that she seldom wore cologne—it would be too socially overt, a signal that could be misinterpreted as a come-on. Hannah liked to live under the radar. Now, though, she'd opened up to him, taken a risk. Her bravery, as much as her personality and beauty, made his heart swell.

As he drove to the secret destination, they talked about their dull days. He suspected she'd been marking time as much as he had. He begged the universe that this date went well, because he'd fallen hard for her already.

He pulled into the empty car park and killed the engine.

She glanced around. 'Either you're brilliant, or you've lost the plot.'

'Yeah. Big risk. Huge. Not like bugging my employer's lift, though.' She poked out her tongue.

He wanted to hold her hand as they approached the huge building with the domed adjunct. He didn't.

She pinched her lip. 'You do know it's closed, right?'

'Err... yeah! Div.' He gave a gentle nudge. 'I have a man on the inside.'

They reached the main entrance of the Winchester Science Centre, and he checked his watch. He hoped Pirin had communicated the plan clearly to his mate.

Or I'll look like an idiot. Again.

'So, you couldn't already get enough derring-do from hanging out with me?' she said.

'I nearly got hit by a car for you. This is a breeze.'

The wind eddied around them. It was approaching dusk. The silence was unnerving, not counting the spectre of being discovered... for the second night running.

A figure appeared in the building's gloomy interior. The guy checked around, then unlocked the door, and they slid inside. 'Pirin's mate, right?'

Drew nodded. His heart hammered. He could only imagine how Hannah felt.

The security guard—"Oli" was stitched on his breast pocket—scanned the area behind them, then closed and locked the door. He was about twenty-five, and his uniform was a size too large. 'I'm off in an hour. Night shift comes on at nine. You've got until then. IT are doing a systems upgrade, but Adam won't leave his little geek box.'

'Good. Thanks,' Drew replied.

'Don't go nuts. My cock is on the block for this.'

'Thank you, Oli,' Hannah piped up with unexpected confidence. 'You're a diamond.'

He beamed at her. 'Oh, well, thank you, miss.' Oli put his shoulders back. 'Right. Got to do my rounds.'

Drew gave the guy a thumbs up. 'Cheers.'

The security guard, who'd mercifully turned out to be a million times more amenable than Len, left.

Drew gazed around the deserted Reception area, which opened into the modest science education zone. That wasn't their destination.

'I'll assume you've been here before?' he asked.

'Yeah. Like, when I was *nine*.'

'You said you wanted somewhere with space.'

She rolled her eyes. 'Very punny. Come on then, potential boyfriend. Unless we get arrested, in which case,' she counted on her fingers, 'I don't know you, this was your idea, and, if your sister's a therapist, she earns more than I do, so she can bloody well put up your bail money.'

'Clyde never had to put up with this shit from Bonnie.'

'Whatever.'

She led him into the Planetarium. They stopped, gazing at the vast dome above. A few ceiling lights burned around the perimeter of the dark circular room, gently illuminating a podium and rows of reclined seats.

She explored his face. 'I think I know why, but... why?'

'Private. Spacious. Dark—so you can take your glasses off and rest your eyes.'

'And you can gaze longingly into them?'

'No,' he said truthfully. 'All this danger for that? This is for you. And,' he shrugged slowly, 'there's a little stage there. I thought... maybe... I could sit—in the dark, hidden, unthreatening but supportive—and you could do a brief set?'

She leant back. 'You want me to do a *gig*?'

'Want? Absolutely not. But it's a no-obligation, risk-free, unpaid, guaranteed-rave-review chance to show me your best material. The absolute minimum social anxiety amphitheatre I could offer. A way to practice—like being in a club. Do you want a chance to change your life? I'm right behind you, Hannah. You're the funniest person I've ever met. And I met Barry Chuckle—so there.'

Her face cycled through a gamut of emotions. 'You're a hell of a catch, Andrew Flower.'

'I know. It's mutual. Now—get up there and roast me.'

She smiled, took a deep breath, put her shoulders back, and—best of all—her chest out, then walked, somewhat nervously, to the tiny stage area.

He sank into a nearby chair, made an inconspicuous silhouette, and waited. After a few nervy seconds, in which he wondered what the hell he was doing with this crazy plan, she spoke.

Initially, things were timid stop-start fragments, and she focussed on the floor.

He crossed his fingers and toes for her.

Then, she grew in confidence. She had observations, one-liners, puns, a shaggy-dog story, plenty of jibes at his expense, and a good dose of swearing. When she finished, the tears he wiped away were of laughter, pride and the deepest affection. He applauded and cheered like a packed house at the Apollo.

She gingerly perched on the adjacent chair, quivering. 'Well?' she murmured.

'Honestly? If Charlotte was still going out with Sam, I'd be haranguing him to get you an audition.'

'Sam?'

'Char's ex is a talent scout.'

She shrank back. 'That's not baby steps, Drew. That's scary fucking shit. This was a seat-of-the-pants five minutes—'

'Ten minutes.' He showed her his watch timer.

'—ten minutes at the request of my boyfriend, who is hardly an unbiased audience.'

'"Boyfriend"?'

She waved it away. 'Placeholder term. "Friend"—okay?'

'Fine. Okay. This isn't about me. I wanted to give you a chance. And, more importantly, a decent, interesting, relevant, well-thought-out date. Sorry.'

She shook her head. 'No sorry needed. Actually, I had fun—after a bit. Was I too... cutting?'

'If that's how you see me but still want to give this a go, I'm game. You have to accept people's faults, right?'

'Why, do you want to roast *me* now?' She smirked, giving him a noose to put his head in.

'No point. We've only got an hour. Well, forty minutes.'

She poked her tongue out. 'So, what now? I see you didn't bring snacks. Prosecco would have been a start. You're pretty shit at this, you know?' She winked.

'And you're amazing.'

She mimed sticking a finger down her throat. 'Don't. Oli will hate cleaning this carpet.'

The lights flicked on and off. The ceiling speakers crackled. Hannah tensed. Drew glanced around, concerned.

Music began to play. Stirring, introduction-type music. The lights dimmed.

'Oh, Drew, this is so sweet. Our own private show?' There was appreciation in her eyes.

'Nope. Not me. Far too organised and grand a gesture.' He tried to peer into the unlit projection room, begging that they hadn't been discovered.

'System reboot?'

'Bloody hope so. Or we'll soon find out what it's like to be tasered for trespassing.'

'Fuck it.' She lay back in the chair. 'I'm geeking out until we get dragged out.'

He wished he possessed balls to rival hers. Still, he lay back, and the presentation began.

The film flew them through the solar system and out to other galaxies. He let himself become immersed in the 3-D experience yet kept glancing over at Hannah, who was also rapt. This date might not be a complete washout... prison permitting, of course.

The audio commentary rolled on. "...binary stars like these orbit one another in a dance of mutual attraction, destined to be together for their entire lives..."

Something made him glance across. She was looking at him. She smiled awkwardly. He beamed. Her chest fell in a happy sigh.

Unspecified time passed. He found himself stroking the chair arm, wishing it was something softer. A few moments later, something softer rested on his hand. He looked. Another reticent smile, then she splayed her fingers and entwined them with his. She shifted her body against the near edge of the wide seat.

Endorphins came out to play in his brain.

He watched the spinning galaxies, then looked at her again. A million pinpricks glittered in her wide eyes. Then she turned to him, and a familiar something passed between them.

She gestured upwards. 'Amazing, isn't it?'

'Yeah. But the stars aren't the most beautiful thing here, Hannah—you know that?'

She swallowed, and her gaze explored his face, landing on his lips.

This was the moment—or at least *a* moment.

He leant over. She reciprocated. His heart thundered.

The auditorium door banged open. She jolted. He sat up, tingling with disappointment and discomfort.

'Time's up,' Oli called.

'Fuck,' she breathed.

Drew gave her a sober look in the shifting light. 'Quit while we're ahead, okay?'

'I suppose.'

They levered themselves out of their seats and went to the door.

'Hope I didn't... interrupt anything,' Oli said, grinning.

Drew patted the guy's crappy epaulettes. 'Don't worry. She didn't want to do it the third time anyway.'

Hannah struggled to contain laughter. 'Take me home then, lover boy. We don't want to press our luck with the Nookie Police.'

Oli's face was a picture.

Drew cupped her shoulder, led her out of the Planetarium to the main atrium, and waited while the security guard unlocked the door.

He shook the guy's hand. 'Legend, Oli.'

'Pirin owes me one. Sorry if the reboot startled you. Always runs whatever's next on the playlist.'

'It was... fun, thanks.' Hannah flashed him a smile, and Drew guided her out into the cool night.

FLOOR 39

The journey home was reflective, filled with banter, and neither of them mentioned the saved-by-the-bell near miss. He avoided repeated glances at her—this was no time for another horrific prang.

By the time he parked under the streetlight outside her building, she'd retreated inside herself a little. Was it nerves, sadness that the evening was done, or something else?

He took the bull by the horns. 'Do you want me to walk you to the building?'

Hannah nodded faintly. 'That'd be nice.'

He locked the car, and they paced up the path.

He stopped at the main door and glanced inside. 'Do you want me to see you right to your flat?'

She nodded enthusiastically. 'Yes.'

In a few steps, they were at Number 1. She eased a key into the lock, cracked the door, and leaned on the frame. 'Thanks for a nice date, Drew. It was unexpectedly lovely and... competent.' She winked.

'High praise indeed.' He swallowed hard. 'So... see you very soon?'

'Very.' She pushed the door open.

'Hannah?'

'Yeah?' she said softly, turning to him.

Blood roared in his veins. 'Do you want me to kiss you goodnight?'

A light went on in her face. 'Yes.'

'On the cheek?'

She eyed his mouth. 'No.'

He leant in, paused in case she changed her mind, then, when she didn't, he kissed her. Few things—in fact, nothing—in the last three years had delivered the same hit of utter joy. It was a lightning strike. A supernova.

He wanted to keep kissing her forever, but this was Hannah, and even two seconds of lip-locking was a huge step, so he broke off.

Her happy brown eyes roved his face. 'So, it's official, okay?'

'Very okay.'

She beamed. 'Good. Now, to be honest, I need to collapse in a heap, generously topped by wine.'

'Understood. Tonight was massive for you. I'm impressed, grateful, and pleased I didn't disappoint.'

She squeezed his fingers. 'Hardly at all.'

Drew glanced across the hall. 'I assume you'll discuss the date with Amy.'

'In about two minutes.'

'And... the kiss?'

'Yep.'

He grimaced. 'Will she ask for marks out of ten?'

'Probably.'

'Hmm. Okay. Night.'

'Night.'

At the main door, he pivoted. She'd been watching him walk away, which was a good sign. 'Just for my peace of mind, you know, and good night's sleep, do I get at least a 7?'

She did a so-so of her head. 'Yeah. And for the kiss, at least an 8.'

That comforted him. 'Oh, good.' He gave a lame wave. 'Night. Again.'

'Night. Again. Div.'

He emerged into the streetlight-spattered evening, buoyed, his mind whirring and full of possibility. The air was clean, sweet and life-affirming. The car locks thunked open.

There were footsteps behind him. He spun, alarmed.

Hannah came to a stop, a query on her face. 'And will you grade *me* with Pirin?'

He grinned. 'Definitely.'

'Do *I* get a 7?'

'Don't worry, Hannah, you're at least a solid 5.'

She poked his shoulder. 'I make the jokes around here.'

'Okay, at least a 7.5. Deal?'

She pursed her lips in thought, then glanced around. All was quiet. 'The defendant would like to enter more evidence for the jury to consider.'

'Would it?' His pulse quickened.

'It really would.'

'The jury allows.'

She moved in, laid a hand gently on his chest, and her lips, less gently, on his.

Kissing is always good, but kissing Hannah is better.

Sadly, she stopped.

Drew licked his lips. 'That helped your case.'

'Good.' She looked over her shoulder. 'Walk me back to the door?'

'Sure.' He tabbed the remote key, and the car locked.

At the main entrance, she asked, 'See me to my flat?'

'A pleasure.'

She pushed the ajar door of Number 1, then faced him, licking her lips.

'Do you want me to kiss you goodnight?' he asked, pretty sure of the answer.

'Definitely.'

Tentatively, he put a hand on her waist, eased down and kissed her. Five seconds later, his arms were around her. After five more seconds, her arms were around him.

It was twenty seconds of ambrosia.

'8.5,' she said.

'Ditto.'

'Good.' She tapped his chest in a farewell gesture. 'Night. Again, again.'

He beamed cheekily. 'Say hi to Amy.'

She rolled her eyes. 'Whatever. Now, fuck off.'

Churchill was a wise sod, Drew mused as he drove home. "If you're going through hell, keep going". Drew had kept going through a dark tunnel for three years, and now he'd burst into a blinding golden light. Hannah had reinvigorated him. She was feisty yet vulnerable, adorable and moreish. He licked his lips, trying to hold onto the taste of her.

A tiny circle of orange lit on the dashboard. He tutted.

A mile further on, he pulled into the Shell station. Petrol had gone up a penny. He brimmed the tank. Hopefully, he'd use it to take Hannah on further romantic adventures. In the small shop, he bought water which he could have drunk for free at home in ten minutes, and a Twix Xtra because he'd burned plenty of calories being shit scared about getting arrested for entering the Planetarium after hours and without a ticket.

'Drew?'

He jolted. The last uneaten inch of Twix slipped from his grasp onto the forecourt. 'Bollocks!'

He ignored the fifteen-second rule and followed the voice. 'Sam?'

Sam holstered the adjacent pump and closed his petrol cap. 'Alright, Drew. What're you doing in town?'

Drew swung the water bottle under his armpit, and they shook hands. 'They closed Bristol. I'm at Head Office now.'

'Living in town?'

'Yeah. Er... with Char, actually. Temporarily, you know, until I figure out a place. Bit of a rush, it was.'

'Ah, right.' Sam nodded. He was five-eleven with enviably thick black hair and a Mercedes. The talent scouting business was treating him well.

Drew's nerves crackled. *How long before the topic of Charlotte is pursued?*

There was an awkward silence. 'Still at the agency?' Drew asked.

'Yeah. Just on my way back from a gig. New signing. Died on his arse. Never mind. Win some, lose some.'

Like girlfriends. Please ask about Char, Sam. Please. Free her from Dick the dick.

'Out late on a work night?' Sam noted.

'Yeah. I was... meeting someone.'

Sam's brow raised. 'Ah. Meeting? In a non-work sense?'

'Yeah. Just a thing. Girl from the office.' He coughed awkwardly. 'Not a date... as such.'

Sam patted Drew's shoulder. 'Good for you, mate. I always hoped you'd... get back on the horse. Really shit, what happened. Awful. It's good to see you again. If you ever want a drink—'

A horn blared. Someone in a black 4x4 wanted Sam to stop holding up the pump queue.

'Shit,' Sam said. Then, 'Dick,' under his breath. He pumped Drew's hand. 'Take it easy.' He moved towards the kiosk.

'Yeah, sure. You too.' Drew opened his driver's door.

'Drew?' Sam had stopped.

'Yeah?'

Sam's face was resigned, even melancholy. 'How is Char?'

'She's... good.' Drew smiled. 'Talks about you,' he lied.

'Really? Oh. Okay.' Sam sighed.

'Obviously, she has to put up with me around, but can't have everything—right?'

Sam beamed. 'Yeah.' He jangled his keys. 'Look, send her my... regards, okay?'

'Absolutely.'

'Cheers.' Sam headed off, past the rear of the 4x4, flicking the driver an unseen finger.

Drew smiled. The bloke was a thoroughly decent sort, almost like an older brother he'd never had. Certainly, a suitable brother-in-law that he could have had... and still might.

FLOOR 40

On Sunday, Drew and Hannah chatted on the phone. She was more reserved than in person but more natural than on text. He wanted to see her, hold her, but didn't push it. He took solace by imagining kissing her again. Holding her. She was a drug, and he was sky high.

Most of Monday was taken up with a budget meeting for a new show called "Knowledge Wins" —a working title Drew thought was shit. However, he didn't mention it to his peers and superiors.

The show centred around finding out whether the famed "Knowledge" of the London cabbie was still relevant—and the best navigational method—in the technologically advanced 2020s.

Three cabbies of different generations would compete with members of the public, armed with their own approaches. Some locals with a decent grasp of the city would wing it. Others would use various GPS devices. For "scientific fairness", six episodes would be recorded on different days and under random traffic conditions, each journey with a different start and end point. Inevitably, character backstories would emerge, hopefully, some tension and, ideally, a prang or two.

Drew, with promotion imminent, was allocated the role of budget oversight. This was a big deal. It was a complex show, with a ton of crew, stacks of gear, and doubtless reams of expenses from people eating at various Pret outlets.

After the emotional high of Saturday, Monday seemed to be its career equivalent.

Ordinarily, he would have invited his girlfriend (*wow*!) out for a celebratory lunch. However, Hannah was Hannah and religiously ate a packed lunch at her desk, away from the pressing hordes, sunshine, and men in suits discussing strategy, leverage and running things up flagpoles for expected salutes.

Instead, Drew ate at a café and took away a double chocolate muffin for the afternoon.

As he returned to the building, a contretemps was underway in Reception. He recognised the protagonist—Sian Bright, producer/director of "The Lock Keeper". The antagonist was Marc—a guy who seemed to habitually rub people up the wrong way, though emotionally rather than physically, unlike his buddy Kevin Yates.

Sian's arms were full of belongings. She was beetling away from the lifts.

'You were warned about the policy on fraternisation with cast members,' Marc called.

Drew's skin prickled at the spectacle.

'How about a bit of leeway?' Sian replied. 'How about some understanding? It didn't affect the production!'

'You can't be impartial about a person in a doc you're... involved with.'

'Yeah—tell the whole bloody building, why don't you?' she yelled, barging past the main desk.

Marc pursued. 'This isn't the company's problem.'

'Yeah, but you're the ones standing in the way of *love*. I didn't bloody *plan* for it to happen. It can come from anywhere, any time.' She looked Marc up and down with disdain. 'If a person's worth it.'

'Sian. It's simply not allowed.'

'If it's Henry or this, then you can stick my job up your arse!'

'This won't help you,' he cautioned.

She halted, glowered, and raised a finger. 'Yeah? Well, I'll find somewhere. I've got a fucking *Bafta*, remember?' Then she strode away and clattered through the front doors.

Marc glanced nervously around, then slunk away to the lifts. He seemed to be adept at coming off second best against feisty ladies.

Drew waited for the blast zone to clear, then headed to his desk.

In the middle of the afternoon, he received an unexpected text from Hannah: "The best news ever! See you at 7. x"

He replied, "Intrigued! xx"

At seven o'clock, he met her in the Elle lift on B.

She was simultaneously guarded and fizzing with excitement. She pecked him on the cheek. He went in for the full snog.

She put her hand on his chest. 'Not at work, Drew, okay? I hate being talked about. It's not because I'm embarrassed about being with you.' Her eyes were intoxicating pools of supplication and affection.

He sighed. 'Okay. But this weekend coming, can we do something? Something couple-y, okay?'

She smiled. 'I'd love to. Think of another amazing, Hannah-friendly plan, and I'm there.'

He kissed her forehead and imbibed her scent. 'Cool. So, what's this "best news ever"?'

The contained, nervous energy resurfaced. She looked into the lobby, checking for interlopers, then pulled out her phone and accessed a piece of media. She tapped the tiny Play icon.

It was a video of her PC screen, showing the wide-angle spy camera from their lift. His heart raced.

Kevin Yates was with a female. After a few seconds, he grabbed her backside. She rounded on him. He wagged a single finger in warning. The woman quivered, then turned away. Yates smiled.

Hannah's recording ended.

She lowered the phone. 'We've got the fucker, Drew. We've got him.'

They stayed for a few minutes. Hannah needed a long hug, and he was delighted to offer it. She'd put the recording in an anonymous folder on her work PC, sent the file to her personal email, and wisely deleted the outgoing message. She'd also put a copy on a USB stick, which she handed him, saying it was safer if all the data wasn't in one place.

The question was how to approach the CEO with evidence of one crime and get him to admit to others? Her earlier plans had been to speak to him via the secret link while alone in the lift. She could be anonymous, reveal the evidence, and threaten to out him unless he resigned.

Drew wasn't convinced. What if, in response, Yates ordered that the lift be torn apart in search of the mysterious voice? He'd go to the ends of the earth to keep his secret. He'd instruct HR to interview everyone. He'd commission a trawl of security pass data to narrow down the potential candidates.

Hannah was initially riled up by his attitude and then saw his point. The waters between them calmed. Still, they were no nearer an answer.

He suggested they sleep on it. No reason to go at it like a bull in a china shop. They needed to be clever—at least as clever as her spy-camera plan.

She gave him a long peck on the cheek. 'Couldn't have done it without you—helping me put the system back in.'

'Will you take it out now?'

'No. Yates might do it again—then we've more evidence, in case he claims it was a "one-time" thing, a "misunderstanding", or some weasely high-price solicitor bullshit argument.' She bared her teeth. 'I'm not giving up now. Not when I'm—we're—so close.'

He kissed the top of her head. 'I hope we can tread the right line, that's all. It's playing with fire.'

She shook her head. 'No. Yates is the one who played with a fucking *furnace.*'

If he didn't know before, it reaffirmed that Hannah wasn't a woman to be messed with.

He walked her to the bus stop, which was busy, and she wasn't ready to be publicly demonstrative yet, so after a shy peck, he headed back to the car park and drove home.

As he breezed into the hallway, the lounge erupted into exclamations and kerfuffle.

He darted in, fearing for Charlotte's safety.

She was hastily pulling a throw blanket over her chest. Richard was writhing beside her on the sofa, scrambling into his underwear.

Drew's retinas were seared.

'Bloody hell, Drew!' she snapped.

He retreated into the hallway. 'I live here too!'

Richard clattered past, his arms full of clothes. 'Thanks a lot, *mate,*' he hissed, thumping up the stairs.

Drew peeked into the lounge. Charlotte was decent, with the throw wrapped around her and a cushion in her lap.

'Look, Char—'

She tutted hard. 'I know you live here too, bro, but...' She sighed. 'Honestly.'

'You think I *like* barging in on you and Dick like that?'

She glowered. 'His name's Richard.'

'You say tomato...'

'Leave it. Anyway, I thought you'd take Hannah out for dinner or crash at her place. You did *say* it went well on Saturday.'

He thumped down beside her. 'Don't be presumptuous. She's not a "boning on the sofa at any opportunity" girl.'

'Yeah, that's right—make *me* the villain here.'

'Want me to make Dic—*Richard* the villain?' he sniped.

'Piss off.' Then she cocked her head and changed lanes. 'You and Hannah *are* getting along, right?'

'Yes. Amazing,' he said from under hooded eyes. 'Sorry I caught you testing the springs.'

Charlotte's nose flared, but then she calmed. She plumped a cushion. 'Look, Drew, this can't go on forever. You need to get your own place. Do you *know* how uncool it is living with your sister?'

'Probably as uncool as living with your brother. Besides, why do you want to be cool? Why do I? I've never been cool. There's more to life than being cool.'

'Yeah. There are *relationships*.'

This sounded serious. 'Are you throwing me out?'

She laid a hand beside him. 'No. But the writing is on the wall. We're separate people, both with love lives now, which is great—but so is privacy.'

'So, stay at Richard's,' he suggested.

'Why don't you stay at hers?'

'We're not at that stage yet.'

'Well, when?'

He sprung up before saying something he regretted. He pulled off his tie and tossed it away. 'I don't want to fight, sis.'

'Me either. But you need to work on it, okay?'

He sighed hard. 'It'll be okay when the promotion goes through. I can scrape a deposit on a place.'

'You're not *hard up*.'

He plopped into an armchair. 'I'm not flush! Why do you think I stay here? I paid for a lot of bloody therapy after Katie died, and I burned my savings during my compassionate leave.'

Her face creased into sympathy. 'Look, I'm not *blaming* you. I'm saying it's time to focus on moving out. You're in a good place with a great girl. Lots of things in your life are much better. Work on *this* now.' She glanced at the ceiling. 'Or Richie will get pissed off with his girlfriend's little brother hanging around.'

That was the scratch of a dagger in his back. *Bloody Richard.* 'It was never a prob with Sam,' he pointed out.

'Richie is not Sam.'

Drew wrinkled his nose. 'Too bloody right.'

'Look, he's like... a sorbet to clean my palate after a bad break-up.'

'Ha! More like a Mr Whippy—artificial, insubstantial, and bad for you.'

Charlotte's eyes flared, but somehow she smiled. 'Maybe, but you should see the size of his flake.'

'I think I almost did,' he muttered, shivering.

'They're different men, okay?'

'Well, I never caught you on the sofa with Sam, if that's what you mean.'

'It's not at all what I meant.'

'I know.' He picked at a loose cushion feather and let it flutter onto the coffee table.

He sensed the wind of change blowing through 22 St Andrews Crescent.

Charlotte sighed. 'Look, bro, I'm considering leaving the therapy practice and going solo. Better income, less business rent to pay.' She looked at him with what was, for her, the closest thing to puppy dog eyes. 'I'll need a room here to bring in clients to see. Not yet, but soon. So that's a big factor, too.'

Shit. She's throwing me out by stealth.

I suppose it could have come at a worse time. Hannah has a place. Broaching the subject will be... tricky, let alone that it's rushing into something.

'So... you'd have lots of different men on the sofa, eh?' He winked.

She rolled her eyes. 'Crude and wildly inaccurate, but seeing a smile on your face is worth it.'

'Thanks.'

'I am *so* happy for you. Regardless of my work decision, I hope the promotion—and the Hannah situation, when the time's right—means you'll get a place very soon.'

'Does "Richie" want to move in?'

She gave a faint shrug. 'No, he isn't showing those kinds of signs.'

Good. Maybe there's hope for her yet.

FLOOR 41

On Tuesday morning, Drew's fingers moved robotically around the keyboard and mouse. His mind was too distracted by the prospect of house hunting, possibly having to find a flatmate, and discussing the whole thing with Hannah.

Also, if he was shelling out tons more in rent every month, he wouldn't be able to spoil her with treats and weekends away. He wasn't entirely sure that such devotion dovetailed with her personality, but his inclination was to shower her with love.

After lunch, his heart was pierced—and not in the way he liked.

Her text read, "Shit! Shit! Shit!" followed by a crying emoji.

He replied, "What?!".

There was no response, which had him shaking.

His concern only lasted ten minutes because his desk phone rang.

'Hi, Drew.' Lotus' voice was flat. 'Kevin wants to see you. Now, please.'

His heart skipped. 'On my way.'

Quickly, Hannah was forgotten. Whether this was news of the sabbatical initiative or notification of the pay rise related to his promotion, it would immediately add a sorely needed lustre to a decidedly meh day.

He went to the CEO's suite with a spring in his step.

Lotus' expression remained sober while he waited for her to grant him access to Yates' room. Perhaps it was a poker face. After all, she'd be happy for his success in either matter, wouldn't she?

'You can go through,' she said.

'Thanks.'

He closed the door and sat in the leather chair opposite Yates. It was odd, knowing what he did about the CEO whilst appreciating what the man was doing for his career.

Yates pushed a small plastic tray across the desk. Drew peered in, and his stomach lurched.

'Last week, the lift engineers found this little box of tricks. On Friday, the Productions Director stumbled upon you and Miss Thomas in that same lift.' Yates fingered the wiring. 'I don't know what this is, but I'm told it could be some kind of surveillance system. Designed for what nefarious purpose, God only knows.' He leant forwards. 'The bare fact is that it's subversive interference with company premises. And that's *very* serious.'

Drew clenched his sphincter for all he was worth.

Yates sat back and steepled his fingers. 'You are suspended immediately, pending a full investigation. On a personal note, I'm very disappointed. You were on a path, Andrew. You had a promising policy idea. However, things don't look good, and your job is hanging by a thread.'

Drew corralled a desire to hurdle the desk and lay a fist in the man's face. Sure, it couldn't make matters much worse, but he struggled to see how it would improve things.

Yet, he had a weapon at his disposal, and it was probably the only option. 'Understood and noted, Mr Yates. However, am I the only one in this room with something to be worried about? Potential impropriety in the workplace?'

The CEO's jaw hardened. 'I have no idea what you're talking about.'

'Physical impropriety. Multiple instances of it?'

There were daggers in Yates' eyes. However, the man was wise. 'I don't know what you *think* you know, Flower, but I have nothing to hide.'

Drew's pulse raced. This was do-or-die time. His job was on the line. He now understood what Hannah's text meant—the CEO had spoken to her too, which was heartbreaking. He tried to channel the kind of balls she sometimes displayed. Would she have made the same gamble he was about to? He doubted it. She'd probably frozen in fear.

'I think multiple women in this building would disagree,' Drew said.

Yates thumped his elbows on the desk. 'Even the suggestion of what you say is bullshit. All the same, if you let this go and throw whatever you *think* you know in the metaphorical dustbin, I'll *consider* keeping you on. Maybe even honouring that promotion *and* moving ahead with your laudable initiative. Alternatively, if you pursue these ridiculous claims, you're fired. Mention this to any other employee, and you're fired. Think it over.'

That sounded like a cue to get the hell out of Dodge, so Drew did. He didn't even glance at Lotus. She couldn't know that he'd risked his career to protect her mental health as well as Hannah's. That wasn't his lookout. Lotus would have to stand on her own two feet.

He felt sick to the stomach and riven with indecision. He went to his desk, collected the necessary belongings, switched off his computer and went to the lobby.

The left-hand lift came. He couldn't face it. He didn't wait for the right-hand lift. The bloody contraptions had got him into this shit, and he was done with them. Talking to Elle was about to cost him his job.

He trudged down the stairs, passed G, and took the untrodden flight to B and traversed the corridor to a room marked "Archiving". This was the storehouse for millions of hours of raw footage, finished programmes and related collateral. It dated back to Park Productions' genesis in the Seventies, albeit under another name. The vault also housed material for other companies that didn't boast the state-of-the-art temperature-controlled facilities which lay in the bowels of the building.

This was Hannah and Jim's domain. They handled the deposits and requests for information, updated catalogues and monitored CCTV in the vault. It met her need for near-solitude, controllable light, and a data-oriented mind.

Nervously, he went through the door into the three-person office.

She was the sole occupant. She looked pale and broken. Her eyes were red. He wanted to give her a bear hug, but her body language said no. He clenched his jaw in hatred of Kevin Yates, and anguish that their plan—Hannah's plan—had failed.

She looked up. 'I'm suspended.'

'Me too.'

That surprised her. 'Really?'

'Accomplice to the crime.'

'Fuck.'

'You could say that. Going home. You?'

Her voice cracked. 'Yeah. Need to work out how to fuck Yates up. Throw in a grenade on my last day.'

He leant on the nearby chair. Its wheels moved. He nearly spreadeagled on the floor. 'Shit!'

She gave a short, forlorn chuckle at his uselessness.

'Huh?' he continued. 'Did you get the same ultimatum as me—drop the accusations or take your P45?'

'What? No. What the *fuck* did you do, Drew?'

'I said we know what he did, and he should reconsider my suspension. Why, didn't you?'

She smacked the table, then winced. 'Didn't fucking think of that.' She snorted. 'And I'm supposed to be the smart one.'

'Don't forget beautiful and funny,' he said with a wink.

'This isn't a *joke*, Drew. I'm fucking losing my job. At least you've got a way out. Maybe he'll reconsider when he sees my evidence, and we'll both be fine, right? Right?' There was desperation in her eyes.

He grappled with the slippery chair and sat. 'I don't think that's an option. He was pretty bloody clear. I walk away from this scandal—that he denies—and I might be okay.'

'And you'd *do* that?!'

'I can't lose my *job*, Hannah! We're fighting a battle we can't win. You *know* he's a sneaky bastard, and I bet he'll bury anything we throw at him. I'm about to be promoted. I'll get my employment initiative through. I can move out of Char's place.'

She snarled. 'And all you have to do is drop the accusation—everything I've worked so fucking hard at.'

'Look—' He reached for her.

She recoiled. 'What happened to helping with this? You drop it all in a heartbeat to save your job?!'

He swallowed hard. 'I'm thinking about us. Our future.'

'And I want you to stand up for me. Is that so hard?'

'I thought you were the one who wanted to be the stand-up,' he chirped—inappropriately.

'Ha fucking ha. I like my job here. It's not sexy or on a promotion ladder to the executive bathroom, but it's safe, predictable, and all I've got. If I accuse him, he'll fire me. My anonymity is gone! You blew the fucking secret, Drew. At least have the decency to follow it up!'

A sour taste entered his mouth. 'You know what it sounds like? You're using me to get to the CEO. Exploiting a man, like he exploited you.'

'Piss off, Drew. You have no fucking idea what it's like.'

'We can't both lose our jobs!'

'But you owe me,' she spat. 'Or I thought you did.'

He threw everything at it, desperate to rescue this. 'I care about you, Hannah. We belong together. We've talked. We laughed. We had a great date—'

'Ha!' She sprung up, hurt and sarcasm in her eyes. 'Don't you know that binary stars are destined to never meet! Did you not *get* that, you fucking div?'

Drew backed off, wounded and seething. 'At the time, you thought it was sweet—don't deny it. And we *did* meet—in person, after your scaredy-cat charade. *I* made that happen. *Me.*'

'I didn't ask to meet, you know. That was never the plan.'

'Well, you bloody started this by talking to me!'

'And you got obsessed over a fucking talking lift.' She sneered. 'Should have known your judgement was off.'

He raised a rigid, cautioning finger. 'And if you think I'm like other men, especially Yates, your judgement is off too.'

'Well, *he* put his career ahead of the mental welfare of women employees, so I think I have my answer.'

His nerves sparked. The implied equivalence was disgusting and wrong. He sought to even his breath. 'I'm going. I'll see you around.'

'Don't bother talking to the lift. I won't fucking answer.'

He shrugged. 'Whatever. They probably ripped out our new system anyway.'

She was eying the floor. 'No. This suspension is from what the engineers found last week. They wouldn't know about the new system... unless you told them, mister blabbermouth?'

He was stunned at this new lack of faith. 'I did not! Why the hell would I?'

'To save your job,' she snipped disdainfully.

'Well, we're not all fortunate to have a fallback career, unlike *you*.'

She batted back his cheap shot. 'No, but at least you have your sister to live with. I won't be able to afford the rent. I'll get fucking evicted.'

'Move in with Amy.'

Her nose wrinkled. 'If you want to help me, the best way to bury the past is to get Yates arrested. If you can't do that, you don't *really* care about me.'

'It's my job! My career! I need to honour Katie's memory and see her initiative through.'

Hannah nodded disparagingly, blinking back tears. 'Right. To put a dead girl ahead of a living one. I see where I stand now. You haven't *really* moved on.'

'Look, Han—'

She shook her head hard. 'No. We're over.'

'But—'

She was shaking uncontrollably. Her eyes were devilish—and not with her usual biting humour. 'Read my lips, Drew. Fuck! Off!' She descended into tears and collapsed into her chair, a quivering mess.

He backed away. He was out of arguments and comebacks. He'd broken only the second thing he'd ever adored. He scuttled out of her office and ran. He didn't wait for the lift. He bounded up the stairs to Reception, his mind whirling, on the verge of sobs.

How can she not see it my way?

FLOOR 42

He paused in the stairwell, gathering his composure. Nobody else needed to know that he'd lost his job and girlfriend in the space of fifteen minutes.

Through the partition door, a lift arrived with a *PING!* Three people exited.

He wanted to hate the lift but couldn't. After all, he'd overcome something apparently insurmountable. His elevatophobia was gone—and Hannah had done that.

He shook his head. *No.* The pull of the possible—and his inner strength—were instrumental in that victory. It showed that even the tallest mountains could be scaled. This wasn't over. He'd fought so hard and long to get his career, the Katie initiative, and the Hannah relationship to such a good place. To give up on all three simultaneously was cowardly.

He had to *try* to rescue something.

He took a deep breath and walked into Reception. The other lift pinged. Lotus exited.

At that moment, Drew needed a friend. An arm round his shoulder. Support.

He also had an idea. It was unlikely to be as outlandish as threatening to shop the CEO to the police, so it was worth a stab.

'Hi, Lotus.'

'Oh, hi, Drew.'

'Popping out?'

'Yeah. I need a cuppa. It's been a stressful day.'

He checked his watch: 3:36. 'Tell me about it,' he said forlornly. 'Um... can I buy? I could do with the company.'

She eyed him sympathetically. 'I think I know what happened. Yeah. Come on.'

Even walking two minutes to the café with an attractive blonde raised his spirits. *Sometimes, it's the simple things in life: a beautiful sunset, a perfectly cooked bacon sandwich, Lotus' lovely smile.*

They sat at an outside table.

Sensing that she was concerned, he revealed that he'd been suspended for property damage. He didn't mention the lift or Hannah, and she didn't ask. He wanted to keep his powder dry. They chatted about other stuff—the support group, Sian Bright's departure, and the productions Drew was working on.

The other outdoor customers had left. A suitable moment arrived for him to take a brave pill. She seemed quite sober about his suspension and might guess he'd confronted Yates. After all, she'd alluded to the CEO's tainted character.

He reached across the small table but stopped short of her hand. He asked if Yates had ever sexually assaulted her.

She leant back, taking offence. However, it was due to the question being asked, not because her answer was No. He saw a brief echo of

Hannah—a mild panic overlaying the innate desire to speak up, do right, or push back.

He clasped her hand supportively. She squeezed back. For a split second, there was something in her eyes. Drew, because he was weak and in an emotional pit which couldn't possibly go deeper, did something pretty stupid. 'Look, Lotus, do you maybe want to go out tonight?'

She gave an embarrassed snicker and patted his hand. 'Oh, Drew, that's sweet, but no. I like you and everything, but I'm already seeing someone.'

Despite expecting this outcome, he died a little inside. He could have styled it out as a mere trifle or a misunderstanding, but she'd see the lie. He'd already screwed up one relationship today and couldn't afford to lose Lotus as a friend and ally. 'Okay. Sorry, that was a stupid thing to ask.'

'No, it's fine, really. Flattering.'

'Well, I always thought it was impossible, though we get along, and I was... interested. You're too good for me anyway.'

'That's sweet.'

He took a deep breath. 'Look, forget it. You need to know that... other people have told me about Yates creeping on women in the office. You're not alone, and it mustn't stand. Do me—and yourself, and them—a favour, and please think about telling me—soon—if there have been any problems.'

A pained expression flitted on her face.

He took out a pen and scribbled his personal mobile and email address on a business card.

Nervously, she took it. 'What would you gain from this?'

'I told Yates that if he sacked me, I'd blow the whistle on him.'

'He'd sack you anyway.'

'Almost certainly. And if there's no evidence against him, it's lose-lose.'

She bit her lip. 'So what are you going to do?'

'I've no idea. I'm a bean counter, and right now, the sums don't add up. There's a formula error in the spreadsheet.' He sighed. 'The whole bloody file might be corrupted.' He put on a smile. 'So, I need to revisit the data and see how to balance the budget of my life.'

She sniggered. 'You're a real geek, you know that?'

Her pretty, happy mouth buoyed him. 'I've been told. Maybe I'll be told again by someone, somewhere.'

She checked her phone. 'I should go. Don't want Yates to fire me too.' She leant in and murmured, 'Because you need a person on the inside, right?' There was a sad beseeching in her eyes.

'In an ideal world, I want the good people at Park to stay there and the bad ones to leave. And you're a good one, Lotus.'

She rubbed his shoulder. 'You too, Drew.' Then she pecked him on the cheek and left.

Drew went home. He hoped Char wasn't spreadeagled on the sofa again.

Luckily, she wasn't in. He was suffering such mental discombobulation that any discussions with her—veering between sisterly care and professional advice—would be unlikely to turn out well. He couldn't ask for help if he didn't know what he wanted.

He spent until six thirty trying to work out what he wanted. He failed. There was a gaping hole in his insides. A vortex which had sucked out his professional goals and personal contentment.

All from one ride in a bloody lift. It would be funny if it wasn't laughable.

With no sign of Char—and a shoulder to lean, if not cry on—he left the house to grab a cheery dinner for one. A self-pitying indulgence which echoed with lovelorn, low days that he thought had gone forever.

For the full-on wallow, he went to the restaurant where Hannah had taken him. He sat in the same booth. He ate the same meal.

He felt like shit. Things had moved from self-pity to emotional self-flagellation.

When he couldn't stand his own sorry company anymore, he paid, then went to the loo.

As he exited the Gents, he stopped dead.

In the far corner of the restaurant, a couple were sitting down to eat. The guy gave the girl an unnecessarily enthusiastic kiss and chivalrously pulled her chair out.

Drew's neck hairs prickled.

Lotus was indeed in a romantic relationship with someone. Unfortunately for Drew, but much more tragically for Charlotte, it was Richard.

FLOOR 43

Drew's short drive home was even less fun than the previous few hours. How the hell could he tell Charlotte that part of *her* life was also in the toilet? He'd barely formed a plan for revealing his own shitstorm of a day.

The silver lining was that catching sight of her flailing naked limbs wouldn't happen tonight.

She was on the sofa, but the only thing she was getting her lips around was a toasted sandwich. She made a great ham and cheese toastie. He hoped she wouldn't barf it up in the next five minutes.

'Hiya,' he said, as if life was unicorns and rainbows.

'Hmm-hmm,' she replied through a mouthful of calories.

'Back in a sec.'

He went to his room, changed into joggers and a tee, and returned. 'No Richie tonight?' he asked absentmindedly.

'No. Working late. Deadline.'

Richard was an Account Manager of some sort—Drew didn't really give a shit—but the guy's excuse was at least plausible. Not so good if he'd been a milkman.

Drew perched beside Charlotte.

She frowned. 'What's up?'

Apparently, his poker face wasn't great at concealing a dud hand. 'I've got some bad news.'

She snorted. 'What, the lift's pregnant? She caught you inside another lift?'

'Don't be a div. We did this. Hannah's a real person.'

'Okay. Sorry.' She fell serious. 'The real Hannah is seeing another *lift occupant*?'

He fought the sick feeling in his gut. 'No, Char. She's not the cheating one. Nor am I.'

Then he took out his phone and showed her the photo he'd surreptitiously snapped in the restaurant.

She arched back and laughed it away.

He clasped her hand supportively and described what he'd seen.

'Bullshit,' she said.

'What? You don't believe me?' He pointed at the door. 'Go on—it's ten minutes away. They'll still be there. Look through the window.'

'I'm not *spying* on him.'

'So you take Richard's word over mine?'

Her eyes flared. 'I don't know.'

'Text him. Or—you have that Find Friends thing—look where his phone is. A million quid says he's not at the office.'

'Oh, piss off, Drew.'

She was riled, in denial. If he'd accused her ex of a similar stunt, she would have replied calmly because it couldn't possibly be true: Sam was a thoroughly decent guy.

Now, Drew sensed anger in her, having been let down by someone she must have known, in her heart of hearts, wasn't squeaky clean. 'I said you should have fixed things with Sam instead of rebounding. At least *I* had the sense to avoid relationships altogether until the right one came along.'

'Right, so you're the psychologist now, Mr holier-than-thou?'

He inspected the floor. *Bugger.* 'Actually, Hannah and I broke up.'

She scoffed, shook her head and laughed. That hurt. He strode to the kitchen and pulled a beer from the fridge. She could get her own. *Cow.*

She appeared in the doorway, contrite. 'Sorry, Drew. Really?'

'Yeah. Really.' He gave her the whole story.

'You want my advice?'

Earlier, he had. Now, he wasn't so sure. 'Maybe.'

'Screw your job. Throw yourself on Hannah's mercy. You never know, it might work.'

'And what happened to me getting out of your hair? Leaving you and Richie to shag yourselves into a paper-thin relationship? No problem there, now, I suppose? Given he's shagging Lotus,' he sniped. 'Still happy to have an unemployed brother loafing around the place?'

She jabbed a finger. 'No. I'd much rather you were employed and in love. The difference is I give a shit about your relationship. All you do is try to jam spanners into mine.'

'He's cheating on you, Char.'

'No—you're just pissed off because Lotus, your own fallback woman, is dating, and you're taking it out on me.' She fluttered a hand. 'That picture was ropey. It could be anyone.'

'So, you don't believe me?'

'Says the person who was asking about *ghosts* two weeks ago?'

He threw his arms up. 'You know what, Char? For someone who's supposed to help people through their emotional car crashes, sometimes you're really, really shit.'

She stepped in close, her nose wrinkled in disgust and hurt. 'In that case, get out of my bloody house. Now.'

As Drew pulled up outside Pirin's house, he consoled himself that at least he hadn't hit a telegraph pole or suffered a puncture on the way. He was bordering the drink-drive limit, so he might have been facing a night in a prison cell rather than the hospital. Crashing at Pirin's bachelor pad wasn't exactly on his bucket list, but it was a bloody sight more palatable than the alternatives.

It was also a gift horse he couldn't look in the mouth. Amazingly, Pirin didn't have *company* that night.

Drew hadn't given his friend any details on the phone, but dumped chapter and verse in the first ten minutes after arriving.

'Shit,' Pirin said, casually sipping his cat's piss while processing Drew's life meltdown.

Pirin was a calm sod. His heart rate never seemed to exceed 25.

Drew blew out a cataclysmic sigh as a full stop to the expulsion of the demons. Then he realised there was an appendix to his story of woe, so he blurted that out as well.

'You asked Lotus out on the rebound?! After five bloody minutes? Jeepers, man.'

'Yeah, it was dumb and desperate—I get that. Me and Lotus would have never worked out.'

'You mean because she's drop-dead gorgeous, and you're fair-to-middling on a *good* day?'

'No. I mean, she'd never marry me. Lotus Flower?' He shook his head. 'Everyone would think she was a porn star.'

'Hmm. Fair.' Pirin gazed pensively at the ceiling. 'Lotus Dharwal? That works.'

'Stay away, mate. Enough going on in her life right now.'

He held up a palm. 'I know. I'll avoid.'

'So what's your advice?'

'Which bit? The family snafu, the career nosedive, or the love life implosion?'

'Thanks for your sympathy.'

Pirin beamed. 'It's a talent.'

Drew peeled at the beer bottle's label. 'Char's right. I should move out, stop being a burden. I'll have to see if there's a few quid down the back of the sofa. Maybe call on the bank of Mum and Dad.'

'Which means you'll need to explain everything to them, right?' Pirin shook his head. 'You could move in here?'

Drew laughed. 'I'd seriously cramp your style.' He sighed. 'I can sell the old engagement ring and make a few hundred quid back.'

'You should have sold it ages ago. It's an albatross around your neck.'

'Yeah. Seems I'm destined to never have another girl anyway.'

'Except you thought that before, and you were wrong,' Pirin pointed out.

'Then I lost this one too.'

'But also, like last time, you didn't do anything wrong in the *relationship*. It's no different to Charlotte's argument with Sam—right?'

'And your point is?' Drew asked. 'They're still not speaking.'

'You said they didn't even *try* to patch up their differences. Besides, you're giving up after one bloody week! You've carried a candle for Katie for three years! And then you thought you could have a relationship with her as a *ghost?* Trying to regain something after all that time?' Pirin shook his head in amused disbelief. 'Don't tell me you've suddenly learned your lesson and gone from moping and pining to making a clean break?'

Drew scowled. 'Why should I take relationship advice from someone who's never held down a girlfriend for more than a few weeks?'

Pirin grabbed Drew's arm. 'Because, mate, for the first time since Katie died, you've actually been happy. I'm not giving you advice based on *my* experience, what *I* would do, or what's best for *me*—but what's best for *you*.' He poured more not-real-tea down his throat. 'Besides, how am I supposed to vicariously live the "happy ever after" vibe if you won't do the decent thing and settle down?'

Drew laughed. 'What am I, some life role model?'

'Hell, no.'

'You're unbelievable.'

'No, *you* are. I've never been stupid enough to find happiness and then chuck it away like a used johnny. If bouncing from one fling to the next is shallow and socially objectionable, then at least I won't be waking up every morning for the next three years—maybe more—thinking what an idiotic mistake I made. Last time, you losing Katie was an accident. This time, giving up on Hannah will be deliberate, and you'll be even more of a nightmare to hang out with. If you get sacked, that'll be a blessing, as I won't have to watch you drag your miserable sodding knuckles around the office.'

Drew's shoulders fell. 'I suppose.'

'Besides, if you want the P-dog's honest advice, you should at least sleep with Hannah before you dump her. It's worked fine for me for years, and I'm about the jolliest, well-adjusted guy I know.'

Drew was nonplussed. 'I think if Char dug around inside your head, she'd disagree.'

'And she might be single by tomorrow morning.' Pirin fluttered his perfect jet-black eyebrows.

'Yeah—but still have full use of her mental faculties.'

'Love comes from the strangest places,' "P-dog" pointed out.

Drew frowned. 'Hmm. That's what Sian Bright said.'

'Really? Oh—did you hear she got the sack?'

'Hear? I saw it.'

'Wow. Poor girl, right? Love or the job, what a bloody choice.'

Drew fell sober. 'Tell me about it. At least she'll get work. She's very good. Bafta, you know?'

'Yeah, but you'll get work, too, mate—you're only an accountant. Millions of 'em everywhere. You could get another job tomorrow. Another office. New women to meet...'

'Well, thanks for the vote of confidence.' Drew drank, downcast. 'But I wouldn't be chasing women. I want Hannah, and I can't even think beyond that.'

'You used to say you'd never think beyond Katie.'

He shrugged. 'Things change.'

'I'm glad.'

Drew rapped the bottle down on the table. 'But I pushed so sodding *hard* for this.'

'Something has to give. You can't have both. Besides, you said Hannah's sacked anyway, whatever you do.'

'She doesn't deserve to be sacked for trying to get justice.'

'Neither do you, mate, but Yates won't see it that way.'

Drew's heart ached. 'I fear for her. She has a safe space there. It's ideal for who she is. She'll struggle to find a better company.'

'But you said she wants to do stand-up? And that she's bloody hilarious.'

Drew balled up the damp label. 'Well, it's not like I can magically make that happen, is it?'

'I suppose not.'

Then, a lightbulb went on inside Drew's skull. He jolted.

'What?' Pirin asked.

Drew shook his head. 'No. It's a long shot,' he murmured.

'Well, the P-dog may not know much, but I don't see how you can keep your jobs and get Yates taken down.'

'Then I suggest you sleep on it too. Otherwise, I'll be crashing here permanently, and neither of us wants that.'

'Amen, buddy. Amen.'

FLOOR 44

By the time Hannah got home at three fifteen, her migraine was ebbing. She'd blamed Drew, but on the bus ride she realised that the five minutes in Kevin Yates' office had induced the crushing pain. When she returned to her desk, she'd taken a triptan, but the headache hadn't waned when Drew arrived. Her discomfort—and the shock of her suspension—were a large part of the row with her new boyfriend.

As soon as she arrived at the flat, she had another good cry, a strong cuppa, and fell asleep on the sofa. Sleep always helped her pain to fade. Besides, there was no way she could force an incapacitated brain to work through the day's problems. Even a fully working mind would struggle with the current shitshow.

When she woke, it was six-ten. The wall clock was a chintzy thing Amy had bought in Marrakech and given to Hannah as a joke birthday present.

The flat felt artificially empty, but it only mirrored her gutted soul. There was no escaping a need for company, a sounding board. Someone to extinguish the fire of disappointment and defeat. Someone well-qualified in that discipline.

She knocked on the door of Number 2.

After a muted curse, the door opened—but only a foot. 'Oh, hi. What's up?' Amy was nervy. She darted a glance behind.

Hannah tried to peer around the door. 'Bad time?'

'No... er. Well, yeah. Look, Han—'

A much-needed smile broke on Hannah's lips. 'Have you got a man in there?'

'No,' Amy rapped, offended but defensive. She narrowed the gap.

'You... lying, cheeky... so-and-so! All that "I don't need a man to make me happy" while cheerleading for me, forcing me out of my comfort zone, and now—'

'Who is it, Jonesy?' came a woman's voice.

Amy flushed red as a Welsh dragon.

Hannah's anxiety went off the scale, crashing into her incredulity. 'Oh. Really? Oh. God, I'm so sorry. I didn't know that you... I mean—'

Amy's jaw locked. 'Right—one of *them*, are you?'

'No! I just... didn't....' Hannah quivered, lost for words.

Amy scowled. 'Thanks for nothing.' Then she slammed the door.

Hannah's throat clogged. She pelted across the corridor, her eyes blazing, rimmed with tears.

She stumbled into the kitchen, whacking her foot on the end cupboard.

'Fucking hell!' She grabbed a nearby mug and dashed it onto the floor. 'You stupid cow, Han!'

Then she hobbled into the bedroom, rudely pulled off her clothes and jumped into bed. She curled up foetal, pulled the covers around like a cocoon, and sobbed.

When Hannah's tired pupils focussed on the bedside clock, it was 19:32. She was starving.

She showered, dressed, and made a mushroom omelette. The flat felt oppressive and stale, so she opened the French door. Cool evening air fluttered in from the gated garden.

As she was washing dinner down with a much-needed crisp Chenin Blanc, the doorbell rang.

'Shit,' she breathed. Then she brightened. What if it's Drew, come to apologise?

She went to the spyhole. It wasn't Drew. All the same, it would be a self-destructive and churlish act to ditch her best friend on the same day she'd lost her job and a wonderful man—assuming Amy was still speaking to her.

Luckily, Amy's expression was contrite and forlorn. Hannah unlocked the door.

'I'm so, *so* sorry, Han. I can't leave it like this. I was flustered, embarrassed. I'm a mess. This was my first time. It's not serious—'

'No, no. It was me. Oh God, *please* forgive me.' Her lip trembled.

Amy's expression was supplicating. 'Hey, hey. I *know* you're not a prejudiced person. It was a shock—that's all.' She closed her eyes and took a breath. 'Please, I can't be mad at you. Let me in and let's have wine, or tell me to fuck off forever.'

'You should go back, so she doesn't think you've bailed on the date.'

'It's okay. She's gone now anyway.'

Hannah knocked the side of her head on the door. 'I scared her away? Fuck. Sorry.'

'No, she has a shift.'

'Is... she from your station?'

Amy shook her head. 'Another one. I met her on scene. Had a bit of a turn. Smoke got into my mask. She made sure I got home safe.'

Hannah instinctively reached out in sympathy, and then her wicked mind kicked in. 'And she checked your chest was in good condition?'

'Might have started there, yes.' Amy shrugged, almost coquettishly. 'Look, you've been crying, so I'll—'

Hannah grabbed Amy's sleeve. 'Fuck's sake, Ames, come in. *I* was out of order. Panic attack. I just didn't...' she looked away. 'You know.'

Amy kissed the top of her head. 'Yeah. Come on then.'

Amy went to the kitchen, found herself a glass, and they plopped onto the sofa.

Hannah picked at her trousers, feeling awkward as hell. 'So, you already knew her?'

'Maddie?' Amy nodded. 'We've met at incidents before.'

'I've heard of eyes meeting across a smoky room, but not like that!'

Amy fell unusually introspective. 'I've been struggling with this for a while. Suppose you noticed.'

Hannah actually felt like she'd let her friend down. 'Not really. I don't know what was more of a shock, seeing you in that... situation or discovering that my gaydar is so bad. Thought I knew you, babe.'

Amy fiddled with the stem of her glass. 'If it's any consolation, I'm not sure I've been giving off those vibes. Probably hiding them. Didn't want to... scare you off. Because we're friends.'

Hannah saw nerves and an unfamiliar mirroring of her social anxiety.

Amy smiled awkwardly. 'Then, when I realised you weren't likely to let me get as close as I wanted, it told me that I did want something with... someone.'

Hannah got the oddest feeling in her tummy. 'You mean... you... me?'

Amy stood, flustered. 'Sorry. I'll go. This is too weird for you.'

Hannah grabbed Amy's hand and hauled her back down. 'You fucking well won't. Because that would mean I'm not supporting you while you figure stuff out.' She gripped Amy's hand. 'You supported me *so much*. Especially these last weeks.'

Amy relaxed. A smile appeared. 'Thanks, Han. You're the best.'

'Maybe not the *best*, but living opposite means I'm *literally* your closest friend.'

Amy laughed. 'God, I love you, babe.' She cocked her head. 'So... bring it in? Or is that too creepy now? Worried I'd hit on you, right?'

'You won't. I think you know it's a non-starter and only likely to kill our friendship.'

Amy nodded. 'And neither of us can afford that. Please don't let this be weird now, okay?'

'Yeah.'

Amy opened her arms. 'So?'

Hannah beamed. 'You *do* have my favourite pillows.'

Amy beckoned, reclined, and Hannah laid her head against Amy's chest. Listening to the heartbeat was calming. Amy stroked Hannah's head. Relief was settling, and Hannah hadn't even dropped the day's bombshells.

'I s'pose I was holding a little candle for you,' Amy murmured.

'Like a tea light.'

'Exactly. Reckon I stupidly hoped you'd jack it in with men and try... the alternative.'

'So why were you encouraging me to pursue Drew?' Hannah glanced up, tummy still somewhat fluttery.

'I wanted you to be happy, somehow. Maybe it was reverse psychology or the last throw of the dice.' Amy offered a sober smile. 'Or I knew deep down it would never work between us.'

'Because I'd get a constant crick in my neck from kissing you, you... towering inferno.'

Amy laughed. 'We're so much better as friends.'

'Absolutely.' Hannah winced. 'Especially now I've lost my man.'

Amy jolted, pushing Hannah upright. 'What?!'

Hannah shook her head. 'In a mo. I really fucking need that hug.'

'Okay.'

Amy pulled her into a deep embrace, which was an unguent on Hannah's wounded soul. Still, it reaffirmed that she wanted strong, reassuring, loving arms around her more often. A man's arms. Drew's arms.

She had a short, quiet sniffle, then calmed herself, sat up, and took a long slug of wine. 'So how was it? With Maddie?'

Amy was mildly embarrassed. 'Good.'

'Do me a favour? Spare me details—for now. Not that I'm super-curious. Or completely disinterested.' Hannah clutched her head. 'Shit. I'm making this worse.' She took a deep breath. 'Just... maybe when I have sex news of my own, we can compare notes.'

Amy chinked their glasses. 'Deal.' She clasped Hannah's shoulder. 'So, *you* ready to spill? Worse news than mine, I'm guessing.'

Hannah gave her chapter and verse. Midway through, Cat wandered in, made a nuisance of itself, then hopped onto the sofa and curled up beside Hannah. She stroked it absentmindedly as she talked, which relaxed her.

Amy pondered. 'I'm assuming you want my advice—reason you let me in.'

'It's also why I barged in on the middle of your sexual revolution.'

Amy patted Hannah's knee with deliberate patronisation. 'Let's do you, honey. Don't reckon there's time for us both to deal with "what the fuck do I do with my love life?" tonight.'

'Agreed.'

'Good. Here's my sense. You've lived the last couple of years like men can't be trusted, and they're selfish, sexist, opportunistic arseholes. I *have* been there too, you know?' She sighed happily. 'Though maybe that's not a problem anymore.' She clasped Hannah's hand. 'For fuck's sake, don't use the past behaviour of a few people to judge everyone. Drew wasn't sexist, plus he fell in love with you as a *person* first. It's the exact *opposite* of how things normally go. Look at Stuart—he picked you up in a bar.'

'Because I got conned into staying late after a birthday dinner.'

'And, no doubt, flashing the girls more than was wise.' Amy gestured to Hannah's chest.

Hannah jolted in a spike of self-conscious anxiety. Cat was disturbed, so it stood, stretched, and then curled up on her lap. 'Drew really gets me,' she admitted.

'It doesn't sound like he gets how important the Yates thing is.'

Hannah sipped her wine. She was feeling mellow. 'He does. He was just... making a choice. Not him over me. His life instead of... not even my *life*. My... *crusade*. Which was probably doomed to fail anyway. Certainly is now.'

Amy stroked Cat. Hannah reckoned Amy wanted to stroke her, but this was safer. 'He wasn't dissing you, honey. I'll bet a million on it. He wasn't even saying what you did was wrong, invaluable, or stupid. At worst, very worst, it was self-preservation after he'd been given a "frying pan or the fire" choice. A gut reaction. A panic attack. He only just got back on his feet. New town. Big stakes. New hot girlfriend. Lotta pressure. He wasn't thinking straight.'

Hannah nodded slowly. 'He can be a clumsy sod. Fucking adorable, though. Considerate. Attentive. And God, can he kiss.' She tickled Cat under the chin. It purred. 'Drew gives me... unconditional love.' That's what she wanted, she realised. To be taken for who she was.

'He kissed the bloody lift even before he met you, for fuck's sake, Han. He's got it *bad* for you.'

'Hmm.' Hannah put her head back and inspected the ceiling, hoping the answer was magically there. 'How do you know when you're in love with someone?'

Amy patted her knee. 'I reckon when you ask your best friend that question, it means you're already at that point.'

'*Best* friend?'

'Best neighbour, at least?'

'Definitely.' Hannah beamed, then winced. 'I'll try not to barge in on you again.'

'I'll put a scarf on the door handle next time, okay?'

Hannah laughed. 'Did *you* do that in college, too?'

'Yeah—though I didn't get much action in college.'

'Promise me you'll make up for it now?' Hannah nudged her.

'Only if you do.'

Hannah fell serious. 'You might have to keep me posted by text. Yates will sack me either way, right? So, bang goes this place. Have to downsize. Get a studio apartment.'

'I'll put you up, honey.'

'Just when your sex life has turned the corner?' Hannah shook her head. 'You can push friendship too far, you know. I'd definitely be more likely to blunder in on you... *in flagrante.*'

'We'd work something out. Besides, if I pull a millionairess, I'll be sure to kip over at her mansion.'

'Ah—then I could stay in the servant's wing.'

'And pull the servant.' Amy waggled her eyebrows.

'I don't want a servant. I want Drew.'

'Rather than your job or nabbing Yates. Or both?'

'Grrr!' Hannah buried her head in her hands. The choice!

Amy put an arm around her shoulder. 'Look, let's figure out how to get at least *one* of them—because right now, none are certain.'

'Well, I've got plenty of bloody time to figure it out.' A worry hit her. 'I hope Jim doesn't go fiddling around on my PC while I'm not there.' She clenched a fist. 'Should have disconnected the new link. If anyone goes into my office, they'll get extra evidence of my spying, and I'm toast.'

'From what Drew said, Yates believes he's got you both where he wants you. Besides, Drew copped to the crime. If that's not chivalry, I don't know what is.'

Hannah nodded firmly. 'Then that's it. He's number one priority.'

FLOOR 45

When Drew woke on Wednesday, "hump day", he definitely had the hump.

Pirin's spare bed was comfortable enough, but the whirling conundrums in his mind had made for broken sleep. *At least I don't need to go to work*, he reflected sadly.

He took his phone from the bedside table.

"1 New Message."

He begged that it was from Hannah. He opened it, heart pounding.

It was from Charlotte.

> I confronted Richard. He admitted it. He's dumped. You were right. I am so sorry. Please come home. Sis x

That brightened him. Then he hoped Lotus wouldn't be the next in line for Richard's two-timing. He ought to warn her. Except it was none of his business. On the other hand, he needed her help. Or rather, Hannah did.

He showered, put on the mismatched clothes he'd hurriedly grabbed before being booted out of home, and went to Pirin's breakfast bar.

Pirin lived in relative upper-middle-class luxury. He even had a conservatory. Drew had once met Pirin's father. The man owned a very profitable food supply business. Pirin may not have been the apple of his parents' eye through finding a nice girl, settling down and providing grandchildren, but it hadn't stopped them from jointly creating a house that a suitable girl might find herself in one morning... Or possibly two consecutive mornings, if she was a real hit.

Pirin, dapper as ever, was gathering momentum towards his departure for work. 'You've got ten minutes, mate. Want my pearls of wisdom?'

'Yeah, I slept fine, thanks for asking,' Drew replied.

'Don't mess with your hotel manager, dude. You need a place to crash, remember?'

'Actually, Char retracted her eviction. I'm going home.'

Pirin brightened. 'Oh, good. One less pile of shit for you to shovel. So, you want to hear? I mean, before I roll in late, get sacked too, and have to crawl to *you* for a bed?'

'On the basis that that would put you in the same house as my sister, speak. Now. Quickly.'

'Okay. This is the P-dog's take. Hypothetically, in a year's time, you'll be in one of two situations. You'll have collared Yates but be in the doldrums because you wish you'd chosen Hannah. Or you'll be shacked up with Hannah, wishing you'd pursued the boss instead. Which is it?'

Drew's eyes widened. 'You know what, mate? That's a brilliant summary.'

'Editing, innit? Taking the full story and boiling it down to a dramatic, what-will-happen-next trailer.'

'Well, the good news is I already decided.'

'It's the fit brunette, isn't it?'

Drew winced. 'That's *too much* editing. But, yeah, it's the girl. I'll go into the office later, tell Yates to shove his job, and give him an ultimatum for Hannah. I can get another job. I can't get another *her*. Sian was right.' He chuckled. 'I may not have a Bafta, but I can make the smart decision too.'

'Right on. And Katie's initiative?'

'I can take it to my next job. There'll be another outfit that can use it. Hannah was right—I was clinging to the past rather than embracing the future. Trying to do my best for an old girlfriend rather than a new one—and I'll lose the new one. The old one's already...' He sighed. 'You know. So, I'll honour Katie's memory with something else. I have an idea... *if* the pieces fall into place.'

Pirin inspected his tie knot in the microwave's shiny door. 'You suppose Hannah will forgive you for ditching the harassment accusations just because you threw yourself on your sword?'

'I have another idea.'

Pirin looked Drew up and down. 'Honestly, I doubt you can beat Yates. He's got away with this for so long. He thinks he's untouchable. Plus, he's mad as a box of wasps, with the divorce payout hanging over him. Don't poke the wasps' nest, mate.'

'I'm not going to. I'm going to play it clever.'

'Then I bloody wish you luck.' Pirin grabbed his BMW car keys. 'I may not be angelic when it comes to office sex, but it's always consensual. That guy is a prick of the worst kind, and I'll do whatever it takes to support you.'

Drew followed him to the front door. 'Cheers. The best bet is to make him think he's won when he hasn't. He's an arrogant shit but doesn't know what I know.'

'Wish I could hear the whole plan, but I agree. Yates needs to win his little battle against you and Hannah. Any victory will feel sweet after he's about to lose two mil in that settlement.'

'Then let's hope he's distracted and makes a mistake.'

Pirin patted him on the shoulder. 'And let's hope you're *not* making one.'

'It's a punt, sure, but I gambled when I got in the lift, and won. I gambled tracking down Hannah, and won. Even if I lose something out of all this, it just needs to be the *right* thing.'

'Amen.' Pirin stepped out into the sunshine. 'Mum sometimes pops in to run a hoover round. Can't let go.' He rolled his eyes. 'So, don't leave the TV on the porn channels, alright? See you later.'

Drew made breakfast from the contents of Pirin's cupboard and fridge, then headed home.

Charlotte was out at the clinic, as expected. However, there was a bottle of French wine—it even had a serif script on the label—sitting on the table. On it was a Post-It note saying simply,

Sorry. C x

As it was only ten thirty, he decided to forgo the wine. Things weren't "morning drinking" bad just yet.

Instead, he picked out his only "power suit". It was five years old and tight around the waist. It probably wouldn't help his cause, but it couldn't hurt.

He gathered his wits, logic, and bravado, and headed to the office.

By rote, he took the left-hand lift to the 9th floor. He found himself stroking the **B**. He wanted to call out, but she wouldn't be there, so he took out his phone, paused at the precipice of a hopeful gamble, then texted,

> I'm trying to make this right. Even if you don't want to chat, please at least reply. I'm about to gamble everything. I wanted you to know. And I'm sorry. Drew.

He took a deep breath and hit Send.

The lift slowed.

PING!

He went to the CEO's office. He'd told Lotus he was coming.

She was nicely welcoming. 'Hi, Drew. They let you in the building—that's a good sign.'

He chuckled. 'I suppose. And they didn't even have to check my pants.' Lotus frowned. 'Never mind.'

Before he could ask if she'd contemplated their café conversation, she waved him through.

His nerves crackled as he sat opposite the man who held two people's careers—and possibly love lives—in his hands.

'Andrew,' Yates said curtly. 'You have two minutes. What is it?'

Drew laid the USB stick on the desk. 'This is footage of one of your... gropes.'

Yates' nose wrinkled in hatred. 'Go on.'

Interesting. He didn't deny it.

'It was my idea to bug the lift. Someone I... know in the office is one of the people you *interacted* with.' He swallowed down acid reflux and pushed the USB stick across. 'This is the only copy. The only hard evidence of the things you've done. All the rest is, "she said, he said," and I'll bet you can afford a bloody good lawyer to make those circumstantial claims go away.'

'You bet your arse I can, Flower.'

'So, this is the lynchpin. Without it, I doubt anyone will come forward. Especially as you'll sack them too, right?' Yates shrugged. 'I hear you've suspended Hannah Thomas.'

'Well, you were seen together.'

'She was helping. She did it because she... fancies me, the stupid girl. What's more important is that she's a bloody fine archivist. She keeps the vault ticking over. The company gets a lot of income from the vault.'

'That's as may be.'

'I'm only a bean counter. She's one of a kind. In many ways.' He pushed at the USB stick again, playing mind games.

'Your time's up. Get to the point.'

'I resign. You don't need to sack me or risk me suing for wrongful dismissal. I'll go quietly. Take that stick and... burn it, erase it, whatever. That'll make the women think again. The matter's closed.'

'You know—I might just do that.' Yates stood, dropped the USB stick on the floor, and pounded it with his thick black sole until it was a shattered mess. 'Right, you can go.'

'One last thing. Sir. You reinstate Hannah Thomas.'

'Why?'

'Because you've met her. You know what type of person she is. Without hard evidence, there's no way she'll say a word against you—much less in a packed courtroom. She *hates* the spotlight. Being cross-examined by your people would put her in therapy for months. It's not worth it for her. Give Hannah her job back. You've got a scapegoat in me. Justice is seen to be done for the lift tampering. The other thing... never happened.'

Yates stared for an eternity. 'Clear your desk. I'll expect your resignation letter by Friday five P.M.' He thumbed towards the door.

Drew stood. 'And Miss Thomas?'

'I'll reconsider. Decision by Friday five P.M. as well.'

'Thank you.' Drew went to the door.

'What about your... sabbatical initiative? Giving that up too?' Yates called. 'You fought hard for that.'

'It's only an idea, Mr Yates. Hannah is a person with hopes, dreams and a job she loves. Besides, firing a timid little woman because you're *scared* of her?' He shook his head. 'You didn't build Park Productions into the successful business it is by running away from things, did you?' He gave a sober smile. 'Anyway. Thanks for getting rid of that bloody USB. It's been an albatross around my neck. Have a good week. I hope your divorce works out. I'll go and clear my stuff.'

A somewhat conciliatory frown broke on Yates' forehead. 'That's decent of you, Flower.'

With a shrug, Drew left.

Lotus was on the phone, but he wasn't planning to speak to her anyway. What surprised him was Pirin sitting there, calmly waiting.

'Oh. What... not you as well?'

Pirin smiled faintly. 'No. Something else. Go on. You look like you need to neck a bottle of vodka or smash Yates' windscreen. My advice? Do neither.'

'Yeah. I wasn't going to, but... okay. Have a good... whatever.'

Pirin nodded sagely. 'Cheers.'

Drew scuttled to the Gents and let out five minutes of pent-up breath. Would his brown-nosing, misdirection-filled gamble work?

He didn't discuss the situation with anyone in his department. He simply cleared his things into a Sainsbury's Bag-for-Life he'd brought, then took the left-hand lift down to G for the final time. On the way, his phone beeped.

Good luck. Hannah.

Better late than never.

At least they were communicating. Besides, they'd turned a voice-only dialogue into the beginnings of a romance, so maybe they could kick-start a reconciliation using text only?

He sat in the car park for a few minutes, corralling his thoughts about the last piece in the puzzle. Then he pulled out his phone and dialled.

'Hi, Sam. It's Drew.'

FLOOR 46

D rew stopped off at the supermarket and filled the trolley with necessities.

Is this my life now—weekday daytime shopping?

I bloody hoped not.

As another sop to Char, possibly motivated by a desire for ongoing tenancy, he spent the afternoon doing chores. It was tedious as hell but preferable to agonising over things which were out of his control. He'd done his best.

He made a cuppa and switched on Countdown.

His phone pinged.

> How did it go? H

That raised his spirits—they were talking. She cared.

I played every card I had. Waiting game now.

I'm sorry I shouted.

Sorry I hurt your feelings.

I miss you

Miss you too

How's unemployment treating you?

Bored shitless

Ditto

Watching sodding Countdown

I got 432. Two away

I got 434. Boom!

That's cos you're a fucking accountant

!

Or were :-(

Production accountant. Still am. Just an unemployed one

He sipped his builders' tea.

INDELIBLE

?

The conundrum

Oh. Right. Smart arse

Pissy pants

!

x

He laid the phone on the sofa. His hand quivered. Either that was an oddly coincidental typo, or she'd blown him a kiss.

Perhaps things aren't over?

He munched on a chocolate digestive to calm his nerves. Then he replied with a smile emoji. She responded in kind.

A glint of sunlight illuminated the dank cave of his soul.

The Messages app fell silent for a few minutes. He didn't know where to go with the conversation. He certainly didn't want to count his chickens or push too hard for a commitment to meet. Yet, he felt the door she'd slammed in his face was now ajar.

Got to go

Ok

Ames has been promoted to Crew Manager! Going out to get pissed

You? Out? :-)

I'll be safe. I've got a fucking six-foot firefighter for company

Okay. Have a nice time. But promise you'll take care?

Promise

I won't text you too early!

Why had he presumed that this detente would continue until tomorrow? Too late. The message whooshed away.

Okay. But do text. H x

He took a deep breath.

Okay. D x

There were no more replies. She was probably getting changed. Having a shower.

His mind wandered to an image of her in the shower. His heart thudded. His boxers stretched. He scoffed. Only he would choose that moment, the worst point in their relationship—if they still had a relationship—to mentally undress her for the first time.

It did no harm, but he stopped. No point in projecting an uncertain future. Besides, even exchanging messages had nourished his ardour.

He plugged his phone into the charger in case she needed to be in touch later. He desperately wanted to hear from her but hoped she'd let her hair down and have a good time. She needed to wash off the invisible sheen of cack that Kevin Yates' behaviour had deposited on her—their—lives.

At six thirty, Char veritably bounced into the lounge, wielding a bunch of roses. Yellow. Someone was obviously feeling passion towards her. He had an idea who.

'Hey, Drew.'

'Hey, sis. What's the occasion?'

'Tell you in a sec. Got to get these beauties in water.' She went into the kitchen.

Drew smiled to himself.

'Hey—can I borrow your car tomorrow?' she called. 'Mine broke down this morning. Sodding thing. Had to get towed to the garage. No parts in stock. Useless place.' She returned with the flowers in a tall glass vase. 'You don't need it, right?' She grimaced. 'Sorry—didn't mean to belittle your—'

He waved it away. 'It's fine. Besides, my car for your house is more than a fair swap.'

'Not forever—okay?' She winked.

'No, sure. But easier being here now that Richard is out of the picture. Shit. Sorry—didn't mean to belittle *your*—'

She swatted him on the arm. 'Good riddance to bad rubbish. Besides, I still want to go solo at work.'

'Oh. Yeah.' He brightened. 'Anyway, there might be a glimmer with Hannah.'

Char beamed. 'Really?'

'I'm only joining dots, but...' He shrugged.

'I'll keep my fingers crossed.'

'Thanks.' He indicated the vase. 'So, did Richie try to win you back after twelve hours in the doghouse? Tut.'

'No, thank Christ.' She encouraged him over to the sofa. 'You won't believe this, but Sam turned up at the clinic. Out of the blue. No text, no call, nothing. With those.' She pointed at the dozen roses.

So, Sam hadn't been particularly inventive with his romantic gesture, but he'd made one, which was the important thing. Drew mentally fist-bumped himself.

'Bloody hell,' he exclaimed, feigning surprise.

Her eyes narrowed in suspicion, but she continued. 'Yeah. He caught me during my lunch hour. Threw himself on my mercy. Said it was stupid for us to break up like that. Said he didn't care that I couldn't have kids. Said he'd never stopped loving me.'

'Begged to have you back?'

She smiled and shook her head. 'He didn't need to beg. Never got that far. I crumbled like a bloody sandcastle. You were right, Drew. I should have patched this up ages ago.'

'I'm not going to say, "told you so". Especially as I'm no expert on smooth relationships. But I'm happy. More than happy.'

She embraced him. 'I don't think this was a coincidence,' she murmured. 'Was it, Andrew David Flower?'

Shit. Rumbled. 'No comment.'

'You're the best brother.'

'I have my moments.'

'I wish you'd spend as much time on your own sodding happiness as you do meddling in mine.'

He broke off. 'Meddling?'

'Okay—matchmaking.'

'I'm just trying to get everything to... add up. Balance the debits and credits. Put things where they belong.'

Char smiled. 'You're such a bloody geek.'

'I get enough of this from Hannah, thanks.'

'And you want to keep getting more of it, right?'

'Like you wouldn't believe.'

She rubbed his shoulders. 'Then how can we get the two of you back together?'

'Well, with respect to Sam, I can't just turn up at her house with a bunch of flowers. There's a lot to smooth over—and a lot still up in the air.'

'Like what?'

He told her what he'd done at the office and what he'd said to Yates.

'Shit, Drew, that took balls. You *have* to tell Hannah what you did.'

'She'll find out when she gets called in to get her job back.'

Char gave him a sober look. 'And if she doesn't? If Yates goes back on his word? You said he was a slippery, untrustworthy dick.'

'Here's the thing, Char.' He pulled a USB stick from his pocket. 'I can be sneaky too.'

Her eyes widened. 'Shit. What do you plan to do with that?'

'It's ammo in case he doesn't keep Hannah.'

'You're playing with fire.'

He chuckled. 'Luckily, I know a firefighter who'll ride in and help.'

She put a hand on his knee. 'You'll still only know what happens if you meet her. Plus, you'll only get any proper... *thanks*,' she winked, 'that way.'

'Baby steps, Char. We're still broken up, technically.'

'I'll say again—and take it from the Sam thing today—don't leave it to chance. You don't have to go big with a public display of affection. No aerial signwriter, no celebrity lookalike-a-gram. Hell—what you did today, chucking your career away to save hers—that's the bloody gesture. Take her a box of chocolates. Women are suckers for lame shit like that. You're not giving her the chocs—you're offering back *yourself*, and *that's* what she has to decide if she wants.'

'Bloody hell, you're wise sometimes.'

She whacked his knee. 'I'm wise all the time, thanks very much.'

'Including breaking up with Sam over a misunderstanding?'

'It's an emotive subject, okay?' She smiled awkwardly. 'You wouldn't understand.'

He pondered. It was time. 'Hold on.'

She frowned. 'Okay.'

He went to his room, collected the requisite item, and laid it between them on the sofa.

'Drew—' She wore a disbelieving, almost panicked expression.

He clasped her hand. 'It's only an offer. You aren't under obligation. I won't be offended if you say no. How can I be? It's not *really* my property. But it is your life, your body, and your happiness.'

She pushed at the envelope. 'I can't, Drew.'

'At least consider it. Please. For me.'

Her gaze explored his face. 'But if you and Hannah make up, and—'

'Absolutely. If we get that far, and she wants kids, and can't, and doesn't feel weirded out, then, yes, maybe this is a lifeline. But, honestly, it would be a worse-case fallback. You and Sam are further down the road. I swear you weren't far from the big white dress. Besides,' he winked, 'You're not getting any younger.'

She shoulder-nudged him. 'It's... amazing, and odd, and hard to process, and a million other things.'

'It's a chance to give it a shot. The ammo, in fact.'

She bit her lip. 'Hmm. Okay.'

'At least keep this in *your* room. I don't want Hannah stumbling on it. If she freaks, that could be curtains.'

'That sounds like you anticipate Hannah being in this house. In your room.'

'What can I say? She's a sucker for clumsy, uncool geeks who live with their sister and are bent on career suicide.'

She kissed his forehead. 'Then what impeccable taste she has.'

FLOOR 47

Drew was up in time to see Char leave for work. She still had that spring in her step. He hoped to have a similarly vibrant gait by the evening—if he could engineer a second reconciliation in 24 hours.

He double-checked the weather forecast and Google Maps. He couldn't find a flaw in the plan that had entered his mind just before midnight. However, it relied on Hannah being receptive and in a good mood. Hopefully, a girls' night out had improved her temperament, building on their very civil text exchange.

Mid-morning, he walked to the Little Waitrose to gather the items for that night. She may have joked about his picnic-planning rubbishness last time, but he wasn't going to forget anything now.

At 13:45, which he considered late enough for any ill effects to have worn off her, he took the five-minute bus ride to his destination. This next step was the weak link in his plan. He crossed his fingers for a stroke of luck—he was undoubtedly due it.

As he walked up to the fire station, he clenched a fist. Amy was on the front apron, running a cloth over a fire tender's frontage. As he approached, she stopped work.

He froze, hoping they were still on speaking terms. After all, she'd threatened to knock his block off if he hurt Hannah, and the jury was out on whether that had happened.

She put her hands on her hips. He could see her triceps. His stomach tensed.

'Alright?' she said guardedly.

He stopped, more than an arm's reach away. 'Congratulations on your promotion.'

She brightened. 'Thanks.'

'Did you have a good night?'

'Bloody fine, actually. Three coffees this morning is helping.'

'Hannah okay?'

Amy moved closer. 'After last night, or generally?'

She wrung out the rag. Now he could see her biceps.

'Er... I suppose... both, really. Obviously, you were there last night, so I have complete faith about that. But... before....' He took a deep breath. 'When I... let her down, and said stupid stuff, and got my priorities backwards, and made her cry, and—'

'Gave her a migraine,' Amy added. 'I *wasn't* there.'

'No. Yeah. Right. Shit. So...?'

'How is she *emotionally*? Rather than in terms of being hungover?'

'Yeah. I mean, I don't know if she said, but we chatted a bit—by text—yesterday, and she seemed pretty... fine. Level-headed. Not ready to rip off my head and piss down my neck, I think. Or even ask you to do it. Which you totally could. Not here, though. You're on duty. And recently promoted, too. Congratulations on that, again, by the way. So... Jonesy... Can I still call you Jonesy? Amy. Look, Amy, I know you're her best friend and very protective, and—'

Amy stepped *very* close. Drew flinched. His pulse quickened. He tensed his tense stomach even further.

Mercifully, she smiled. 'Hannah's fine, Drew.'

He exhaled hard. 'Thank Christ for that.'

'Didn't get wasted, fall down and crack her pretty head open. She also didn't tap off with some grunt just to spite you.'

'Good. Well, that's a relief.'

Amy glanced around. 'She likes you. A fucking lot.' She looked him up and down. 'Can't see it myself. Bag of nerves, aren't you?'

'Well, you know—the whole "rip off my head" thing.'

She cocked her head. 'You here for my bloody *permission* or something? Want me to ask her out for you? Do the grovelling apology?'

'God, no. I can do that myself.' *Probably a cinch after going up against Yates.*

'Oh, right.' She pursed her lips. 'Were you after a ride in the appliance, then?'

His face lit up. 'Could I?'

She belly laughed. 'Course you fucking couldn't! More than my job's worth.' She clasped his shoulder. 'So, you here to find out the lay of the land, Drew? Test the water? Cos if you are, the water's warm. I get the feeling you're a "once bitten, twice shy" person. She's the same. You bit each other this week. I know you won't do it again.'

'Because of the best friend, firefighter, "piss down my neck" danger?'

'No. Cos you're a smart, decent bloke.'

His mouth opened and closed. 'Wow. Thanks, Jonesy.'

'No problem. Now, gotta get back to work.'

'Would you... er... do me a favour? Tiny one. That's really why I was here.' He pulled a folded piece of paper from his pocket.

She eyed it suspiciously. 'Passing love notes in class? Could have sent her a text.'

'No. This is more romantic. Plus, no chance for searching questions.'

'Is it private?'

He pondered. *Best to have Amy onside.* 'No. Just an invitation. I mean, I'm sure when she reads it, she'll tell you anyway. And give you the full story tomorrow morning—however it turns out. Maybe have you on speed dial later, in case I screw up again.'

'So I can jump in this thing,' she thumbed at the fire tender, 'howl over to your big make-up date, whisk her to safety from the big bad man, then shove the hose up your arse and turn it on?'

He beamed. 'I'd be disappointed if you didn't, Jonesy.'

Suddenly, he was in a bear hug. He couldn't have hugged back if he'd tried; his arms were pinned. She smelled of car polish, coffee and latent violence.

'You're a good bloke, Andrew Flower,' she murmured into his hair. 'We're joking around right now, but don't fuck up this date. She's like a sister to me and deserves the world.' Amy broke off.

'I'm trying bloody hard to give it to her.'

'Good.' She waved the paper. 'I finish at six. That be enough time to make herself beautiful for your date?'

'You're kidding, right? Hannah could turn up hungover, without makeup, un-showered and in a burlap sack, and I'd still be the luckiest man alive.'

'Fuck, you say the sweetest things sometimes.'

Drew nodded sagely. 'Thanks. Might write that one down, actually. Use it later if things need a boost.'

She chuckled in disbelief, then pocketed the note. 'Go on then, piss off.' She fluttered a hand.

Drew pissed off. The die was cast.

FLOOR 48

When Drew got home, he prepared the picnic, selected an outfit, and texted Char to check that she'd be home in time for him to reclaim his car. She would.

For something to do, he rang Pirin to reveal the plan and ask for a critique. Whilst romance wasn't really Pirin's bag, he was a logical, practical sod, so he would point out any glaring screw-ups in Drew's attempt to win back the girl.

Pirin was obviously bored shitless, so he took an impromptu early-afternoon coffee break, and they talked for half an hour. Apparently, "The Lock Keeper" had turned out well. The only question was whether Park Productions would release the programme or shelve it to protect themselves from any bad press if the Sian Bright issue went public.

Drew made a very late lunch and charged his phone. No point in running out of battery in the middle of nowhere—which is where he'd be with Hannah later on... all being well.

The phone buzzed: "Voicemail".

'Yesss,' he said to the empty room.

Then he realised that Hannah could have rung to tell him to forget the whole thing.

He didn't recognise the caller's number. That was good—in the sense that it couldn't be her. Acceptance was still possible.

He listened.

"Mr Flower. This is Jane Unsworth. I'm the Director of the Winchester Science Centre. A matter of concern has been drawn to my attention, and you're requested—strongly requested—to come to my office at four o'clock today to answer some questions. Thank you."

He dropped the phone and pelted to the bathroom before his bowels let go.

Sodding Pirin. Sodding Oli. He ground his teeth.

You try to take the girl of your dreams out for a quirky date—without breaking and entering, remember—and bloody Big Brother looms over you to whip your arse for daring to reanimate your love life.

Shit. Shitting shit.

He finished up and darted back to his phone. It was 15:22.

His mind raced. He had no car. The WSC was out of town, and the necessary buses were only hourly. Who knows how long it would take to get a cab?

He couldn't rankle this Unsworth woman any more than he already had. As it was, there would probably be actual police—not some wannabe like Oli—waiting in the Director's office. He mustn't be kept late, even if he wasn't thrown in jail. He had the big date with Hannah. Make or break.

Shit!

What if Unsworth has got hold of Hannah, too? Oli would have blabbed our descriptions to his boss—almost certainly to avoid getting sacked himself.

Shit.

If Hannah was in trouble, Drew was in deeper trouble. Amy would release a million gallons of water into his rectum, and the courts would have difficulty pinning a conviction on a few scraps of sodden flesh.

Panicking, and seeing only one solution, he dressed hurriedly, pulling on the power suit and tie he'd used for the Yates summit. It might make the difference between forgiveness and incarceration.

He grabbed his phone, wallet and house keys and pelted to the bus stop.

He arrived at the fire station at 15:36.

Someone was reversing a gleaming tender into the garage. It was Amy.

He frowned. He'd never considered her as a driver, only a suited-and-booted firefighter. Still, it gave a solid gold opportunity. He waved his arms like a lunatic, flagging her down. The tender lurched to a stop with a hiss of air brakes.

Startled, she threw up her hands in a silent, "What?"

He jogged over. She clambered down the cab steps. 'The fuck is it?'

'I need a ride. Emergency.'

She sputtered a laugh. 'You're not serious.'

'I'm in trouble.'

'Who with now? Hannah?'

'No. With the sodding Director of the Science Centre.' He growled. 'Maybe only a slap on the wrist for an illicit after-hours visit. Maybe cuffs on the wrist.'

'Take the bus,' she said.

'No time.' He checked his watch. 'Twenty minutes.'

She looked at him like he was an idiot. 'Drive.'

'No car.' He glanced at the fire tender.

She guffawed. 'You're having a fucking laugh. Got yourself and Hannah sacked, and now you move on to me? I don't like you *that* much, Drew.'

'Shit.' He pondered. 'You drive?'

She jammed her hands onto her hips. 'Not as such.'

'You drive that,' he pointed out.

'Not to commute in, funnily enough.'

'I meant—'

She tutted. 'You're fucking useless. You know that?'

'Yeah, but a heart of gold, right?' he suggested hopefully.

She pondered. She raised a single finger. 'Stay.' Then she trotted into the fire station, yelled, 'Taking a late lunch break, Terry!', and disappeared through the back door.

Drew's insides were a mess. Then came a noise which filled him with dread.

'Oh, Jesus,' he groaned.

A motorbike rounded the corner of the building.

With quaking arms, he pulled the helmet over his buzzing head.

If there had been more time, he would have explained the situation to Amy. How, the last time he'd been a passenger in a vehicle with a woman, the woman had died. How he'd never been a passenger with anyone since—he'd always insisted on driving. How motorbikes were death traps.

Plus, he'd rather not be a jelly-legged, blubbering mess when he met this bloody Unsworth woman.

However, if he'd had more time, he would have called a cab or taken the bus. He shouldn't have been yakking to Pirin. Equally, if he'd taken Hannah somewhere sensible for their first proper date—the cinema, for instance—he wouldn't be putting his life in the hands of someone whose middle name was probably Danger.

He wanted to tell Amy to ride safely. There was no point. She already considered him a wuss.

'Okay?' she yelled over the sound of the engine.

'Yes.' What he meant was "No".

'Hold on!'

He grappled frantically for the bar on the seat behind him.

She pulled away, thankfully with minimal theatrics, then accelerated up the main road. Thirty miles an hour felt like three hundred.

After ten seconds, his bent-back arms hurt like buggery.

'Bollocks to it,' he grouched into his visor. He took a bottle of brave pills, let go, and threw his arms around Amy's sturdy waist.

She accelerated into the 40 zone.

He clung on like a limpet. He hoped she didn't mind. Other people had surely clung to her, fearing for their lives. The difference was that they'd been rescued from flaming death. He was merely on a slow-moving motorcycle.

He couldn't hear over the roar of the engine and the whistle of the wind, but she was probably tutting like a machine gun. He didn't much care. He wasn't trying to impress her or be her type of man—only Hannah's. Hannah should be bloody appreciative of the latest in a long line of hurdles he was jumping to win her love.

He wondered if Amy would help him break out of prison in time to make his date. Perhaps Char would kindly pay his bail?

He dearly wanted to check his watch to see if they'd be on time for the Director's dressing-down session. It was pointless. After all, what was he going to do—ask Amy to ride *faster*?

FLOOR 49

I t felt like it took a week to reach the Science Centre.

Amy pulled up outside the main entrance. She snapped up her visor. 'You go in. I'll park.'

'Thanks a million.' He unpeeled himself from her waist, gingerly dismounted on wobbly legs, and levered off his helmet.

She stuck out a hand. 'Gimme your lid.'

He handed it over.

She jerked her head towards the main entrance. 'Go on. Woman in there wants to hear what you've to say for yourself, right?'

He swallowed. 'Thanks, Jonesy.' He checked his watch: 15:54.

She yanked him towards her. 'You'll do fine. My advice—tell the truth. You might get forgiven.'

'Right.'

She tugged the throttle, slipped the spare helmet over her other wrist, and purred away. The world fell ominously quiet.

Come on. Breathe. Unsworth can't be worse than Yates. Can she?

He went inside. The silence was replaced by the buzz and chatter of hundreds of people milling around the cavernous building. Children darted and squealed, parents laughed, and various experimental exhibits rattled and beeped.

He didn't know where the Director's office was, but he made a beeline for the electronic turnstiles.

'Oi!'

He stopped.

'Excuse me, sir. Ticket?' An officious security guard, "Barry", eyed Drew with chastisement.

'Oh, I'm only here to see someone.'

'A likely story.' Barry thumbed to the Ticket Desk. 'Join the queue.'

'I'm here to see the Director.'

'Family, are you?'

'No.'

'You have a business appointment?'

'Not as such. Actually, I'm here to be berated, banned and jailed. I'll only be five minutes.'

'You still need a ticket to enter the venue, sir. Doesn't matter how long you spend at the Interactive Zone.'

Drew opened his mouth to protest. *Is this Len's brother, for Christ's sake?*

Then he noted a spare till at the Ticket Desk and decided not to risk further confrontation and potential additional jail time.

He checked his watch: 15:56.

'One, please,' he said to the smiley young female clerk.

'Any Planetarium shows?'

He growled. 'No, thanks, just the entrance fee.'

'Oh-kay,' she chirped, tapping at the computer. 'Would you like an Annual Pass? It saves thirty pounds compared to four visits over the year. Plus, you also get priority invitations to—'

'I won't be here for the rest of the year! I'll be in jail! Your boss will ban me from this place for having a secret after-dark date in the Planetarium!'

The poor girl's eyebrows leapt. She gave a nervous smile and glanced around.

'Went very well too, I hear,' said a voice nearby. Oli walked over.

Naturally, he's on duty today because things needed to be even more sodding awkward. What is it about security guards lately?

Drew laughed nervously. What he really wanted to do was pin Oli to the wall and ask if he'd squealed about the whole matter, but Common Assault would be an unwanted bonus on his sentence.

'Impressed with your stamina, mate,' Oli continued. 'Twice, right?'

'Shh,' Drew hissed.

A man nearby was eyeing him with amusement.

'What? It wasn't *my* idea!' Drew rapped.

A family with two young children were passing. They slowed, like motorway drivers ogling a crash on the opposite carriageway, which was a fair comparison.

Oli was giving Drew a look of disbelief.

'Okay, it *was* my idea! Not the sex, the coming here at night.' Drew looked beseechingly at the parents. 'You all should. The Planetarium show is great.' He flashed a shaking double thumbs up.

The father frowned. 'You were watching the show at the same time? Blimey. How does your girlfriend feel about that?'

'Ah. I... er... I don't know. We broke up.'

Oli snorted. 'Maybe if you paid her more attention during sex, that wouldn't happen.'

'Look, this isn't Jeremy Kyle! Besides, we didn't have sex,' Drew clarified.

'A likely story,' the father said.

'It was our first date.'

The father ushered his children backwards. 'Look, mate, did you have sex on those chairs?' he murmured. 'I'm about to take my family in there.'

'His girlfriend said they did it twice,' Olli offered.

'We didn't have sex!' Drew yelled.

More people stopped.

'We... held hands,' he protested.

'Aww, that's so sweet,' said the girl behind the counter.

'So why did she break up with you?' asked the lone man.

Drew held up his palms, which quaked in time with the rest of his body. 'I think we're getting off-topic here. All I know is I'm here to see the Centre Director, to be banned or whatever.'

The mother of the family touched her chest in shock. 'Oh my Lord, did you *break in*?'

'No! We were let in.'

Oli conspicuously backed away.

'And you *didn't* have sex?' the father enquired desperately. His son, maybe eight years old, looked up, curious.

'No!' Drew pleaded.

'Did you want to?' the girl behind the counter asked.

'Not you as well! Look, please just give me a ticket, and let me go and see the only person who should *really* care what happened and let me explain myself to her. Okay?' He glanced around, a pleading expression on his face.

Amy was standing there. Her lips were pressed together like a mangle.

Finally, a ray of bloody sunshine in the middle of a deluge.

He shot her an expression which said, "Please kill me".

She rolled her eyes theatrically. 'Sorry, everyone,' she called, a firefighter clearing the scene. 'Nothing to see here.'

People mumbled and began to disperse.

'Fifteen pounds twenty-five, please,' the ticket girl said.

He tapped a quivering debit card against the reader, took the paper stub and let Amy march him unsteadily away.

'How much of that did you see?' he squeaked.

'Enough, mate. Come on.'

At the barriers, he waved his ticket. Amy produced a fancier item from her wallet and held it under the reader.

'You have an Annual Pass?' he asked in weak disbelief.

'Course. Love coming here. Saves thirty pounds—'

He snapped up a hand to silence her. She sniggered. He would have taken issue with that, except she'd got him here in time. Plus, he'd seen her biceps.

Amy waved towards the far corner of the bustling atrium. 'It's this way.'

'Don't you have a shift to get back to?'

'It's two more minutes, Drew. Besides, you're a bloody one-man disaster area at the moment. Wouldn't want you to clock someone. Especially the woman you're here to see.'

'Yeah,' he sighed. 'Thanks, Jonesy.'

They zigged and zagged. He checked his watch: 16:00. Despite the crippling nerves at what was about to happen, at least he hadn't made things worse with Unsworth by being late.

Amy slowed her pace, allowing him to walk alongside. He looked for an office area or a suitable doorway marked "PRIVATE".

He stopped as if there was a landmine in the way. There wasn't.

There was Hannah.

FLOOR 50

H e didn't know whether to be more relieved or less. His poor brain was ready to wave the white flag.

'But... but...' He checked behind.

Amy gave a knowing wink and waved. 'Got to get back.'

'Thanks, Ames,' Hannah called.

'Hannah?' he said, stating the bloody obvious.

A few people milled around. The Centre was becoming less crowded as families ended their visit, ready to potter home for tea, clutching souvenirs and listening to their kids chatter excitedly.

Hannah beckoned. He walked to her, zombie-like, his mouth moving like a fish.

She was standing beside a table on which were scattered a few large metal cuboids. 'Science lesson for you, Andrew Flower.'

She picked up two of the sturdy magnets, held their ends apart, then relaxed her shoulders. The magnets were invisibly sucked inwards, joining with a clunk. 'We're not binary stars, you and me. We're magnets. Impossibly, eternally, drawn tight together.'

She pulled hard, with effort in her face, but couldn't part the duo. She tossed them on the padded table with a heavy thud.

'The... Director?' he asked, nervous but with an inkling of the answer.

She smiled and shook her head. 'No.'

His mind cartwheeled. *All this... show and stress... for me?* Now, he was relieved, but she hadn't leapt into his arms, so was the jury still out?

'How did your gamble go?' she asked.

'Oh. I... er... resigned. I said the lift stunt was all my idea, and I resigned and... insisted they re-hire you, or I'll kick up a fuss.'

Her fingers came to her mouth. 'Oh, Drew, but you can't.'

He shrugged. 'Too late. Sorry. Again. Shit.'

'No. You don't get it. You can't because...' She moved closer. 'Because I went to Yates and resigned. I said it was all *my* idea.' She met his gaze. 'And I demanded they give *you* your job back.'

An inadvertent chuckle burst from his throat. Then from hers. Quickly, they were laughing.

People gave them curious looks.

Her eyes danced with a familiar sparkle. She took his hand and led him to a quiet corner. His palms tingled with the feel of her skin.

'What did Yates say?' she asked.

'Don't know. A decision by end of Friday. What did he say to you?'

'Same. But... you resigned to save *me*.' She shook her head in disbelief.

'Of course I bloody did. I can't leave you hanging around, waiting for some other... magnet to come along.'

'Me either.'

'So, you brought me here for a *science lesson*?'

'Yeah. And to say I shouldn't have told you to fuck off. Or compared you to Yates. And to say that if it's my job or you, I choose you.'

'I choose you too, Hannah.' He restrained the impulse to hug her.

She chuckled. 'Then we can live in poverty together, right?'

'I suppose.'

'What would you have told Unsworth?'

'Is there an Unsworth?' he asked.

'No idea.'

'Are you asking whether I would have gone to jail for our illicit liaison under digital stars?'

She shrugged her petite shoulders. 'Well, at least a criminal record wouldn't have affected your current employment status.'

Now, more than anything, he wanted to tickle her. To bundle her to the floor and create a spectacle in a public space. To have her laughter fill the building and go some way to repaying the social torture he'd been subjected to.

However, this was Hannah, and one doesn't do things like that to a Hannah.

'It's a bloody relief not to have to grovel to another suit.' He grimaced. 'Still, less embarrassing than admitting to the front desk, the security guard, and a lot of surprised families that we had sex in the Planetarium.'

She frowned. 'But we didn't.'

'They think we did. Or assume.'

'Why—do they know you? Have you done it before in there?' She put her hands on her hips and looked at him in cheeky amusement. 'Are you some kind of local sex legend?'

'No! Did you tell them the whole voice-in-a-lift courtship thing?'

'Funnily, no. I was on my way to being barred and arrested. Didn't want to be late to Unsworth's office on the excuse of recounting the history of my last relationship.'

She bit her fingernail. 'Last? Not current?'

'We aren't current. We broke up. Remember?'

Her face fell. 'So, all this,' she glanced around. 'Was I wasting my time?'

'Honestly? I'd love to say it was, and burst your balloon, but I don't have the chops for deadpan delivery like that.' He took her hands. 'So are we... un-broken up?'

'I'd have to be a real fucking bitch to say No, right?'

'Then it must be a Yes because I don't think you have it in you to be like that.'

'Oh, believe me, I can be,' she said with steely determination. 'But not with men I'm trying to seduce.' She winked.

'And you did well, too. A fake phone call, the spectre of legal reprimand, a crazy bike dash, public humiliation, and a recap of GCSE magnetism? That's about the most romantic gesture on the planet.'

She shot him daggers. 'So, you'll have me back?'

'You'll have *me* back?'

'Is this a game of courtship chicken, you chicken?'

He poked out his tongue. 'Potty mouth.'

'Pissy pants.'

He squeezed her into a bear hug. She clenched back. He kissed the top of her head.

She pecked him on the cheek. 'Right. Let's fuck off.'

'Bus home?

She nodded. 'Bus home.'

They held hands , crossed the Interactive Zone and mingled with the dribble of people making for the exit.

'Look, Daddy!' A child pointed at Drew. 'That's the sex man!'

They chose the back seat for the bus ride into the city. Drew didn't let go of Hannah the whole way.

Apparently, she and Amy had organised the reunion stunt during the previous night's revelry. Hannah had recorded the "Unsworth" phone message using her voice changer. Nobody had planned for Drew to make a mercy dash. She thought he'd simply drive over. They certainly hadn't expected him to broadcast a false sexual adventure to half the visitors.

She apologised profusely for putting him through hell. He didn't care. Nothing worth having comes easy, he said. She feigned gagging. Again.

Amy had told Hannah about Drew's note. She hadn't read it, but said Drew was planning a surprise at eight o'clock.

'What was it going to be?' she asked.

'Nothing special. I mean, nothing as simple and touching as what you just did,' he joked.

She jabbed him in the ribs. 'What was it, Drew?'

'A picnic under a clear sky, up on Cheesefoot Head.'

'Hilltop stargazing? Ohmygod that's so sweet!'

He scoffed. 'Something would have gone wrong.'

'Really?'

'Well—that's how you see me. A hapless buffoon.'

She squeezed his arm and laid her head on his shoulder. 'No. But you are... imperfect.'

'And you're so perfect?' he jibed, then touched his nose to hers. 'Except, you pretty much are.'

'No way. Very far from it. But because you chose me anyway, I accept you.'

He glanced out at the passing streets. 'There's still time for *my* date.'

She clenched his hand. 'Mind if we don't? Still a bit wiped out after last night. Plus, you know, the stress of wondering whether you'd turn up. And whether you'd say yes.'

He stroked her cheek and beamed adoringly. 'Good. I'm glad it screwed with your mind too. Only fair.'

'You're a fucking snake, Andrew Flower.'

'And you're a rancid, foul-mouthed, preying hermit, Hannah Thomas.'

'You say all the nicest things.'

He held her close as the bus lolled along. 'You and Jonesy are a real force of nature, aren't you?'

'She's a bad influence.'

'Hmm.'

She narrowed her eyes. 'And Pirin is the total angel?'

'No. But he made me see the error of my ways. So did Char.'

'She's a smart cookie,' Hannah said.

'She is. I think she'd probably like you.'

Hannah's brow arched. 'You mean if we last beyond the end of the week? When you finally get the courage to show me off in polite society? The sweary-Mary schemer who's having you jump through hoops, make a fool of yourself, and jack in your job?'

'What's your point?'

'I want to meet her. Now.'

'Ha-ha.'

She pinched his ear like he was a truanting teen. 'I'm serious. Give me a chance to get the Charlotte Flower seal of approval. Show her the ghostly voice that nearly drove you to drive her to distraction.'

He looked behind her eyes and found only seriousness. *It couldn't hurt, could it?*

FLOOR 51

They took a second bus to Drew's house. His car was parked outside; Char was home.

Hannah gripped his hand, and he sensed nerves, but she was masking well. In fact, he was probably in more trepidation, not counting the possibility that they'd burst in on Char and Sam on the sofa, making up for lost time.

Happily, his sister was in the kitchen. So was the unused picnic.

The introductions were cordial, and Drew's muscles remained tense until Hannah cracked the first tentative joke. Char laughed.

They sat in the lounge and recounted the day's events. Afterwards, he asked if Hannah was peckish and whether she wanted to go out or get a takeaway. She mentioned the picnic and pointed out a perfectly serviceable patio and garden beyond the back windows.

So, although it was quirky and a bit crazy—very Hannah—the three of them tossed the picnic rug on the small square of urban grass and had an early dinner. He'd bought lemon drizzle cake for pudding. Apparently, that was her favourite: instant "boyfriend points".

After an hour of explanations, backstories, and laughter—some at his expense, Drew spotted Hannah checking her watch three times in five minutes. For a girl with social anxiety, she was pretty good at giving subtle signals.

They packed the detritus into the bin and dishwasher, and Hannah excused herself to the loo.

Charlotte ushered Drew into a corner. 'You want my opinion? It's okay if you don't.'

'Of course I bloody do. Whether I take it, that's a diff—'

'She's a keeper, Drew. I have no notes. Don't screw it up.'

He beamed. 'She's great, right?'

'You're kidding? She's way too good for you. You're batting well out of your league, bro.' She gave him a smacker of a kiss on the temple.

'Couldn't have done it without you, Char.'

'Likewise. And you know what? I'm mentioning her to Sam.'

'What?'

She shrugged. 'He's a talent agent. She has talent. Come on—it's not rocket science. Or magnetism.'

His eyes were wide. 'But—'

A theatrical sigh led Hannah into the room. 'God, I was pissing like a horse.'

Drew sniggered nervously. 'My girlfriend, ladies and gentlemen. Five-foot-four of pure class.'

Hannah jabbed him with her elbow. 'Could be worse. Jonesy's six-foot and barely much better.'

'Thank Christ I'm not going out with her,' he murmured.

'Unlikely. Not her type. Too...' she gestured vaguely '...dangly in the genital department.'

Five quid's worth of pennies dropped in Drew's head. 'Plus the whole aspect of me being shit scared of her.'

Hannah beamed. 'I know—great, isn't it? And that's when you *haven't* done anything dickhead-ish.'

Char patted Drew's shoulder. 'I can see my brother is in good hands.'

'Thanks.' Hannah reached for his arm. 'Come on then. Do something decently fucking romantic for once and drive me home.'

He was pulled into the hallway. 'I'm either going to kill her or marry her,' he called to Char.

He drove her home under early-evening skies. The weight of the day pressed heavily, yet his heart was in the orange-tipped clouds.

'What do you think?' he asked.

'Your sister?' She grimaced. 'Fucking awful woman.'

He didn't rise to that because he knew it was bollocks.

As he'd done twice before, he parked by the kerb outside her building.

'Drew?'

'Yeah?'

'Thanks. I'm not the easiest person.'

'Me either. Look, about the whole Yates thing…?'

She closed her eyes. 'Not now. Don't spoil today. Monday's a long time away. Let's just be… boyfriend and girlfriend, okay?'

'Okay.'

'Thanks. So… walk me to the building?'

'Always.' He held her hand as they strolled to the entrance lobby door.

'Walk me to my flat?

'Yeah.'

They went through to Number 1. She fished out her key and slid it into the lock.

She looked up at him with big brown eyes behind gently tinted lenses. 'Kiss me goodnight?'

'Okay.'

It was a long, intense kiss. An oasis in the desert. He'd missed that.

She frowned and bit her lip. 'Help me check there are no axe murderers in the flat?'

'Definitely. Safety first, right?'

She led him in, closing the door. She put the light on low.

He took in the surroundings. 'Seems all clear.'

'That's a relief.'

She pulled him into an embrace. He felt pent-up energy in her frame but didn't know its cause.

'Look under the bed for monsters?' she asked quietly.

His pulse quickened. 'A wise precaution. I mean—only together for four hours, and I wouldn't want you gored or squished or eaten whole. At least, not until I've helped you finish the rest of that lemon drizzle cake.'

'Good plan.' She kissed him, full and long on the lips. As she did, she slipped off his tie. 'Hold on.' She broke off, went to the front door, and attached his tie to the outer handle.

She walked back, matter-of-fact. 'Ames is such a nosy parker. Don't want her knocking on the door asking for a cup of fucking sugar.'

He moistened his drying lips. 'Right. So she doesn't disturb the... monster checking or us having a nice mug of cocoa on the sofa.'

'Absolutely,' Hannah replied earnestly.

'Phew. Good. I don't want to get ahead of myself.'

'Very sensible, sweet and romantic.' She glanced at the bedroom. 'Well?'

'Oh. Yeah. Right.'

He went through, quickly assessed the layout, and turned the dimmer switch to minimum. Then he got down on all fours and peered into the darkness under the bed.

'What the fuck are you doing?' came her amused voice.

'Checking for monsters. What does it look like I'm doing?' He stood. 'All clear.'

'That was a joke. Div.'

He feigned surprise. 'Ah! Sorry, I've never heard you tell a joke before.'

'Fuck off.'

He shook his head so slowly. 'Absolutely not.'

He slipped off her glasses, noticed a stand on the bedside table, and set them down. Then, for the first time, he took a good, long look into her eyes. He stroked her cheek and kissed her softly. Endorphins charged through him.

'Anything else you need a hand with before I leave?'

She shrugged so teasingly. 'You could help me with these silly buttons on my shirt?'

He glanced at the five small buttons which led down from the slight V in her plain navy blouse. Naturally, it was an impossible invitation to resist. 'Before I do, I need to tell you something.'

Hannah cocked her head. 'You're a woman in drag? You're a cop, and this was a police sting to catch the mystery lift tamperer?'

He smiled, cupping the small of her back. 'No. I'm in love with you.'

'Thank fuck for that.'

He suppressed a laugh and put on a serious face—because this part was important. 'I wanted you to know... er... *beforehand*, so you don't think whatever happens influences how I feel about you, Hannah.'

She stroked his cheek. 'That's very sweet.'

Calmly and methodically—fighting rampaging desire—he unbuttoned her blouse. She pulled it off and cast it aside. In the split second that her attention was diverted, he clocked her bra. Electricity surged through him.

'Anything else?' he murmured.

'No. I've got the next bit.' She unbuttoned his shirt and discarded it. Her fingers skipped on his chest, giving him goosebumps. 'I need to confess something too.'

'You're a man in drag?'

Amusement flitted on her face. She kissed him, just once, so briefly. Then she unclipped her bra and slid it off. He studied her face.

She frowned. 'Not looking at my tits, are you?' she chastised wickedly.

'No,' he said truthfully. 'I don't want to misread the signs, you know?'

She smirked in disbelief, held his temples, and tilted his head down.

He imbibed the picturesque view. 'Probably not a man in drag.'

She lifted his chin. 'No.'

He swallowed a mouthful of the sexual tension that crackled in the air. 'How are you with compliments?'

A tic of social awkwardness flitted on her face. 'Honestly? Not great.'

'Good, cos your tits are fucking horrendous.'

A belly laugh burst from her. She hugged him tight and stroked his neck. The feel of her chest against his was comforting and heady.

Her eyes locked on his. 'Do you want my real confession?'

'Okay?' he replied nervously, drunk on her beauty.

'I'm in love with you too.'

Relief swamped him. 'Thank fuck for that.'

Her body creased in amusement. He pulled her in, kissing wantonly for the first time. Her lips were as intoxicating as her personality. He pressed his cheek to hers, stroking her soft shoulders.

'It's been three years, Hannah. I hope you...' He coughed nervously, so desperate for this to go well.

'Shh. It's been two years for me. But I think I remember where everything goes. Do you?'

'I can give it a shot.'

Her kisses moved from his cheek to the side of his neck, then to his lips. He clasped her bottom, and she responded in kind. They were pressed together so tightly, a North Pole and a South Pole.

'Beep! Beep!' she trilled suddenly. She looked him up and down. 'Oh, dear. You've set off my security alert.' Mischief flitted in her face.

'Does this mean I need to strip off?'

'Well, I need to check that you *are* carrying a concealed weapon.'

He glanced down at his groin. 'It's not as concealed as it was.'

'Hmm.' She bit her lip coquettishly.

He wanted to let his hormones off the leash, to explode into desire for her. However, this was much more... Hannah—adorably inebriating.

She removed her trousers. He didn't bother averting his gaze.

Neither did she. 'Hmm. I see the problem is getting worse.'

He pulled her close, kissing her long and full. He slid his palms inside the back of her panties and stroked her soft backside. Her breathing quickened.

'You feel much less metallic than when we first met.'

She raised a single eyebrow. 'Do you want me to put on a suit of armour before we do it?'

'Maybe next time.'

She kissed him hard. 'Then take off my underwear, Drew, before I burst.'

FLOOR 52

When Drew awoke, the bed was empty. For a second, he thought it had all been a dream—everything from the voice onwards.

Then he realised it wasn't his bed. Daylight peeked through the blind, bathing the room in an almost ethereal glow. He listened for the shower, checked the bedside clock, and then looked for messages on his phone. None of them gave him a clue.

Her glasses rested on the stand. He smiled.

Hannah entered, wearing only briefs. Oddly, she was carrying a takeaway coffee cup.

He inhaled sharply. The smell of decent, fresh, expertly prepared morning coffee was as intoxicating as the view. 'Bet you made the barista's morning, dressed like that.'

She perched on the bed and handed over the cup. 'Yeah. This was free. He said if I came starkers next time, he'd give me a free pain au chocolat.'

'Why are you up early, running errands? Bit overkill, isn't it?' He sipped the delicious brew.

'Trying to make up for creating yesterday's fiasco.'

'Already forgiven.'

He put the cup down and encouraged her under the duvet. They slid into a loose embrace.

'Seen Jonesy?' he asked.

'Not yet. What, you think I'd be over there like a shot?'

'Don't deny that you'll be discussing last night. Grading me.'

'Like you will be with Pirin?' she said knowingly.

'Shall we make a pact that it's a solid 8 all-round?'

'Someone has a very high opinion of themselves.' She offered a single raised eyebrow, paired with that impish smile.

'Can the accused submit more evidence?' He pulled her closer.

'I need breakfast.'

'I'll make it quick.'

She was wide-eyed in amusement. 'And you think that will help your case?'

'I'll risk it.'

He kissed her. It developed into a snog, which lasted long enough for his coffee to be at the ideal temperature for fast-paced consumption.

When he was done, she sighed theatrically and sat up. 'Well, that was all a hell of an adventure.' She held out her hand. 'It was good to meet you, whatever your name is. Feel free to have a shower before you leave.'

His chest shook with sniggers. 'You are fucking unbelievable, Hannah Thomas.'

'*Now* who's the potty mouth, Andrew Flower?'

'Still you, I think.'

She frowned. 'Why "Drew"?'

'I didn't want to be called Andy.'

'Hmm. Yeah. You're not an Andy.'

He played with her hair. 'We should find pet names. Do you have one?'

'Ames calls me Han.' She wrinkled her nose. 'But that won't work with you.'

'Why?'

'Because I'd have to call you Chewie.' She cocked her head. 'On second thoughts...'

He growled and pounced. She squealed with fake alarm. He scooped her up and rolled on top of her. He sat up, astride her waist. 'You're impossible, Han.'

'Why, you stuck up, half-witted, scruffy-looking Nerf-herder!'

'That does it!'

He dived in, all ten fingers coming to her waist to deliver an overdue tickling of cataclysmic proportions. She writhed and squealed, giggling like a girl.

He only stopped when he couldn't resist her any longer, pressing his lips to hers gently, then more lustfully. Then he corralled his efforts for a shot at a score of 9 or above.

At eleven o'clock, they went for brunch at a little place Hannah knew.

On the way back, they called in at the fire station. Hannah gave Amy the headlines and promised to fill in the sordid details over the weekend. Drew rolled his eyes, then said he'd give Charlotte and Pirin his version of the sordid details too.

Amy gave Drew a huge hug. She didn't reiterate her warning vis-a-vis treating Hannah properly in return for the safety of his bollocks.

They returned to Hannah's flat to veg on the sofa and see who'd win at Countdown.

At two-fifty, Drew's mobile rang. He'd recently saved the incoming number, hoping this person might become a friend.

'Hi, Lotus. This is unexpected.'

'Hi, Drew. Mr Yates asked me to give you a call.'

'Mmm-hmm.' Drew jabbed the Speaker button. Hannah leant in.

'He'd like you to come in on Monday,' Lotus said.

'Oh. Oh, great!'

'Sorry, Drew. There's no decision yet. He's so tied up with his divorce case. He'll decide over the weekend, then let you know on Monday.'

Drew tutted. Yates had said Friday 5 P.M. Again with the slipperiness. This was going to keep him and Hannah on tenterhooks for even longer.

'Oh. Okay, thanks. How... does it look?'

'I've no idea. How are you coping?' Lotus asked.

'Fine, thanks. Did you have any further thoughts about... our discussion?'

Lotus paused. 'It depends on what happens with your and Hannah's job situations. Anyway, I have to go. I need to call her too. Yates wants to see her on Monday as well.'

Hannah's eyes widened.

Drew put a finger to his lips. 'I'll... thanks, Lotus. I think there's a chance I'll see Hannah before Monday, so I'll pass on the message. You know—save you some time.'

'That's very sweet.'

'Well, if I scratch your back, maybe you help me. Not me, obviously. Your fellow employees. Anyway, I'll let you go. Thanks.'

'Okay. Thanks, Drew. Have a good weekend,' Lotus said cheerily. The line cut.

'"I'll see Hannah before Monday",' she mimicked. 'You can *tell* people, you know. We *are* a couple.'

He embraced her. 'Maybe I should have said, "I'll see Hannah naked before Monday", then she would have got the message. And also got the message that I'd be giving you the message.'

'Ha! If you think you're seeing me naked again this weekend, you're absolutely... right.'

He let her kiss him for a while.

She fell serious. 'You know, if Yates does offer me my job back, I'm not sure if I want to take it.'

'Why?'

'If we don't get him sacked, arrested, or both, he'll still know I've got dirt on him. How the fuck will I get treated then? Longer hours. No more pay rises. Replaced by a younger, cheaper, shitter archivist? Forced out by a method cunningly designed not to fall foul of unfair dismissal claims?' She flopped against the chair back. 'What you did is laudable, Drew. Sweet and selfless, but I don't know if Yates has soured that place forever. I certainly did by pulling that lift stunt.' Her eyes became sad.

He pulled her close. 'It's not over until it's over. If Lotus helps us—maybe even other victims speak up too—he can't punish them all.'

'So what you're saying is, it's him or me.'

'It's your decision. This was your idea. Do you want to walk away, find another job, and hope Yates gets kiboshed by someone else? Or, on Monday, do you want us to go in there together and—regardless of his decisions—tell him the game is up?'

She bit her lip. 'He'll make your life hell too. Plus, he'll call foul that you lied about destroying the evidence.'

'True. Unless... we get more evidence. And maybe a witness or two.'

FLOOR 53

D rew had the best weekend in ages. They did annoyingly coupley things like holding hands across the table in the café and kissing on a park bench. He felt ten years younger.

He stayed at Hannah's, keeping out of Char's hair and allowing her free rein to rekindle her romance with Sam.

On Sunday night, Amy popped across for a couple of hours of wine, laughter, poking fun at Drew, and concocting a scheme for Monday.

As they walked to his car the following morning, bellies swarming with butterflies, Drew's phone pinged. It was from Pirin.

> Best of luck, mate. I have a good feeling.

He didn't show Hannah the text, not wanting to get her hopes up. This was a huge punt.

After grabbing a takeaway coffee, they passed smoothly through Reception. Drew remarked that as their security passes hadn't been voided, things looked hopeful. Nevertheless, Hannah remained muted, her anxiety as if they were re-entering a dragon's lair.

He ached to hold her hand but didn't want to make her uneasy or set tongues wagging. Besides, what was five minutes of handholding after three days of intense, heart-warming proximity? He was utterly smitten. She was perfect. Even better if her emotional baggage could be thrown on the conveyor belt to hell.

They went to Yates' office.

Lotus was at her desk in the adjoining anteroom. She was guarded and tense. The greetings were oddly superficial. She'd worn a short skirt and a push-up bra, which was both helpful and brave. She was giving their plan a good chance.

Drew perched on her desk. He'd try not to fall off this time. 'What's up?'

Lotus' nose wrinkled. 'He's like the cat that got the cream.'

Drew's spirits soared. 'So... that's good for us, right?'

'Probably. But he fucking hugged me when he came in.' She shuddered.

Hannah clasped Lotus's shoulder. 'Supportively, or like a creep?'

Lotus glanced at the adjoining door. 'I want to *get* him,' she hissed.

Hannah eyed Drew. 'So, we'll do this. Whatever he says in there, I don't give a shit. If it was just me, I could maybe move on, but not if Lotus is going to be in the firing line.'

'Will it work?' Lotus whispered.

'Not a fucking clue, honey,' Hannah replied. 'But let's give the prick enough rope to hang himself.'

Lotus' desk phone buzzed. 'Are you both going in?' she asked.

Hannah grabbed Drew's hand. 'Yes. We stand or fall as one. Right, my love?'

His face flushed. He glanced awkwardly at Lotus.

'You're adorable together,' she said, managing a smile.

'Er... thanks.'

'Come on.' Hannah tugged his hand. 'Best poker faces. Let's see what our illustrious CEO has to say about our careers.'

Into the valley of death rode the two.

When they emerged five minutes later, Drew was nonplussed. 'Did that just happen?'

'Ours is not to reason why,' Hannah said, yet she was reeling too.

'What are you going to do?' Lotus asked. 'Stay?'

'I don't know. Ask me later. After...' she glanced at the door. 'You know.'

'But at least you have the option, right?'

Hannah sighed. 'Yeah. He's even more fucking insufferable when he's happy, though. Why do good things always happen to bad people?'

'They happen to good people, too,' Drew said. 'Come on, let's get some pastries inside us.'

She was still unsettled. She wouldn't get to an even keel until this whole mess was sorted, one way or another.

Love? Tick.

Jobs? Tick.

Justice? Not yet. And the desire for justice had started this whole adventure.

In the corridor, they bumped into Pirin. Hannah excused herself to the loo.

'What happened?' Pirin had a glint in his eye.

Drew's Spidey senses tingled. 'Why do I get the feeling you already know?'

'Tell me anyway.'

'Yates said he was all set to give us the heave-ho, then this morning, he got a call from his lawyer saying they were going to win the divorce case. He's like a pig in shit.' Drew wrinkled his nose. 'Pig being the operative word.'

'Why so glum? You and Hannah got your jobs back, right? So it only happened because Yates was in a good mood? Don't knock it.'

Drew took Pirin's arm and marched him into the Gents. They were alone. 'Okay, spill. Is this anything to do with you? It smells more rotten than the egg salad Simon left in the fridge for two weeks.'

Pirin's smooth, woman-luring smile appeared. 'Maybe.'

'Bloody hell, *you* didn't offer to resign too? I mean—'

'Take it easy. I love you, mate, but there are limits.'

Drew was perplexed. 'So, what, then?'

'Mrs Yates broke the terms of the prenup on Sunday evening. It absolves him of responsibility. Neutralises his infidelity. She has no leg to stand on. So, Yates saves two mil and is happy as, I don't know, a fifty-year-old lockkeeper banging a fit young Bafta-winning film director.'

Drew's mouth hung open. 'How the hell do you know what Mrs Yates did?'

Pirin slid out his phone. 'Well—'

Drew recoiled. 'I don't want to know.' He looked his friend up and down, riddled with disbelief, wonder and possibly gratitude.

'Just proving I have evidence, that's all.' Pirin shrugged and put his phone away.

'Bloody hell. How did you...? I mean...?' Drew asked, wincing.

'Tracked her down to a bar where she was celebrating her last night of being married to the lecherous shit. He has taste—I'll give him that.'

Drew scoffed. '*She* bloody doesn't.'

'Rude.'

'Oh, what, you're going to see her again?'

Pirin grimaced. 'Doubt it, when she finds out I diddled her out of two million quid.'

'Or she's glad to get shot of Yates, she forgives you, and is happy to continue the May to December boinking, or whatever.'

'You mean she'd rather have me than two mil? Be sensible, mate.' Pirin winked. 'I'm worth double that.'

Drew didn't rise to that. 'But you did that for me—me and Hannah? Threw Yates a lifeline so he'd go all gooey and forget the whole sacking thing?'

Pirin patted Drew's shoulder. 'I may have subtly quizzed him on the divorce situation. Offered him a hypothetical outcome.'

A penny dropped. 'When you were waiting outside his office last week.'

'You and Hannah aren't the bad people here. She played to her strengths—setting up that surveillance system. You played to yours—being a good guy. Me? I just shagged someone. Same old same old.'

'You're a bloody reprobate.'

Pirin clasped Drew's arm. 'I know you don't approve, but maybe my powers *can* be used for good occasionally. You believe I'd never do anything which wasn't consensual, right? And you'd call me out if you thought I'd crossed a line?'

'Absolutely.'

'Good. Plus, I'm not saying I *won't* see Mrs Y again. We got along. She's only nine years older. Let's say... May to September. Stranger things have happened.'

'A second date would be strange enough for you.'

Pirin gestured to the room. 'This whole thing fixed your hang-up about never wanting another relationship.' He shrugged. 'Maybe it's opened my eyes too? I can't deny I'd kill for what you and Hannah have.'

'Wow. Stranger things indeed.'

'Meantime, I can still live vicariously through you?' Pirin offered a hopeful smirk.

'If you must.'

'I do a killer Best Man speech.'

'Now you really *are* being a bloody reprobate.'

Drew spent the afternoon in Hannah's small, dark office space. At four o'clock, a friend of Amy's joined them.

Shortly after five fifteen, Lotus texted. They fired up Hannah's system, exchanged sober looks of comradeship, and gathered around the screen.

A couple of minutes later, Lotus and Yates entered the left-hand lift. The CEO was very loose-limbed. Lotus was anything but. Still, she subtly shielded her actions and thumbed B instead of the G that Yates had demanded. Their voices came through the intercom clearly.

Drew tingled with hopeful yet hateful nerves.

The lift descended.

'So, good news about your settlement,' Lotus said anxiously.

'Yep. That's right.' Yates exhaled dramatically. 'Free and ready to celebrate.'

'I'm sure.'

'So... how about I buy you dinner?' Yates entered her personal space.

Beside Drew, Hannah's grimace was a mixture of determination and disgust.

'No, thanks, sir,' Lotus replied, cringing.

From the wide angle of the secret camera, the three watchers could easily make out Yates' eye-line, which wasn't on Lotus' face. 'Even for your boss, who's now single? And who pays your wages?' He stroked her hair.

'I... don't... Please.'

'Lobster and champagne is just the ticket. Especially for a girl like you.' Then Yates gently cupped her breast. She was quivering.

Hannah's jaw was clamped so hard it might break. A tear rolled down her cheek. Drew squeezed her hand.

'You dirty bastard,' Amy's friend murmured.

Lotus pushed Yates away.

'Now, that's not very nice,' the CEO said.

Lotus glanced up at the floor indicator.

'Hold on, Lotus,' Drew beseeched.

'That'll do.' Amy's friend rose. He put on his cap. He spoke into his radio.

The three of them went out to the lobby.

PING!

The doors opened.

'You pressed the wrong bloody button!' Yates rapped.

Lotus bolted from the lift. 'No, I didn't.'

Yates stepped out. He froze. For a disgusting sexual predator, he was at least smart. He knew immediately what had happened. He scowled at Lotus.

PC Aaron Wilson read the CEO his rights.

Hannah went to Yates and raised a finger. 'Gotcha.'

'Circumstantial bollocks.'

'Do you wish to press charges, Miss Brown?' PC Wilson asked.

'Yes, I do,' Lotus replied.

'Me too,' Hannah said.

Yates snorted. 'You'll never stand up against me in court. Timid little thing like you.'

'If I don't, ten others will. But, you know, take your chance. The reputational damage from even being *involved* in the case will be huge for you, let alone for this company. My advice—resign and pay damages. Two million spread across all the victims should do it. Or see you in court.'

'You bitch.' He turned to Lotus. 'And you.'

'Getting this all down, PC Wilson?' Hannah asked calmly.

The man looked up from his jotter. 'Every word, Miss.'

PING!

The right-hand lift opened. Two more policemen exited.

'Aaaand... Cut.' Hannah flashed Yates a wink.

Drew gathered her up, took Lotus in hand, too, and they headed for the stairwell.

ROOF

On Tuesday morning, after sleeping like logs at Hannah's flat, they went out for breakfast.

She was relaxed like he'd never seen, as if a ton weight had been lifted from her shoulders. She was still an adorable blend of shy and comedically mouthy, but now he didn't fear for her soul.

They agreed to take the rest of the week off. Lotus had emailed their updated employment contracts, which had been approved before Yates hoisted himself by his own petard.

Drew would be back in the office, bright and breezy, on Monday morning. Hannah would take a few days to decide. He was ambivalent: so long as she was happy, he didn't need to bump into her every day.

At eleven o'clock, Char texted.

At two thirty, Drew took Hannah for a "surprise date", which wouldn't be anything of the sort.

When they parked outside another nondescript high-rise building in an Enterprise campus across town, she remained none the wiser.

He checked them in at Reception. Nobody asked to see his pants. The company's name gave a clue, as did the name of their contact, and Hannah started to retreat inside herself.

He stroked her shoulder blade. 'It'll be fine. You'll be amazing.'

'I can't. I can't do this.' There was supplication in her face.

'Yeah. You're right. Actually, you aren't really that funny. I faked all my laughter.'

Her eyes flared, and she jabbed him in the belly. He embraced her and kissed her hard. He didn't care who saw. Then he led her to the lift and waited.

Admittedly, Drew was also nervous. Not because he was going in a lift—he wasn't. Anyway, those were fine now. He was anxious on her behalf.

BING-BONG!

The doors opened.

Sam stood there. 'Step into my office?' he said.

Hannah looked at Drew with a worried query.

He took her hand. 'Going in a lift changed my life, Hannah. Go in this lift. Please. It might change yours.'

She bit her lip.

Sam's foot was across the door, preventing it from closing. He shot Drew a glance which said he approved of Drew's girlfriend.

Drew pulled her head to his chest and whispered in her ear. 'This is *literally* an elevator pitch. An audience of one. You did that already, in the Planetarium. And you were awesome. You can do it again. Go on—I dare you to rip me to shreds in there. Roast me alive, Hannah. Tell him I couldn't find your clitoris if I had a scale map and a torch. I don't care. I love you.'

She broke off, sniggering. She kissed him. 'Okay.'

He let her go. She stepped into the lift.

'Six floors, Miss Thomas. Make me laugh.' Sam thumbed the button, winked at Drew, and the doors closed.

On the drive home, Hannah was like a four-year-old after two bags of Haribo.

'I can't believe it,' she kept saying.

'I can.'

'No, but...' There was so much love in her gorgeous eyes. 'And I can't believe you did this. Charlotte did this.'

He stroked her leg. 'It's only a try-out, baby.'

'But it's something, Drew. Don't you get that?' She couldn't stop smiling.

'"The journey of a thousand miles starts with just one step".'

'Oh fuck. Not you, as well. I swear, Andrew Flower, if you ever look at a motivational poster—let alone suggest putting one up in either of our homes, I'll dump you like a fucking plummeting lift.'

'Alright! Calm down, potty mouth.'

'Pissy pants.'

He took her to his place for the first time since their impromptu garden picnic. Char was at work. He'd pass on the good news later unless Sam did so first.

Hannah explored his bedroom.

Luckily, he'd thrown the Churchill poster— "Success is not final, failure is not fatal: It is the courage to continue that counts" —away when he left Bristol.

'Too... bachelor?' he wondered.

'No.' She embraced him gently. 'You'll do.'

After the most lingering, hair-prickling kiss, her attention wandered from his face to beyond his shoulder.

He wondered what item hadn't passed the checklist.

She went to the shelf, gingerly fingered the small box, and then lifted it down.

His heart thudded. This was a bad misstep. He should have consigned this tainted token to the cupboard, or ideally a scrapheap. 'I'm sorry. I should get rid of that. Like, now.' He shook his head in disappointment. 'Hanging onto bad memories is stupid. Especially after... you and me. I can't believe I bloody kept it. What an idiot.'

She turned the box over in her hands. 'It's fine, Drew. I understand. Truly.'

He scoffed at his past ridiculousness. It was so clear now, in the light of a new dawn. 'I thought I'd never meet anyone as good as her. I was wrong. So, so bloody wrong.' He hung his head.

She raised his chin. 'It's fine. No shame or forgiveness needed, okay?'

He sighed with relief. 'Okay. Thanks.'

She opened the box. The oddest feeling rattled through him—a mixture of guilt, embarrassment, and regret.

She prised the ring out, peering at it curiously. 'Actually, I like it.'

'Really?'

'I can't be a bitch about this.' She held it up to her eye, scrutinising the diamond. 'Besides, you have good taste.' She set the ring back in the box. 'But I'd never want this one. Obviously. I know you'd never—'

Drew shook his head. 'No. It's a keepsake, that's all. Or it used to be. I'd never offer it to anyone else. Insensitive to Katie and... whoever.'

'I understand. Good answer.' She pecked him on the cheek, then returned the box to the shelf.

Still, his skin fizzed with that curious sensation.

She stroked his chest. 'I'd like something similar, though. When the day comes.'

He swallowed hard. 'You said "when", not "if".'

Her pupils danced. 'Hmm. I did, didn't I?'

'You mean you think that... someday... we...?'

She took both his hands and looked him in the eye. 'Yes, Drew. I do.'

THE END

A GAME OF TWO HALVES

The new, pitch *purr*fect, sports romcom from Chrissie Harrison

Out 10.10.2024

In order to save lower league Cattingley Town FC from relegation—and demolition of the football ground, hapless mascot Tom must regain his cheerleading mojo and catalyse the team into a successful FA Cup run. What he really needs is love.

When feisty physio Laura joins the club, Tom is instantly smitten. However, she's already dating The Cats' deadly rival team's hotshot striker and thinks Tom, like the whole team, is a work shy loser.

Can they forge a fragile romantic alliance to overcome the odds on and off the pitch before the season ends?

For updates, early notice of future releases, free excerpts and more, join my Readers' Circle at https://www.chrissieharrison.co.uk/newsletter/

ACKNOWLEDGEMENTS

Where to start? At the front?

I'm indebted to Alexandra Allen for such a superb cover design. I'm blessed to have found her and look forward to many more projects together. "Dress for the job you want", right?

I'm fortunate to have, in Mark and Nicki Thornton, not only great friends but two people who have offered so much advice and support over countless years. Please help me to help them by following Nicki's writing career at nickithornton.co.uk and please consider supporting your local independent bookshop by choosing bookshop.org rather than... *other* suppliers. On the topic of independent bookshops, I'm indebted to Rachel, Gaynor and all connected with Parade's End Books for their help.

Another two longstanding friends, Stu Moore and Ingrid Weel, put up with me blathering on about this and other book projects, and their input as beta readers is always appreciated. Also a special mention for Sarah Saya, whose support around the launch was invaluable.

That said, my favourite beta reader feedback session was sitting in a Copenhagen hotel bar until midnight with my amazing sister. Hopefully she'll like the next book, whose main character she inspired...!

Through social media I have found many great fellow indie authors. Elizabeth Holland has been kind enough to champion this book, and her feedback is always welcome. If you fancy a great escapist romance read, do head to elizabethhollandauthor.com. Another valued writing buddy and supporter is Deborah Klee, whose contemporary & women's fiction books can be found at abrakdeborah.wordpress.com.

This book was roughly two years in the making, and it wouldn't be in the shape it's in without the input of editor & coach Beth Miller (www.bethmiller.co.uk), and the expertise of Becca and Maddy at Softwood Books (softwoodbooks.com).

Lastly but most importantly, my constant beavering away at a keyboard is only possible due to the support of my family, chiefly my spouse. Hopefully that faith in me will—eventually—be repaid not only in my contentment but also in a growing readership... and a couple of pennies to rub together.

ABOUT THE AUTHOR

I'm an incurable romantic at heart, and a sucker for great humour. I've been writing for many years, and all the stories contain love, or humour, or both. It seems I'm unable to stay away from comedy and romance!

I have a soft spot for stories with strong women and nerdy or hapless guys – and sometimes pathos or bittersweet vibes. I like the connection between my protagonists to be more than physical; a way for them to bond and help solve each other's problems. I'm also keen to shine a light on mental health issues, especially anxiety and neurodiversity.

Fundamentally, I try to write the books I like to read – those with wit, heart and intelligence.

Outside of writing, I enjoy photography, great scenery, a relaxing train ride, delicious coffee and cake, and catching up with friends and fellow writers.

Chrissie Harrison is a pen name.

To get early notice of future releases, free excerpts and more, join my Readers' Circle at https://www.chrissieharrison.co.uk/newsletter/

Find out more, or follow me on social media;

https://www.chrissieharrison.co.uk
https://www.instagram.com/authorchrissieharrison/
https://www.facebook.com/AuthorChrissieHarrison
https://www.tiktok.com/@authorchrissieharrison
https://www.goodreads.com/chrissieharrison
https://www.youtube.com/@AuthorChrissieHarrison

ALSO AVAILABLE

When a travelling salesman stumbles on a secret town, he must choose between love and a long-held promise of untold riches.

In this stylistic and mysterious romantic comedy, meet the most unique characters and get pulled into the colourful world of Sunrise.

"A gripping yarn - quirky characters, a pacy plot and a setting like you've never read before. A fun ol' read." - *Paul Kerensa, Comedian & British Comedy Award-winning TV writer – Miranda, Not Going Out*

Printed in Great Britain
by Amazon